THE
Tilbury Poppies

Also by Sue Wilsher

When My Ship Comes In
The Empire Girls

THE
Tilbury Poppies
SUE WILSHER

sphere

SPHERE

First published in Great Britain in 2018 by Sphere

1 3 5 7 9 10 8 6 4 2

A CIP catalogue record for this book
is available from the British Library.

ISBN 978-0-7515-7084-7

Typeset in Bembo by M Rules
Printed and bound in Great Britain by
Clays Ltd, Elcograf S.p.A.

Papers used by Sphere are from well-managed forests
and other responsible sources.

MIX
Paper from
responsible sources
FSC® C104740

Sphere
An imprint of
Little, Brown Book Group
Carmelite House
50 Victoria Embankment
London EC4Y 0DZ

An Hachette UK Company
www.hachette.co.uk

www.littlebrown.co.uk

For Mia, my darling

If I die, they can only say I have done my bit.

First World War munitions worker
FLORENCE GLEAVE,
who died from TNT poisoning,
May 1917, aged twenty years

1

February 1916
St Clere's Hall, Stanford-le-Hope, Essex

Lily Pavitt reached down between the kitchen dustbins and picked up a dead rat by the end of its tail. She opened the lid of the bin and dropped the limp brown body on to the breakfast scraps. Its eyes were open and fixed and there was a froth of poison around its yellow teeth. She looked at it for a moment, rubbed her finger and thumb on to her apron and clanged the lid back down.

'I trust you'll make good use of that, Pavitt.' The Housekeeper, Mrs Coker, appeared at Lily's shoulder.

Lily jumped and lifted the lid off the dustbin to reach in for the carcass. The housekeeper's fist was closed tightly over the bunch of keys on her belt – it was how she managed to sneak up on the staff. Lily slipped away to find John the hall boy. John would have to skin and boil the rat to render its fat into tallow for the servants' candles. It had to be done *by order of the mistress* – that was the excuse Mrs Coker always used. Of course the housekeeper herself had the use of an oil lamp in her own quarters. The hierarchy at St Clere's Hall was strictly observed, both above and below stairs.

'And, Pavitt?'

'Yes, Mrs Coker?' Lily turned around, not wanting to hold the rat's cold, scaly tail any longer than necessary.

'The library has not been dusted; do it before the family come in.'

Lily nodded and stepped inside. Dusting the library wasn't her job by rights, but they were all pitching in, since another housemaid, Mary, had left to do war work at the Tunnel Cement works in West Thurrock. It sounded other-worldly to Lily. She'd heard that Mary was wearing trousers and was hefting heavy sacks around on barrows like Lily's husband Sid did at the docks.

The mistress had been furious when Mary left. Everyone knew the real reason why Mary had to go, and it wasn't because of the good money she was earning lugging sacks of cement around. Lily was married and didn't live in. The only reason they kept her on was because of the so-called 'servant problem' – there weren't enough of them to go around and the big houses were struggling.

Taking the dead rat into the tiny room where John tended to the lamps, she deposited it on his table with an apologetic look and went to fetch her feather duster. Holding her long skirt, she trudged up the familiar back stairs. She crept into the empty library and went about her work in the cavernous room lined with dusty bookshelves. Dust was said to be mainly fragments of dead skin. Funny how this dust was the dead skin of the family and of the staff, mixed together; the staff moving quietly about the place, preparing the rooms as though by magic, never using them themselves.

Lily paused at the sound of female voices but before she could slip away, the mistress, Lady Harrington, and the younger of her two daughters, twenty-year-old Lady Charlotte, swished into the room.

'Attending a ridiculous march does not entitle you to make decisions detrimental to this family.' The mistress spoke sternly, holding her temper with a glance at Lily.

'Sorry, milady,' said Lily in a whisper and an awkward curtsey.

She made to leave the room, but the mistress jerked her finger to her lips in an angry shush and waved Lily back to her work. She shouldn't have spoken in Lady Harrington's presence.

'Carry on, Jane.' The mistress called all of the housemaids Jane and if ever she saw the kitchen maids she'd call them Anne.

It was their dresses that Lily always noticed: a light rattle of beading work over lace and silk, exquisite items, things that Lily would never wear.

'It was not a ridiculous march, Mother. And serving our country overseas is hardly detrimental to the family,' Lady Charlotte flamed, her red hair matching her mood.

Their hair, dressed expertly by the lady's maids each morning, was coiled and pinned up into its proper place around hair rats stuffed with remnants from their brushes.

'Of course it is. Endangering your life on a whim is unnecessary and frivolous. A woman shouldn't be doing anything so dangerous.'

Their voices, like their lives, were clear-cut and refined.

'Not on a whim, Mother,' said Lady Charlotte through gritted teeth. 'What about Bertie? He is serving our country overseas; he couldn't wait for a promotion.'

They ate extravagantly several times a day, called for tea with the pull of a bell, went without meat once in a while to do their bit for the war.

Lady Harrington sighed. 'Your brother is a man, my dear; it is different, as well you know.'

Charlotte sat down on one of the leather armchairs. Lily moved silently as she dusted, trying not to make a sound or attract attention, doing her best to be invisible as she had learned to do when she first went into service seven years ago at the age of fourteen.

'You know Elizabeth, you know her family; it's only in Le Touquet, it's not exactly on the front line.'

They lived in a world that was always the right temperature, always clean, always in a good state of repair.

'Yes I do know her family, and why they would allow the Duchess of Salisbury to help in a military hospital in France is beyond my comprehension.'

'She's not *helping*, Mother,' snorted Charlotte. 'She set it up.'

Lady Harrington shrugged, unwilling to compromise her position. 'This is absurd, when we are establishing an auxiliary hospital here in our own home and your sister is training with the Red Cross as we speak. We've been notified that men will be sent the moment we are ready . . .'

'It's the same old thing, Mother. You assume I will follow in Harriet's footsteps when you forget I am my own person. What if I were to join the WAC in France?

4

They only consider women of good character. That should satisfy you.'

The mistress gave a dismissive sigh. 'There are plenty of safe war jobs you could do here. What about interpreting for the Belgian refugees? I read in the paper that another boatload of them landed at Tilbury only yesterday, together with those unfortunate English students from the Brussels conservatoire . . . you'd have a chance to use your French . . .'

'What about the Women's Police Service?' countered Charlotte. 'They maintain good moral standards; you'd like that, wouldn't you?'

Lady Harrington shuddered. 'Those disgusting suffragettes. And those awful *land girls* wearing breeches. At worst, if you must, be a lady clerk at the Bank of England. Anything of that nature could be arranged for you in a trice . . . It'd be a splendid novelty for them and I'm sure Lord Nevill wouldn't mind too much.'

'Oh!' Charlotte jumped out of her chair and strode over to the window. 'Lord Nevill may do as he pleases and let me do the same.'

'Charlotte, really! Be mindful of your duty. You were extraordinarily lucky to have gone to court before presentations were suspended for the war, you should capitalise on that. Your father would be devastated if you went to France now.'

Charlotte looked out of the window and Lily wished there weren't so many books to dust in the library; it really wasn't very good to be working in the mistress's presence.

'Why? Because I'd be witness to him trotting around on his silly horses planting turnips on the French farmland behind the lines and pretending to be involved in the action? The Cavalry aren't even in this war!'

She had gone too far. Lady Harrington strode out of the library leaving her daughter there at the window. Lost in her thoughts, Charlotte looked past Lily without really seeing her and then she too left the room.

Breathing a sigh of relief that Mrs Coker hadn't come in to see her there with the mistress, Lily finished her dusting. Downstairs she delighted in telling the staff what she'd heard. Lady Charlotte didn't often reveal so much about herself in their presence. They all preferred her sister Harriet to snooty Charlotte.

'You'll never guess, Lady Charlotte wants to go and do war work in France,' she told the others in the servants' hall.

'Like the ladies in the paper?' asked Martha. They all loved to read about the strange suffragette types: rich and educated and having wild adventures. Women like Elsie Inglis, the Duchesses of Sutherland and Westminster, Dorothie Fielding and the 'Angels of Pervyse', Elsie and Mairi.

'Sounds dangerous,' said one of the kitchen maids.

'An adventure, though,' said Lily. Perhaps it *was* something Lady Charlotte would do.

'Makes more sense for her to stay and help when the hospital's set up here,' said one of the footmen.

'What took you so long in the library?' said Mrs Coker, coming in to crack the whip. 'The stairs need doing.'

On her hands and knees at the top of the grand staircase, Lily swept each step diligently with her dustpan and brush. As she swept she wondered how things would change once the hospital was up and running at St Clere's Hall. She'd probably be given even more work to do, but then it'd be a chance to help the war effort in her own little way. She coughed as the dust puffed into her face and she tasted it on her tongue. A door closed upstairs and her heart raced, it was too late in the morning to be doing such work. At the sound of heels on the wooden floor of the landing, Lily stopped mid-brush. The mistress started her descent and Lily jumped up to 'give room', averting her gaze and facing away. She pressed against the banister, looking out over the hallway until the mistress had passed. It was the only time Lily was allowed to step foot on the main stairs.

'I'll see that dust, Jane,' said the mistress, stopping at the foot of the stairs.

'Yes, milady,' said Lily, rushing to finish her sweeping while Lady Harrington waited tapping her foot on the bottom step. She liked to remind the staff who they were working for. Lily's armpits dampened with the anxiety of the mistress waiting there; she wanted to be quick, but needed to fill the dustpan. Checking her starched apron was straight and clean, she stood before the mistress and held the pan out for inspection. But first, the mistress peered at Lily's face, holding her gaze, looked at her sweaty forehead, at her chapped lips. She stared at a strand of brown hair that had escaped from Lily's cap until Lily pushed the brush under one arm to free her hand so that she could slide the hair back into place. And finally the mistress looked down into the pan. She sighed, her nostrils flaring as though at a foul smell, then she turned and walked away into the sitting room.

Lily let out a breath, relieved not to have displeased the mistress, who'd been in a fairly good mood of late, what with the master away in France. Lily hoped he wouldn't be back anytime soon – he was known to prey on the help. The housemaid Mary had been a particular favourite of his. She'd confided to Lily that he had threatened to sack her without a reference if she made a fuss. The opportunity for war work had come up in the Tunnel Cement factory while the master was in France and Mary had taken her chance and left. Lily had noticed the master's eye on herself on more than one occasion and she was worried she'd attract that unlucky duty before long.

'How's your friend doing, the one with the brother?' Sarah, the lady's maid, whispered to Lily, as they stood behind their chairs in the servants' dining room, waiting for the butler to be seated.

'She's holding up, thanks.' Lily's friend Margaret had lost her brother Tom in the war. 'He was like a brother to me too. It's awful how they don't bring back the dead, isn't it?'

Sarah rubbed Lily's shoulder and gave her a sympathetic smile. They all hushed as the butler came in and took his place at the head of the table and they too sat down for their six o'clock supper. The youngest of the kitchen maids served them, her hands shaking, afraid she'd make a mistake.

'Their mum Phyllis has gone a bit loopy with the grief of it all, losing her only son, she's started handing out white feathers to the neighbours, it's horrible.'

When the butler took up his knife and fork and began to eat, the rest of them did too, mindful that he was a fast eater and once his cutlery went down, so would theirs.

'Your Sid'll be all right, though, won't he?' said Sarah, chewing fast around her words.

'Yeah, course, he's a docker, it's a starred job.'

Lily stopped talking to concentrate on her food. It was important to clean her plate – one of the main benefits of being in service was the three decent meals a day. Of course their boiled mutton stew made from the family's leftovers was nothing compared to the sumptuous five-course dinner that would be taken upstairs at eight o'clock, but at home if there was meat there'd only be enough for Sid.

Once the family and their guests had been seated for dinner, Lily had to do the first maid's job of tidying up the bedrooms again, laying out the nightclothes and carrying any chamber pot slops away. All in all the family changed clothes at least four times every day. She checked the fires in all the rooms and waited for the family to retire. She had the new duty of helping the lady's maid get the mistress ready for bed. It was a job she would have preferred not to do. Lady Harrington would find fault in everything she did. *Must you, Jane . . . not that way, Jane . . . too tight . . . too loose . . .*

At last Lily was allowed to leave for the day. She wriggled into her coat and slipped out of the servants' entrance, up the stairs and into the biting cold. Pulling her coat and shawl across her chest, she crossed the drive. She frowned at the approach of a motor car so late in the evening and squinted to see through the dark. As it went past she saw a uniformed driver and seated behind with his unmistakable rod-straight back and large moustache, she saw the silhouette of Lord Harrington.

Lily rushed down the drive into the darkness of Hoford Road. The whole house would be roused by the unexpected arrival of the master and she was glad not to have to stay any later. It was already past eleven and it would take her nearly an hour to walk home. To arrive back at work in the morning in time to make tea and toast for Mrs Coker's breakfast and get the fires going all round the house, she'd have to wake up at five. It was no wonder her boys ran to Sid's mother, Ada. They hardly saw their own.

The thought of the master returning from France made her feel uneasy. With first housemaid Mary gone, she'd have to make sure she stayed out of his sight. Lily quickened her pace. Shining between the clouds, the moon afforded enough light for her to find her way. She shivered and pulled her shawl tighter across her shoulders. It was a good night for the baby-killers, the German Zeppelin airships that flew over and dropped bombs on people. They liked some cloud cover to hide behind. The thought of it always struck terror into Lily's heart.

The heels of her boots crunched along the dirt track road, the mud silencing her step here and there and snagging on her long skirt, weighing it down. She passed Sutton's farm on her left on the Mucking marshes and the gravel pit on the Tilbury marshes to her right. It was a long walk home and Lily was already exhausted from the hours she'd put in for the Harrington family. This was the only time she had to herself; it might have been a chance to clear her head and breathe the air, but her pace was rarely slow, she always hoped that one or both of her boys would have a restless night and wake up when she returned home. Robert, three years old, and little Joe, only two years. She'd gone to get her job back only a month after Joe was born. Sid did his best for his wage but it wasn't enough. His father Gerald had a bad chest and his mother Ada looked after the little ones while Lily worked, and made sure Lily was grateful for it even though she and Sid were supporting his parents. It all meant that Lily hardly ever saw her boys, except on her one afternoon off a week. Although even then, Ada would save some of the housework for Lily to do.

A rustling sound in the hedgerow made her jump. Her mind flashed with thoughts of German spies and escaped prisoners of war. A woodpigeon flew awkwardly out of the side of the hedge and recovered, flying across her to get away. She laughed at herself. Stupid bird. It was safer than she was. The shooting of wildfowl had been prohibited along this stretch of the Thames from Tilbury Fort to Hole Haven, which meant she was more likely to be shot than the pigeon was. It also meant they were without the occasional bird for the pot at home on a Sunday.

The sound of an aircraft overhead made the smile drop from her face. It wasn't the throb of an airship, more of a whining sound, perhaps one of the new aeroplanes. She froze, and hunkered down near the ground, putting her face in her knees, her fingertips supporting her on the gritty road. Her hat wouldn't afford her much protection, lucky it was dark all around her: no lights to attract attention. There were regular Zeppelin raids in those parts, what with all the local factories and them being on one of the routes to London from the Continent. The Hun had flown a plane up the Thames in 1914. The hum overhead was a deathly sound when Lily didn't know for sure if it was British or German. As it receded towards the river she listened for the pop of anti-aircraft guns from one of the forts, imagined the shrapnel falling from the skies like metal rain. No sound came and she relaxed, it must be one of theirs.

She stood up and continued her walk home, quickening her pace to get there, skirting around Mucking village and the George and Dragon pub, on to Cooper's Lane. She often worried whether the boys were safe here in Tilbury with the air raids. Dropping bombs on people sleeping in their beds . . . it was too awful to think about. The papers said that four hundred and fifty people had died in Zeppelin raids so far that year, including a woman in Southend the previous May. It scared the living daylights out of you.

Lily sighed and stuffed her hands deeper into her pockets. Nothing was the same, the country hadn't known anything like it; even the German butcher in Tilbury had been forced to leave by an angry mob. Women in the street handed out white feathers like they had a right to do it, shaming men, making them feel like cowards. It all made Lily's stomach churn. But the thought of the Germans winning, coming here and violating women, killing babies . . . German warships were creeping around Britain's coastline firing bombs into people's homes, blowing children to bits in their beds. What about the British Navy, weren't they supposed to be the best in the world?

Heading down Fort Road, the smell of the river grew stronger. There were houses dotted along the road, some with thatched roofs. She tensed when she heard the sound of running feet and saw the figure of a man coming towards her in the dark. She didn't know whether to quicken her pace or dive into someone's front garden. With relief, a familiar voice called out to her.

'Lil!' Her husband Sid ran panting towards her.

'What're you doing, Sid? You frightened the life out of me.'

'Sorry, love, I came out looking for you when I heard the plane go over – thought you might take fright from it.' He laughed when he saw her face. 'But looks like I was the one who scared you.'

Lily grinned. 'You silly sod, where's your coat?' She threaded her arm through his and snuggled into his side. He had on his docker's clothes – dark trousers and waistcoat, white shirt and scarf, cloth cap. The man was never cold; he joked with the boys that it was his magic moustache kept him warm. If ever he shaved it off he'd need his coat, he told them. He was a big man, a gentle giant, made of sturdy stuff but stringy with muscle and not an ounce of fat on him. Smaller men would challenge him to arm wrestles and try to provoke him into fights, take advantage of his good nature. But he wouldn't be goaded; he hated violence and even shied away from smacking the boys when they were naughty. He'd had to develop an air of authority when he was around other men, but with Lily he was a love, always worrying about her. 'It was one of ours, I listened for the anti-aircraft guns from the fort,' she said.

'Good girl, you were right. Still, I don't like you walking back in the dark with all this going on.'

Instead of carrying on down Fort Road they turned right towards Civic Square. Since the war had started, you couldn't walk too far across the Tilbury marshes to the river – if you were caught anywhere near the docks or the fort after hours you were challenged by the guards. The Royal Dublin Fusiliers protected the docks with bayonets fixed. There was talk of machine guns and a six-pounder anti-aircraft gun at the pier head locks. Part of the river was mined. Everyone was afraid of a German invasion, everyone thought Essex would be taken first and everyone was suspected of spying, you had to be careful.

'The Chittocks' youngest signed up today,' said Sid.

'Never,' said Lily, shocked. 'But that's all four of their boys now.'

'I know, and Harry's worried sick, says he's thinking of signing up too, maybe he'll get posted with one of them.'

'What'll his wife do? She'll be out of her mind with worry.'

Sid nodded. 'Yep, but at least she'll know they're all doing their bit.'

Lily shuddered. 'It gives me the shivers. I don't know why you'd volunteer now, when you know how bad it is. Fair enough when it first started and no one knew it'd last this long and kill this many.'

'All the more reason, in my book.'

Lily frowned and looked at her husband. *It's almost like you're thinking of doing it yourself,* she wanted to say, but stopped herself; she didn't want to have that conversation. Sid's job was protected – it was essential for the war, thank goodness – but there were plenty of builders, police constables, tailors, wheelwrights and shoemakers from the local area who'd enlisted. And now the Chittocks' youngest, too.

They were coming into the town centre but the gas lamps were out because of the wartime lighting restrictions. Lily had walked this way often enough to be able to do it blind-folded. Left down Montreal Road and right on to Dock Road. In the old days there might have been men rolling around drunk at this time but Lloyd George had curbed drinking hours because the war workers were turning up drunk in the factories. Chucking out time was now eight o'clock in most of Thurrock, a restricted area.

'Are the boys down?' Lily asked as they turned left on to the hairpin railway bridge. She wanted to change the subject.

'Yep, unless you shut the door with a slam, but you'd never wake them up on purpose, would you now?'

Lily smiled; Sid knew her better than anyone. They'd been sweethearts at school. She'd gone into service and saw Sid on her one afternoon off a week. She was seventeen when they got married, and had her first baby the year after. It seemed like an age ago. She couldn't imagine being without Sid, she was one of the lucky ones.

They ·crossed ·the bridge together and the Dwellings loomed in the darkness, the four-storey tenement blocks for the dock workers. Up the stairs to the second floor they went and along the communal balcony. Sid opened the door of the two-bedroomed flat that they and the children shared with Sid's parents, Ada and Gerald. All Lily really wanted to do was fall into bed but she was desperate to lay her eyes on the boys, even if they were asleep.

It must have been nearly midnight. As she stepped into the kitchen she didn't expect to see Ada and Gerald sitting at the table by the range, they'd normally have been in bed hours ago. Her first thought was that something terrible had happened to the boys. Without a word she rushed past them to her bedroom, saw that little Joe and Robert were safely tucked up on their mattress on the floor, sleeping soundly. With a sigh of relief she stroked their hair, felt the warmth of their skin against her cold fingers, kissed their cheeks and crept quietly out of the room.

'What's happened?' she said. Sid had pulled out a chair for himself and sat with his parents in silence. Lily walked over to them and saw in the middle of the table there lay a white feather. It was such an innocent-looking thing. Ada and Gerald were staring at it like it was a white snake about to rear up and bite them. Lily frowned and looked at Sid, who returned her gaze, his face serious now.

'What's that, Sid?'

'You can see what it is, can't you?' snapped Ada.

'Yes, but where did it come from?'

'That friend of yours, Margaret, her mother gave it to him,' said her mother-in-law.

'Phyllis? But she knows you're a docker,' said Lily, looking at Sid. 'What do you all look so blue for?'

'He's going to enlist, that's what for,' said Ada, folding her arms at Lily as though it was her fault.

Lily went cold with dread. 'Don't be daft. Sid, you're not, are you?'

2

'Well, don't look like that. You know I'll have to go sooner or later.' Sid smiled and held out his hand for her to join him at the kitchen table.

'Why didn't you say anything?' said Lily, sitting down. 'And no, I didn't know that, your job is starred, that's why you wear that badge, isn't it?' She nodded at the silver On War Service badge pinned to his waistcoat. 'I thought that was supposed to protect you from being given a bloody white feather.'

'Tell that to your friend's mother, then,' said Ada, slapping the table and making the teacups rattle in their saucers.

'I suppose she's just being patriotic, wanting everyone to do their bit,' said Sid to his mother.

'She's bitter about her losing her Tom and wants everyone else to suffer for it,' said Ada. 'It's cruel. Just because she gives you a feather, doesn't mean you have to be goaded by it.'

Ada looked to her husband for support but he was strangely quiet. Sid ignored her comment and turned to Lily. 'You know conscription's coming in for single men. It'll be married men before long, and then they'll be combing through the essential jobs for more. You see the way this war's going, the men we've

17

lost—' Sid stopped, knowing he was only making it worse. 'I might as well join up now, King and country need me, Lil.'

'Yeah, they need you here working in the docks,' said Lily, panicking and realising now why he'd been talking like that on the walk home. Maybe he'd even used that plane going over as an excuse to come out and butter her up for the news that awaited her.

'There's less and less work for us dockers, Lil . . . '

He gave her a resigned look; she knew the situation at the docks. With shipping disrupted since the outbreak of war, the work had dropped off. Now the docks were being used by the services to convert civilian ships to military. Lily had seen the hospital ships that had a green line painted around the hull and a large red cross on the sides. Other ships were fitted with guns. Lots of native crews were without work too and living in one of the storage sheds. Sid had to stand on the stones each day waiting to be chosen by one of the foremen and Lily could always tell when he hadn't been picked and would spend the day hanging around. It didn't happen often but he'd be ashamed to admit it, just like the other men, playing penny up the wall to kill time. And it wasn't as if the docks were any safe haven either. There were lots of accidents – falls and drownings – there had been one only last month: a labourer had fallen to his death from a crane. Lily's own brother Bill had died working under a railway wagon when he was only fourteen.

'Well, what about looking for something in one of the workshops outside the docks?'

Sid frowned. 'But those jobs aren't protected, Lil. I'd get called up anyway.'

Lily felt the panic rise from her gut. She didn't want Sid to enlist. She'd be left here with Ada, and working at St Clere's Hall with damned Mrs Coker and the mistress. Without Sid around life would be unbearable. And he might get hurt, or worse. So many men were leaving and not coming back, or coming home blind or with limbs shot off and unable to work. It wasn't fair.

'For heaven's sake!' She struck her lap with her fists. 'Our lives are hard enough as it is. The bloody Germans, I hate them!'

'I know, love.' Sid put his hand on her cheek and looked so sad. She was being selfish; it was Sid who was going to have to go out there, he was surely terrified but too good to show it. She leaned her face into his large hand and couldn't stop the tears from coming. She loved him so much. The thought of him in uniform shooting someone to protect himself . . . He'd hate it, it would ruin him. He was the type to put himself in the firing line to save someone he hardly knew. And what about their boys? They'd lose their dad, and then what? She closed her eyes and tried to swallow the tears away. Ada was watching her.

'We'd best get to bed, love,' said Sid, 'both got to be up at the crack of dawn as usual.'

'You'd better do that washing before you turn in,' said Ada, nodding towards the scullery at the back of the flat.

'Mum, can't she leave it tonight?' Sid appealed to his mother's better nature but Lily knew she didn't have one.

'What, do I have to do everything around here? It's enough looking after those boys, let alone all the shopping and clean- ing I have to do at my age, queuing up for the grocer and baker every day and then get to the front and nothing's left.'

She looked at her husband and threw her hands into the air. Gerald shook his head – it was unclear who he disapproved of. He picked up his paper and waved it above his head to say goodnight as he headed to his bedroom.

'It's all right, Sid.' Lily got up and went to the wooden dolly tub, looked in at the clothes soaking there. Luckily the kettle was still warm, so she poured in the water and started scrubbing the clothes against the washboard. Her knuckles rubbed against the hard ridges of the board, the skin on her hands already chapped and raw from work. She tried to think what it meant to do the washing at home, what it represented. It meant she had a family, she had her boys, washing their clothes was something she could do for them. Robert's little vest, he only had two and he was always spilling something down himself or falling over in the mud. That's what Ada would tell her anyway. Lily had a warped view of her children; she didn't see enough of them and had to rely on Ada's reports. She just hoped they were all right and as happy as they could be living in the Dwellings with no treats and not enough food. The stark contrast between her own life and that of the Harrington family at the Hall was something she tried not to think about. It was a privilege to work for a good family like that.

Pulling a pair of short trousers out of the water, she wrung them out with her hands and wound them through the wringer over the sink, hung them up on the lines stretched across the scullery ceiling. She thought how everything just hung in the balance waiting to fall when something went wrong. If Sid got hurt or worse they wouldn't have his wage. Hers alone wouldn't be enough to support all of them. They might lose the flat, which was tied to Sid's job. Where would they live? The damned workhouse would take them. She shuddered; she hoped it wouldn't ever come to that.

When she'd hung up the last of the washing, she slipped into bed next to Sid. She could tell from his breathing he wasn't asleep. He lifted his arm to let her snuggle on to his chest.

'I don't want you to do it, Sid. Does that mean anything?'

He laughed. 'Course it does, you daft bird, but a man's got to do his duty. Why should other men do it and not me? It ain't fair.'

'None of it's fair, but sometimes you have to think about your own and that's that. Your dad was quiet,' she said, wondering why Gerald hadn't said his piece about any of it.

Sid stroked her arm but remained silent. He hadn't even said anything against Phyllis, who'd given him the feather. Lily felt sick when she thought of it. How could Phyllis do such a thing? Her daughter Margaret was Lily's friend, more like a sister, and when they'd lost her brother Tom in the war it had hurt Lily too. Poor Tom, cut down so young. You heard words like slaughter, devastation, massacre when people talked about the fighting. She couldn't imagine her Sid caught up in that.

'It's all well and good for Kitchener to ask for volunteers,' she whispered. 'What about that time when some of them died when they had to stand in the cold rain on parade without their coats waiting for him?' Sid made no answer. 'And that was here, before they'd even left for France.'

There was no point now, Sid wanted to go to sleep, and so should she but she felt like going to knock on Phyllis's door, telling her to take it back. When you gave someone a feather you were calling them a coward. How dare she try to shame

21

Sid into enlisting? She'd lost her son and Lily was sorry for her, but not so sorry that she'd want Sid to put his life in danger.

'That awful Vesta Tilley, whipping crowds into a frenzy, dressing up like a soldier and getting men to enlist. It's all right for her, she doesn't have to go and fight on the front line; she hasn't even been to France to perform for the boys.' She paused, thinking of more damning evidence. 'And it won't be like in the beginning with a fanfare of trumpets to see off the crowds of volunteers, conscription will stop all of that.'

Sid turned to her, a tinge of impatience in his voice.

'Lil, everywhere I look I see reminders that I'm not doing my bit in this war. There are soldiers guarding the docks at work; there are garrisons camped out on the marshes training for France; lads billeted all around here, even some in schools; boat loads of injured men coming into Tilbury for the ambulance trains, the military funerals. I can't open the *Gazette* without seeing the call to arms and appeals for volunteers. There are posters everywhere, Kitchener pointing his finger telling men to volunteer, telling women to let their men go, to be ashamed if their boys don't take the King's shilling. Men released from German camps docking here. Can't you see how it is for a man, how you get looked at if you're not in uniform, even if you're in a starred job? You see the sacrifices being made by our lads—' Sid's voice caught in his throat. 'Well, you feel it's your duty to help protect the country, to protect our women and children. What if they invaded, Lil?' He paused, as if to let it all sink into his own mind, as well as hers. 'Now go to sleep, I've got a lot to think about.'

Lily's eyes swelled with tears. She tried to bite back a reply but couldn't stop herself.

22

'But they don't even bring the dead back home!' As soon as she'd said it, she wished she hadn't. 'I'm sorry,' she whispered and put her hand on to Sid's chest. He turned over without a word, leaving Lily feeling dreadful.

She couldn't sleep for the worry of it, and next to her Sid was silent, not the sound of his usual soft snores. They were both engaged with their own frightful thoughts in the dark. And everything was worse in the dead of night. There was no point of reference to compare things to, only the fear itself, amplified, growing and growing in your mind with nothing to stop it, no reality to jolt it back into perspective.

She remembered the shock of reading the paper at work when the HMS *Clan MacNaughton* had gone down in a storm. All on board were lost at sea. Thirty-five had been local men. She thought of poor Tom, Phyllis's son, who had been one of Kitchener's early volunteers, shot by a sniper in the Gallipoli trenches. She wondered whether he had suffered much, if anyone had held his hand at the end or reassured him with words of comfort. They used to run around the streets together and play on the marshes when they were growing up. Phyllis must have worried about him every day, must have looked down the street waiting for his letters from the post woman, dreading the sight of a telegram bicycle wending its way to give her bad news.

The only thought that gave her comfort was that Sid might get up in the morning and decide he'd carry on as he had been, wait to see whether he'd be called up to enlist, instead of volunteering. He might listen to reason, Lily would talk to him, persuade him to see sense. She looked over the side of the bed at the boys asleep on the mattress on the floor beside her. Joe had pushed his blanket off and had stretched his legs out on top. He looked so skinny. Lily felt a pang of guilt. She had given up trying to steal food from the Hall for the boys, she couldn't risk getting the sack, so she went without on her afternoon off to make up for it. If only Sid could get more hours they'd have a bit more to give the boys. But from the sound of it, things at the docks would only get worse not better. Gerald was eating food he wasn't earning. She bit her lip at the ungenerous thought. Her father-in-law had worked hard all his life; she shouldn't begrudge him now. She reached over to pull Joe's blanket back on but disturbed Robert in the process.

'Ma?' he said.

Lily's heart lifted with joy. She put a finger to her lips to shush him and held out her arms. He climbed over his brother and crawled into bed with her, the two of them snuggled together. If Sid saw it he wouldn't approve. His parents frowned on showing the boys too much affection. But she didn't see them often enough. Robert's warm little body next to hers made her cry again. Her head filled with thoughts of the Germans sailing down the Thames to capture London, the reports of the Belgians being raped and murdered, babies being killed. It was all so horrible. The brave Tommies going out to beat the Hun, protecting the country. The letters in the *Gazette* from the boys in the trenches, their jovial way of talking about things when really they must have hated it out there. Lily could see how that would play on Sid's mind when he looked at his own family. She could understand how he must have been thinking about enlisting all this time. She gave Robert a last squeeze and whispered for him to get back into bed.

The next morning Sid had already left for work when Lily got up at five. He must have heard about a boat coming in and gone to be called for work early. Lily had wanted to talk to him about the white feather. It was her afternoon off today, she planned to go and see Phyllis when she got home from work, ask her what the hell she'd been thinking when she'd called Sid a coward. The boys were sleeping soundly and Lily resisted the urge to wake them up. She dressed quietly and slipped out into the darkness, the bracing wind off the river taking her breath away. Once out on to Fort Road she picked up her pace to get her blood pumping. It was so cold. Her mind went to the men in France sleeping in the trenches; she wondered how they kept themselves warm. The houses became further spaced out, large green verges and post and wire fences showing boundaries. She nodded at a man passing on the way to the docks, breathing through a cigarette on his lip, his hands jammed deep in his pockets.

'Brass monkeys this morning,' she said, coming into the warm kitchen below stairs at St Clere's Hall.

'What do you expect in February?' said the cook, Mr Tween, stirring a saucepan of stock.

Lily ignored him, grumpy sod. 'Mrs Coker's breakfast ready?'

Mr Tween nodded at a tray on the table. 'Don't blame me if the tea's cold, you're five minutes late.'

Lily gave him a look behind his back and took the tray up to the servants' quarters. Pushing the door handle with her elbow, she entered the dark room, placed the tray on Mrs Coker's bedside table and opened the curtains. The housekeeper stirred and sat up, her greying hair tied in a loose pony tail at her shoulder, her nightdress done up to her neck. Lily didn't expect any thanks and didn't receive any either. Her stomach rumbled but she had the fires to do yet.

Downstairs she collected a bucket of cleaning things and a scuttle of coal, trudged up the back stairs again to the first floor of the house and tiptoed into Lady Charlotte's rooms. Cleaning out a fire and setting a new one without making a sound was a fine art, but it was imperative she didn't wake Lady Charlotte up. She lay the dust sheet down before the hearth and swept out the grate, taking care not to clang the dustpan. Arranging the kindling and coal, she lit the fire, blowing on it to get it going. It was always satisfying to light a nice clean fire. It wouldn't be long before the chill came off the room.

As she tidied the things away, the brass brush slipped out of her hand and clattered down on to the hearth. Lady Charlotte jolted awake, sitting up in bed.

'What in heaven's name?'

'Oh, I'm so sorry, Lady Charlotte. I dropped the brush.'

'Pavitt? Oh!' She fell back on to her pillows and closed her eyes. 'I shall report you to Lady Harrington, you clumsy oaf.' Lily froze, not knowing whether to speak. Lady Charlotte opened one eye. 'Well, go on, off you go.'

Lily grabbed the bucket and scuttle and left the room as quickly and quietly as she could. There was a chance the mistress would have her wages docked if she was reported. It was really bad luck. She went back down to refill the scuttle, and proceeded to clean the fires in the remaining bedrooms. Once she'd done that she went down for some breakfast. The other staff had already eaten, so she had to beg the cook for a plate and endure the scornful looks from Mrs Coker, who could not abide tardiness. The housekeeper kept her busy until three, when she begrudgingly let Lily go home for her one afternoon off a week.

The housekeeper's words rang in Lily's ears as she walked home: 'I've a good mind to keep you back after the way you've worked today. Your wages will be docked for waking up Lady Charlotte – yes, you needn't look so surprised, she told the mistress and it got back to me. You're too slow and too noisy doing the fires; you'll have to pull your socks up tomorrow.'

The words made Lily's eyes sting with angry tears. She always did her best, and did a good job, but nobody noticed until she made a mistake and then she was ripped to shreds for it. Since Mary had left, Lily had her work to do as well, and with no difference in her measly wage of half a crown. Her back and legs ached from the bending and lifting and she could have killed for a few hours' sleep but she trotted home, looking forward to seeing the boys, and dreading the task of giving Phyllis a talking-to about the white feather.

There was no one else walking on Hoford Road and the sun was out. She walked faster, checked behind her for anyone there and broke into a run, shaking off thoughts of Mrs Coker and white feathers. With her hand on her hat she laughed and ran like a lunatic and didn't care, it felt wonderful. At the sight of the first house on that road, she slowed to a walk, her secret moment of madness cheering the rest of her way home. To add to her joy, her boys were playing in the tenement courtyard when she got there. They ran up to her, folding themselves up in her skirts and calling out, 'Ma, Ma.' She picked them both up, all thoughts of aching shoulders forgotten, until they wriggled to get down to carry on their games. She left them there and walked up to the flat.

'Well, I hope you're happy,' said her mother-in-law Ada, sitting at the kitchen table, as she had been the previous night.

'What?'

'He's gone to sign up, hasn't he?'

Lily put her hand to her stomach, feeling sick. 'Sid? He hasn't.'

'Yes he has, my girl, he left a good hour ago; Gerald walked with him.'

'Watch the boys, I'm going after him.' Lily turned on her heel and made to leave.

'It's too late for that, and you've work to do here, miss. And your children to look after, I'm not your slave, you know.'

'I'm sorry, Ada, I'll be back in a minute.'

'You damn well won't . . .'

Ada rose from her chair, her face a picture of rage, but Lily made it to the door and sped down the stairs and out on to the road. She ran over the hairpin bridge, thinking fast. The recruiting office was in Grays, the next town, everyone knew that, the posters were in the paper every week, and plastered everywhere you went. It was an emergency; she could spend the money on the train fare to get there. Up ahead she spotted Mr Motherself's horse bus. It was a stroke of luck. She ran to catch it, waving at Mr Motherself, who saw her and pulled the reins to stop.

'You going to Grays?'

He nodded and tipped his cap when she rooted in her purse for a penny. Sitting in the covered wooden carriage that always reminded her of a gypsy caravan, she tried to catch her

28

breath. It took an agonising twenty minutes to get to Grays. She got off at Joyes' Drapers on New Road and walked as fast as she could around the corner to the High Street. Mitcham's Furs had been taken over for the purpose, a large sign saying RECRUITING OFFICE plastered over the original shop sign. There was no queue of hundreds of men down the street as the paper had shown when the war had started two years ago. When the government told them the war would be over by Christmas. There was no queue at all. But there was a group of boys in uniform from the TS *Exmouth* training ship sitting on the pavement, with various musical instruments at their lips, the sound of a brass band tuning up. They gave Lily a strange look as she passed.

The door bell rang when she entered the office. The shop had been sectioned off with the front half for the army's use. A man in uniform sat at a desk on one side and at the other side of the room there was another soldier standing up. With him was Sid, wearing a funny pair of eye test glasses, telling the recruiting officer the letters on the wall. Gerald stood nearby and Lily gave her father-in-law a quick wave, not wanting to speak and be reprimanded by the officers.

'Jolly well done,' said the officer when Sid had finished his test. He turned and saw Lily and the smile fell from his face.

'Lil? What're you doing here?'

'Sid,' she said, taking a step towards him, but painfully aware of the officers watching her. 'Please, Sid.' She shook her head at him and tried not to cry.

The officer at the desk seemed to have the long and short of it and spoke before Lily could.

'Well, Sergeant, we have another two willing and able

recruits. They'll be defending our glorious country and our womenfolk and children before we know it. If you would please step over here?'

Lily blanched when he handed Sid and Gerald a Bible each. What did the sergeant mean by two recruits? She wanted to reach out and pull them both away but she couldn't. A woman had no say in a place like that.

'You first,' he said to Sid. 'Do you read?' When Sid nodded, the officer handed him a piece of paper. 'Raise your hand and read the allegiance.'

Sid gave Lily an uneasy glance, raised his hand and read from the paper. 'I, Sidney Ronald Pavitt, do make oath, that I will be faithful and bear true allegiance to His Majesty King George the Fifth, His Heirs and Successors, and that I will, as in duty bound, honestly and faithfully defend His Majesty, His Heirs and Successors, in person, crown and dignity, against all enemies, and will observe and obey all orders of His Majesty, His Heirs and Successors, and of the generals and officers set over me. So help me God.'

Avoiding Lily's eye, Sid nodded and passed the paper to Gerald, who read out the oath too. 'Splendid,' said the officer. 'You'll be pleased to hear you can join the next lot of men going to Warley for training tomorrow. Report to Drill Hall at ten hundred hours sharp. Civilian clothes. You'll be provided with everything you need.'

It was all happening so fast; Lily felt sick at the thought of them going to Warley for training. The officer saluted and Sid and Gerald raised their flat hands awkwardly to their eyebrows.

As the three of them left the office, the TS *Exmouth* band

jumped to attention and started playing 'Fame and Glory', one boy smashing his cymbals together with extra zeal. Sid and Gerald seemed to stand taller at the sound of the song but Lily hated it, she wanted to knock the hats off the boys playing the instruments, wanted to throw their cornets and euphoniums down the High Street. Several passers-by stopped to see, applauded the two new recruits, some children waved and cheered. And Sid and Gerald seemed to stand straighter still. They walked a short way to the train station, Lily unable to speak until out of earshot of the patriotic onlookers. They bought their train tickets in silence, Sid paying for the three of them, and once in the platform waiting room, Lily let forth.

'I can't believe it, Sid. I thought we were going to talk about this. And Gerald, what in heaven's name? Does Ada know about this?'

Sid and Gerald exchanged glances. 'We'll tell her now, love,' said Gerald.

'Oh my good God,' said Lily, slumping back against the seat, too shocked to be able to think straight. The two of them were going off to war. What on earth would happen to them all?

They made the train journey in silence, each lost in their own thoughts. Lily was afraid to say anything, what was done was done and she didn't want to make things harder for them. Sid reached across to hold her hand and they sat like that until they disembarked at Tilbury. When they reached the tenements the boys saw them coming and ran to meet them, but soon ran off to play when they caught the mood of the adults.

Ada was lighting the range with a match to boil the kettle when they came in.

'Well, have you done it, then?' she said to Sid.

He nodded. 'Yes, Mum, it's done. We leave for training tomorrow.'

Ada put her hand over her mouth but then frowned. 'What do you mean, we? There are some others going with you, then?'

'It's me, love,' said Gerald. 'I'm going with him. I have to, I'm sorry, love.'

Ada gave a disbelieving laugh. 'Very funny, Gerald. I can just see *you* out in the trenches with *your* chest.'

He stepped towards her, took her hands in his. 'I have to go with him, love, with our boy, I'm sorry.'

'But you're too old!' Ada blurted. 'Too old and not a picture of health, I don't mind saying.'

'Forty-one is the maximum age,' he said, 'and I'm forty, and they didn't listen to my chest, just checked my eyes.'

'No! You can't, you silly old sod, you can't.'

Gerald gave a small shrug and an apologetic smile and Ada came at him. Lily stepped away as the woman banged her fists into Gerald's chest, knocking him backwards until he fell clattering against the range, the kettle making a metallic grinding sound as it was pushed across the hob. Gerald grabbed his wife's wrists, pulled her struggling into his arms. He held here there until she stopped thrashing against him and let out one anguished sob. The kettle came to the boil and rattled violently, no one taking it off the heat, the scalding water bubbling up and over the spout.

3

Normally Lily would sneak out of bed and feel around in the dark for her clothes but this morning she struck a match and lit a candle. She wanted to watch her family sleep, wondering if it might be the last time they were all in the same room together.

Sid stirred, the light playing across his face, and then relaxed and put out his arm for his wife. Lily held his hand, her face crumpling into tears. Her darling Sid, what would she do without him? She scrutinised his sleeping face, peaceful and kind, his dark eyebrows and moustache, the stubble on his chin, his hair tousled and boyish. She wanted to beat his chest and beg him not to go, the way Ada had with Gerald the night before, but she couldn't do it. He was going to war because he needed to.

She glanced down at the mattress on the floor where the boys slept. Robert was half on the floor, a chip off the old block, kind to a fault, even in his sleep he was making room for his brother. And little Joe was sprawled across most of the bed, arms and legs at angles like he'd been challenged to take up as much room as possible. Her stomach convulsed at the thought of them saying goodbye to their father, at how hard it would be to make light of it so they would be proud and not worried.

'Sid, love,' she whispered, rubbing his arm gently. He grunted and opened his eyes to slits. 'I'm off now, love.' She waited the two seconds it took his mind to register what was happening today and his eyes opened fully. He pulled her towards him on to his chest. 'I'll be there to wave you off, though.'

'But the old bag won't let you,' he mumbled. It was a joke between them. They couldn't decide who was worse, Mrs Coker the housekeeper or the mistress herself, so he referred to them jointly as the old bag.

'They bloody well will. They'll have to,' said Lily, feeling the sting of tears. She had to be there to wave Sid off at the train station.

'Say goodbye now, just in case.'

She sobbed. 'No, I can't.'

'It's all right, I'll be all right and so will you.'

She stifled her sobs and nodded into his chest. 'I'd better get off then, if I've any chance of leaving early, I'd better not be late to start with.' She stood up and looked down at him. 'Tell your mother to be there with the boys at Grays station, and I'll come.' She leaned over to kiss him. He grabbed her arms and held her there. Letting out a sob she pulled away and with one last look back at him from the doorway she left.

Through her tears, the walk to work was a blur of black trees. She jogged along, determined to arrive on time, tripping on unseen rocks and sticks in the road, the cold air burning her lungs. There was only one thing she could think of – she had to be at Grays station to see Sid off. Panting, she came in at the servants' entrance of St Clere's Hall, shook off her coat and went straight into the kitchen. Mr Tween turned in surprise.

'Early today, is it? Making up for yesterday, I suppose?'

'Is Mrs Coker's breakfast ready?' Lily said, ignoring his remark.

'She'll not be wanting it yet. It'll be ready in ten minutes.'

In ten minutes she could get the coal up the back stairs for Lady Charlotte's fire. She grabbed the scuttle and filled it quickly at the coal shed, ran with it up the stairs, the sense of urgency propelling her forwards. Creeping into Lady Charlotte's room, she glanced at the bed, its occupant sleeping soundly. She had the fire swept out and laid in a fraction of the time it normally took her, and she was back down in the kitchen in time for the cook to set the cup and saucer on the tray. She bumped her way through the door and up the stairs again to the housekeeper's room. Setting down the tray, she stood back, waiting for Mrs Coker to rouse herself and sit up.

'Well? What do you want standing there, girl?' Mrs Coker picked the crust from her nose and flicked it on to the wooden floor.

'I've got something to ask you, Mrs Coker, but it'll keep until you've come downstairs.'

'Oh, ask it now and be done with it,' she said, with a flicker of curiosity.

Lily took a deep breath. 'My husband has volunteered for the army and he's leaving town for the training camp today. I need to leave work early to go and see him off, please.'

Mrs Coker made a humph sound in her throat. 'Your

husband is only volunteering now to avoid being fetched under conscription. You should be ashamed when so many of our boys have already perished.' With that, she poured herself a cup of tea from the pot, her eyebrows raised in indignation.

'No, Mrs Coker, he's a docker; he's not expected to enlist, he's doing it out of pride.'

'Pride, eh?' The housekeeper hacked the crown off her boiled egg and dipped in her spoon, sucked off the yellow yolk with a slurp. 'And there's no white feather involved in his decision, I don't suppose?' The woman watched sharply for Lily's reaction as if to catch her out.

'No, Mrs Coker,' said Lily, knowing if she admitted the truth, the woman would only use it against her. She cursed Phyllis silently for causing all of this and vowed to confront her about giving Sid that damned white feather.

'Well, you can't go; there's too much to do.' The yolk had run down the handle of her spoon. She stuck out her tongue that was dotted with rags of congealed egg white and ran it the length of the handle.

Lily wanted to tell her to stuff her job, but she daren't. It was precious, she was lucky to have it. And now with Sid going, she needed it more than ever.

'I'll make up the time . . .' She faltered, the sight of Mrs Coker's face stopping her.

'You'll get on with your work, that's what you'll do, unless you want me to tell the mistress that we need to look for a new housemaid, one that can live in, which would be a darn sight more convenient, I don't mind saying.'

'Yes, Mrs Coker.' Lily ducked her head and left the room. Going down the corridor, she felt sick at the thought of missing Sid leave. Coming back downstairs, she grabbed the coal scuttle and chewed her nail, gave Sarah the lady's maid a tight smile and went back up to do the mistress's fire. She crept into the lavish bedroom and started when she saw two people asleep in the bed. The master must have sought out the mistress's company and not gone to his own room as he might normally have done. Taking extra care to be quiet, she swept out the ashes from the grate and desperately thought how she could get away early from work. A barmy idea suddenly occurred to her and she thought she might act on it, not knowing what the consequences would be if something went wrong. The master liked her, didn't he? Not in a decent way, of course, and she'd intended to steer well clear of him, but there might be a way of using it to her benefit.

She picked up the coal shovel and held it above the stone hearth, glanced at the sleeping figures, and dropped it. The loud metallic clang woke them up instantly.

'What the devil?' called out Lord Harrington, sitting up in bed and looking about him. Lady Harrington did the same, and when she saw Lily there at the fireplace, her face was a picture of wrath.

'Jane?' She put a hand on her husband's arm to reassure him. 'It's all right, dearest, you needn't be alarmed; it's silly Jane and her clanging bucket. The stupid creature woke Charlotte the other morning.'

Lord Harrington leaned back on his pillow and reached out for his pipe. He seemed quite amused by the sight of Lily standing there holding the offending brass shovel and took the opportunity to look her up and down.

'I'm sorry, milord, milady, I'm just nervous this morning.'

'Hush!' said the mistress. 'You will not talk in our presence. Finish your work and leave us in peace, if you please.'

'Hold your horses, old thing,' said the Lord to his wife. 'What do you mean by nervous?' he asked Lily.

Lily's heart leapt, her plan might work. 'Sorry, milord, it's my husband, he's leaving for army training and I wanted to see him off at Grays station but Mrs Coker says there's too much work, so . . .'

'Oh, righto, righto,' he said, frowning and pulling on his pipe, the smoke obscuring his face for a moment. 'Well, it's a bloody bad show if we can't see our boys off, don't you think?'

'I think,' said the mistress, scowling, 'that if Mrs Coker says there is too much to do, then I trust her implicitly.'

'Yes, quite right, quite right, but even so. Righto, come on, I've made up my mind.' With that, the master pulled back the bed cover, swung his legs down to plant his feet in his slippers, and stood up, his pipe still in his mouth.

'Where the devil is my dressing gown?' he said, looking around uncertainly.

'Shall I fetch the valet, milord?' said Lily, stepping forward.

'I'll be damned if a man of the army can't find his own dressing gown,' he said, striding around the room. 'Damned if he can't.'

He couldn't locate the dressing gown, and Lily took her opportunity and ran downstairs to fetch the valet, who was eating his breakfast in the servants' hall and looked like his trouser braces had given way when he heard he was wanted earlier than dressing time. He ran upstairs with Lily on his heels, the two of them entering the Lady's room out of breath.

'I do apologise, my Lord,' said the valet, bowing as he held out the gown for the master to slip his arms into.

'Yes, well, humph,' said the master. 'That will be all.'

The valet backed out of the room and Lily felt sorry at the sight of his wretched face, but her need was more important today.

'Righto, come on, Jane; let's sort this thing out.'

He waved Lily ahead of him out of the door. Out of habit she put her hand on the servants' door to the back stairs, but hesitated.

'Yes, we'll go down the back way,' said Lord Harrington, ushering her through. The green baize swung shut and Lily paused on the landing, gestured that they needed to go down the back stairs. Before she could move, the master stepped towards her, blocking her way. As he looked down at her, he seemed enormous, the pungent aroma of his unwashed body overpowering, his moustache obscuring his mouth.

'I had better know your real name. It's not Jane, I suppose?'

He spoke around his pipe – the smoke on his breath was repugnant. 'No, milord,' said Lily, trying not to look him in the eye. 'It's Pavitt.'

He nodded. 'Pavitt, I see. Well, look here, Pavitt, I am a man of the world – even more than that, I am a man of the Essex Yeomanry. And I am in a position to offer you some advice, if I may.' He didn't pause for her consent. 'The army is a life of comradeship, of hardship, of brutality and loyalty, but also of loneliness. An army man must do what he must to see himself through, if you understand my meaning. And the people he leaves behind must do the same.' He took a step closer to her. 'You do understand my meaning, Pavitt?' he said, taking his pipe out of his mouth.

The sound of footsteps clattered on the stairs above them. They looked up to see Mrs Coker emerging from the servants' quarters for the day. When she saw Lord Harrington on the back stairs, she broke from her reverie and squeaked a surprised greeting.

'Oh, my Lord, goodness me, you took me by surprise.' She glanced at Lily, cornered like a trapped rat, and back at the master.

The master took on a stern tone, which Lily knew was to divert attention from the way he was standing so close to her.

'Now look here, Mrs Coker, what's all this about Pavitt here not being allowed leave to see off her husband going to war?'

He waited for her response, which she gave while the colour drained from her face.

'Oh, my Lord, I do apologise, I was only thinking of the house and the family. Of course she must go, if you consented to it.'

He didn't deign to reply, but pushed back through into the main landing. Lily's shoulders dropped an inch and she would have laughed out loud with relief if the housekeeper hadn't been approaching her in a quiet rage.

'And what time do you intend on shirking your duties this fine day?' said Mrs Coker, straightening her skirt and continuing her descent down the stairs.

'Thank you, Mrs Coker, my husband reports to Drill Hall at ten this morning, so if I leave at ten I'll be sure to be there at the train station in time to see him off.'

'Well, you'd better get on with your work then, Pavitt. I

expect all the fires to be done and all the slops to be emptied before you go. And we'll need to sort out when you'll be giving back the hours you are taking today.'

'Yes, Mrs Coker, thank you,' said Lily, ducking her head and cantering down the stairs, thinking about the risk she had taken, and how it had paid off, for now at least. She'd have to be extra careful about avoiding the master in future.

The minute Lady Charlotte and the master had come down for breakfast at nine, Lily was upstairs to empty the chamber pots and tidy the rooms. The mistress took breakfast in bed, and this morning she really took her time over it. Finally her lady's maid, Sarah, called for Lily at a quarter to ten to help attend, and the mistress was so indecisive about what to wear and how she wanted her hair that Lily wasn't finished with her until half past.

'I'm off, Mrs Coker,' she said, poking her head into the housekeeper's office. The woman made no reply and Lily ran away, getting out before anyone changed their mind. She gathered up her skirts with one hand, held on to her hat with the other and ran down the London Road. The cold didn't bother her; she just had to get to Grays on time. She'd even spend thruppence on the fare from Stanford-le-Hope station to get there for Sid. And as her train pulled into Grays, she knew she hadn't missed him – there was a crowd waiting for the new recruits, she could see them down the High Street from the train window.

There was no sign of Ada and the boys. Lily ran down the platform on to the High Street, pushing through the throng, rushing on tiptoe to see above the heads. The sound of a brass band drifted towards her and she knew they were coming down Quarry Hill. The crowd parted to make a wide walk-way through the middle of the road and the boys from the TS *Exmouth* training ship came marching along with their trumpets and drum. A marching officer led the recruits, all kitted out in their new khaki serge and Lily scanned their faces for Sid. A hand closed tight on her arm and she turned to see Ada standing next to her. The boys were there, enthralled by the occasion and looking for their father.

'Oh, boys!' said Lily, leaning down to encircle them in her arms. 'Aren't you just as proud as punch of your dad?' They looked at her uncertainly, excitement and fear drawn across their faces. 'Let's look for him, come on.' Lily turned away to compose herself, saw the same strained look on Ada's face. They were pushed back as the recruits drew nearer, but Lily resisted, and got the boys to the front for a good view, looking at each row of men as they came filing past, at each uniform, as bland as pea soup, at each face, controlled and tight.

'Pa!' called out Robert, pointing to two rows back. Lily jumped to see, and there he was, her Sid, and only the second man in the row – what luck, he'd be sure to see them there.

'Sid! Sid, love!' called Lily, not caring about decorum or decency.

Gerald was there too, marching shoulder to shoulder with his son. Ada waved her handkerchief at him and called his name. *Those who enlist together serve together.* That was Kitchener's promise. Father and son had on their uniforms; they must have been measured up that same morning. The hobnail boots, the webbing, the brass buttons, the peaked cap. The puttees wound about their legs like bandages, as if a premonition of what was to come. For an instant Lily's chest swelled with love and pride at the sight of her Sid looking like a soldier, and then she saw him look sideways at her as he passed and he looked like a little boy, being bullied into a fight he didn't want. A shiver of terror shot through her, it was as if they both saw what might come at the same time, they both fully realised it at that moment.

Ada started to sob. 'They can't go,' she said. 'What will I do? Oh, what will I do? Gerald! Gerald!'

Lily held her mother-in-law's arm. 'Stop it, Ada. Let him go. Smile, for goodness' sake, just smile.'

Ada started to wail, and Lily just hoped that Gerald wouldn't hear her above the din of the band and the people's cheers.

'Oh, what will I do? I'll go to my sister's, I'll not stay here, I'll not.'

Lily looked at the woman in horror, but Sid had gone by. 'Wave to your pa, boys; did you wave to your pa?' Robert and Joe looked up at her, Joe's lip trembling. The crowd was too much for him, and Lily wasn't sure they'd seen Sid properly, because of Ada's nonsense. She grabbed them both up in her arms, so heavy, but she stumbled forward, pushed through the people next to her to get to Sid, calling after him. His swinging arms lost a beat but he didn't turn around, it wouldn't have been allowed.

'Come on, boys, one last word, say goodbye to your pa.' Joe was crying now, and Robert looked near to breaking down too. She surged forward until she came up by her husband and matched his stride.

'Bye, love, bye. Say bye to your pa, boys. Bye, love, bye.'

Sid had all manner of things etched across his dear face but he didn't say a word. He had seen them, though, that was certain and Lily had to be happy with that. She stopped and put the boys down. They clung to her legs and cried. No tears fell from her eyes, she was numb. The scene played out around her. The waving wives and triumphant band, more boys had been claimed for the cause, more lives to be used as artillery shells and bullets. And her Sid was one of them.

She made her way back to Ada, pulling the boys along with her. Her mother-in-law had her hankie to her face, watching the men march past. When the boys saw her they rushed to her side. Ada said to Lily what she'd said before.

'I'll go to my sister's. I can't stay here without him.'

Lily knew why she said it. It wasn't because she couldn't cope on her own without Gerald. After all, they'd have each other: she and Ada and the boys would manage. It was because Ada couldn't read and wouldn't be able to read the letters Gerald would send her. It was something she'd never admit to Lily for the shame of it.

'We can help each other,' said Lily, putting her hand on Ada's arm. But Ada took her arm away and turned to go, the boys going with her and leaving Lily to follow. She had managed to smile and wave Sid off to let him go with a light heart but now what would they do? The thought of being left at home with Ada was bad enough, but the thought of Ada leaving was worse.

Once the army train had pulled away to the sound of 'Auld Lang Syne' played by the band, they were allowed into the station. Waiting on the packed platform, Lily looked at the posters plastered along the fence. Posters appealing for war workers and recruits. One of them showed a man in his armchair at home, one child on his lap and another playing at his feet; the caption read, *Daddy, what did YOU do in the Great War?* Lily was pleased that her boys knew their daddy was doing his bit. Another poster had a woman munitions worker wearing an overall and pushing her hair into a cap. In the background, there was a battle scene with a Tommy putting shells into a field gun. The caption ran, *On her their lives depend . . . Enrol at once.*

'Come here, boys,' said Lily. Robert and Joe didn't want to leave Ada's skirts and Lily felt a prickle of anger and shame. 'Come here, I said; do as your mother tells you.' Lily looked to Ada for support but the older woman gave her none. Rather, Lily sensed her pleasure that the boys wanted their nanny. Lily grabbed Robert's hand and held it tight against her, squeezing his hand to let him know she was cross.

'There's no need for me to write to my sister,' said Ada. 'I know she'll say yes.'

Lily swallowed away her frustration. How did the woman think Lily would manage without her?

'But what'll I do, Ada, if you go?' Lily indicated the boys without them seeing.

'What, Nanny?' said Robert, sensing something was wrong.

'I'm going away to live with my sister,' said Ada, and Lily cursed her silently.

A shadow fell across Robert's face as he processed the information. He'd just seen his father and grandfather go off to war and now this too. He pulled his hand away from Lily's and went to Ada. He didn't need to say anything; it was clear how he felt. Looking away to save her dignity, Lily saw their neighbour Phyllis a little way down the platform. At the sight of her, Lily's hackles rose and she strode towards the woman without a thought. Seeing Lily push through the crowd towards her, Phyllis started with surprise and straightened her shoulders in defence.

'What were you thinking about, Phyllis, giving my Sid a feather?' said Lily, her hands trembling with anger.

'So what if I did? He's gone, hasn't he, to do his duty? Good on him, I say, it's only what he should have done.' She nodded to a poster on the fence, the picture a silhouette of two Tommies armed with rifles and bayonets, climbing a slope to battle, with the caption, *Don't stand looking at this, GO and HELP!*

'But you know damn well he's a docker in a starred job; he wears the badge, doesn't he?'

Phyllis shrugged and Lily wanted to push her over the edge of the platform on to the track.

'You should be proud of him going,' said another woman behind Phyllis, who Lily didn't know. 'I'm proud of my husband, we all are.'

The next train made its arrival known with loud grunts of smoke and screeching brakes. Lily leaned in so no one else could hear. 'It's on your hands, Phyllis, if anything happens to him.'

'Oh? And what about my boy, whose hands is that on?' said Phyllis. Lily shook her head, she was sorry for Phyllis's boy, of course she was, he had been her friend, but Phyllis had acted out of spite when she gave Sid a feather – a sad kind of spite that wished her boy's fate on everyone else.

Lily made her way back to Ada and they piled on the train and found seats, the boys giving up theirs for other adults crowding into the carriage. They both squeezed on to Ada's lap. Ada grimaced at the weight and pushed Joe across to his mother.

'What did she have to say for herself?' said Ada.

'Not much,' said Lily, aware of the families who'd just waved off their boys. She looked out of the window as the train pulled away. The thought of Sid marching past her made her throat tighten. 'What on earth would I do if you left, Ada?' she said again. Ada shifted Robert on her lap when his arms knocked her hat sideways. 'I mean, how would I work?' said Lily. 'Who'd have the boys? No one will take them with the hours I do at the Hall. I wouldn't be able to work, would I? We need the money.'

'I'll take them with me. My sister wouldn't mind.'

'What? No, what do you mean, take them with you?'

Ada shrugged as if it was the best idea she could think of. Lily's shoulders sank when she looked at her children. She'd been so worried lately that they were in danger in Tilbury with the Zeppelin raids. Ada's sister lived in a little village in the Kent countryside. But the thought of them all leaving her on her own . . .

'I'll read the letters, Ada,' she said in a low voice. Ada blushed a deep red. It was as if she'd accused her mother-in-law of harbouring a German. 'I'll read Gerald's letters, it's all right,' said Lily, 'and I'll write them for you, too.'

'I'm going to my sister's, and that's the end of it.' Ada drew her mouth into a tight bunch and looked out of the window. 'And I'll take the boys with me so you can work and send us their keep,' she went on, still staring out, 'they'll be safe in the countryside.'

'But I'll be on my own,' said Lily, knowing that the boys being safe would be a weight off her mind.

'You can go and live in up at the Hall, like you used to; they'd much rather you do that anyway,' said Ada, turning to look at her. 'The docks can let our flat out for the time being but keep it for when we all come home.'

Lily stared at her mother-in-law. She'd worked out a plan pretty quickly since finding out the day before that Sid and Gerald were both going. The woman was panicking, making rash decisions. Her reason for living had been looking after Gerald, doing everything for him. Now Ada's only communication with him would be through letters, letters that she wouldn't even be able to read herself.

'That way we won't be paying rent, you'll just pay your live-in board at the Hall and you can send me the rest. You'll be able to send me Sid's separation allowance and I'll have Gerald's and that will do for our keep at my sister's.'

It was all new to Lily; all of a sudden there was the prospect of her being alone without her in-laws, without her children and without Sid. And Ada wanted her to go and live at St Clere's Hall and be a proper live-in housemaid, which was what Mrs Coker kept on at her about. It would secure her job, there was no doubt about that. And, looking at the boys clinging to Ada like she was their mother . . . Lily fought back her tears; in one fell swoop everything she held dear was slipping away.

A thought occurred to her. 'What about if I came with you? I'd be able to get a little job somewhere there, wouldn't I?'

'Oh no, I don't think so, there wouldn't be enough room for you at my sister's. It'd be a pinch with the boys there as it is.'

They weren't close, Ada and Lily, and Lily should have known Ada wouldn't want her to come. She was probably right that there wouldn't be the room, but she hadn't even given it a moment's thought.

The train slowed down as it pulled into Tilbury station and Ada got up to ready the boys to leave.

'It's for the best and it's not for ever, is it, just while Gerald and Sid are away.' She tugged at the boys' hands to get them to look up at her. 'You'd like to come and stay with Nanny at Auntie Dolly's, wouldn't you? In the countryside where you can run around the fields?'

'Well, we haven't decided yet, boys,' said Lily, frowning at Ada.

'I would, Nanny,' said Robert, while Joe looked uncertainly from his brother to his nan, not understanding.

'See?' said Ada. 'It's for the best.'

The train shuddered to a stop and Lily kissed the boys' heads, staying on the train to get back to work. The train pulled off again and Lily watched the backs of the woman and two young boys as they waited with their tickets at the exit. From the back Ada could have passed for their mother. Lily felt angry tears spring to her eyes. She didn't know if Ada really wanted the boys to go with her out of affection for them or if it was her way of keeping what was Sid's close to her. Either way, Lily knew the boys would be all right with Ada, she always treated them better than she treated Lily. And if they went with her to Nettlestead Lily would still be able to see them sometimes. She could get there and back on her afternoon off, she'd not see them for long but she'd be able to keep in touch. She shook her head; she couldn't believe she was even making these plans. As usual she had no say about what happened in her life and that alone made her angry. But if Ada went, Lily really had no choice.

It was half past one by the time she walked into Mrs Coker's office to tell her she was back.

'It was good of you to make an appearance,' said the housekeeper, not looking up from her desk. 'I shall make a plan of when you will return the three hours you have taken.'

'Yes, Mrs Coker, thank you,' said Lily. 'And, Mrs Coker?'

'What is it now?'

'I wanted to ask you if – and I'm not sure if it'll happen yet – but if I wanted to live in again, would there be room for me here?'

Mrs Coker put down her pen and looked up. 'Well, well, is there trouble in paradise?'

Lily frowned and shook her head. 'My mother-in-law might take my boys to her sister's, so I'd be able to move back in here – it's what you'd rather, isn't it?'

'Well, never mind what I would rather. The family would certainly want you to be doing your job to its full capacity. Yes, certainly you can move back in.'

'Thank you, Mrs Coker.'

'It'll be a good chance for you to make up those hours, too. Off you go now, there's the bedroom floors to do.'

Lily grabbed a tin bucket and dustpan and brush. It would just be a quick sweep today, a more thorough brushing on Fridays. She made her way up the back stairs and pushed through on to the first-floor landing. On the way to Lord Harrington's bedroom, she looked over the banister to the ground floor and saw the master move from the library to the sitting room. He glanced up at her as he went and she shivered, remembering how he had cornered her on the servants' stairs that morning.

In the master's room, she got down to sweep the rug, glad he was safely out of the way. It was looking like she would be moving back into the servants' quarters. She hadn't lived there for over three years; it would be strange going back. There was still a chance Ada would change her mind and stay. Lily would just have to wait and see. Even if Ada took the boys, she might stay at her sister's for a week and decide she'd be happier at home. She tensed when she heard a man cough on the landing, and turned to see Lord Harrington come into his room. She was on all fours on the rug, and quickly sat up on her knees.

'I'm sorry, milord, I'll come back later.'

'Oh, it's all right, er, Pavitt, I just needed to pop in for a book.' He strode to his bedside table and picked up a book that lay there. 'Did your lad get off all right?'

'Yes, thank you, milord. Thank you for letting me go.'

'Not at all, Pavitt, happy to.'

Lily stood up, wanting to leave the room and the awkwardness of the situation. The master seemed to take it as an invitation to move closer, and Lily glanced at the door.

'Mrs Coker tells us you'll be moving back into the servants' quarters now your man has gone off.'

'That's right, milord,' said Lily, blanching as he took another step closer. He could have touched her if he'd raised his arm.

'Gosh, you're a pretty little thing, aren't you, Pavitt?' he said, appraising her face and figure.

'I don't know, milord,' she stammered.

She winced as he reached out to her. With the back of his hand he traced the shoulder strap of her apron, downwards to the bib to settle on her chest. She froze rigid and stared into his hooded eyes.

With a sudden breath in, he let his arm fall to his side. 'Righto, Pavitt, I'll leave you to get on with it.' And with that, he turned and left the room.

Lily waited there for a few seconds to make sure he'd gone, then she dropped to the floor to finish sweeping as quickly as she could. She bit her lip and blinked, sweeping up her tears with the dust into the pan.

4

'Can't you at least leave on my afternoon off next week?'

Several days had passed and Ada had shown no sign of changing her mind.

'No, we need to get an early start, take the ferry over to Gravesend, then two trains down to Nettlestead.' Ada busied herself packing her things into boxes for storing once she'd gone. 'This lot can go in the tenement basement,' she said, implying that Lily would be carrying it down for her. 'I've arranged a short-term tenant from the docks.'

'What? But I told you I can't move into the Hall for a week or so.' Lily's plan to stay in Tilbury in case Ada changed her mind didn't seem to be panning out.

'Well, you'll have to board with a friend in the meantime. You need to get your things packed up and stored for when the new tenant comes tomorrow.'

Lily put her hands on her head. The woman was infuriating.

'Ada, you're only just telling me I need to move out tomorrow. Didn't you think I'd need more time to get myself sorted out and to have some time to see the boys?'

'It's your afternoon off today, isn't it? You'll have plenty of time to get packed up and take all this down to the basement and see the boys.'

Lily bit her tongue and imagined her hands around Ada's throat. 'Robert, Joe, come here,' she called out of the door down to the tenement courtyard where they were playing in the bitter cold.

They trudged up the communal stairs with red noses and streaming eyes. Lily sat down and called them to her.

'My dears, this is going to be such an adventure, going to Auntie Dolly's.' She beamed at them and they smiled back. 'You know what? You're going there tomorrow with your nanny.'

'We know,' said Robert. Lily nodded and kept her composure.

'Ma has to go to work in the morning, so I will say good-bye to you really early before I go, all right?'

'Hungry,' said Joe.

'Hang on, Joe; did you hear what Ma said?' The little boy nodded and went to watch Ada packing up, his brother followed him. Lily watched them and her heart pinched with sadness.

She went out to beg some apple crates from the green-grocer and got back to pack up their things, bundling some clothes for herself to take to the Hall – she'd have to move in there tomorrow. She laid Sid's clothes into a box, folded them slowly, thinking about him. She'd had a letter from him the day before telling her about training at Warley: the drills and the early starts, getting into shape ready for war.

How their lives had changed in just a few short weeks. He'd asked after the boys, of course, but she'd held off replying. Now she'd have to tell him his mother was taking them to his aunt's at Nettlestead. She'd phrase it so it would sound like the right thing to do – he had enough to worry about. She stood up and looked at the boxes, picked up the first one and struggled down the stairs with it to the basement.

The next morning she woke up with a shiver of dread. She'd let the boys get in the bed with her and they were sleeping soundly – one squashed and one sprawled, as usual. Not wanting to wake them yet, she dressed quietly and checked the flat. It was tidy enough for the tenant. She'd been up till late sluicing and scrubbing the floors.

'Boys, wake up,' she whispered, stroking their heads. They stirred and looked at her through gummy eyes. 'I'm off now, boys, give Ma a kiss.'

They crawled into her lap, still half asleep and she clutched them to her, kissed them over and over, the last kiss never being enough, squeezed them and let them lie back down. It was early for them, they closed their eyes and went back to sleep. She was glad they didn't see her face crumble.

She crept into Ada's room to say goodbye. She had to shake the woman's arm to wake her up.

'What is it?' she said.

'I'm off now, Ada, I've said goodbye to the boys. Take care of them for me, won't you?'

'What time is it?' said Ada, squinting at the draped window. She moaned and lay back down.

'Bye, then,' said Lily, but Ada gave no answer, she just moaned again and rolled over back to sleep.

Lily heaved her bundle of belongings knotted into a sheet

on to her shoulder and walked out into the darkness. It was bleak and cold and she could see no sign of the dawn on the horizon. She'd never felt so empty in her life.

'I'll be moving back here today, if that suits you, Mrs Coker?'

Lily set the housekeeper's breakfast tray down on the bed and stood back, holding her breath at the stench of wind puffing from the bed sheets as Mrs Coker sat up.

'Never mind what suits me, Pavitt, it's what suits the family that counts. There's a room for you but it needs airing and setting, so you'll do that in your own time.'

'Thank you, Mrs Coker, I'll go and do the fires.'

'Yes, Pavitt, it's what you'll do every morning – you needn't announce it.'

Lily was supposed to start with the master's room when he was at home, and then the mistress's, and she thought that was probably best. The earlier it was, the less likely he would be awake. She had managed to avoid him since the time in his room the previous week when he had touched her. He was a heavy sleeper, thank goodness. Creeping into his room, she was relieved to see he wasn't in his bed. She looked around quickly but there was no sign of him. She breathed out a sigh; he must have slept with her Ladyship last night. Without delay, she laid down the dust cloth and started to sweep out the fire.

'It's a wonderful morning, Pavitt.'

Lily jumped and let out a small shriek. Lord Harrington stepped out from behind the drawn curtain.

'Oh dear, I'm afraid I've startled you. I do apologise. I often wait for the dawn to come in. When you're in the field you go by nature's clock and wake up with the birds; it's force of habit, I suppose.'

Lily regained her composure, tense with worry that he would try something. She dumped the ashes into the bucket and set about arranging the kindling in the grate.

'Now, you mustn't worry, Pavitt. About me, I mean. I'm a harmless fellow really, and you've a good position here, I'd say?'

'Yes, your Lordship,' she squeaked, desperately arranging the fire. She gathered everything into the bucket, took up the dust sheet, and made to leave.

'No rush, Pavitt; join me at the window, it's a glorious sight.'

'But I've the fires to do, milord, I must get on,' she said in the strongest voice she could muster. But her guts were melting with fear and her mouth was as dry as anything.

'Pavitt, I insist,' he said, commanding her to come.

She set down her bucket and looked back at the closed door. He held the curtain aside for her and to her dismay they were soon hidden behind it at the window. He stood behind her, his breath in her hair.

'What did I tell you? Glorious, isn't it?'

The sun was hiding beneath the horizon but had reached up to touch the charcoal sky with its pink fingers. It was beautiful but Lily was scared to death. She flinched when Lord Harrington put his arms around her from behind and leaned down to kiss her neck. 'It'll be a good hour before the sun is up. It's so very beautiful,' he breathed. 'Keep quiet, now, Pavitt,' he said in a hushed but determined voice.

He pulled her left hand behind her back and pushed it

against his groin. She felt his hardness through his pyjama trousers and made to move sideways to get away but he put his other hand on her shoulder and held her there, his fingers digging into her skin. Panicking, she tried to pull her hand back but he had it too tightly in his. A coldness crept over her, her feet frozen to the floorboards. She wanted to cry out but her voice was stifled by fear. This was something Lord Harrington wanted to have from her and she was helpless to do otherwise. She focused on the pink clouds as he rubbed her hand against his privates and grunted into her hair. His hand hurt hers with the force of it, rubbing, rubbing, harder and faster, the smell of his stale sweat and sour breath, he rubbed and grunted and then he stopped and let out a long juddering breath. He released her hand. She sobbed and fled, fumbling her way through the opening of the curtain and back into the room. Grabbing the tin bucket and cloth, she wrenched open the door to run down the landing and on to the servants' stairs.

When she reached below stairs she ran to the scullery, turned on the tap and scrubbed her hand with Borax and the stiff clothes brush until her skin was red raw.

'Are all the fires done, Pavitt?' It was Mrs Coker, look-ing up from a piece of paper as she went past. Lily let out a wretched sob and pushed past the woman, grabbed her coat from the peg and bolted for the back door. 'Where do you think you're going?' Mrs Coker called after her. Lily didn't reply. All she knew was she had to get out. Her survival instinct was now making her run instead of play dead.

She ran, crying, along the drive and out on to London Road. The tenement flat was given over to another tenant from today so she couldn't even go home. A man walked by and took a second glance at her. She sniffed and wiped her eyes on the cuff of her coat and slowed to a walk. She thought of Lord Harrington and shivered. Never would she have imagined he'd be capable of something so crude, so sickening. If Sid knew he'd go mad. She wouldn't be able to tell him, it'd have to be her secret. The previous first housemaid, Mary, who'd left to do war work at the cement factory, had been the object of the master's attentions. It was awful to think she'd been made to do things like that and Lily wondered how long it had gone on for and whether it had got even worse over time. No wonder the poor girl had left.

Walking in the direction of Stanford-le-Hope town, she passed some quiet houses, a woman pushing a milk cart along the dirt road, a sight she'd never have seen before the war. She rarely had cause to come this far into town – St Clere's Hall was on the outskirts and she lived south of there in Tilbury. Crossing over the railway track, she saw a poster pasted on the side of an end-of-terrace house. It was one of those she'd seen at Grays station – the munitions worker pulling on her overall, and the slogan, *On her their lives depend*. She continued on up the hill towards the church and sat down on a bench in the square, put her face into the lapel of her coat and wept. She felt soiled and as though she were to blame somehow, she wanted to run away from herself. Someone tapped her on the shoulder.

'You all right, love?' It was a woman carrying a basket. She looked with concern down at Lily and Lily nodded up at her. If she said nothing, the woman would think she'd had some bad news from the front or some such, and that was acceptable. What Lord Harrington had done to her was not fit for conversation, polite or otherwise. Forcing a smile, Lily sniffed and dried her face again and the woman rubbed her shoulder and moved on. Aware that the sky had grown brighter, Lily glanced up and saw a magnificent sunrise the colour of tinned peaches. The sight did nothing to lift her spirits.

Dragging herself up from the bench, she wandered aimlessly around the streets of the town centre. She felt utterly despondent at the thought of not being able to go back to the Hall, not being able to go home, and not being able to see Sid or the children. She stopped at the haberdashery and looked in at the window at the meagre offerings and high prices there, moved on to the butchers where the meat was being arranged in the window. There were stories of butchers selling dead cats, the food shortages were getting so bad. Shuffling on, she went past the labour exchange and stopped to look at the multitude of war recruitment posters on the outside wall. They made a moving sight. Pictures of men in trenches, of Zeppelins caught in searchlights, of an upper-class and working-class woman shoulder to shoulder, urging their boys to go to war. And there was that poster again: *On her their lives depend*. As she stood there, half in a daze, a woman in a smart coat and hat came up to unlock the door.

'Good morning,' said the woman, in a posh voice. 'I shan't be a moment opening up. Come in, if you like?' She held the door for Lily and smiled. Lily had had no intention of entering the labour exchange but still, something made her step forward and go inside. She pushed through the blackout curtain and squinted in the darkness. 'I'm not allowed to switch on the light just yet, but I'll give you a lamp and you can have a look round until I'm ready. You're lucky you caught me opening up so early, I was on patrol duty last night and couldn't get to sleep for the life of me this morning.' The woman lit the wick of an oil lamp, placed the glass chimney over it and passed it to Lily.

'Thanks,' said Lily, speaking for the first time since being in Lord Harrington's bedroom. Her voice wobbled and she turned to walk around the room. Boards were placed up on tables with situations vacant pinned on to them. There were a quantity asking for men for farm work and other manual work — these were hard times for farmers and others who had lost their workers to the war. Lily had heard about the land girls who had stepped in to help — well-bred types who were prepared to get their hands dirty. Good on them, too, thought Lily, seeing the gravity of the situation in a new light. Being in the labour exchange was like seeing a potted view of the world as it was.

There was a board for the Greygoose Munitions factory, which was just south of there on the edge of the East Tilbury marshes. She'd heard about it somewhere — in the local paper, perhaps. They were asking for women workers to train to drive cranes, of all things. Lily was taken aback. She had heard talk of women doing factory work but here it was in black and white. Women were needed to do proper men's work — welding, using machinery, working with dangerous explosives. Lily felt both repelled and thrilled by the thought of it; it didn't seem respectable, but it did sound exciting. And the wages! She blinked and looked again. Surely not. They were paying men four pounds and six shillings a week and women two pounds and two shillings plus overtime. She was on half a crown at the Hall. Food was so expensive now, Ada and the children would be struggling and Sid would need food parcels sent once he was posted. Lily shook her head, wondering why on earth she was thinking that. Her thoughts flicked to the master's hand on hers, pushing against his trousers. One of the adverts on the board was for a lady overlooker at the munitions factory. *Of good social status*, it said, *no experience necessary, but the ability to be tactful and exert control with the correct tone is essential.*

'Ah yes, Greygoose; they need more women now that conscription's come in,' said the smart woman, appearing at Lily's shoulder. 'Come and sit down and I'll see which positions they are offering.'

The woman smiled and gestured towards a table. She took her seat on one side and Lily followed her, mutely to take a chair facing her. 'And we don't want a repeat of last year's shell crisis, which was an absolute disgrace, I'm sure you'll agree.'

Lily nodded, remembering the scandal of the men in the trenches in France being without enough ammunition.

'Now then, let me see,' the woman went on, sifting through some papers on the table. 'Yes, here we are. There are a couple of positions of authority, charge hand and over-looker, but do you have any similar work experience? What do you do now?'

'I'm in service at St Clere's Hall,' said Lily, not committing herself to anything.

'Housemaid?' said the woman, watching Lily's face, and Lily nodded, knowing that the woman had the measure of her now she'd spoken. 'Ah, yes, in that case, you'd go in at the lowest level. It's dirty, exhausting work, but you're used to that in service. It's dangerous too. But the money's good. Let's see, two pounds and two shillings for a six-day week, twelve hours per shift, days and nights alternating, and Sundays off. What do you think?'

Lily could only shake her head. 'I'm sorry, I don't know what I'm doing here, I didn't really mean to come in ... I was just looking at the posters.'

'Oh, I see,' said the woman, sitting back in her chair. She gave a little laugh. 'Well, you certainly gave the impression of someone looking for work.' She considered Lily silently for a few moments, glanced down at Lily's wedding ring. 'You're married, I see?'

'Yes.'

'Is your husband away at war?'

The mention of Sid made her stomach turn over and tears threaten to fall. 'He's training now; he'll be posted before long.'

The woman nodded. 'If you work at Greygoose, you'll be making ammunition for him with which to defend this country against the Hun. What an opportunity!' she said, sitting forward and holding out her hands. 'This war is giving women the chance, at last, to prove themselves able to do other sorts of work. These women are proud women, proud of themselves and what they are doing for their country. It's a sea change and I'm all for it.' She waited for Lily's reaction, but Lily could only listen and had no idea what to say to this unusual woman. 'These are the munitionettes you've heard about. They wear trousers and do men's work. They are *the girls behind the men behind the guns*,' she continued, indicating a poster on the wall with the same slogan.

'Thank you,' said Lily, pushing up from her chair, 'I think I'd better go.'

'Very well,' said the woman, 'but before you go, let me leave you with one more thought. If you worked at Greygoose, you'd have more money and more freedom and, yes it's a privately owned company and you'd have to work jolly hard, but you'd not be beholden to a family the way you are now, at their beck and call for a pittance of a wage. You'd be important, part of a large team of workers with camaraderie, doing patriotic work for your country and our boys overseas. It's the chance of a lifetime.' She smiled at Lily. 'Come back any time if you change your mind. You'd need to be interviewed by the welfare supervisor at the factory before you're offered a place, but I don't think you'd have any problem. Now, it looks like I have some others to attend to,' she said, nodding behind Lily at a short queue of people. 'Be a dear and pull those curtains aside, would you?' the woman called out to a man there. Lily hadn't noticed them come in, and she was suddenly worried that someone would recognise her and tell Mrs Coker or the mistress that she'd been there.

'Thank you,' she said again, and made her leave out into the bright morning.

Not knowing how to go back to the house and explain herself to Mrs Coker, Lily went and sat down on the bench by the church again. The woman at the labour exchange had had a strange effect on her. She was one of those funny suffragette types, Lily was fairly sure of it – the way she'd spoken about women doing men's work and all that. But the thought of not being beholden to the family and at their beck and call . . . and the staggeringly high wages . . . and yes, being away from Mrs Coker and the mistress . . . and especially being away from the master and any future plans he had for her. But wearing trousers seemed very odd to Lily, she wrinkled her nose at the thought of it.

As she sat there, a line of men came up the hill flanked by armed soldiers. The men were dressed in field-grey German uniforms. She'd heard a rumour that there was a prisoner of war camp nearby. They filed past and stopped at the post office. The postmaster opened the door for them and Lily wondered whether it was already nine o'clock or whether there was a special arrangement for the Germans to use the post office out of hours. The men looked healthy and relaxed and Lily felt a rush of anger at the thought that some of them could have killed or wounded some of the British boys out in the field.

The POWs brought back to mind the thought of war work but the whole idea of leaving service was strange to Lily. It was a respectable position, a privilege to be a housemaid in a large house like St Clere's. Sid was always proud of her for it. She'd never contemplated leaving. But now, this funny woman had been so excited about the prospect of her going for a munitions job. She tried to imagine herself working in a factory with lots of other people and the thought scared her. But, she reminded herself, Mary the previous first housemaid had done it. She was working at the cement factory, and that sounded just as far from service as munitions. The woman at the labour exchange had said she'd be important if she was a munitionette, she'd be serving her country and helping the boys overseas, helping her Sid. As she sat there, slowly chewing it over, her brain seemed to get used to the idea, it even sounded appealing.

But it was dangerous work, the woman had said. Lily had heard of accidents at explosives factories. What if something happened and she was hurt ... or worse? What about the children and Sid? No, it wasn't for her. She'd just have to go back to St Clere's. She stood up and turned to walk down the hill. As she approached the station she saw two well-dressed women standing on the corner. One of them shook a tin at Lily.

'Could you spare some change for a new dormitory hut for the munitions workers?'

'Yes, course,' said Lily, digging a penny out of her pocket. The other woman handed her a little card with a pressed poppy sealed on to it with wax.

'It's from the Western Front, the Battle of Loos,' said the woman. 'The poppies grow in the shell holes on no man's land. My husband picks some when he can and presses them to send back for our fund-raising.' She smiled with pride but her eyes looked haunted.

Lily took the card and swallowed away a lump in her throat. 'Thank you,' she said. 'How lovely.'

She continued across the level crossing on to London Road, looking at the poppy. As she walked she remembered the woman at the labour exchange talking about an interview with someone from the factory. There'd be no harm in going for an interview, even though the thought of it scared Lily to death. She surprised herself by turning around and walking back up the hill.

When she got to the front of the line at the labour exchange the woman looked up at her and exclaimed in recognition.

'Ah, I had a feeling I'd be seeing you again. Sit down, please,' she said, gesturing to the chair.

'I'm still not sure, but I think I might go for the interview for the munitions job, if that would be all right?'

'Indeed it would be. Righto, then,' she said, looking through her papers. 'Here we are ... the interview is with a Mrs Sparrow.' At the name, she put down the paper and gathered her thoughts. 'The formidable Mrs Sparrow is the welfare supervisor for Greygoose Munitions factory. It is a position of considerable authority. She works with the management to oversee the welfare of the women workers, a job which covers a multitude of things, including conducting interviews and making deployment decisions. In short, you'd be wise to stay on her good side.' The woman tapped the side of her nose and winked. 'Greygoose is a private enterprise but it does fall under the regulation of the Ministry of Munitions, who have some control over wages and working conditions for the so-called diluted labour force.' She waited for Lily to indicate she understood but Lily shook her head. 'It's what they call the employment of women and unskilled men in skilled jobs, for the duration of the war. Don't worry, they give you training and the machinery these days is wonderful so you'll be fine. Mind you, it does beg the question of why it's taken a war to realise women can do these jobs,' she went on, half to herself.

'It's dangerous work, though?'

'Oh yes, it can be, of course, by its very nature. But in reality, accidents are rare and in the main it is a healthy place to work because of the high standard of living made possible by the good food and high wages.' Lily nodded and wondered whether the woman was playing things down. 'There is a wonderful social life too. They have piano and singing at mealtimes, a gramophone in the rec hut; they have games, theatrical societies, dances, classes in sewing and typing and so on; they have film screenings, sometimes they go on outings together to the theatre, they even play sport for fun, it's all very wholesome.'

Lily was taken aback. It sounded like some sort of holiday camp. 'That sounds nice,' she said.

The woman beamed. 'You'd sign on for three years or the duration of the war. Bear in mind you'd need a leaving certificate if you wanted to leave before that, which would be at the discretion of the employer. If you don't have a leaving certificate you can't work for six weeks.'

Three years sounded like an awfully long time to Lily. Then again, the thought of working for Lord Harrington for the next three years made her shudder.

'Mrs Sparrow will be conducting interviews here on Saturday morning.' She paused. 'Might I say, you are perfectly entitled to join a union if you wish. Mrs Sparrow may advise you not to, but you are entitled to. I marched for Women's Right to Serve last year and saw Emmeline Pankhurst speak, it was really quite marvellous.'

Lily's suspicions were right, she was a suffragette. But she didn't seem too bad really. Lily wondered whether it was the same march that Lady Charlotte had attended.

'If you could be here at ten o'clock on Saturday?'

Lily wondered how she'd manage to leave work, but she felt a sudden sense of abandon, which she'd never experienced before.

'I'll be here, thank you.'

'Thank *you*,' said the woman and looked past Lily for the next person waiting.

On the walk back to work, Lily's feelings swayed between revulsion at the master's brutality and elation at the notion of going to a new job. So much had happened in one day, she'd hardly had time to wonder how the children were doing on their journey to Nettlestead. They might be there by now, maybe they were running around in the fields like Ada said they could. Underlying it all was her sadness that Sid had gone. She wanted desperately to talk to him about it all. She'd written to tell him Ada was taking the children to her sister's, wording it in such a way that he wouldn't worry. His latest letter from the training camp had been jolly and positive and she didn't want to make things harder for him, he was probably putting it all in a good light for her too.

Just the thought of him there in his uniform doing drills and such inspired her to do something more useful than emptying the family's chamber pots and cleaning their shoes. Women didn't go to war and if truth be told she was glad of that. But there were other things she could do. A pulse of energy pumped through her. She didn't usually let herself reflect on her position of servitude in life because she'd been taught the value of hard work and a steady job. But she was on her own now and perhaps she didn't need to be told what to do this time, perhaps she could make a choice of her own for once. Her head was spinning with it all. For now, she must get back to work and face Mrs Coker. She just had to hang on two days until the interview on Saturday.

By the time she'd got back to St Clere's Hall, she'd made up a story that she hoped would wash with Mrs Coker. She tapped on the housekeeper's office door and went in. The woman was drinking a cup of tea at her desk.

'Oh, you deigned to come back, did you? And do you mind telling me what on earth is going on? One minute you're saying you're moving back in and the next you're running out of the door.'

'I'm so sorry, Mrs Coker,' said Lily, wringing the front of her skirts in her hands. 'I found out that my Sid will be going to France once his training is up, and I was upset. I'm really sorry.'

Mrs Coker pursed her lips. 'Yes, well, you'll be upset on your own time from now on otherwise you'll be handed your cards, do you understand?'

'Yes, thank you, Mrs Coker. I'll go and finish the fires.'

'Humph, it's too late for that, the family have taken breakfast by now. Martha had to finish the fires. You'd better go and help Sarah dress the mistress and then do the bedrooms.'

'Thank you, Mrs Coker.'

'His Lordship has taken an early train to London, he'll be gone for several days,' the housekeeper added, volunteering the information. She gave Lily a knowing look and Lily shrank from it. The thought that Mrs Coker had guessed what the master had done to her made her squirm with discomfort. She didn't know what to say, so she simply ducked her head and left the room, relieved beyond words that the master wasn't in the house, and grateful to Mrs Coker for telling her, even though she had probably done it to gauge Lily's reaction more than from any sense of sympathy.

As soon as she'd lied about Sid going to France, she wished she hadn't. What if she was tempting fate and bringing it upon him? She went up to help Sarah, and she tidied the bedrooms, glad that there was no chance of encountering the master. The housekeeper had seemed to imply that his London trip was unscheduled. Perhaps he left because of what he had done to Lily. Her stomach turned to water whenever she thought about it.

That night she moved into a room in the servants' quarters and slept in the single bed in a quiet room, without Sid's snores and the children's snuffles. She felt they were scattered to the winds. The lack of contact with them felt so strange, as if they weren't real, that she'd have to touch them for them to spring to life again. It was as though she'd gone mad and had imagined her family, as though she'd been living at St Clere's all along.

The next day was uneventful; she kept her head down and got on with her work, anxious that she'd need to find another reason to leave work for the interview on Saturday. Mrs Coker's levels of patience were low at best; she didn't know how much further she'd be pushed. Lily couldn't jeopardise her job at St Clere's without knowing if she had something else to go to.

The morning of the interview, she got up early to get some of the fires done before taking Mrs Coker her breakfast. She had only been able to think of a weak plan to get away to the labour exchange. She placed the tray on the housekeeper's bed and stood back to root in her pocket for a handkerchief. She sniffed into it. Mrs Coker wrinkled her nose.

'Don't stand there snivelling, girl, get on with your work.'

'I'm sorry, Mrs Coker.' Lily let out a little sob. 'I've started the fires already. I couldn't sleep last night for worrying about Sid, so I got up early to start work.'

The housekeeper considered her for a moment. 'I've worked here a long time, Pavitt, and I have seen it all, trust me. Now get on with your work.'

Lily ducked her head and left the room, kicking herself for thinking she could fool the old bird. If Lily did get another job – and the thought of that was still strange – she'd need a reference from Mrs Coker. By then, she'd know Lily had sneaked around but Lily couldn't very well ask for time off to attend an interview.

By half past nine, all the fires were done, the family had eaten breakfast and Lily and Sarah had finished dressing the mistress. Below stairs, the butler handed her a letter.

'One for you, Pavitt.'

Recognising Sid's handwriting, she opened it quickly, scanning the words.

Training going well . . . food is terrible but plentiful . . . heard a big push by the French is due . . . talk here that we'll be sent over once trained . . . might end up in the trenches . . . don't worry, I can use a rifle now . . . they've taught us how to stick the Hun with a bayonet . . .

Lily's shoulders sagged as though all the air had been squeezed out of her. Poor Sid. How he'd hate the idea of sticking a German with a bayonet. He was a gentle soul. Bless him for making light of it for her sake. He wouldn't have mentioned going to France if he wasn't sure; he was trying to break it to her gently. Poor, dear Sid.

'Well, don't stand there staring at the floor, Pavitt, get on with your work, for goodness' sake.'

Mrs Coker stood with her arms crossed. Lily looked up and the woman's mask slipped at the sight of Lily's stricken face. For the first time Lily wasn't scared by her, she was able to look right through her as though she didn't matter.

'I'll get the coal for the library,' she said, standing up in her own good time and making her way to the back door, the coal bucket swinging in her hand. In the back yard she leaned against the coal shed and took Sid's letter from her apron pocket. She'd wished it on him, she'd lied to Mrs Coker about him being posted to France and now it would come true. She hated herself for it and there was only one thing that would make up for it – she'd go for the interview, she'd get a job at the munitions factory and she'd help Sid, she'd make bullets for him to use in that damned rifle so he could protect himself and come home when it was all over.

Leaving the bucket inside the shed, Lily walked around the side of the house to the front road. Without her coat, in the freezing cold, she strode purposefully. Mrs Coker would realise sooner or later that she was missing but she didn't care.

With ten minutes to spare, she arrived at the labour exchange. The woman she'd seen before showed her to a chair to wait and before long she was called over to a table in the corner. A smartly dressed woman stood up to shake her hand.

'Mrs Sparrow, welfare supervisor at Greygoose Munitions factory. Pleased to make your acquaintance.' She wore a smart blouse and long skirt, her wide-brimmed hat was on the table. Her square face was set with small eyes and a mouth that was hard to read, as if it was amused when she wasn't happy.

'Mrs Lily Pavitt, pleased to meet you,' said Lily, her new strength and determination melting into feelings of doubt.

'Please,' said Mrs Sparrow, indicating the chair and smiling. Lily sat down, pleasantly surprised at the woman's manner. From the way the labour exchange woman had been talking, she'd been expecting someone stern. The woman sucked her lips together as though wetting a clarinet reed before she spoke. 'Let's get started. Could you tell me what you are doing for work currently?' She glanced at Lily's uniform and down at her notes as if she already knew the answer.

'I'm a housemaid down the road at St Clere's Hall.'

'I see. How long have you been there and why do you wish to leave such a good position?'

'I've worked there for seven years; I started there when I left school at fourteen.' Lily paused, wondering how best to answer the next question. 'I don't want to leave there; as you say, it's a good position. But my husband Sid has enlisted and he'll soon be posted, and I want to do my bit for the war.'

The woman sucked her lips with unwavering confidence that her audience would wait for her to speak. 'But isn't St Clere's Hall converting to an auxiliary military hospital? Wouldn't you play some part in the war effort by staying on there?'

The woman was sharp. 'Yes, I suppose. But I think if

I worked in a munitions factory I'd be doing more for the boys overseas than if I stay at St Clere's. It's a chance to do my bit to help my husband and the rest of the boys in service.'

'Well, it's laudable to think you'll be helping all of the boys in service,' Mrs Sparrow said, a strange smile playing on her lips, 'and I commend the sentiment. Ordinarily I would frown on a girl leaving service. The big houses need their staff. And it's the girls whose work has dried up in the tailoring and shop trades and so on, who have seen their training wasted, the slightly better class of girl, who does well in a factory like ours.'

Lily frowned and didn't know what to say.

'But, with conscription now in place,' Mrs Sparrow continued, 'and more of the men being called to the colours, we are in need of more workers, and I should think you are no stranger to hard work and discipline?'

'No, Mrs Sparrow, I work hard at the house, very hard.'

'Well, currently the factory manufactures cartridges, shell cases, detonators, cordite, guncotton and gunpowder. Of course, working at the factory is inherently dangerous but we have strict codes of conduct to avoid accidents. The factory is heavily guarded by the West Kent Regiment and the East Anglian Brigade of the Royal Field Artillery, and the site is surrounded by barbed wire and blockhouses. I see you are married?'

'Yes, and with two children.'

'I see.' Mrs Sparrow frowned, looking back at her notes. 'And where do you live?'

'My husband recently enlisted, and my mother-in-law has

taken the children to her sister's in the country so I moved back into the staff quarters at St Clere's.'

'We have single accommodation for workers in what we call the colony – dormitory-style huts in what has become a model village a mile across the marshes from the factory works. We call it Goosetown. A light railway takes workers to the factory from there. There is strict segregation of the men and the women. There is no provision for children of new workers at Goosetown, the houses are all taken by long-serving employees, but you would be given a bed in the colony if you would like?'

Lily couldn't help but smile. She'd been worried about where she'd live. 'Yes, that sounds lovely, thank you.'

'I'm not sure it is lovely, but the girls make the best of it. Each hut has a matron to oversee housekeeping, which also adheres to strict codes of conduct, but the girls are jolly enough there.' She paused, seeming to choose her next words carefully. 'We do ask, when we take on a married woman, that they are very careful not to . . . corrupt . . . the unmarried women . . . We would not want the moral tone of the factory lowered, you do understand?'

Lily was shocked and wanted to laugh at the thought that she would be able to corrupt anyone. She felt herself redden. She looked at her lap and nodded. Mrs Sparrow seemed suitably satisfied by her embarrassment.

'Do you have any reason to believe that your current employer would not provide you with a favourable reference?'

'I don't know. I mean, I'm a good worker, very good, else they wouldn't have allowed me back once I got married, but they wouldn't want me to leave, so I don't know what kind of reference they would give me.'

Mrs Sparrow wrote something down in her notes.

'The position would be for three years or the duration of the war.'

Lily nodded.

'I would like to offer you a job, Mrs Pavitt, and a bed in our colony. You would be in a factory workshop within a small team, with the appropriate charge hands, overlookers and supervisors and so on. You will be placed as need dictates and will have no choice in the type of work you will be required to do. If you are sent to work in the danger zone, you will receive an additional halfpence per hour.'

'Well!' said Lily, her pleasure at passing the interview diluting her apprehension about the 'danger zone'. 'Thank you very much, Mrs Sparrow.'

'You'll find it hard work, just as every other worker there. But we are thoroughly grounded in the welfare of our workers and have a YWCA canteen providing good quality meals; there is also a recreation room with various societies and functions. I would advise you to take advantage of the self-improvement activities, but take care to avoid any immoral goings-on outside of the factory – the consumption of alcohol, and so on. At Greygoose the workers give their all and are rewarded with rest and comfort. The wage is very high indeed: you will be on two pounds and two shillings per six-day week. We do advise that you give any spare money over to war certificates and benevolent collections and that you avoid joining unions and suchlike, which is wholly unnecessary at times of war. The shifts are twelve hours, alternating between day and night on a weekly cycle. Sundays off. Do you have any questions?'

'I don't know,' said Lily, momentarily stumped by the strange thought of 'spare money'. 'When would you like me to start?'

'I presume you would work out a week's notice at St Clere's Hall?'

'Yes, I think so,' said Lily, nodding and immediately anxious about telling Mrs Coker that she'd be leaving.

'Then, let's say . . . ' Mrs Sparrow consulted her notebook. 'Monday week, the twenty-eighth of February.' She looked at Lily for agreement and Lily could only nod and smile. 'Take the Corringham Light Railway from Fobbing Road and you'll get off at Greygoose Munitions station. I shall meet you there at ten o'clock sharp. You'll be able to find your way?'

'Yes, I expect so. Thank you, Mrs Sparrow.'

'You'll have a health check and be kitted out in your uniform. I'll then get you settled into the colony at Goosetown, you'll have your dinner there and you will start work the following morning at six o'clock – you'll be on shift team A.'

They both stood up. 'Assuming there is no problem with your reference, allow me to welcome you to Greygoose Munitions,' she said, shaking Lily's hand again. 'You will now be considered a valued national employee doing her duty for King and country – it is a privilege indeed.' Lily wondered whether she was still asleep and dreaming.

It had been her first interview in seven years. Even back then, it hadn't been proper questions, just a quick talk with Mrs Coker with Lily's mother in attendance. She was proud of herself for having answered Mrs Sparrow's questions so well and elated at being offered the position. It gave her the boost she needed amidst the upheaval and trauma she had been through of late.

As she walked back to work she took Sid's letter from her pocket and kissed it. The thought of him going to France made her go cold. At least Gerald was with him, although Sid would be more likely to give his life to protect his father than the other way around. Her new job would feel like being at his side in some way. She'd been given the chance of making her own choices for once, and this is what she'd chosen to do. In the back of her mind she wondered if Sid would be worried about her working in munitions and cross that she was going to leave service. But it was only as much of a sacrifice as the men in the trenches were making. It would be like being on the front line at home. She'd show him it was the right thing to do.

The most pressing matter now, though, was Mrs Coker. Lily wondered whether she should have asked Mrs Sparrow when she'd be seeking the reference. She didn't know how much time she had before Mrs Coker found out. It was Saturday so she had at least until Monday before a letter arrived, and she'd have to hand in her notice no later than that. She resolved to say nothing for the time being.

Collecting the bucket from the coal shed she slipped back in through the servants' entrance and walked through into the library. Unnoticed by Mrs Coker, she filled the scuttle there, gave silent thanks to God for helping her and went up the back stairs to sweep the bedroom carpets. At luncheon, taking her seat in the servants' hall, Mrs Coker made a poor attempt at concealing her surprise when she saw Lily at the table.

'Pavitt, where have you been?'

'Sorry, Mrs Coker?' she said convincingly. 'I've been sweeping the bedroom floors.'

'I'm glad to hear it, Pavitt,' said the housekeeper, eyeing Lily suspiciously.

Lily was glad to get through the rest of the day without event. At church the next morning, she prayed for Sid and Gerald, and all the boys overseas, and she asked God to help her in her new job, to give her the strength to do it well and without fear. She asked for forgiveness for hiding her plans from her employers and fellow workers and assured Him she would give them the news on Monday. In her room that night she tried to compose a letter to Sid to explain what she was doing but gave up and went to sleep.

When Monday morning came, Lily took the housekeeper her breakfast tray as usual, elated at the thought that she would only need to do it another six more times. She set down the tray and stood back, waiting for Mrs Coker to rouse herself and sit up in bed.

'What?' she said.

'Good morning, Mrs Coker. Can I please see you later when you've got time?'

'What's it about?' she said, taking a bite from her toast and chewing while she spoke.

'Er, shall I talk with you later?'

'Spit it out, Pavitt, the world does not revolve around you.'

With a small pang of anger, Lily realised she would feel some satisfaction in telling Mrs Coker.

'I need to hand my notice in,' she said.

Mrs Coker threw her toast on to the tray. 'What?' she

demanded. 'After everything we've done for you, you're waltzing off? To do what, may I ask?'

'I've got a job in munitions,' said Lily, in a voice barely above a whisper.

Straining forward to hear, Mrs Coker had a fearful look of disgust on her face. 'Munitions?' she shouted. '*Munitions! What on God's earth do you think you are doing?*'

Lily took a step backwards. She hadn't often seen the woman look quite so red in the face. 'I'll just be off to do the fires then,' she said, backing out of the door.

'Well, I'll be damned!' shouted Mrs Coker through the closed door.

Lily ran downstairs feeling sick to her stomach. That was the worst of it over with, she hoped.

When she went back up to do the fires, she realised how many times she had been on her knees sweeping out those same grates. How many times she had had to turn away to 'give room' if a member of the family passed her while she was cleaning up the dirt from their shoes on the stairs. It was only the idea of no longer doing such tasks under such authority that enlightened her as to the drudgery of it, the injustice even. In Lady Charlotte's room, she turned to look at the sleeping figure, thought how her lady's maid would rouse her with a sumptuous breakfast and an ironed news-paper in bed, how she'd then be helped to dress, how she'd go downstairs at her leisure while her room was being tidied and her clothes being washed, and how she would spend her day doing as she pleased in the finest surroundings.

Lily felt an unfamiliar sting of resentment. She was glad she'd be spreading her wings and going somewhere else. She was soon in the mistress's room helping the lady's maid Sarah attend to Lady Harrington. As Sarah pinned the mistress's hair into place and Lily collected her dirty laundry, there was a knock at the door and Mrs Coker walked in.

'Yes, Mrs Coker?' said the mistress, seeing her reflection in the dressing-table mirror.

'Your ladyship, I do apologise for disturbing you but I have an issue I need to discuss.'

'Would you like Sarah and Jane to leave us?' said the mistress, meaning Sarah and Lily.

'No, in fact, it is Jane I need to discuss and it wouldn't hurt her being here. I am afraid to report, your ladyship, that Jane intends to leave us. She has handed in her notice today.'

'Oh, Mrs Coker, why do you bother me with such things?'

'Because, milady, we have only two housemaids remaining after Jane and it is proving quite difficult to find replacements.'

'Jane, what do you have to say for yourself? Why on earth are you leaving? Are you getting married?' All the while she spoke, Lady Harrington regarded her own reflection.

Lily ducked her head. 'No, milady, I'm already married. I'm leaving to do munitions work for the war.'

'But our hospital will be open soon; you'd be helping the war if you stayed here. How will we manage with fewer staff?'

'I'm sorry, milady, I've committed to it now.'

'Well, retract your commitment; you are already committed to St Clere's.' The mistress applied some face powder in the mirror. 'Honestly, Mrs Coker, do these girls not know the value of a decent position? Why do they want to do a man's job? Making weapons is unladylike; women weren't designed for such things.' The mistress looked in the mirror and patted her hair haughtily. Sarah shifted awkwardly, caught in the firing line. 'And those hideous trousers they wear, good grief, how unfeminine to imitate men in such a way.'

Lily stood holding the mistress's dirty laundry, she wanted to take her leave but she was caught there between the sharp tongues of Mrs Coker and the mistress, the collective 'old bag', as Sid would have said.

'You know, Mrs Coker,' continued the mistress, 'those munitions factories contain dangerous explosives.' Lily ground her teeth together, the mistress was going to try her best to undermine Lily's decision – it was low to use scaremongering. 'One spark and they could go up at any moment. What was that place last year that blew? Dozens died, if I recall. Not to mention all the accidents that must happen that we are not told about in order to protect national security. I must say, if I were married and . . . Jane, do you have children?'

'Yes, milady,' said Lily, nodding meekly.

'Well, if I were in your position and married with children I certainly would not put myself in such a precarious circumstance. I might question the risk of leaving my children motherless.'

Lily wanted to turn around and throw the dirty laundry into the fire. The spite of the woman! Did she think Lily would change her mind on hearing her venomous words? Did she think they inspired Lily to stay working for her? How she wished she could speak her thoughts aloud and tell the mistress what a vile shrew she was. How she craved the courage to recount the master's treatment of her behind that curtain. But Lily needed a reference and she would not be goaded.

'Thank you for your wise words, milady, but my husband may be sent to France and I want to help him protect himself. I'll be leaving in a week's time. Thank you for providing me with work these past seven years.' With that, she dropped into a shallow curtsey and left the room. On closing the door she heard the mistress say:

'Has she really worked here for seven years? Well, I'd hardly have known it.'

5

Warley army training camp,
28 February 1916

My dearest Lil,

I don't know about you leaving St Clere's but you'll be pleased to get away from 'the old bag'. Take good care – it doesn't sound safe to me. Dad says the same. Mum writes to say the children are all right. Terrible news about the SS Maloja. It makes Dad want to teach the Hun a lesson – he wants to get out there, show them a thing or two.

You said you start the new job next week, well write to tell me how it went.

Your loving husband,
Sid

Painfully aware of the armed guards at the station entrance, Lily stood on the platform of the Fobbing Road terminal of the Corringham Light Railway and, despite having spent a frivolous one and halfpence on the train ticket, wanted to take her bundle of belongings and run away. It was all suddenly very real and very frightening.

The last days at St Clere's Hall had been tense. Mrs Coker had her doing the dirtiest, lowest jobs she could find, to the extent that the hall boys and scullery maids were twiddling their fingers. On her afternoon off she'd gone down to Nettlestead to visit Ada and the boys. The boys had been pleased to see her, and Ada seemed contented there with her sister. It was a small cottage, crowded inside with all sorts of bits and pieces that made Lily feel suffocated.

Yesterday, her fellow servants bid her a fond farewell with a small tea to mark the occasion but when Mrs Coker got wind of it, it was put away. *So that's what you get for giving a place seven years of service, is it?* she wanted to say, but didn't, she had the all-important reference to think about.

Every day she had worried that the master would return from London but he hadn't, thank goodness. And now here she was, stepping into the unknown.

Two young women, one with blonde hair, the other mousy, came on to the platform, also carrying bags and talking in low voices. They saw Lily and came over.

'Hello, are you starting today?' asked the blonde one.

'Yes, hello. I'm Lily,' she said, holding out her hand. 'Are you?'

'Yes, I'm Rose and this is Marge.'

Lily shook Marge's hand too and the girl gave her a shy smile. Close up, Lily realised that Marge must have been no more than fifteen and was pale and drawn. 'Have you done this sort of work before?' she asked them.

Marge giggled and clapped her hand over her mouth.

'Don't mind her, she's a bag of nerves,' said Rose. 'We were at Orsett Hall together, kitchen maids. They didn't half go mad when we both handed our notice in. We haven't done anything like this before.'

Marge giggled again. 'Oh, they didn't like it, did they, Rose?' she said quietly to her friend.

'No, like I said,' said Rose, with a deadpan expression.

The little train came puffing along and they all got on the third-class carriage, which had hard little seats like a toast rack and was open to the elements at the sides. The cold wind blew through as they rumbled off across the East Tilbury marshes.

Lily looked across the large flat stretch of wetlands and the grey River Thames, beyond the clumps of bulrushes in standing water and great banks of blackberry bushes dominant and untamed. Cows, bullocks and horses from local farms grazed here and there. Fallen branches crawled with lichen and ivy grappled with limes and willows. Nettles, gorse, thistles and coarse grasses grew there – these were hardy plants used to rough weather; there was no place for fragile blooms on these marshes. Lily shivered; it was a bleak, unwelcoming place. It looked like the end of the earth.

The train wheezed to a stop at a station signed GOOSE-TOWN, and Lily made to get off.

'We're to meet Mrs Sparrow at the Greygoose Munitions stop at ten,' said Rose.

'Oh, yes, me too,' said Lily, realising her mistake.

As the train pulled off again she saw the rows of long wooden huts that she guessed must be the workers' accommodation. There were other buildings and houses and some children walking along a road. It looked like a proper little town. Craning her neck as she passed, she noticed a school building.

'Why on earth would they have a school next to a munitions factory?' she wondered aloud. Marge giggled and shook her head.

'It's a little town with a school and shops and everything,' said Rose.

As the train rumbled on towards the factory itself, Lily saw a long tangle of barbed-wire fence along the perimeter, with blockhouses at intervals. Mrs Sparrow was waiting at the next station, Greygoose Munitions, peering at the train from beneath her wide-brimmed hat and looking up at the station clock as Lily and the other two got off with their bags. She wore a smart black belted coat, the hem of her skirt brushing the top of her heeled ankle boots. She was a dumpy woman but held herself with an air of authority.

'Good morning. I'm glad to see you are here on time. If you'll come this way?'

They handed their tickets to the stationmaster and walked past two more armed guards whose presence cast a spell of guilt over Lily even though she had done nothing wrong.

'The women who work here receive a mixed bag of attitudes,' said Mrs Sparrow as they walked towards the factory entrance. 'Some people see it as amusing that they wear trousers and do men's work. Others see it as threatening, particularly some of the men who work in this factory. You'll grow accustomed to it. Just be mindful that people will have their views and that this work is just for the duration of the war – the men will need their jobs back when they come home. Here are your identification cards, you must carry these with you at all times and show them when entering the factory and any other time a guard, member of staff or policeman or -woman requests to see it. And here is your 'on war service' badge. These are issued by the Ministry of Munitions to women doing urgent war work. You are permitted to wear it on your uniform in the factory but only if you work in the safe area.'

Lily took her identification card and the triangular brass 'on war service' badge and felt her cheeks redden with pride.

They approached an imposing set of black iron gates, ten feet high. There was a column on either side, each topped with a statue of a goose carved out of grey stone with legs astride, wings spread and neck stretched forward as if about to strike. Lily looked up at their open beaks and spiteful eyes and shrank back from them. Mrs Sparrow approached the armed guards to announce the new girls. There were two women police constables on sentry too. Lily had seen 'copperettes' patrolling the docks and the town, especially in the evening when the girls would hang around there for the soldiers. They would move on couples in doorways and pick up women drunk in the gutter but Lily had never met one in person. It seemed strange to her that there could be women police, it wasn't proper. They must be suffragette types like the woman in the labour exchange, she thought, using the war as a chance to get their message known. They wore dark blue uniforms: long skirts with military-style jackets and large felt hats. They were gentlewoman types. One of them took Lily's bag, searched through it and returned it to her. 'Your hairpins, please,' she said, in a high-class voice, holding out her hand. With surprise, Lily and Marge removed their bobby pins and handed them over. Lily felt self-conscious with her hair falling around her shoulders. 'Do you have any matches or cigarettes on your person?' asked the police constable. Both Lily and Marge shook their heads and the woman admitted them through.

'Your references were adequate, none of them bursting with praise but that's to be expected given you've all left service,' said Mrs Sparrow as they continued their walk to a building on the left-hand side and Lily breathed a sigh of relief. 'Be mindful that as long as you work hard and obey the rules you'll be happy enough here. At the factory the priority for all of us must be production. It never stops, hence the rotating twelve-hour shifts. The men even work on Sundays. You remember the shell crisis, of course? If we fail our duty here we risk the lives of our boys overseas.'

They entered the building and Mrs Sparrow ushered them through a second door marked MEDICAL. They found themselves in a long room with partitions along one wall; a woman in a nurse's uniform was putting on an apron.

'This is Nurse Jarvis, one of Goosetown's nurses. She will be conducting the health check,' said Mrs Sparrow.

'If you'll please disrobe?' said Nurse Jarvis, gesturing for them to choose one of the partitioned alcoves.

'Pardon?' said Rose.

The nurse sighed. 'Please undress and wait to be inspected.'

'What, take our clothes off?' Rose was ashen-faced.

Marge started to laugh; she tried covering her mouth but couldn't stifle her giggles.

'It is no laughing matter, miss,' said the nurse. 'It is regulation. You need to be checked over and you'll not start work here until you have been.'

'Well, I'm not taking my clothes off for no one,' said Rose.

'Then I'm afraid you must leave,' said Mrs Sparrow.

Lily's stomach turned over. Marge was smiling but her eyes looked scared.

'Well, so be it,' said Rose, and left the room, Mrs Sparrow going after her.

Nurse Jarvis raised her eyebrows at Lily and Marge and waved them forward. The girls exchanged looks of horror but both went into separate alcoves and started to undress. Lily couldn't see Marge but the nurse was in full view. She took off her coat and skirt and waited.

'Everything, please,' said the nurse.

Lily started to shake. She leaned down to unlace her boots and put them neatly to one side, dreading the thought of being naked in front of this woman. She faced the wall and pulled off her underclothes and stood there shivering in the cold, covering her breasts with her arms. She heard Marge let out a whimper next door.

'Keep still,' said the nurse, just behind her. It made Lily think of Lord Harrington standing behind her. She wanted to cry, she was so exposed. She felt the woman's fingers on her head, picking through her scalp, presumably looking for lice. She stopped, looking closely at something, and sighed.

'Lift your arms,' she said. Lily did as she was told. 'Turn around.' Lily turned and looked at the wall behind the woman's head while she inspected Lily's body. Lily bit her lip to stop herself from crying. 'Arms down and hold out your hands.' She looked at Lily's palms and turned them over to look at the tops of her hands. 'Open your mouth,' she said, peering in at Lily's teeth and then into Lily's eyes, holding the pulse on her wrist as she did so. 'You may get dressed.'

Lily put her clothes on as quickly as she could while Nurse Jarvis asked her a series of questions. 'Have you had any disease? Fits? Bad chest? Are you with child?' Lily answered no to them all. 'Are there any other health problems?' Lily shook her head; she didn't want to tell her she always had a cold and was always tired and she had back ache and tooth ache and the veins in her legs itched and hurt since she'd had the boys. Those were things you just put up with and didn't moan about.

The nurse went to repeat the check on Marge. Marge let out a series of nervous laughs. 'For goodness' sake, girl, what on earth are you laughing about?' said Nurse Jarvis.

Good on you, thought Lily, at least she and Marge had been brave enough to go through with it.

Mrs Sparrow came back in when they were both dressed.

'They both have head lice,' said the nurse. 'Otherwise they're healthy enough; underweight and bad teeth but they can work.' Lily was horrified to hear herself described in such a way. She felt like a piece of mutton being inspected by a fussy customer at the butcher's.

'I'll wait while you delouse them,' said Mrs Sparrow.

Nurse Jarvis nodded and beckoned the girls to follow her. They each in turn had to lean over a trough-like basin while the woman shook lice powder on to their hair. When it was done Mrs Sparrow called them over to a table.

'The company is under the legislation of the Ministry of Munitions and requires you to sign this agreement of confidentiality,' she said, handing each of them a piece of paper. 'The operations in this factory are highly sensitive and confidential and you are legally bound not to relay any details of working processes or employee processes to anyone outside of the factory. This includes chats with friends and family, letters to loved ones and so on. I do not need to remind you of the punishment for treason in this country.'

Lily and Marge read the contents of the letter, Lily able to understand most of the words but not all, and signed at the bottom. Lily would have to be careful not to write anything confidential in her letters to Sid.

As they walked outside with Mrs Sparrow, Marge looked at Lily's head and laughed, and when Lily saw Marge's hair free from pins and covered in white powder as though she'd aged thirty years, she couldn't help but smile too.

'I beg your pardon, Mrs Sparrow, but where's Rose?' said Marge meekly.

'Your friend has decided to go home,' said Mrs Sparrow. 'Follow me please.'

Lily gave Marge a look of sympathy and Marge gave a nervous giggle in return, looking back towards the gates for her friend. Lily wondered whether the young girl wanted to go too.

'Any discomforts here at the factory are only as much as the sacrifices being made by our men in the trenches, please remember that,' said Mrs Sparrow. 'Lord Kitchener himself has acknowledged the great work our munitions factories do and has likened them as equal to active service in the field.'

They followed Mrs Sparrow into a long wooden hut that had a twin building on the other side of the road. Inside the walls were lined with rows of thin wooden lockers. At the far end there was a long trough with four taps spaced along it.

'This is one of the change rooms. There is another next to

this one. Those across the road are for the men. When it is time for your shift, you'll wait at the factory gates. When you are let through you will be selected at random to be inspected for contraband items such as matches, cigarettes, tobacco and any metal items – this means hairpins, jewellery, buttons, other metal fasteners on clothes, corsets, unless those with whalebone, everything. Metal causes sparks that cause explosions. If you are found in the factory with any metal items on your person you will be fined and warned. If it happens again, you'll be suspended, is that understood?'

Lily and Marge nodded and Lily looked down at her wedding ring. Mrs Sparrow let the importance of the instruction sink in. 'You are then to come *straight* here to change into your uniform, you will leave your clothes in one of the lockers. When you finish your shift you will come here to wash and dress and you will leave the factory site immediately.' The welfare supervisor looked the women up and down and turned to some boxes on the floor against the wall.

'This is your uniform,' she said, pulling out some garments and shaking them out to inspect them. 'A fireproof tunic and trousers, a cape and a cap,' she said, handing a set to Lily and reaching for another box to find some for Marge. 'The girls wear trousers with the tunic out of practical necessity, not out of any misplaced suffrage ideals. A lot of people don't like it but they don't have to work in these conditions, hence their opinions are of little consequence to us. You must wear your hair without pins tucked into the cap at all times; it is mandatory. If your hair is free it may be caught in the machinery.'

Lily baulked at the idea of her hair getting caught. She looked at the garments – they were a khaki colour with a red trim and made from a thick, coarse cotton twill that was either stained or dirty and frayed here and there. Still, for a reason she couldn't explain, she felt a thrill at the idea of wearing them. From the look on Marge's face, she felt the same way.

'And some rubber overshoes,' Mrs Sparrow went on, handing them each a pair. 'Take these with you to put on once you get to the small change area in your workshop. Do not wear them outside of the workshop. One spark from a piece of grit or the wrong type of heel and the whole place could go up. It is not just your own safety to think of, but that of your co-workers and of the factory itself.'

Lily felt her whole body clutch with fear at the magnitude of making any mistake, when simply forgetting to take out a hairpin could result in explosions and death. There were so many lockers in the room, she couldn't imagine being in there with all of those people.

'Put your uniform in a locker and remember which one it is for when you start your shift in the morning.'

Lily and Marge looked for spare lockers but there didn't seem to be any. They eventually found one and agreed to share it. Lily tried to commit its number to memory. *Three hundred and fifteen.*

'Leave your things here too; you may collect them on your way out. I'll give you a quick look around the factory works now, but please do not touch anything and stay out of the way.'

They followed Mrs Sparrow down what seemed to be the main thoroughfare. 'The whole site is ideally placed, surrounded by water on three sides: the Thames, of course, and the two creeks, Hole Haven and Shell Haven. Any large explosions would therefore be contained within the site and the creeks and river are also used for transporting goods.' Lily wondered why Mrs Sparrow was telling them this; it wasn't to make them feel safe, that was certain.

'There are two areas of the factory,' the woman continued. 'On the right is the safe area,' she pointed at various low wooden buildings, 'including the chemical laboratories, ambulance room and administration buildings. On the left is the danger area.' She stopped to look at the buildings spread out across the site. 'The work huts are around two hundred yards apart and have lightweight roofs that will blow off in the case of accidental explosions. They are also surrounded with banks of earth to minimise any blast, as are the magazines you see further out on the marshes. It's more a precaution than anything else; accidents are few and far between.'

As they walked off the main road for a closer look at the danger area, the ground became muddy and Lily knew she'd be brushing off the hem of her skirt later. She followed in Mrs Sparrow's footsteps and stepped up on to a raised wooden tramway that led from one shed to another. 'You are permitted to walk on the tramway but make room for any trucks that are pushed along by the workers.' There was a foul smell about the place and Lily wondered if they had problems with their drains. 'In these huts we manufacture the guncotton, black powder, smokeless powder, cordite, nitro-glycerine and cartridges. The cordite sheds have recently been expanded to cope with demand.'

In the case of accidental explosions. Lily shivered. It was a frightening prospect. She watched as a woman in uniform pushed a truck of boxes along a stretch of tramway in the distance. She wanted to ask how often the ambulance room was used but thought better of it.

Ignoring the stench and swampy ground, Mrs Sparrow turned back to the main road and continued her spiel. 'When you're appointed to your shop, you'll have no need to see any other shop, which is why I'm showing you around quickly now to give you the lay of the land.'

'Which shop will I be in?' said Lily, unsure whether it was the wrong time to ask.

Mrs Sparrow stopped. 'Well, I was going to put Marjorie here and her friend Rose in the cordite shed, but seeing as Rose has gone, perhaps I'll put you in there with Marjorie.'

'In the danger area?'

'Yes, Mrs Pavitt, in the danger area,' said Mrs Sparrow, her glare daring Lily to contest it. 'Now, if you'll come this way we'll make our way out.'

Lily's heart sank and she wished she hadn't asked. Perhaps she'd have been put somewhere else if Mrs Sparrow had been given a chance to rethink her plans in light of Rose leaving. Lily could have kicked herself. Now she was in the bloody danger area, in the cordite shed. She had not the foggiest idea what cordite was, but hated to ask any more questions for fear of getting herself into deeper water. She glanced at Marge, who looked scared out of her wits.

'You'll have read the newspaper reports of giddy munition-ettes flaunting showy clothes and wasting money in public houses,' continued Mrs Sparrow. 'That type of behaviour is not tolerated here, outside of working hours or otherwise. There are regular patrols by the women's police service around the town and station to deter any immoral goings-on and they will report back to me anything they deem beyond the realm of decent behaviour.'

Lily and Marge exchanged glances and Lily wondered how people had time to go around public houses and so on. She'd had no such opportunities when she'd been in service. It was all work and sleep.

Mrs Sparrow led them back to the change rooms to collect their bags and hairpins and then out through the main gate, where Lily felt those mean goose eyes on her back as they walked to the train station.

'The Corringham Light Railway has been a godsend,' said Mrs Sparrow. 'It saves workers a lot of time without that walk across the marshes. We employ over six thousand workers here currently, around fifteen hundred men and women live in Goosetown, the rest travel from surrounding villages and from as far as Southend and Barking every day.'

They didn't need to wait long for the little train. It rattled along, the fourteen carriages mainly empty between shifts except for two patrolling women police constables. Ten minutes later they stopped at Goosetown. Lily was excited to see where she was going to live; it already looked nicer than the daunting factory works.

'As you can see, Goosetown is a model village – there are forty brick houses here, mainly for management and long-serving employees. The detached house you see there is for Mr Broughton, the factory manager. There is a school for their children, with church services held there on a Sunday. We have a small hospital and our own fire and police stations, a horse-drawn fire engine and a Ford motor ambulance that would bring a patient from the ambulance room at the factory works to the hospital here. The wooden bungalow huts are in what we call the colony, which is where you'll be lodging. The village shop is over there; it has a post office and sells groceries and so on. There is a village hall where dances are held. And there is a large YWCA hut housing a canteen and a recreation area for the women workers that is staffed by volunteers, some very well-to-do ladies who are kindly giving their time for the war effort. The men have their workmen's club on the other side.

'I will say,' she added, stopping to give extra emphasis to her words, 'the YWCA do allow modern activities such as smoking and dancing and even some alcohol, but they advocate the proper pursuits of bible study and teetotalism wherever possible. Please bear in mind that the war has meant change for a lot of us and we must be respectful of this and set a good example to those who need guidance. We'll head to the canteen now for some luncheon,' she said, leading the way.

They entered a large wooden building with a cross on the door. Long dining tables stretched the length of the room with a long low backless bench on each side instead of chairs and beyond there was what looked like another large room.

'This is the canteen, as you can see. The YWCA volunteers staff it, not an inconsiderable task given the number of women working here. At dinner time the society ladies will be here, too. At the moment it's empty because A-shift are working and B-shift are sleeping.'

'Hello,' said a woman behind a counter at one end. She was well spoken and smartly dressed in the YWCA uniform, a fitted army-style jacket and long skirt, a collared blouse and blue cravat tie.

'Hello, would you be a dear and give us some sandwiches for luncheon?'

'Yes of course, Mrs Sparrow, I'll bring them over.'

Mrs Sparrow nodded and beckoned Lily and Marge to follow her along the length of the tables in through to the next room. 'This is the recreation hall,' she said, leading them into a big room with tables and chairs scattered informally across the floor. 'The girls come here after they have taken their dinner to relax and engage in wholesome activities. There is a piano and gramophone too, as you can see. The girls have a penchant for singing and dancing, which we do allow. An entertainment committee organises concerts and dances in the village hall. But there are ample self-improvement opportunities here too: classes in bible study, painting, sewing, typing and so on. Please do take full advantage of them.'

Lily felt excitement bubble up inside her. Was this really all here for her to use? Self-improvement opportunities? She couldn't wait to write and tell Sid about it all.

They followed Mrs Sparrow back to one of the long tables in the canteen. The YWCA woman brought over a tray of tea and sandwiches. Lily tucked into the cottage cheese and corn bread, suddenly famished, but slowed down when she saw Mrs Sparrow giving her the eye. The welfare supervisor nibbled delicately at her own food.

'We do try to have wheat-free and meat-free days once a week to help with the food shortages. We grow our own vegetables on site, too. The fee for your bed and board will be deducted from your weekly wage. It includes breakfast, luncheon and dinner.'

'How much is it for bed and board?' Lily tried swallowing her mouthful before asking the question but didn't quite manage and attracted another look of disapproval from Mrs Sparrow.

'It is twenty shillings.'

Lily did a quick calculation in her head. If she got two pounds and two shillings a week, with twenty shillings taken off for bed and board, that would leave her twenty-two shillings. Plus Sid's separation allowance of twenty-one shillings. She'd be able to send Ada forty-three shillings. She hesitated. It was a fortune. She thought she would keep a bit back for herself. She might need money to buy bits and pieces and felt a thrill at the thought of having her own money but also a stab of guilt. She'd wait and see when she got her first wage and then decide.

They left the canteen and followed Mrs Sparrow to the colony of bungalow huts.

'You'll both be on A-shift, as they are currently doing days and you'll be starting work in the morning. That means you'll be in an A-shift hut. The shift is twelve hours with a break for a mid-shift meal plus two ten-minute tea breaks. If anyone is caught sleeping on shift they shall be fined six shillings and given a warning. Three warnings means dismissal with no leaving certificate.'

They walked along a road with perhaps a dozen two-storey wooden huts in rows, a hundred feet long by twenty feet wide. 'These huts are all for women; the men's colony is on the other side of Goosetown. There is to be no mixing with the men. The women's police patrol the area to ensure no immoral goings-on here either. This is your hut, number ten.'

They stepped up into the hut. Inside there was a main walkway down the middle and perhaps as many as twenty small curtained-off rooms along each side. 'This is Mrs Pratt, hut ten's matron. She oversees the housekeeping here.'

'Oh, hello,' said a woman with a crisp voice and an immaculate hairdo, wiping her hands on her apron. 'And who have we here?'

'Lily Pavitt and Marjorie Cuthbert,' said Mrs Sparrow, looking down at her notebook. 'They'll be in the cordite shed.'

'Ah, righto,' said Mrs Pratt, with a glance at Lily's scruffy boots tied with string and her white-dusted hair that she'd pinned up without a mirror. 'Well, your rooms are along here.'

Lily and Marge followed her along to two rooms at the end. A couple of the current occupants had left their curtains open and Lily glanced in as she passed. They looked cosy and jolly, with photo frames and flowers. In Lily's room there was a single black iron bedstead and mattress, a wash stand and a small chest of drawers. It looked plain but clean. She put her bag down and had a sudden urge to see Sid. She felt quite strange fending for herself without him.

'I'll fetch you some bedding and you can get yourselves settled in. There are two baths and two lavatories at the end of the corridor. I know it's not much but we make do. We are always courteous to one another in hut ten, we take turns and keep the hut and ourselves neat and tidy and we try not to be too noisy. There are penalties if we do not heed these simple rules,' she went on, with a funny kind of smile and making a point of looking at Lily's hair again.

'Right, I shall say goodbye for now,' said Mrs Sparrow. 'The girls will be back from work shortly after six. Go over to the YWCA hut with them for your dinner. Any questions, just ask one of the girls or Mrs Pratt here; otherwise, anything more serious come to see me in my office at the administration building in the safe area of the works.'

'Thank you,' said Lily as the matron and welfare supervisor walked away. 'Right then,' she said to Marge, 'best get unpacked, I suppose.'

Lily didn't have many belongings with her – a few items of clothing and her hairbrush. She wished she had photographs of Sid and the boys but they'd never been able to afford to get them done. She'd ask Ada if she could arrange it and send one on to her and maybe Sid would have an army photograph to send her. She'd noticed a black ribbon draped over a photograph in one of the other rooms and guessed that meant whoever was in the picture had died.

She and Marge laid their beds with the linen Mrs Pratt brought for them, and put their clothes away in the chest of drawers. They went to have a look at the baths and lavatories and filled up their jugs with water for their wash stands. Then they walked to the grocery store to buy paper and envelopes for writing letters. By that time it was three o'clock and Lily suggested they take a nap while waiting for the other girls to come back from their shift. It was something Lady Charlotte might have done – take a nap in the afternoon – but Lily just needed to be on her own for a little while.

She closed the curtain to her little room and sat on her bed. In her solitude her shoulders drooped and she felt herself starting to cry. She tried to do it quietly. It was all so much to take in. She'd kept a brave face when she was with Marge and Mrs Sparrow but really she was terrified. Terrified of all those women coming back to the hut and terrified of going over to the canteen when it was full of people. She didn't know anyone except Marge; what if the others didn't take to her? The thought of starting work in the morning was the worst. If she couldn't do the work they would ask her to leave and then she'd be out of a job with nothing to send to Ada.

She lay down on the bed, it was comfortably sprung and the pillow was soft. She wanted to write to Sid but thought she'd wait until she felt better – she didn't want to worry him. She desperately wanted to see her boys and wondered what they were doing. If she managed to do the job and get paid, she'd buy them a toy to take down on her next visit to Nettlestead. A small whimper escaped her lips and she hoped Marge hadn't heard it. Her eyes closed and she curled up like a child and drifted into sleep.

6

Lily could hear the sound of singing. She sat up in bed and wondered what time it was; she felt like she'd had quite a decent nap. The singing got louder as it came through the door and into hut ten. Women's voices, laughing and chattering.

'Ooh hello, who have we got here, then?'

Lily tensed, listening. Marge pulled back Lily's curtain and ducked into her room.

'They're back,' said the girl, white with fear.

Lily got up, straightened her clothes and gathered her wits. She nodded to Marge and led the way out into the corridor.

At least a dozen women with their hair falling down their shoulders in loose scruffy plaits rushed towards them down the hall.

'Hello!' they called. 'Welcome,' 'What are your names?' 'Welcome to hut ten.'

They stopped short of Lily and Marge, smiling and chatting, each trying to get a word in.

'Hello,' stammered Lily, feeling herself redden. 'I'm Lily and this is Marge.'

The girls reached forward to shake their hands; some even embraced them in warm hugs.

'I'm Eliza,' said one girl. 'Have you had your dinner?'

'No,' said Lily. 'We were told to wait for you to come back from work.'

'Oh, who said that, the old bag?' laughed another woman.

Marge stifled a giggle. 'Er, Mrs Sparrow,' said Lily.

'Yes, that's her,' they chorused. 'Let's get washed and changed and we'll all go over to the canteen,' they chimed, busying themselves and disappearing into their curtained rooms. Lily's heart soared. She needn't have worried after all, the girls were lovely. And how funny that they called Mrs Sparrow the old bag – the same name that Sid used to call Mrs Coker and the mistress at St Clere's. She smiled at Marge and put her arm around her new young friend's shoulders, sharing a quick hug of relief.

The girls appeared from their rooms looking fresh and smart in nice clothes and hats.

'So where will you be working?' asked Eliza. She was tying a scarf around her head and Lily tried not to watch – the girl had a bare patch of scalp with no hair, the skin on her head red and puckered.

'In the cordite shed,' said Lily.

Eliza looked to Marge for her response but the shy girl could only nod.

'Pressing room or mixing room or what?'

'We don't know yet,' said Lily, glancing at Eliza's head without meaning to. 'Where do you work?'

'Oh, they've put me on packing in guncotton, ever since I got scalped by a drill in the cartridge shop. Come on, let's go.'

Lily swallowed, glad Eliza had changed the subject. *Scalped?* Good grief. She exchanged a look of horror with Marge. They joined Eliza and the others as they headed to the door of the hut. Two thick blackout curtains had been pulled across the doorway, with a space in between them. Mrs Pratt stood there to supervise the girls going out, leaving two at a time and pausing between the blackouts so as to avoid showing any light from inside. The sun had gone down and it was dark but for a bright moon. They picked their way through the unlit colony and into the village, chatting all the while.

'The food's not bad,' said one girl. 'They give you plenty of it, anyway.'

Someone started up 'Pack Up Your Troubles in Your Old Kit Bag' and everyone joined in, marching over to the YWCA hut arm in arm. Lily linked arms with Marge and sang along, her spirits rising even higher as more women from other huts made their way over to the canteen.

Inside, the atmosphere wasn't dampened by the dark drapes covering the windows. The long tables were set with cutlery, flowers and brown teapots. Lily followed Eliza to the serving hatch where three ladies resplendent in finery were dishing out food.

'Two Zeps and a cloud, please,' said Eliza, grinning at Lily. 'Sausage and mash,' she explained.

'There you are, my dear. Gravy?' said the serving woman with a cut-glass accent.

'Yes please,' said Eliza.

'The same, please,' said Lily. Eliza turned and laughed at Lily's expression. They sat down together with Marge.

'You never worked somewhere like this?' asked Eliza.

Lily shook her head. 'No, I came from service, so did Marge. Who are those women?'

'The toffs serving? Oh, you know, the ladies doing their bit for the war. Funny, isn't it, being served by the likes of them?'

Lily nodded and cut her sausage with her cutlery stamped with the word 'Greygoose'. She didn't know what to think. The women at the serving counter were dressed just like Lady Harrington. They wore beaded dresses and expensive hats, their fingers and necks were crowded with gems. It was a shock and it grated on Lily's nerves. And it was strange how Eliza had made a joke with them about the sausage and mash looking like a Zeppelin in the sky. The thought of Zeppelins always filled Lily with horror.

The tables were soon full and Lily turned her head towards the sound of a piano in the corner. One of the serving ladies had sat down to play and another, standing by her in a fur stole, started to sing 'The Roses of Picardy'. She had a strong, soprano voice which made the hairs on Lily's arms stand up and soon the whole room was singing along with her. It was a rousing sight and tears sprang to Lily's eyes. She'd never known anything like it. The joy and friendship in the room was overwhelming.

The song finished and for a moment Lily thought of the boys at war, of her Sid in training and soon to be posted, of those that hadn't come home and never would. The room fell silent and she knew everyone was thinking of the war and what it meant to each one of them. A quiet sob came from one table and Lily looked to see a friend place her hand on the arm of the girl upset. The piano started again and soon the whole room was singing along to 'It's a Long Way to Tipperary' and the spirits were instantly lifted, everyone laughing once again.

There was an unfamiliar feeling of camaraderie and Lily wondered whether this was how the boys at the front felt. There was a sense of belonging, of togetherness, and she'd only been there one afternoon. She resolved to be strong, to get on with it. As she looked at the women sitting at her table she saw that one had a burn scar on her face, another had rotten teeth. Two women sitting together had yellow skin and orange hair. Lily couldn't help staring. Even the whites of their eyes were yellow.

'What's wrong with them?' she whispered to Eliza.

Eliza followed Lily's stare. 'Oh, they're the cordite girls; it makes your skin turn yellow. We call them the canaries. But that's what you'll be doing, isn't it?'

Lily and Marge both gawped at the canary girls. They were going to turn *yellow*?

'Oh well,' said Eliza, 'we all just get on with it here. We're doing our bit for the boys, aren't we? Look at me, I'm still here.' She patted her scalped head gently. 'I'm proud to be here, I don't care if it's dangerous. Maggie there got splashed with acid, Annie's got septic teeth. Marie over there lost two fingers last week,' she said, motioning to a woman eating one-handed, her other hand wrapped in a bandage. 'That's why we wear these with pride,' she said, touching the 'on war service' badge pinned to her lapel like a brooch. Lily was glad she'd pinned on her own badge too.

'You're all very brave,' whispered Marge.

'Oh, she speaks,' laughed Eliza. 'I'm only doing what the boys are doing for us. We're helping each other, aren't we?

We're supplying them with ammunition and they're killing the Hun before we get invaded by the blighters.'

She said it in such a matter-of-fact way. Lily wondered if Sid was proud of her, or just scared that she was in danger.

'Want to come into the rec room?' said Eliza, getting up. Some of the others were going through too. Suddenly, there seemed to be some sort of commotion at the other end of the canteen and Lily craned to see some of the girls leaning over to look at something on the ground. There was a woman on the floor, her body jerking, her arms and legs flailing.

'Get a wooden spoon!' someone shouted. A spoon was brought and placed between the woman's teeth.

'It's all right,' said Eliza, 'it's just Ella. She gets fits since she worked with the cordite. It does that to some people, but don't worry, it's only if you were prone to fits in the first place. You're not, are you?'

'I don't think so, no,' said Lily.

'No need to look so scared, you two. Ella's been moved, she works in checking now. Like I said, we just get on with things here. Come on, I'll get you some wool in the rec room. We've all got some knitting on the go – socks, gloves, mufflers, to send to the boys in France.'

They sat at a table in the rec room and Lily started off a row of stitches on her needle. She'd make a muffler to send to Sid. One of the workers had put a record on the gramophone and some of them had paired up to dance around the empty floor space where the chairs and tables had been pushed back. Another woman came by shaking a tin.

'For Alice Pearson's family, the crane driver who died last month.'

Lily dug in her bag for a penny and put it in. 'Sorry, I haven't been paid yet,' she said, wondering what happened to Alice Pearson but not wanting to ask. She remembered seeing the situation vacant for crane drivers in the labour exchange and a shiver went through her.

'This is nice,' said another girl who sat down to join them. She was lighting up a cigarette and chewing on some cake she'd carried from the canteen in her hand.

'Nellie,' she said, putting her cake straight down on the table and holding out the greasy hand. 'Someone tells me you'll be in the cordite shed. That's where I work. I wonder which room you'll be in. I reckon it'll be in with us in the new press room, we need another couple of workers in there.'

'Oh?' said Lily. 'Yes, maybe, I don't know yet.'

'Did you have a good dinner?' asked Nellie. Her accent wasn't local. Lily had met a couple of East Londoners in Tilbury; Nellie sounded the same as them. 'The YWCA opened the canteen last year because we were all eating our dinner down the pub and coming back worse for wear,' Nellie went on, not waiting for an answer. She smiled wryly. 'The church ladies have reformed us,' she said, adding, 'or that's what they think anyway,' with a wink. 'They look after our morals.'

She looked across the room and narrowed her eyes as a woman walked by. Picking off a lump of cake, she suddenly threw it at the woman's back. The woman spun around to see where the weapon had come from.

'Nellie! Was that you?' she said, striding over to their table. Lily shrank back, horrified.

'What?' said Nellie. 'I don't know what you're talking

about.' She took a puff from her cigarette and winked at Lily. Lily looked away quickly, not wanting to be pulled into someone else's tiff. The woman leaned down to Nellie and poked her in the shoulder.

'Just because you're rough and fast, Nellie Watts, it doesn't mean I'm not equal to you in a fight.'

'Oooooh,' laughed Nellie, seeming genuinely amused and loving the confrontation. 'Fighting talk from the lady, is it? Well, come on then, outside, let's be having you.'

Lily looked from one to the other, her heart pounding. Were these girls really going to have a fight? The other one looked well brought up, she could tell from the way she held herself and spoke, whereas Nellie slouched in her chair and cackled with laughter.

'Oh, I wouldn't give you the satisfaction, you horrid little tart.'

'Oh! Ha ha ha!' laughed Nellie. 'Well, off you go then, you've probably got bible practice or some such, haven't you?'

The other woman flounced off, giving Nellie a dirty look.

'Who was that?' asked Lily.

'Oh, that's Agnes, or *Miss Harknett* as we've got to call her. Got a rod up her backside she has. Thinks she's better than the rest of us because she was apprenticed in ladies' tailoring when the war started. She's my charge hand at work. She might be yours too if you're in our gang.'

Lily was mortified. What a way to start. She might have just made an enemy of her boss already.

It was half past nine when Lily made her way back to hut ten in the dark. Some of the girls were still in the rec hut dancing, but she was exhausted and knew she'd better get a good sleep for the early start in the morning. As she walked, she saw the searchlights sweep the sky for Zeppelins. It was a good sign. If there had been a sighting of the enemy further out to the coast there'd be an air raid siren. As it was, the searchlights were patrolling the skies as a precaution. She looked across the marshes towards the factory works, all in darkness as the blackout rules dictated. But she knew the sheds were full of workers and that production never stopped. She thought of them in the sheds, toiling round the clock behind heavy curtains and shutters, and she felt scared to join them. She would be one of them in the morning.

Back in her little curtained room, she took out her paper and pencil and wondered what to tell Sid, mindful of what she couldn't tell him by law and what she didn't want to tell him to make him worried. She certainly wouldn't mention that she might turn yellow.

7

The girls hadn't been quite as gay the next morning when Mrs Pratt the matron had woken them all up at five o'clock. They had whined and dressed and dragged themselves over to the YWCA canteen for breakfast. Lily and Marge had been sombre and nervous throughout and now were standing with what looked like thousands of other workers – men, women and teenaged children – at the gates of the Greygoose factory works.

Lily shuffled to the front, was asked to show her identification card to the woman police constable and then, because it was her first day, she had to go along to be searched by another constable. She'd wound her wedding ring with string as Eliza had told her to do and she'd worn her hair in a long loose plait because no hairpins were allowed, but still the woman checked her hair for rogue pins, checked her clothes for any metal fasteners and her pockets for matches and cigarettes. Lily had forgotten a button at the back of her skirt. The police constable cut it off and told her off for it, writing down her name in a little book. When she came out, she saw the constable pick out another worker for a random check. The girl rolled her eyes and said it would make her late.

They went into one hut to check in then on to the change room where they found their locker and uniforms. The room was overcrowded with girls trying to get changed. It felt strange to Lily to pull trousers over her legs. She looked around her to check the others were doing the same. Tucking her hair into her cap and pulling on the tunic and cape, she stood up and wished there was a looking glass.

'How do I look?' she said quietly to Marge.

'The same as me, I suppose,' said Marge with a nervous giggle. 'I wish my mother could see me now.'

'How old are you, Marge?'

'Eighteen.'

Lily frowned, the girl looked much younger. 'And your mother doesn't need you to live at home?'

'There are too many of us. I'm more of a help earning a wage for them and not living there. I'll go home on my day off to help.'

Lily nodded. 'Here, don't forget these.' Lily picked up the rubber overshoes and handed Marge her pair.

Mrs Sparrow was waiting for them outside the change room and led them along to the danger area. Lily was so nervous she felt sick. The trousers felt funny and bulky between her legs but it was much easier to step up on to the raised wooden tramway to the cordite sheds than when wearing a long skirt and petticoat.

'Yours is range thirty-eight,' said Mrs Sparrow. 'The pressing huts where the cordite dough is pressed into cords. The foreman of range thirty-eight is Bernard Nash. You'll be in the new hut with experienced workers. There is no overseer for your hut as yet – we are currently recruiting for the position – but your charge hand is a Miss Agnes Harknett.'

Lily grimaced. That was the woman from the rec hut last night, who Nellie had thrown the cake at.

'Bernard Nash and Miss Harknett will be responsible for your training. Well, don't stand there gawping like fish, go on in and put your rubber shoes on. I need to get on.'

With that she left them, holding up her skirt to walk back along the tramway.

Lily looked at Marge's white face and pushed open the door to the long wooden building. She held a blackout drape aside and stepped inside. The stench of chemicals made her recoil.

'Oi! Stop!' A man in a khaki uniform with green trim and a flat cap came rushing towards them. 'Get your bloody shoes on!' he shouted.

Lily and Marge jumped to it, Lily nearly wetting herself with fright. They stooped to put the overshoes on and stood up to face the man's wrath.

'Bloody hellfire, what you doing coming in here without them on?'

'Sorry,' stuttered Lily, 'we didn't know where to put them on.' She glanced at Marge who was biting her lip, tears in her eyes.

'You put them on as soon as you come in the outer door and before you come past the curtain,' he said, taking off his cap to smooth back his ginger hair. He puffed out his cheeks, seeming to calm himself down, and swept where they had been standing with a broom propped against the wall. 'Who are you then? What's your names?' His voice was gruff and curt.

'Lily Pavitt and Marge Cuthbert,' said Lily, knowing Marge wouldn't want to speak.

'Right then, I'm the foreman here – Bernard Nash.' He was only as tall as Lily and his face reminded her of a potato, it was a dark yellow colour – cordite yellow – with broad cheeks pitted with scars and wide-spaced eyes. 'Come on then, this way,' he said, waving them on. 'Bloody war,' he muttered.

It was stiflingly warm inside the shed and the air was thick with the smell of chemicals, which made Lily feel faint. She could see several women working in the room, all in khaki and red trousers and caps. There were two large machines on the back wall and women standing on raised platforms operating them. Long strings of something were coming out of the bottom of the machine and being laid across tables by the women below. Most of the workers had a yellow tinge to their skin, some more than others. They looked up and smiled at the new girls as they came in. Mr Nash led them through this room and through an identical one next to it and into a third the same again. Here there were fewer women. Mr Nash took them over to the haughty girl Lily had seen in the rec room, who was talking to another older woman operating one of the machines.

'Miss Harknett, these are your new girls, Lily and Marge,' he said, looking at them with disdain. 'Miss Harknett will be training you until the new overlooker is taken on. Argh, what the bloody hell are you doing there?'

He charged up the steps to the raised platform where the older woman was fiddling with something on the machine.

'The gauge is off a bit; I'm adjusting it, that's all,' said the woman.

'What have I told you about setting the machines? Call me or Alfie to do that. I won't tell you again.'

The woman folded her arms with indignation but kept

quiet while Mr Nash set about correcting the machine. There was an awkward atmosphere in the room and Lily was glad when Miss Harknett spoke to them.

'Hello, I'm Agnes Harknett,' she said, straightening her shoulders. 'But you shall address me as Miss Harknett as I am in a position of authority here.'

Someone sniggered and Lily looked round to see Nellie, the girl who had thrown the cake in the rec room, standing at a table arranging long cords of something and also trying to arrange her face.

'I think you and Nellie have already met,' said Miss Harknett. 'If I were you, I should choose my company wisely around here; there are far too many rough types for my liking.' She looked Lily and Marge up and down and seemed to make up her mind about them. 'I think you two are no strangers to hard work, though?' She said it as though it was a bad thing and Lily shifted uncomfortably.

'This is Jessie,' she said, indicating a girl of about eighteen also standing at a table, a froth of orange hair escaping the front of her cap. Jessie smiled and said hello. 'This is Mabel,' Miss Harknett went on, pointing up to the woman on the raised platform. Mabel was older, late thirties perhaps, and looked worn down by life, with sunken cheeks and dark circles beneath her eyes. She uncrossed her arms and smiled at them and gave them a wave, pointing at Mr Nash and making a talking gesture with her hands behind his back. Lily noticed one of her front teeth was missing. 'And that's the sum of our gang. There's Alfie the press hand and machine setter who flits between the three pressing rooms, and Mr Nash there the foreman. We'll have a new overlooker soon but until then

I'm in charge of this room. I'm sure it will take some time to find the right sort of person for overlooker.'

'Right, that'll do it,' said Mr Nash, wiping his hands on his trousers and coming down the platform steps. 'Call me or Alfie if anything needs doing to the machines, otherwise it'll be a penalty.'

'Yes, Mr Nash, thank you,' said Miss Harknett. 'Oh Mr Nash, would you set up the other machine, I'll train the new girls on it today.'

Mr Nash gave her a look of disdain and climbed the steps again and when he was done, Miss Harknett took them both up.

'Have either of you worked in munitions before?' she said.

'No,' said Lily, and Marge shook her head.

'Well, this is a cordite pressing hut. Cordite is a smokeless explosive used in ammunition. It is made with nitro-glycerine, guncotton, ether and other things. It is mixed into a dough in another part of the danger area and brought here along the tramway in bags. These processes are so dangerous they have to be done in separate buildings,' she added with an air of importance. 'Here we put the cordite through a hydraulic press to make cords of various thickness and length for use in shells and bullets. The cords are dried and gauged for length then packed and sent on a barge along the river to the Woolwich Arsenal where they are put into the cartridges and shells, which of course are then shipped out to the front lines.

'These machines are the hydraulic presses.' The two big iron presses were intimidating; Lily nodded and tried not to look scared. 'We carry the bags of dough very carefully in from the tramway, and up the steps and we pull the bag open and lift out handfuls of it with great care and place it into the drum of the press.' She demonstrated, pulling open a rubber bag, which had orangey-brown coloured paste inside. She put both hands into it and put it into the press cylinder. 'You each try,' she said. Lily went first. The dough was moist and thick, like brown porridge. She was scared to touch it in case it exploded. 'It would take a sharp bang with a hammer to make it blow but we handle it carefully nevertheless,' Miss Harknett explained.

'Right, now we swing out the press and turn the wheel and Jessie down there will catch the cords coming out and pass them to Nellie who'll arrange them on the slatted trays and cut them off. When the trays are full we carry them through to the ovens in the next room where hot air is passed through to dry off the ether. That's why it's so frightfully warm in here. And it's worse at night when the blackout drapes are up too.' Lily watched as the long strings of cordite came out of the bottom of the press and Jessie guided them on to the table.

'While they do that, you'll fill the other cylinder with more dough.' Lily and Marge did it together. 'You'll get quicker at it in time. But keep it slow and careful for now.'

'Yes, sorry,' said Lily, feeling hot and light-headed from the fumes. She swung the cylinder out and started to fill the empty one that had come back, going quicker this time.

'Marge, you come down and I'll show you what to do. Lily, you carry on.'

Lily could hear Miss Harknett showing Marge how to lay out the cordite strands, but Lily was too caught up in what she was doing to pay a great deal of attention. Careworn Mabel was operating the other press, with Marge and Miss Harknett arranging the cords on the trays from that one.

'You got kids?' Mabel called over to Lily.

Lily tried to answer without looking up from her work. 'Yes, two boys, Robert is three and Joe is two; they're with my mother-in-law in the country. And you?'

Mabel cackled. 'Oh yes, I've got six. On my own, too, since I lost my John a year ago,' she added soberly. 'He was on HMS *Formidable* when it was torpedoed.'

Lily noticed the black armband on Mabel's sleeve. 'Six? Blimey, that must be a job, and I'm sorry about your husband, that's dreadful.'

'Yes, he was a boiler stoker here in Greygoose but he joined up when the war started and then, you know . . .'

Lily gave Mabel a look of sympathy. Poor woman; and all those children, too. With alarm, Lily stood back from the press. It was making strange chugging sounds.'

'Alfie! Mr Nash!' screamed Miss Harknett.

Mr Nash came running, dashed up the steps and shoved Lily aside. He switched off the machine and started pulling the cordite dough out of the cylinder by the handful.

'Bloody hellfire, you put too much in!' he shouted. 'Do you want the whole shed to blow? You're lucky you didn't start a bloody fire, woman.'

'Oh, I'm sorry, I'm really sorry,' said Lily, trembling at the suggestion she might have caused an explosion.

'Well, take better care. You only fill it to there,' he said, pointing to a line on the inside of the cylinder.

'I'm sorry, I thought I did fill it to there,' she said, looking at Miss Harknett for support, but the charge hand just frowned at her.

'Well, you should have been paying more attention,' said Mr Nash. 'That's how the last girl lost her hand.'

'Who?'

'Mary. She lost her hand when an explosion in the cylinder blew the die off. It started a fire too. Bloody war.'

Lily felt sick. 'Is she all right?'

'She's in the hospital in Goosetown,' said Mr Nash. 'There, it's fixed, now get on with it. And don't work too fast.'

He stomped down the steps and into the next room. Lily was terrified she'd make a mess of it again and cause an explosion. The thought of causing an accident like that, getting someone's hand blown off . . . Her head was pounding from the fumes and her hands itched from the acid in the dough. She started to refill the cylinder and was careful to mind the line, as she thought she had done before. She swung it out and pressed the lever and there was a shout from Jessie below.

'It's on the wrong setting,' she said. 'It's coming out too fast and uneven.'

'Oh, what now?' said Miss Harknett. 'Someone get Alfie.'

Jessie disappeared and came back with a young man who was much easier on the eye than Mr Nash. But he was just as abrupt and came up to set the machine without introducing himself to Lily. He moved with an awkward gait as though he had pain down one side of his body.

'Don't touch the pressure settings,' he said to her.

'I didn't,' said Lily, frowning.

'Oh, you're new. Well, don't touch any of the dials; if you want to change anything call me or Mr Nash.'

Lily could have cried. She was trying so hard to do well but it kept going wrong.

'*He's* doing it,' Mabel said in a loud whisper once Alfie had gone. Lily thought she had misheard and shook her head. '*He's* doing it. *Mr Nash* is setting it wrong to make you trip up.'

'What?' Lily was so light-headed from the fumes. Her cap was tight and hot. She took it off and grabbed hold of the side rail and closed her eyes.

'Put that cap back on immediately,' called Miss Harknett, looking up at her. 'And go outside for a breath of air, we can't have you fainting around the machinery.'

'Thanks, I need the lav anyway,' she said. 'Where is it?'

'I'd hold it if I was you,' said Nellie, laughing.

'Out the door and round the back of the shed,' said Miss Harknett, ignoring Nellie.

Lily got herself down the steps and remembered to take off her rubber overshoes before going outside. The brightness made her blink, she felt as though she'd been in the shed for an age. It was freezing but she was glad of the fresh air. She picked her way through the mud round to the back and found the lavatory: just one, with a corrugated-iron roof. She sat down on the pot with relief but something brushed against her backside and she stood up with a shriek. Looking into the bowl she saw a brown rat standing up against the inside of the toilet bowl and she flung herself out of the door as fast as she could.

She ran away from the lavatory, her tunic covering her immodesty. She was mortified to see that the tops of her trousers were wet but luckily when she pulled them up, the tunic covered the dark patch. She'd just have to go the rest of her shift in discomfort, it was too shameful to mention it to Miss Harknett – she had already proved herself unworthy of the job. Leaning against the side of the building, she gulped some air, trying to clear her head, and when she was feeling better she went back in.

'Sorry, I feel better now,' she said.

'You'd better take some of the drying trays into the next room, there are too many fumes in here,' said Miss Harknett. 'Nellie, you help her.'

'Yes, Miss Harknett,' said Nellie, dropping into a sarcastic curtsey and picking up one of the trays. Lily followed suit.

'Did you find the lav?' asked Nellie, slotting the tray into what looked and felt like a large stove.

'Yes, and there was a rat in there, inside the bowl,' said Lily, slotting her tray in too and leaning back from the hot and stinking air coming from the drying oven.

'Oh dear,' said Nellie, laughing. 'There are always rats in there, that's why we only go if we really have to. It's worse at night in the dark. Well, at least you're a local girl. I came down from London and they used to put nettles under the toilet seat for me. So I had nettles *and* rats.'

'What? Why?'

Nellie shrugged. 'Dunno, because they were wary of me, I suppose. The pranks didn't last long; it's just something they do here.'

They walked back into the pressing room to get another tray each and Lily remembered what Mabel had said about Mr Nash fixing the machine. She decided not to say anything – it was too strange – she had probably imagined it because the fumes had been so strong.

'I don't remember reading about that accident in the local paper,' she said when they were back in the drying room.

'What accident?'

Lily looked at Nellie's yellow eyes. 'The one Mr Nash talked about, the girl who got her hand cut off by the press.'

'Oh, Mary. No you wouldn't have heard about that. Everything here is hushed up because of spies and public spirit. In any of the munitions factories, it's only if there's a big explosion that can't be hushed up that anything's said in the paper. There's a war on, don't you know!'

'It must have been horrible.'

'Yes, it was.' Nellie shuddered. 'I think about it at night, it gives me horrors.'

'What caused it?'

'Dunno.' Nellie shrugged. 'Mr Nash said the pressure of the hydraulics was wrong, caused an explosion in the cylinder and it blew the die off, the metal thing with the holes in. He doesn't like girls in the factory,' she added, with a wry smile, 'always cusses the war, but when he says "war", he means "women".'

'How do you mean?' said Lily.

'You know, "bloody war" and all that.'

'Blimey, do you get used to this stink?' said Lily, putting another tray into the oven.

'Sort of; it's worse at night, though. Chin up, it'll be tea-time soon.'

At nine their room stopped for tea, while the other two pressing rooms carried on. Lily and the others went outside to get a cup of tea and a bun from the mess hut. There was nowhere to sit down so they had to take it back to the cordite range. They sat outside on the platform of the tramway to eat it even though it was cold.

'Right, come on: back in,' called Miss Harknett before Lily

had finished her bun. She stuffed the rest of it in her mouth and chewed as she went back inside. Taking her place at the cordite press once again, she filled the cylinder with dough and went to wind the wheel to apply the hydraulic pressure but pulled her hands away in disgust.

'Urgh, what's this?' she said, looking at her hands. They were smeared with what looked like black engine grease.

Everyone looked up at her and shrugged. Marge went to cut the cord lengths with the tool they used, a thin length of wood with a thick rubber blade attached.

'Urgh!' she exclaimed and dropped the tool, looking at her hands, covered in the same stuff. Marge looked around at the other women, who all wore expressions of surprise, and up at Lily who returned her gaze of disgust.

Lily was glad of the forewarning from Nellie that the new ones had tricks played on them. She wondered who had done it, and looked at the faces as she climbed down the steps for a rag to wipe her hands on.

Jessie was biting her lips together and Mabel looked too innocent by far. Lily waited for them to say something but when they didn't it felt awkward and unpleasant. She passed a rag to Marge and took hers back up the steps to wipe off the press wheel, wondering if anything else would be done to the new girls.

Her back ached despite the short tea break and her head hurt from the fumes. There was a poster on the wall that showed an aerial photograph of the German trenches on the Western Front before and after they'd been blasted by Allied shells. The caption read: *Munition workers see the effect of your work!* It kept her spirits up no end to think that she was helping the boys over there; she was helping them directly, making cordite for their shells. She was one of *the girls behind the men behind the guns*. It was a feeling she'd never had before, one of importance and dignity; she got a lump in her throat thinking about it. She'd certainly never felt like that working at St Clere's for the Harrington family. On the contrary, she'd practically been a slave for them.

When lunchtime came, they went to collect tea and sandwiches from the mess hut and took it back to sit on the platform again.

'I fancy getting my photograph taken in my uniform to send to my Sid so he's got something to look at,' said Lily.

'Is that your husband? Where is he?' asked Nellie.

'Training at Warley but he'll be posted somewhere before long and I want him to have a photograph to take with him.'

'There's a photographer on Orsett Road in Grays. He puts a painted screen behind you to make it look nice,' said Jessie. 'I had it done to give to my sweetheart,' she said, beaming.

'Oh? Who is that, then?' asked Lily with a smile.

'Oh, blimey, don't ask her that, she'll never shut up about him,' said Mabel, laughing. 'This one's got a bad case of khaki fever.'

'Don't mind her, she doesn't mean it,' said Jessie, and Mabel rolled her eyes. 'He's a guard here, one of the West Kent's. Edward his name is,' she went on, closing her eyes with ecstasy at the thought of him.

'It's immoral,' said Miss Harknett, 'a young woman leaving home before she's married, going round with a man without her father's permission.'

'She's having a bit of fun. You're just jealous,' said Mabel.

'I know I am.' She let out a cackle, showing her missing front tooth and ulcerated gums.

'I am not,' said Miss Harknett, grimacing at the sight of Mabel lifting her trouser leg to scratch the thick blue varicose veins on her calves. 'These girls, getting a bit of money and going around looking fast in make-up and wearing clothes like the mistresses they used to work for. It's not respectable.'

'What did you two do before this?' asked Nellie.

'I worked in service,' said Lily, looking at Marge to encourage her to say something.

'I did too,' said Marge quietly, with a nervous laugh and turning red.

'Oh, you do talk, then,' laughed Nellie. 'So when you get paid are you two going to go round dressing like your old mistresses?'

'I'll be giving my pay to my mother,' said Marge quietly.

'Oh? I reckon you'll be out with the soldiers in no time, getting cosy in the bushes like they all do,' laughed Mabel, and she dug Lily in the ribs, as though the two married women could share a joke.

Marge laughed, trying to hide her face which had turned even redder.

'You'll not go around like a prostitute or I'll report you to Mrs Sparrow,' said Miss Harknett, her voice steely.

'Oh and what do you know about prostitutes?' said Nellie.

'Quite enough, thank you, and I urge you all to have more concern for your own morality and not let these new freedoms overshadow your sense of right and wrong.' She stood up. 'Now, there's work to be done.'

They trooped back inside, worked another three hours

and Lily just kept on going. Mabel started singing 'Keep the Home Fires Burning' and they all sang along, even Miss Harknett, and it gave Lily the energy she needed. They stopped for the ten-minute afternoon tea break and then soldiered on for another three hours before coming off the twelve-hour shift.

'I'm knackered,' said Lily to Marge, who also looked asleep on her feet. 'Have you got a headache?'

'Yes, a shocker, it's pounding, and I kept thinking I'd faint.'

'I know, bet you're glad you're staying in the colony and not travelling home.'

'Too right, I just want dinner and bed.'

Lily lost Marge fighting for a space in the change hut. She tried to wash her hands at the trough sink but there was no soap, and she was carried along with the crowd out through the gates. She saw two little boys there, ragged things, their clothes worn and dirty, no shoes on their feet in this cold.

'What are you doing here?' she asked them.

'Any bread please, missis?' they asked and Lily's heart almost broke. She crouched down to their height. 'I'm sorry, loves, I haven't got a crumb on me, nor no money. They don't let us bring coins into work. Where's your mum?'

'It's all right, missis; thank you, missis.'

Lily stood up and walked away reluctantly, looking back at the two boys. They can't have been from Goosetown. They must have walked miles across the marshes to beg there. They reminded her of her Robert and Joe, and her heart nearly burst with wanting to see her boys at that moment, to hold them against her. She resolved to save some bread at breakfast to bring tomorrow in case the boys were there again.

8

For the next four days, Lily was on the cordite press and Marge was laying out the cords on the drying racks. It was exhausting work. On Wednesday they had come back from morning tea break to find rats' tails in their rubber overshoes. On Thursday and Friday, there was more grease on their tools and Lily began to wonder how much more of it she could take. It was the silence surrounding the pranks that got to her: no one would admit guilt, no one apologised, it was like she and Marge just had to put up with it. Lily was getting ever angrier but didn't have it in her to say anything, and Marge was even less likely to cause a fuss. It was Saturday today and nothing had happened so far but it was tea break soon and judging by the past few days there'd be a surprise waiting for them when they got back.

Lily noticed the pressure dropping on the cordite press but didn't want to ask Mr Nash to fix it. Miss Harknett hadn't come to work today because of illness.

'It looks like this pressure is dropping,' she said. 'Does anyone know how to fix it?'

'Oh, you don't touch it, that's only for Mr Nash and Alfie

to touch,' said Jessie. 'They get very cross if we do it. It needs a new cylinder anyway, and they're heavy.'

'Why can't we do it?'

'Because they don't want us to get the same pay as them,' said Mabel.

'But we have to ask them every time,' said Lily.

'Best to go and find one of them and ask them to do it,' said Jessie.

Lily went into the next pressing room. Alfie was up on the platform at the back operating one of the presses, doing the job Lily had been doing for the past week.

'Alfie, we need a new cylinder.'

'Well, I'm busy; go and ask Mr Nash. I can't stop here, they're a girl short.'

Lily went through into the first pressing room but there was no sign of the foreman.

'Where's Mr Nash?' she asked one of the girls.

'He's sorting out a delivery of dough,' came the reply.

'They're both busy,' Lily told the others when she got back to her room.

'Well, we can't stop work, we'll fall behind our levels,' said Jessie.

'I know where the new cylinders are,' said Mabel. 'Come on.' She beckoned to Lily, who followed her back to the first pressing room and into an ante room. Mabel found a barrow and they both lifted the heavy cylinder on to it.

They wheeled it through the first room, past the second room, where Alfie was too busy to notice them, and into their room.

'What are you doing?' said Jessie, as they hefted the cylinder up the steps to the press. 'We're not allowed to do that.'

'Well, it's here now, isn't it? And we can't stop production,' said Mabel. Lily looked at the worried faces of the other girls and wondered whether she should have helped Mabel.

'I know how to set it,' said Mabel. 'I've watched them do it enough times.'

'Mabel, are you sure you know what to do?' said Nellie. 'You're not going to blow us all up, are you?'

'Don't be daft. It's just putting a new cylinder on, that's all.'

Mabel got the depressurised cylinder off and the new one on and started setting the dials while the others looked on.

'Right, I think that's it,' she said finally, standing back and frowning.

'What do you mean, you *think*?' said Jessie from below. 'Heavens above, you'll blow us sky high, I'm getting out of here.'

She trotted out of the room and the others looked at each other.

'Well? Shall I switch it on?' said Mabel.

'What's all this?' said Alfie, striding into their room. 'What the hell is going on?'

'No one was here to help us so we put on a new cylinder,' said Mabel defiantly.

Alfie said nothing but raced to get up the steps to check the machine, his lame side hindering him. He looked at the connections, the dials, the pressure and he stood back.

'You done it right,' he said, rubbing the back of his neck and frowning. Mabel beamed with pride.

'I told you,' she said. 'I've watched them do it enough times.'

Alfie's expression changed from surprised to hostile. 'Mr Nash isn't going to like this,' he said. 'You'll be in big trouble, I tell you.'

'Alfie, you don't have to say anything. You've checked it now,' said Nellie.

'Course I have to say something. We can't have girls changing the cylinders, it's too dangerous.'

'But we did change it,' said Lily, taking her chance to speak up, guessing that if they were reported, the fact that they had been able to change it wouldn't make any difference.

'Yes, you did that all right,' said Alfie, his expression changing again when he looked at Lily. She thought she might blush and fought it. Going red would give her away. She'd developed a fondness for Alfie even though he was Mr Nash's sidekick. Not in that way, though, she told herself.

'Please, Alfie,' she managed to say. 'We don't want Mrs Sparrow telling us off.'

Alfie took off his cap, smoothed back his hair and put his cap back on. He instinctively reached into his pocket, as though he'd take out a smoke, but of course they weren't allowed to bring their tobacco into the factory.

'All right, then. I suppose this once. But you mustn't do it again, all right? I'll be in trouble myself if anyone finds out about this, especially Mr Nash.'

'Thanks, Alfie,' they all said in unison.

He couldn't help but grin and got himself away down the steps and into the next room. Lily watched him go and felt a glow of friendship for him. He was all right after all.

At tea break, Alfie sat with them to eat his bun.

'You took a big risk doing that,' he said.

'Well, maybe you should train us girls properly then we won't have to keep asking you,' said Mabel.

'We're not allowed to do that,' said Alfie. 'It's Mr Nash.

I shouldn't be saying this, but he doesn't like having girls in the factory doing men's work.'

'Oh? You could have fooled me,' laughed Nellie.

'But we want to do it and we proved today that we can do it,' said Mabel.

'Yes, but then you'd want paying the same as us and that wouldn't do, would it?'

The girls fell silent. Of course women weren't paid the same as men. Men had to work hard for years to work up to skilled jobs. It was obvious to Lily they wouldn't want the women taking all the jobs. But still it didn't seem fair. Why was it so bad for them to be trained to do what they were doing anyway?

'Where're you from, Alfie?' she asked, not wanting to cause him any further awkwardness.

'He's a northerner, can't you tell by his funny accent?' said Jessie, grinning.

Alfie smiled. 'That's right, I'm from a mining village near Newcastle. Worked in the mines with my dad when I left school.'

'Did you, Alfie? I thought you'd served,' said Nellie.

'Yeah, I did. Volunteered for Kitchener's army to escape the coalmines. Served with the Northumberland Fusiliers until I was stuck with shrapnel in Ypres.'

'You were on the front, Alfie?' said Lily.

'Yes and a bad job it was too. Can't say I'm sorry to be invalided out. I've done my bit,' he said, his face clouding over. 'And I've got this to show for it,' he went on, indicating his left side.

Lily wanted to ask him where he was hurt but it didn't

seem proper. His injuries affected the way he held himself and walked. It must have been hard for him.

'Course, the biggest price I paid was that I'll never play football again.'

'Football?' the girls chorused.

'I was professional. On Newcastle's reserve team. It was the only thing that kept me from going mad when I was in the mines. I dreamt of playing on the first team but then the war started and ruined it all.'

'Blimey, Alfie, you must be really good.'

'Yeah,' he said with a dry laugh. 'I was. Not no more.'

'Munitionettes play football,' said Nellie.

'What?' said Lily.

'Women like us in other factories, they play football, properly in teams. I quite fancy that.'

'She's right,' said Alfie. 'There are women's teams up north. They're quite good an' all.'

'What are you lot up to?' said Mr Nash, coming out of the press hut to see them sitting on the tramway. 'Don't you know the next gang are waiting for their tea? Is this what happens when the charge hand is away sick? I'll be reporting this to Mrs Sparrow.'

They all jumped up and, with murmured apologies, got themselves back to work.

When Lily and Marge put on their overshoes there were no rats' tails in them. And when Lily climbed the steps to the cordite press, there was no black engine grease smeared across the wheel. She looked over the rail down at Marge, who picked up her cutting tool, inspected it and looked up at Lily with a little smile. This was the first day since they'd started that there had been no pranks played on them. Of course, there were still three hours to go until the end of their shift, but Lily thought it would stop now. She had a feeling that they had been accepted into the gang.

Sure enough, six o'clock came around and there had been no more tricks played on them. They made their way wearily to the change rooms and when they got through the factory gates the air around them buzzed with the joy of the end of the working week. Lily had saved some bread from the canteen every morning for the boys she'd seen begging at the gates on Tuesday but they hadn't been back. Now she looked for them again and saw them there. They made a pitiful sight. She made her way through the crowd towards them. They looked at her with no recognition. Their eyes seemed blank to Lily, lacking any spark of life. They held out their hands.

'Any bread please, missis?'

She crouched down to them. 'Yes, boys; I saved you some from breakfast.' They took it from her and started to eat it immediately.

'What are your names?' she said.

'Albert,' said one, through his chewed bread. 'Charlie,' said the other.

'I'm Lily. How old are you, Albert?'

'Ten,' he said, and Lily recoiled. Ten? He looked no more than six. She nodded and smiled.

'And you, Charlie?'

'Eight,' he said.

Charlie looked much younger than eight. They were stick thin and dirty. Lily just wanted to take them to the canteen to feed them up but that wouldn't be allowed.

'Where's your mum?' she said tentatively.

Albert pointed north towards Fobbing. He pulled at his little brother's sleeve and they walked away. Maybe they were afraid the lady was asking them too many questions, that they would get into trouble.

Lily caught up with Marge, threaded her arm through hers and joined in the rousing chorus of 'It's a Long Way to Tipperary' with all the other workers happy to be off shift at the end of the week. When they got back to hut ten, Mrs Pratt was there handing out their pay packets for the week. Lily took hers with a thrill of excitement. In her room, she opened it to find twenty-two shillings – the cost of bed and board had been taken out. They had even paid her for that first Monday when she hadn't done any work. It was such a lot of money; she clutched it to her chest and closed her eyes, so proud to have earned it in such an honourable way.

She washed and changed and joined the others in the walk over to the canteen for dinner. Faggots and pease pudding and a lot of it. Served by the usual ladies done up to the nines in their finery. They were serenaded by one of them while they ate and then they went through into the rec room. The atmosphere was jolly and high, someone sat at the piano and thumped out a waltz and Lily grabbed Marge to dance, they swung around and around having a ball.

Jessie gestured from a table for them to sit down and poured something from a brown bottle into two teacups out of sight under the table. She gave them each a cup of stout that she'd bought from the village shop. 'Cheers, ladies, and welcome to the gang,' she said, holding hers up.

'Cheers,' said Lily and Marge together, sipping their drinks.

'Shame your Edward can't come in here for a dance with you, Jessie,' said Lily.

'I know, but I'm lucky to see him as much as I do.'

Lily nodded and felt a sudden urge to see Sid. 'So, does this mean there won't be any more rats' tails in my overshoes?' she said, changing the subject and laughing. She wasn't used to drink and it was going straight to her head.

'Or engine grease on our tools?' said Marge, standing up and draining her second cup, the stout finally making her let her guard down. She laughed around with everyone, but misjudged her angle as she sat back down and fell giggling to the floor. Nellie helped her up.

'I don't know what you're talking about,' grinned Nellie. 'You know what, though,' she said, making sure she had their attention, 'how about we ask Alfie to teach us football? Then we can have teams and matches.'

'Football? For women?' said Marge with a look of disbelief that quickly changed into one of drunken adventure. 'Yes!' she cried. 'I'll do it! Don't tell my mother, though,' she said in an exaggerated whisper. 'She'll think it's immoral.'

'Would we wear football shorts?' asked Jessie. 'I quite like the sound of that. Oi, Bonny!' she called to a girl walking by. 'Bonny, how'd you like to be in a women's football team with us?'

Bonny sat down with them. True to her name, she was pretty with blonde hair and she was dressed as nicely as any lady, she even wore a fur stole, but when she started to speak, Lily knew she was one of her own sort, salt of the earth.

'Football? Yes, I should think so. There are a couple of work teams around here, I think: the cement works in West

Thurrock and one in Ilford. We could play them when we get good enough.'

'Who else can we ask to join?' said Jessie. 'Mabel?'

'Mabel won't, she's got all those kids to look after,' said Lily.

'Hold your horses, we haven't even asked Alfie yet,' laughed Nellie. 'Lily, you ask him, he's got a soft spot for you, I reckon.'

Lily felt her face flush hot. 'I'm married, Nellie.'

'Yeah, I know, but it doesn't hurt to use your assets to our advantage, does it?'

'You're lucky Miss Harknett isn't here, she'd be raging,' said Jessie.

'Oh, I'm not scared of her; I've seen a lot worse, I can tell you.'

'Have you been drinking, young lady?' One of the YWCA volunteers was at their table, directing her question at Marge.

'No, she's just tired, it's her first week,' said Jessie, downing the contents of her cup before the puritanical volunteer realised what was in it.

'Right, we'd better get you back to the hut, Marge, before you fall asleep under the table,' said Lily, glad of the diversion, seeing Marge slouch in her chair with her eyelids heavy with sleep and drink.

'I shall ask a police constable to escort you,' said the volunteer.

'No it's all right, I'll be all right with her,' said Lily and the volunteer nodded with pursed lips, clearly not believing a word of it.

Back in hut ten, Lily tucked Marge into bed and looked down at her. The young girl looked so drawn and pale but this evening she had also looked happy and Lily was glad to see it. Settling into her own bed, she reflected on her first week at work. It had been exhausting but good. She suspected that Alfie had been responsible for the pranks and hoped they would stop now that the group had accepted her. Although it didn't explain how the cordite press had gone wrong twice on her first day – if someone had done that on purpose it wasn't a prank, it was a dangerous trick and she couldn't imagine Alfie doing something like that.

She'd taken a big risk helping Mabel put that new cylinder on. Giggling to herself about it, she couldn't believe she'd done it. At St Clere's Hall, finding a way to get the job done was what kept you out of trouble. Luckily it had all worked out and they'd made friends with Alfie, which was a good thing for their gang. She yawned and snuggled into her pillow. Now she'd been volunteered to ask Alfie to teach them football. Football! What would Sid say?

9

Sunday, Lily's day off. She woke up excited to see the boys. Some of the girls in her hut would have a lie-in and then walk leisurely over to the schoolhouse for the Sunday service. But she got herself up and got the Corringham Light Railway, walked to Stanford-le-Hope station, got the train to Tilbury, then the ferry to Gravesend and then two more trains through Kent.

Nettlestead was a pretty village and her heart raced the nearer she got to Ada's sister's house. When she knocked there was no answer and she sat on the doorstep to wait. She could have looked for the church, which was where they most likely were, and sneaked in, but it didn't seem right. She must have nodded off against the frame of the porch because she was awoken by Robert and Joe shaking her and calling, *Ma, Ma*. She opened her eyes and grabbed them in her arms, crying into their hair.

'Oh, boys, I've missed you so much. Look at you,' she said, holding them back, 'you look like you've been eating well.' A picture of the beggar boys at the factory gates flitted across her mind and her own boys looked so much healthier in contrast that she was glad they were here, safe and sound and eating well. They looked at her with bemused expressions and she realised her reaction was a little strong given they'd only seen her a week ago.

'How're you doing, Ada, Dolly? The boys are looking well.'

'We are as to be expected,' said Ada, drawing herself up. 'How am I supposed to be doing without my husband?'

What did Ada expect her to say? Should she have apologised again that her friend's mother gave Sid a white feather and Gerald volunteered to enlist with him? It was hardly Lily's fault. Instead, Lily met the woman's eye. She wouldn't be drawn into it. Her mother-in-law could at least ask how Lily was. She didn't.

'I expect you'll be wanting a cup of tea?' she said.

'That'd be nice, thanks. Come on, boys, tell me all about everything,' she said, ignoring the stiff old woman who drained the joy out of everything.

They went into the parlour of the crowded little cottage. 'Now, boys, I'm sorry, I haven't had a chance to go to the proper shops yet because I've been doing twelve-hour shifts at work.' She wished she hadn't glanced at Ada and seen the woman's look of satisfaction. 'But I did manage to get some sweets from the shop at work.'

'Sweets!' The boys leapt towards her. She handed them a bag of cream caramels and enjoyed watching them devour the treats. She couldn't remember the last time she'd had the money to treat them.

'Offer one to your gran and great-auntie, boys; don't be rude, I'm sure they would like one.'

Dolly took one, but Ada declined and Lily sighed, knowing her mother-in-law was acting out of pride.

'You're spoiling them. Sweets are a waste of money when there's a war on,' said Ada.

'Here, Ada,' said Lily, in earshot of Dolly, so Ada couldn't squirrel anything away for herself. 'There's thirty shillings in there, for your board and the boys'. Thanks for looking after them.'

Ada took the money and Lily almost laughed at herself when she waited for the woman to express any gratitude. Even superficial gratitude would have sufficed. Lily was grateful she was looking after the boys for her, glad even. She felt a smash of guilt at the thought and squirmed with discomfort. Her job in munitions was changing her, she could see that already and it had only been a week.

'So, what's it like at the factory?' asked Dolly.

'It's . . . ' Lily didn't really know what it was. 'It's hard work but good work.' She settled on that.

'What is it, Ma?' asked Robert, slurping his sweet.

'I work in a munitions factory. We make . . . we make the things that blow up in guns.'

'Kill the Hun!' shouted Robert, and danced around.

'Yes, that's it, to help get rid of the Germans and end the war, that's it,' said Lily, trying to make herself heard.

'What have you been doing this week, then, eh?' she said, calling them to her.

'Kill the Hun!' Robert shouted, dancing around, and Joe joined him. 'Kill the Hun!'

'Yes,' Lily said quietly to herself. 'Kill the Hun.'

She was glad she'd seen the boys, of course, but seeing

Ada left a bad taste in her mouth. The woman couldn't even be civil when she hadn't seen her for a week. It would never change, Lily decided; why did she expect it to?

She slept soundly back at the colony that night, knowing she wouldn't be starting her next shift until the following dinner time and excited at the prospect of having some time and money to go shopping. At the last minute, she'd kept some money back from Ada. She wanted to treat the boys, yes, but she thought she might treat herself too. It felt wrong and wasteful but she was surprised to realise she didn't care. In the rec hut the girls all looked lovely in their new clothes, with their smart shoes and silk stockings, and skirts that swished around their ankles. Lily's patched and threadbare skirts still brushed the floor and her old boots were tied with string. She'd worked hard this week. She was going shopping. And there was no one to tell her any different.

The following morning, Lily wondered whether to rouse one of the girls to go into Grays town with her, as Marge had stayed the night at home to help her mother, but she settled on going alone.

She made her way to the train station at Stanford-le-Hope and took a train to Grays. Her first stop was Orsett Road to the photographer Jessie had told her about. He was able to take her picture there and then. She'd brought her uniform in a bag and stood proudly before the backdrop of what looked like the gardens of a stately home wearing her tunic and trousers, cap and cape. The photographer asked her permission to pull one side of her cape on to her shoulder so as to show her tunic beneath and she agreed, feeling acutely embarrassed.

She smiled awkwardly into the lens and waited for what seemed like an age for him to take the picture.

Glad to get changed behind the screen, she smiled to herself, proud that she'd been brave enough to go through with it. She couldn't wait to send the picture to Sid. The photographer said he'd post it to her when it was ready.

Her next stop was George Davis toy shop on the High Street. She bought the boys a box of tin soldiers to share. And then, her stomach fluttering with nerves, she went on to Joyes drapers. She was dismayed to see a display of mourning wear in the window – it was a depressing sign of the times.

Inside, there was a sale on blouses. She picked out one in cream silk for a shilling. She gave a sidelong glance at the lovely fur sets in squirrel and black mole, thinking of Bonny the girl in the rec hut wearing that fetching fur stole. She would have loved a new hat, but the cheapest trimmed velvet hats were three shillings. It was all so tantalising. Everything she looked at she wanted. And with every new item she saw, her own clothes looked more worn and unacceptable than she'd ever really considered. There was a third off ladies' winter tweed coats, at four and eleven. There were skirts for five shillings in the sale. Gloves, scarves. She wanted all of it. She settled on the blouse for a shilling and a skirt for five. She paid for them and dashed out of the shop before she crumbled with guilt. She'd have to wait for some new boots. But her new skirt was shorter than she'd worn before and her boots would show even more. She shook her head and ran to the station with her bags, almost ashamed to be seen with them. The thought of Ada knowing what she'd done was terrible, but also terribly wonderful.

Back at Goosetown, she and the other A-shift girls went to the canteen for an early dinner at five o'clock. Lily was nervous about doing her first night shift. It was already dark by the time they checked in at the factory gates. The whole factory works were in darkness – any lights would attract Zeppelins. They got changed and picked their way over to the cordite sheds.

Inside the shed it was already stiflingly hot from the drying ovens. The windows were closed and covered by heavy black drapes, which not only kept the light in but also meant no ventilation for the stench of the cordite fumes.

'You'll be on the drying racks this week, Lily,' said Miss Harknett. 'And Marge, you'll be on the press. Nellie, you'll show Lily the racks. Marge, I'll show you the press.'

Nellie made a salute when Miss Harknett wasn't looking and, not for the first time, Lily wondered at her lack of respect for authority. They had all agreed with Alfie that he wouldn't tell anyone about Lily and Mabel fixing the press cylinder last week. It was on Lily's conscience that she had broken the rules and that Miss Harknett would be cross with her if she found out. She would be attentive and respectful to make up for it.

'Yes, Miss Harknett, thank you,' she said, and Nellie raised her eyebrows.

'She won't find out, you know,' said Nellie.

'I don't know what you mean.'

'Yes you do. Alfie won't tell; he's on our side now. Are you gonna ask him about the football?'

Lily smiled. 'I think so, if you're sure it's a good idea.'

'Course it is,' said Nellie. 'We sweat our guts out in here for twelve hours every day; we need a bit of fun, don't we?'

The hum of the cordite press started up and Nellie showed

Lily how to wait for the strands to come out from the bottom of the press and she guided them carefully to Lily at the table.

'Swap with me,' she said, laying the wet cords over Lily's hands. She went along the table and lay the cords along it so there was a little space between each one and then she took the rubber cutting tool and cut them off at the end. 'Guide them on to the next section,' she said, indicating the drying rack, which had three sections to it. 'Here.' She handed Lily the cutting tool. Lily was frightened to use it.

'Won't it blow up if I cut it?' she asked, even though she'd seen the others do it all last week.

Nellie shook her head. 'You'd have to really whack it for it to explode.'

Lily cut the strands, and Nellie took the ends up and passed them along the final section of the rack. Checking that they were laid out correctly, they carried the rack to a table at the side and brought a new rack over while Marge refilled the next cylinder of the press.

'Not too bad, is it?' said Nellie.

'No,' said Lily, relieved. But by the time the first tea break came three hours later, her arms were aching and she had a headache from the fumes. The rash on her hands from handling the cordite was itchy and sore.

It was a relief to be out in the fresh air. They got their tea and buns from the mess hut and found seats inside.

'Mind if I join you, girls?' said Alfie.

Nellie made eyes at Lily and she mustered some courage.

'Alfie?' He nodded at her while he chewed his bun. 'Do you think you might teach us how to play football so we can get a works team going?'

He stopped chewing and looked at them all watching his reaction. He smiled and swallowed.

'And whose bright idea is this, then?' he said.

'Mine,' admitted Nellie. 'Don't you think we can do it?'

'I'm not saying that. I'm just not sure I'm up to it. Have any of you played football before?'

'Well, I haven't and I don't know what all this is about,' said Miss Harknett, putting her bun down on her plate. 'You'd have to check something like that with Mrs Sparrow first; you can't go around arranging things without asking the company.'

'Hold your horses, lady muck,' said Nellie with a frown, and Lily didn't know where to look. 'Of course we'd ask Mrs Sparrow, but there's no use doing that till we know if Alfie wants to do it, is there?'

Miss Harknett pursed her lips. 'Well, you wouldn't catch me playing football. It's bad enough we have to wear trousers for work. Why do you want to be like a man?'

Nellie rolled her eyes. 'Alfie? What do you think about it?'

He took off his cap, scratched the back of his head and smoothed back his fringe, turned cordite-orange. 'Well, I've never thought about coaching. I suppose I could. I can't play myself any more with this damned injury.'

'Good lad,' said Nellie, bouncing in her seat and patting Alfie's arm.

'But coaching a girls' team?' It was like he hadn't heard Nellie, he was still on his own train of thought and Lily watched him with anticipation. 'I suppose it'd be all right. It's not everyone's cup of tea, mind, like Miss Harknett said. But there are some good girls' teams up north so there's no reason why we can't try it.'

'And Bonny said there are some other girls' works teams locally, like the cement works,' said Nellie.

'Is that a fact?' said Alfie. 'Well, they might have a league going, then.'

'Is that a yes, Alfie?' said Jessie, smiling.

'I reckon it is. Yes, I'll do it.' The girls pounded the table with their hands and cheered for him. 'You'll have to train, mind, a lot, and we'll have to clear it with the company, and of course we need somewhere to train.'

'I'll ask Barr the farmer if you can use one of the grazing fields on the marshes here,' said Mabel. 'I'll not be able to join you, mind. It's a shame but I've got the kids to think of, I've got no spare time.'

'Oh go on, Mabel,' said Jessie. 'How much training is it, Alfie? Could Mabel manage it?'

Alfie puffed out his cheeks. 'Well, it depends how serious you are, I suppose. I reckon we could train a couple of after-noons for an hour when we're on night shift. When we're on day shift, though, in the winter . . .' He rubbed the stubble on his chin while he thought. 'It'll be dark after work . . . I wonder if after church on Sundays anyone would mind?'

'I'll have to ask my mum,' said Marge. 'I help at home on a Sunday.'

'Right, so how many girls will we need? It's eleven in a team, isn't it?' said Nellie.

'That's it,' said Alfie.

'Well, there's me,' said Nellie, 'you, Jessie?'

'Yes, and Bonny said she would,' said Jessie, nodding.

'That's three, maybe Marge, that's four. Mabel? Go on!'

'Oh, all right then,' said Mabel, chuckling. 'The kids can

manage without me for an hour every now and then. I'll ask my eldest Hilda to come too, shall I?'

'Yes,' said Nellie, 'so that's six. Lily, you will, won't you?'

Lily looked at them all getting excited. She wondered what Sid would think about her playing football. A man's game. She felt that unfamiliar sense of abandon again, the one she'd had when she went shopping. If she said yes to the football, who was going to stop her or criticise her? She was on her own, she could do as she pleased.

'Yeah, go on then,' she said, laughing.

'Ha! So that's seven. We can get another four, can't we, and in the meantime we can get permission from the factory and start training.'

'Well, what about B-shift getting their own team together?' said Alfie. 'They'd have to find their own coach, mind, I couldn't do that as well. Then A-shift and B-shift can play against each other.'

'All right, we'll talk to some of the girls. Thanks, Alfie; thanks awfully,' said Jessie. She stood up and came to plant a kiss on his cheek. He flushed with embarrassment and glanced at Lily, who looked down at her lap.

Back in the cordite shed, Lily got on with laying out the strings of cordite. Lifting those trays was heavy work. Nellie started up a song, 'Oh Danny Boy', and they all sang along, even Miss Harknett, and then another song and another, and it helped to pass the time and take their minds off the back-breaking work and the fumes. But the songs also made Lily think of the war and the boys in the trenches and how there were sons and husbands and brothers in our trenches and in theirs and how they were blowing each other to bits with the stuff Lily was making with her own bare hands. She was feeding the guns, she was murdering sons and husbands and brothers. Her head spun and she wished it was time for the mid-shift meal, she needed to get outside. She pulled the cords into the trays and her head felt like it was lifting off. She held on to the edge of the table for a second before reaching for the next lot of cords that Nellie was passing to her. It was stiflingly hot in the shed and the air was so thick with fumes, she couldn't breathe. She pulled the cords along and her eyes closed and all she heard was, *Catch her, she's going!*

Lily was lying on her back in cold air with something covering her. She opened her eyes and looked up into the black night sky. Someone had put her down on the platform outside the shed and there was some sacking over her. She sat up, feeling much better for the air. What a strange thing, she thought, to just be carried outside to lie down on the ground. She got up and went back inside. As she did, Mr Nash and another woman from one of the other press rooms were helping another unconscious girl outside. Lily wandered back to her gang.

'How are you feeling?' said Miss Harknett in an unsympathetic way.

'All right, I think,' said Lily.

'Well good, get back to work, then.'

Lily did as she was told and started taking the cordite strands from Nellie and feeding them into the trays. What a strange job this was. She tried to keep her calm, she didn't want to get nervous about passing out again. With Miss Harknett's back turned, Nellie caught Lily's attention. She pulled off a small piece of the wet cordite and put it in her mouth.

'What you doing?' Lily whispered, terrified.

'Just sucking it, why don't you try it? It's nice.'

'How can you eat it? Won't your head blow off? Won't it make you sick?'

Nellie laughed. 'No, as long as you suck it and don't chew it. Otherwise, yes, your head might blow off.'

Nellie was highly amused by Lily's look of horror.

'Why do you do it?' said Lily.

'It tastes nice, sweet because of the glycerine, and it makes you feel drunk.'

Lily frowned and shook her head. She wasn't about to put an explosive into her mouth. She thought Nellie was mad to do it.

'Oi, Lilly,' Jessie hissed at her. Lily looked over and to her surprise Jessie also put a small piece of cordite into her mouth and laughed at Lily's expression. She looked up at Mabel on the press, who was watching them and grinning. She, too, put some of the explosive in her mouth.

If they were all doing it, it must be all right, thought Lily. Especially Mabel, she was a mother, she wouldn't put herself in danger. She pulled off a tiny piece of the soft, brown cordite. She held it to her lips and saw Marge watching her, shaking her head. She put it in her mouth and sucked it. It was lovely and sweet. She left it on her tongue while she worked, and yes, she did feel quite nice, quite happy indeed. Nellie watched her and laughed and struck up a song that she hadn't heard before: 'Knees up Mother Brown'. The song was catchy and made Lily laugh and laugh and when she'd learned the lyrics she joined in. *Ee-aye ee-aye-oh!*

10

The night shift was just as bad as everyone said it was. It was dreadfully hot in the shed and Lily didn't know if she'd ever get used to those fumes. One night, she had passed out again and woken up on the platform outside with a rat sniffing at her arm. When the last shift finished on Sunday morning at six o'clock she was very glad to change out of her uniform and get back to the colony for some much-deserved rest. She'd been thinking during the week that she'd get a couple of hours' sleep and then travel down to Kent to see the boys, but she was so shattered she didn't wake up until three in the afternoon. She couldn't let the boys down, so she ran to get the light railway and then on to Stanford-le-Hope. She got down to Kent and gave the boys their tin soldiers, which they were delighted with, but she could only spend an hour with them before the long journey home. She told the boys to expect her once a fortnight from now on, just in case it happened again and she couldn't manage it.

Day shift started the next morning at six. By then she was getting used to the work. She was back on the cordite press up on the platform and was refilling a cylinder when Mrs Sparrow came into the room. Miss Harknett stood to attention and trotted over to see the all-powerful welfare supervisor.

'How are things in this room, Miss Harknett?' she asked, still with her broad-brimmed hat on and her coat tied with a belt at the waist but with some rubber overshoes on over her heeled boots.

'Very well, Mrs Sparrow, thank you; we are keeping up our production even though we don't have an overlooker.'

'Very good, Miss Harknett. You will be pleased to hear that I have appointed an overlooker and she has gone off for training. She will start here, let me see . . . ' She consulted her notebook. 'She will start in three weeks' time on April the third, which unfortunately for her will be a night-shift week but there we are, there is a war on.'

'Ah, that's good news, Mrs Sparrow,' said Miss Harknett. Lily could see that she wasn't overly pleased about the new appointment. The overlooker would be in charge of Miss Harknett, who looked like she'd rather have been praised for holding the fort than stripped of her authority.

'Who is it, Mrs Sparrow?' said Nellie. Lily wouldn't have dared to ask but Nellie, as ever, was immune to the strictures of authority.

'Who is what, Nellie?'

'The new overlooker, who is it?'

'It is unlikely you would know them, Nellie, so why do you ask? You know that the overlooker will be a lady of particular upbringing, of a suitable education and class. Someone far from your own realm of experience.'

Mrs Sparrow looked at Nellie as though she'd been pulled from the gutter and Nellie let it lie, which made Lily think that maybe she had been.

'Alfie tells me he'd like to start a women's football club here,' said Mrs Sparrow.

Everyone stopped what they were doing to listen.

'I have informed Alfie that we encourage recreational activities here at the factory, in accordance with government guidelines and the welfare movement in general. As such, I have authorised Alfie to coach a team, providing it does not interfere with company work at any time. I shall keep a close eye on the team to ensure this is so. There is the question of where you will practise, though—'

'Oh, Mrs Sparrow?'

'Yes, Mabel?'

'I've asked one of the local farmers, at Barr's farm, if we can use one of his fields on the marsh and he says yes.'

Lily couldn't help but catch Mabel's eye and smile.

'Is that so?' said Mrs Sparrow. 'In that case, I shall inform the West Kent guards so that they do not take you for intruders. They have been known to shoot bullocks on the marshes before now, when the animals do not respond to commands to keep away from our barbed-wire perimeter.'

The girls stifled their giggles.

'I shall also inform the police sergeant. Carry on,' said Mrs Sparrow, leaving them.

'Good old Alfie,' said Jessie, once the welfare supervisor had gone.

'Be careful you don't get taken for a bullock and shot, though,' said Nellie. 'Miserable old cow.'

'Nellie!' reprimanded Miss Harknett.

'Oh, sorry!' said Nellie, making big eyes and shaking her head. 'Don't tell on me, will you?' she said in a mocking tone.

Alfie wandered in after Mrs Sparrow had gone.

'Right, that's settled, then,' he said. 'And Mabel has sorted out a pitch for us, which will be covered in cow muck no doubt, but it's better than nothing. So I'll meet you at seven by the village hall.'

'What, *today*?' Lily almost screeched.

'Why not?' said Alfie, laughing. 'We've got to get you lot knocked into shape. The B-shift have got old Fred the gunpowder manager to coach them and he'll put a shell up their backsides, I can tell you. Excuse me, Miss Harknett,' he said, at her disapproving glance.

'Oh no, Alfie's a taskmaster,' groaned Nellie melodramatically.

'But it'll be dark, won't it?' said Marge.

'Well, you'd better have your wits about you then, hadn't you?' said Alfie, going back to work.

The girls looked at each other and started laughing at the thought of it.

'Yes, all right, back to work now,' said Miss Harknett.

They came off shift and got back to Goosetown for a quick dinner, collected Bonny and Mabel's daughter Hilda and headed over to the village hall. Alfie was already there waiting for them with a football under his arm.

'You can't play in those,' he said, looking at their long skirts.

'We'll have to, Alfie, won't we?' said Jessie. 'Unless we play in our work trousers?'

'You'll need kits,' said Alfie, waving them along with him. They walked past the men's colony of bungalow huts on the other side of Goosetown and headed out on to the marshes. Luckily the moon offered a dim glow over the dark fields.

'Which field is it, then?' said Alfie.

'Um, I think it's this one here,' said Mabel, looking around and seeming to settle on where they were.

'You don't know, do you?' said Nellie.

'Yeah, it's this one here,' said Mabel uncertainly.

There were no barriers to the cold wind, which swept off the river and across the East Tilbury marshes. There had been a lot of rain recently and the ground felt boggy beneath Lily's old boots. She looked around for bullocks, worried that they were in the wrong field, and looked across the marsh to the factory perimeter and blockhouses, hoping they wouldn't be fired at by an over-zealous guard.

'Right, gather round,' said Alfie, dropping the ball at his feet. 'What's your names?' he asked Bonny and Hilda. 'Right then, what we need to do first is get you running about a bit. I'm not saying you're not used to hard work but you've got to get your blood pumping so I want you running up and down this field ten times.'

Marge looked at Lily, her eyes wide.

'Come on, then, I haven't got all night,' shouted Alfie like a sergeant major, and he clapped his hands at them like they were chickens to be rounded up. Off they went, shrieking with laughter, holding on to their hats and running along in their long skirts with their coats flapping in the wind like wings.

'Which way?' they shouted, bumping into each other and laughing even more. Alfie shot past them, faster than they were even though he had to lean to the left because of his shrapnel wounds. 'Keep up!' he called, and they rallied and ran to catch up with him, slipping in the mud and splashing into bogs. When they came to a large bank of blackberry bushes they turned about and ran back and then back again another nine times. They stopped where they'd started, leaning over to catch their breath. Lily and Marge laughed at one another. Lily lifted up her foot; it was encased with a wodge of mud and what smelt like cow dung.

'Well, I've got a good reason to buy some new boots now,' she said.

'My dear, you are a munitionette, you already have a good reason,' said Bonny with a grin.

'All right, now let's see who can kick a ball,' said Alfie.

He arranged them in two lines facing each other and got them to take turns kicking the ball across. Lily managed to kick it despite her long skirt getting in the way. Marge took an overly strong swing at hers and slipped over in the mud, causing raucous laughter all round.

'It's been raining so much, the ground is wet but you'll have to get used to that. We'll train come rain or shine,' said Alfie. 'Have another run up and down and then I think we'll call it a day. We need to get you some shorts.'

'Shorts?' they all cried.

'Yes, shorts, you can't play in those things, can you?' he said, pointing to their skirts. 'Now, go on, up to that bush and back.' He stayed behind this time, Lily glanced back to see him squat on the ground and hold his side, it must have given him pain to run even that distance.

She started running after the others and as a game overtook Mabel at the back, who shouted and sped up, then Lily ran past Jessie and Marge and she sprinted as hard as she could to get past Nellie and Bonny, who screeched at her with joy and raced to catch up. The blackberry bush was looming in the dark and they chased towards it. As it came into better view, it moved and turned and they realised there was a large bullock in front of the bush which squared to face them. They all skidded to a stop.

'Don't move,' said Mabel. 'Bullocks will chase you, you just walk away slowly.'

'I knew it was the wrong field, you daft bat,' hissed Nellie.

The bullock started walking towards them. It was enormous and menacing. Marge screamed and started running back. The scream startled the bullock and he snorted and frisked to a trot, making them all screech and run for it.

'Run!' they screamed to Alfie, and they all tore off back to Goosetown, breathless and laughing.

'Who's gonna ask the old bag if we can have a football kit?' Nellie directed the question to the girls in the press room the next day.

'Not me,' said Jessie, and Marge shook her head too.

'Well, I can't,' said Nellie, 'the old bag won't do anything for me.'

'Why not? What have you done?' said Lily.

'You don't want to know,' said Nellie sourly. 'Why don't you ask her, Lily?'

Lily agreed and once she'd changed out of her uniform at end of shift she went over to the safe area of the works and found the welfare supervisor's office and tapped on the door.

'Come in,' said Mrs Sparrow and Lily entered and stood there nervously, the supervisor looking at her with disdain.

'Mrs Sparrow, the girls and me are wondering if you can get some football kit for us to play football in.'

'Football kit?' said Mrs Sparrow, frowning.

'Yes, our skirts are too long to play in the mud; we can't kick the ball properly.'

'Well, I do not have a budget for football kit, I'm afraid. You'll have to make do for now. Perhaps if you prove yourselves worthy we might consider it at a later date.'

'Yes, thank you, Mrs Sparrow,' said Lily.

At dinner in the YWCA canteen, she told the others.

'Well, we'll just have to buy it ourselves, won't we?' said Jessie. 'We can get some shorts for now. I'll ask my Edward to get them for us; we'll give him the money, they won't cost much.'

'I can't spare any money for football shorts,' said Mabel. 'I've got a family to feed.'

'I'll buy yours, Mabel,' said Nellie.

'Will you, love?' she said, overcome. 'There's a love,' she said, her eyes misting.

'We'll get some football socks too,' said Nellie. 'That'll do for now. We can play in our blouses, can't we?'

'Course we can,' said Lily. 'By the way, I've asked Eliza from my hut to join in too.' She had become quite friendly with Eliza, the girl with the scalped head who had shown her the canteen on her first day.

'Good, and three girls from the pressing shed next to ours want to come, so that's it, eleven, we've got our team,' beamed Nellie.

By the next week, Jessie's sweetheart had got their shorts and long socks for them. The first time she changed into them and went outside, Lily felt naked. The shorts came to the top of her knee and the socks to the bottom of her knee but there was no getting away from the fact that her bare knees were showing in public. She was glad they were on nights that week but still when she walked with the others through Goosetown over to the marshes to train, every single person they passed stopped to stare at them. When they went by the men's colony and YMCA hut, the men called out to them and they blushed and hurried along.

Alfie was waiting for them. 'Blimey, look at you lot,' he said. 'Now I know you're serious about this. Come on, I've found out which field we're supposed to be in.'

They followed him to a patch of marsh adjacent to the perimeter of the factory. When they started to practise, Lily felt the wind on her legs and it was much easier to move around and kick the ball. Two of the West Kent guards at one of the perimeter blockhouses watched them. They shouted things out that the women couldn't hear because they were breathless and running around. But they knew the shouts were jeers and not orders. The women wore their blouses with the shorts, and had left their coats and hats at the colony. Their usual boots would have to do, and their hair was pinned up out of the way. Lily caught sight of Mabel's varicose veins, which stood out in raised lines like the tramway at work. It was from standing up all day, she had said. Despite the dim light, Alfie taught them about positions and rules of play. He'd brought two short stakes to bang into the ground to mark out a goal and he had them shooting goals and passing to each other. It was hard work but Lily loved it.

'Let's go out to celebrate,' said Jessie when they'd finished training.

'To celebrate what?' said Nellie.

'Our shorts, of course!' laughed Jessie. 'We can't go out this week because of night shift, but my Edward will be at the Bull in Corringham next Tuesday, let's go and join them for a drink. Lily? Everyone?'

Lily waited to hear what everyone else said. Marge shook her head with wide eyes, clearly too timid to be thinking about going to a public house.

'I'd have to get back to the children,' said Mabel. 'It's all right for you young ones with no one else to think about – you go on and spend your money and enjoy it.' Lily wondered whether Mabel was lucky to have a house in Goosetown so she could be with her children, or if she, Lily, was better off on her own in the colony, with the freedoms that went with it.

Nellie said she would come and so did Bonny and Eliza and the other press hut girls.

'All right, then,' said Lily, tentatively at first, wondering at the thought of going into a pub and wasting money. She had worn shorts today. She wore trousers at work. She didn't have to ask anyone's permission to go out for a drink, there was no one to express disapproval. She'd been paid and had money in her pocket. She'd damn well go.

Lily got through another week of nights. Sucking the cordite made the time pass quicker but one night it made her feel sick and Jessie did run outside to be sick. She came back in saying she'd have to lay off it for a while and that the soldiers

162

overseas would eat cordite so it would make their hearts bad and they'd be sent home. Lily managed to see the boys on the Sunday for a little while and she gave Ada her separation allowance plus some from her pay packet, but she kept some back for herself again. She needed some new shoes. And she wanted to buy some Oatine face cream. Her skin was starting to turn yellow and the girls said the cream helped a bit. It was funny, though, she didn't even mind too much about turning yellow. Her new life was a revelation to her, and she'd rather be yellow than back in servitude sweeping out Lady Charlotte's grate at the crack of dawn and suffering Lord Harrington's evil ways.

The following Tuesday, Lily put on her new skirt and blouse and scraped the marsh mud off her old boots and met up with the others to get the train into Corringham.

It was exciting to walk into the pub with her new friends. New war rules stated that they weren't allowed to treat each other to drinks any more because workers were getting too drunk, so Lily ordered a stout for herself and sat down at a table with the others.

'This is Edward,' said Jessie proudly, introducing her sweetheart dressed in his khaki.

'Nice to meet you,' said Lily. 'And thanks for getting our shorts for us.'

'A pleasure,' said Edward, taking a puff of his cigarette. 'It's the favourite pastime on watch; we draw straws to see who gets to man the west-facing blockhouses.'

Lily frowned. 'What do you mean?'

'He means, they have a laugh watching us run around in our shorts,' said Nellie.

'Oh,' she said, blushing and taking a sip of her drink.

'So where is your husband, Lily? Jessie tells me he answered the call to the colours?' said Edward.

'That's right. He's training at Warley.'

'Well, I hope he gets a lucky posting like mine.' He smiled. 'That Verdun business in France sounds ghastly and I'm sure our lot will be alongside them in force soon enough.'

Lily nodded and bit her fingernail. She was missing Sid, but not as much as she thought she might. She'd been too busy with work. And every time she wrote to him to try to visit it wasn't the right time for him or she'd be on day shift when he had an afternoon off. It was hard enough trying to see the boys every week or two. Twelve-hour rotating shifts were exhausting. Whenever she felt she had adjusted to the new sleeping pattern, it was the end of the week and it changed again. And then there were the cordite fumes too, which made her feel so low in energy. And the football training, which she loved and wouldn't want to give up now.

'So who's going to the dance on Saturday night?' said Bonny, changing the subject.

'What dance?' said Jessie, her eyes lighting up.

'At the village hall in Goosetown. A big dance. Some injured soldiers have been invited.'

'Ooh, I'll come, I love a dance,' said Jessie. 'Edward, will you be able to?'

'I hope so, love. I'll have to check my shifts.'

'I'd like to come,' said Lily, surprising herself. She looked at her glass, which was nearly empty – the stout had gone to her head. She'd never been to a dance before. There was never an opportunity when she was in service, and Ada wouldn't have allowed her to have any time to herself if there was housework to be done. 'What will I wear, though?' she said, looking down at her boots. 'I need some new shoes but there won't be a chance to go to the shops before Saturday night.'

The girls laughed and looked at Bonny. 'What size are you?' said Bonny.

'Three.'

'Come to hut four after work tomorrow,' she said, smiling. 'I've got something you can borrow.'

The next day there was a heavy snowfall and the light railway seized up. They had to walk across the frozen marshes, ankle deep in snow, to get to the factory gates and spend the twelve-hour shift with wet feet. Alfie still made them practise after work. He was pleased with their progress and their natural tendency for certain positions was becoming clearer. Nellie was good in defence, Lily was good at scoring goals, to her surprise, and Mabel was good in goal. Marge flitted around the centre field, making good passes. Alfie was going to arrange a game with B-shift team soon, which they were all nervous about.

By Friday the snow had begun to melt and the marshes became a sludgy mess. Alfie told them that the B-shift team weren't practising in the bad weather, which gave A-shift the advantage. An advantage 'in here,' he said, tapping his head, 'just as much as in here,' pointing to his feet.

Lily had been working there for a month already. It felt like she'd been there longer. On Saturday the first of April, they sang their way through the last day of shift, excited to be going to the dance after work.

'Are you going to the dance, Miss Harknett?'

'No, Lily, I'm not. My fiancé is on leave from France. We are going to spend the weekend at my mother's.'

'Sounds like fun,' said Nellie, rolling her eyes. 'Why don't you get away for the weekend just the two of you?'

Miss Harknett gave a loud sigh. 'Because, Nellie, it wouldn't be proper. We haven't been able to marry yet because of this dratted war. Believe me, I would much rather be married and living with my new husband than working here and spending the weekend at my mother's.'

'There's a war on, love, don't be so hard on yourself,' said Mabel. 'You never know what's round the corner.'

Miss Harknett didn't answer. She turned her back on the others and continued with her work.

'Our new overlooker starts on Monday,' she said after a moment, her voice strained. 'You'd better be careful with what you say around her, I hear she's a proper lady.'

The others stayed quiet, even Nellie. Lily was worried about having someone new in their room. She was used to the gang now.

They hurried their dinner in the YWCA hut after work and rushed to get ready. Hut ten was a pulsating nest of women trying to get washed or bathed and changed. Lily put on her new blouse and skirt and the lovely shoes that Bonny had lent her. She peered into the little glass in her room to pin up her hair. It was definitely looking ginger now. She smiled; it was a sign of her new life and she was proud of it. She and the others were helping the Tommies end the war and her ginger hair and yellow skin were her badges of honour, her military medals. The rash on her hands and arms was itchy and unpleasant, though, and she was sure her gums felt sore.

Marge had gone home after shift to help her mother; she wasn't going to the dance. Lily linked arms with Eliza who had covered her scalped head with a lovely new hat, and they ran over to the village, picking their way through the mud and sludge on the ground. The village hall had been decorated with bunting. The tables had all been pushed to the edges and a band was playing. Lily's heart rushed with excitement despite the usual patrols of YWCA volunteers and women police overseeing the proceedings.

Lily and Eliza headed over to the table where their football chums were sitting. They enjoyed a natural camaraderie now and were bonded together – they were munitions workers and had also taken the brave leap into women's football together. The other women were somewhat in awe of them. Bonny lapped up the attention.

'Did the old bat give you the talk when you started?' she asked Lily when she sat down.

'Who, Mrs Sparrow?'

'The one and only.' Bonny grinned.

'What do you mean, about spending any spare money on war certificates and doing wholesome hobbies like knitting and bible study?'

'Ha ha, yes, that's it. Well, ignore her. She drains the fun out of everything. As long as you work hard here you can play hard. You'll have a ball and you'll never look back. You came from service, didn't you?' Lily nodded. 'So did I and look at me, I never thought it possible to be this happy. I go out drinking, I go to dances and music halls and all without having to ask anyone for permission.'

Lily smiled and nodded. Bonny sounded fast and loose.

'Immoral', Ada would say. But Lily knew what Bonny meant and she couldn't help being caught up in it all.

'We've still got this lot, though, haven't we?' said Bonny, nodding at the patrols and volunteers. Lily looked at them. One was telling off a girl for her bad language. 'They don't understand us,' said Bonny. 'What kind of lives we've had to lead and what we do to let loose.'

'Do you want a drink?' said Lily.

'Yeah, come on, they won't let you buy me one, I'll get my own.'

They each had a glass of punch, which went straight to Lily's head. The music stopped when a group of injured soldiers came in. The women stood up to clap them and the men grinned and sat down. The music started up again and Bonny winked at Lily and stood up to go over to talk to the soldiers. A police constable immediately went to her and whispered in her ear. Bonny frowned at the woman, said something and continued her conversation. The man she was talking to had a bandage over one eye. He stood up and led Bonny on to the dance floor and soon the other men were dancing too.

'What did that policewoman say to you?' Lily asked her later.

'She said it wasn't good manners to go and talk to a man without being properly introduced. I told her I felt sorry for her if that's the way she lives because I'm the sort who will talk to an injured soldier and make him feel like a man again. That soon shut her up. Bloody toffs telling us how to live, it makes me sick.' Bonny drained her cup of punch and went back for another.

Lily sat happily in her seat, tapping her foot to the music.

She was on her third cup of punch – it tasted so nice and went down so easily – but she still didn't feel brave enough to dance with an injured soldier like Bonny had done. She wasn't sure how Sid would feel about it either.

'Care to dance?'

She started and looked up to see Alfie standing there in a suit. He looked very handsome, freshly shaven with his hair combed back.

'Oh, hello, Alfie.' She gave a nervous laugh and didn't know what else to say. She didn't want to refuse him and cause embarrassment but didn't want to give him the wrong idea either.

'It's just a dance,' he said, sensing her discomfort. She glanced at Nellie, who gave a nod of approval.

'All right, thank you.' She stood up, trying not to look like she'd had three cups of punch. 'But I don't really know how to.'

'Well, you won't do worse than this northern cripple,' he said, smiling.

'You're not a cripple, Alfie, I think you do very well,' she said, slurring slightly and letting him put his hand on her waist and take her hand in his. Standing face to face with him, she was quite breathless. She could tell he was trying not to stare at her.

'Off we go, then,' he said and they moved off slowly, making awkward steps and laughing at themselves.

'What do you think about the dance, then?' he said.

'It's nice, isn't it? Nice that the injured soldiers are here.'

'I'm an injured soldier, too, remember.' He grinned. 'I think you're doing very well at football,' he said.

'I enjoy it, Alfie. You're a good teacher. I don't know what my Sid will say about it when I tell him.'

Alfie tried to arrange his face at the mention of Lily's husband. 'Do you see each other much?' he said.

'No, not really. He's training at Warley and he'll be posted soon. I keep worrying that they'll send him out to France. It sounds dreadful out there.'

'It is. I hope they don't send him there.'

It was hard to talk when she'd had so much punch; what's more, she didn't know how to change the subject without being disloyal to Sid. So she made her excuses and sat back down, telling Nellie to dance with Alfie. The punch was making her drowsy and happy and she found herself weaving over to the table to ask for another one.

'Don't you think you'd better have a glass of water?' said the YWCA volunteer.

'Why? I'm enjoying myself,' Lily was shocked to hear herself say. 'Don't you think I work hard enough here?'

The volunteer was taken aback. 'Yes, of course, but we mustn't get carried away.'

'Why mustn't we? What do you do here, serve drinks? And what do I do? Work with dangerous explosives, standing up all day on twelve-hour shifts risking my health and my life. Why can't I have another cup of punch? Why can't I?'

A woman police constable joined them. 'Is everything in order here?' she asked the volunteer.

'No it is not,' said Lily. 'This ... *lady* in the posh hat is telling me I can't have another cup of punch and I want to know why not.'

'Well, young lady, I think you've answered that question

yourself. You've had quite enough to drink and it's time you went to bed. Now, come along.' The constable took Lily's arm and steered her towards the door.

Lily looked around for her friends and saw Jessie. 'Jessie,' she shouted, 'help me!'

'There is no need for theatrics, it is time you went to bed,' said the constable.

Jessie came trotting over, with Edward in tow. 'What is it?'

'This bloody policewoman is telling me I can't have another cup of bloody punch,' said Lily, not knowing where her voice was coming from or who was saying the words she could hear coming from her own mouth.

'Please do not swear or I shall have to report you to Mrs Sparrow,' said the constable.

'Oh, let her go, we'll take her back, won't we, Edward?'

The constable saw Edward in uniform and agreed to Jessie's suggestion. Little did she know that Jessie and Edward were just as drunk as Lily. The three of them staggered out of the village hall together. The cold air hit Lily and she slipped and fell over in the mud. The other two pulled her to standing, hooting with laughter.

'Oh no, Bonny's shoes,' said Lily in mock distress, looking down at the pale pink satin that was now a dark green mud.

'Oh, don't worry, she's got so many, we call her Bonny-new-shoes,' said Jessie.

Lily laughed and started kicking up the shoes and singing 'Knees up Mother Brown'. She suddenly realised she was on her own and she turned around in the dark not knowing which direction to go in.

A man lumbered by and Lily squinted to see. 'Mr Nash?' she called.

The man stopped to look at her. It was Mr Nash. His hands were stuffed deep into his pockets, his body swaying slightly from his ankles.

'Yoo-hoo, Mr Nash.'

'Who's that? Lily, is it? Why don't you get off home, you silly girl.'

'I am going home,' pouted Lily, feeling very put out.

'Not to the colony, I mean go right home and don't come back.' He pulled a small glass bottle out of his pocket and took a swig from it.

'Well, why don't *you* go home, Mr Nash? You're drunk!'

'You're sending boys to France by being here – women don't belong in the factories, I'm bloody sick of it.'

'Well, why don't you go to France? My husband enlisted – what are you still doing here?' Lily's words hung in the air, she couldn't believe she had said it but her face was numb and she couldn't control what she was saying.

'Because I'm doing essential war work here, you foolish woman. And good luck to your husband – the life expectancy on the front line is three weeks.'

Lily knew he had said something intolerable but it didn't seem to be going deep enough into her brain for her to understand it.

'What's going on here?' It was another woman constable patrolling the area. Mr Nash trudged away and Lily froze dramatically and waited for the constable to approach her. When nothing happened, Lily looked around to see the constable pulling Jessie and Edward out from the doorway of the nearby schoolhouse.

'Get to your barracks immediately,' the woman ordered Edward. He said goodbye to Jessie sheepishly and trotted back the other way. 'And you, are you in the colony?'

Jessie nodded, her head lolling on her neck. 'Hut number nine, ma'am,' she said, and the police constable took her arm and steered her forcefully towards the women's colony of bungalow huts.

'Yoo-hoo, Jessie!' called out Lily, raising her arm in a high wave.

'What is this?' said the constable. 'Another Jezebel? Are you in the colony too?'

'Yes I am,' said Lily, laughing and dancing around in the mud. 'Hut number ten.'

'Well, you'd better come with me too; this is disgraceful behaviour.' And the constable took Lily's arm, digging in her nails, and steered them both back to their huts. Lily vaguely registered being deposited in hut ten and the matron being roused to take her to bed. There were lots of stern-sounding voices but also some whoop-whoops coming from other girls' rooms when they heard Lily singing and protesting. Lily didn't get changed; she didn't even take off Bonny's muddy shoes. She simply lay down on the bed and passed out in a blissful drunken coma.

Lily thought someone must be squeezing her head in the cordite press. And someone had coated the inside of her mouth and throat with a thick cordite paste. She groaned for help but no one came. She groaned louder and Eliza opened the curtain to Lily's room and stood by her bed.

'Get up, you drunken Jezebel.'

'What?' moaned Lily, opening her eyes the width of a matchstick. 'What's happening?'

'You've got a hangover, you daft bird. It's late; I thought you wanted to visit the kids today?'

'Oh no,' moaned Lily. 'No, no, no.' And she closed her eyes and went back to sleep.

Eliza came back with a glass of water and put it by Lily's bed. 'Sit up and drink this; you'll feel better, I promise.'

Lily made a big effort to sit up, grimacing and moaning all the while. She reached out for the water and realised she still had her coat on and it was smeared with dried mud. She sipped the water and felt sick, it tasted of the paste inside her mouth.

'Girls, come and look at this one,' called Eliza.

Lily looked up to see several of her hut-mates crowding in to look at her. They laughed and chatted and hurt Lily's head with their God-awful noise. *Look at her . . . She's covered in mud . . . Must have been a good night . . . Oh, her shoes! . . .*

'Come on, let's leave her alone,' said Eliza. 'Lil, if you're not going to Kent, come to football practice. Lunch is in an hour so drink three glasses of water, come for some food and you'll be all right for practice after lunch. Lily wondered why she was talking such mad nonsense. She downed her glass of water, held it out to Eliza to get her some more, and slumped back against her pillow.

Flashes from the night before started coming back to her. She couldn't understand what was wrong with her mind; she was struggling to remember what had happened. Mr Nash had said something nasty to her . . . a policewoman had taken her home . . . she must have been in trouble . . .

The water did make her feel well enough to get out of bed and have a bath, but she still had a headache. She was mortified to see the state of Bonny's shoes and she felt terrible for missing seeing the boys, but it was out of the question, she couldn't face the long journey the way she felt. She buried her head into her pillow to block out the guilt. She had seen them last week, so she hoped they wouldn't mind too much. In the morning she would have time to buy and post them some sweets before starting night shift tomorrow evening.

Standing outside the hut, she scraped the mud from her coat and from Bonny's shoes. She looked up to see the figure of Mrs Sparrow the welfare supervisor coming her way and she went rigid with fear.

'Good afternoon, Lily,' said Mrs Sparrow, with a strange kind of smirk on her face.

'Hello.'

'I'm afraid I have heard some very disturbing reports about your behaviour at the dance last night.' Mrs Sparrow raised her eyebrows and waited for an answer.

'I'm sorry, Mrs Sparrow. I've never been to a dance before and I drank too much punch. I'm paying for it now, Mrs Sparrow; look at this mud, and my head feels like it's in the cordite press.'

Mrs Sparrow chewed on Lily's words for a moment. 'You are right, you did drink too much punch and you were very rude to one of the YWCA volunteers. You were also heard being ill mannered with Mr Nash and you had to be escorted back to the hut by a police constable. This sort of behaviour will not be tolerated here, Lily. I thought better of you, I really did.'

Lily burst into tears. 'I'm really sorry, I don't know what happened. Please don't sack me.'

'Yes, well, I'm glad to see you are sorry. I hope you are suitably ashamed of your behaviour. I shall have to write a warning on your records. Do not let this happen again, Lily, or we shall have to talk about whether you are the right kind of girl for Greygoose Munitions. Is this understood?'

'Yes, Mrs Sparrow; thank you, Mrs Sparrow,' said Lily, wiping her face on her sleeve.

The welfare supervisor turned and continued along the row of huts. Perhaps there was another girl who needed a ticking-off today.

Lily heaved a big sigh and put on her coat. She headed over to the YWCA canteen for lunch and crept in hoping not to see the volunteer from the previous night, even though she couldn't remember what the woman looked like.

The other girls delighted in recounting Lily's behaviour at the dance. Jessie was there in the canteen with a sore head, laughing about Lily slipping over in the mud. Lily felt ashamed of how she'd behaved but at the same time she liked the attention from the others and she laughed along with them. It made her feel like she belonged. They seemed to think she was fun to be around, she was daring and she spoke back to those in authority like some of the others did. Not that she'd dare to do that when she was sober. She cringed when Bonny walked over to their table.

'Oh, Bonny,' she said, 'I've ruined your lovely shoes. I'm so sorry, I'll get you some more next week, I promise.'

Bonny laughed when she heard what had happened and said Lily didn't need to replace them, it'd give her an excuse to go shopping again. When they'd eaten they persuaded Lily to change into her shorts for football practice and they headed out to the field on the marshes.

It was a bright sunny day; the warm spring light reflected off the Thames and cast a wholesome glow over the wetlands, tempting the grasses and shrubs from their recent slump in the rain and snow. Lily blushed when she saw Alfie, remembering their dance.

'How are you feeling today?' he said with a grin. 'You looked a bit worse for wear last night.'

'Oh, thanks very much,' she said.

'Come on, this'll do you good,' he said, throwing a ball to the ground and kicking it to her. She stopped it with her foot and kicked it along to Jessie. They were soon panting and laughing and scoring goals and Alfie had them running up and down the field. At just after two o'clock they stopped for a rest. 'You're doing very well,' said Alfie. 'I reckon you'll be ready for a game with B-shift soon.'

The girls looked at each other and smiled. 'Do you reckon we can beat them, Alfie?' asked Jessie.

He was about to answer when they felt a strange sensation in the air. The ground beneath their feet shook and they heard a colossal boom that sent terror through Lily's body. She looked around, as did the others, and the first thing she thought was, *The factory has blown.*

'What is it?' someone shouted. 'There's no smoke, where's it come from?'

They all starting running back to Goosetown, terrified they were in danger and just as terrified of what might have happened at the factory. As they approached the men's colony, they saw people standing about in a daze, looking at the ground. The team stopped to see. The windows had blown out of the bungalow huts; there was shattered glass on the floor. They continued on, the windows from the village hall and the schoolhouse were also shattered. 'Thank God it's Sunday,' someone said. 'No children there today.'

'What's happened?' everyone asked everyone else, but no one knew.

'Come on,' someone said, 'let's get over there to help.' Everyone including Lily and the rest of the team started to run over the marshes to the factory. They reached the gates, which had been closed. A number of people were asking the guards what was going on.

'We don't think it's here,' they said. 'We're checking now.'

'Not here?' said Alfie.

'I don't know,' said Lily.

'I'll go and ask Edward,' said Jessie and she headed towards the gates. Lily couldn't see her, there were too many people crowding around now. Everyone was anxious to know what was happening. Lily thought they might all be in danger just standing there. What if there were more explosions? But she just wanted to help like everyone else.

After an age, a ripple of news ran through the crowd. 'It's not here,' voices said. 'It's over the water in Kent, the factory near Faversham.'

'In Kent?' said Lily, panicking. 'But my boys are in Kent. Where's the factory, is it near Nettlestead?'

'Where's Nettlestead?' said Alfie.

'Near Maidstone.'

Alfie rubbed the back of his neck. 'I don't know,' he said and Lily's heart started to pound in her chest.

'Nettlestead must be thirty miles from the Faversham factory,' said a man next to them.

'Oh, is it?' said Lily, grabbing the man's arm and looking anxiously into his face. 'My children are there, are you sure?'

'I'm certain. I used to live in Kent. That factory must be the same distance from here as from Nettlestead, as the crow flies.'

'Oh, thank you,' said Lily, breathing a big sigh and patting her chest. 'Thank you.'

Jessie came back. 'Edward says the explosion wasn't here, it was in the munitions factory in Uplees near Faversham. It's bad,' she said, with tears in her eyes.

'Oh, God help them,' said Bonny. And everyone fell silent.

11

1 April 1916

Dearest Lily,

    I've been sent to Felixstowe to train for France. Dad is with me. I can't write much but I hope you are well. I wish I could see you but now I'm even further away and not even in jolly old Essex any more. I think I shall be here for three months. We've had meat every day so far so it can't be bad. I'm glad to have the photograph. You look very different in your uniform. Trousers! Thanks for the scarf, it's very warm. I've put my army picture in. Write to me here.

    Your loving Sid

'Edward says over a hundred men are dead,' said Jessie at work on the night shift the evening after the Faversham explosion.

Lily put her hand over her mouth and stood in silence with Miss Harknett, Mabel, Nellie and Marge.

'The girls don't work on a Sunday, same as here,' said Jessie, 'so they think it was just the men.'

'There's nothing in the paper,' said Nellie.

'They can't write about it,' said Miss Harknett. 'It would damage morale.'

Everyone at Greygoose wanted more news; they wanted to know how it happened, how many were dead, whether it was something that could have been avoided. It gave Lily the horrors. They all knew they were doing dangerous work but something like this made it all too real. When Sid got wind of it Lily knew he'd want her to find another job. But she didn't want to. She belonged at Greygoose now. She was proud of the work she did for the war, she was important now.

'It is too awful for words,' said Miss Harknett. 'I know my fiancé will tell me to stop working here.'

'Well, you won't get a leaving certificate if you go,' said Nellie. 'Then you won't be able to work anywhere else.'

'Well, I wouldn't want to go anywhere else,' said Jessie. 'I'm proud to be a munitionette.'

The others nodded and started work. It was all to help stop the war, all of it. It was a sombre morning in the cordite shed. Whatever their feelings of patriotism, there was still a lot of fear of what could happen and Lily couldn't stop thinking about the men who had died. Their families. Their children. She had written to Ada first thing that morning, to ask if their windows had blown out and if the boys were all right. She put some sweets in the envelope to make up for not going down there on Sunday. She shivered. What if something had happened to them – or to her – and she hadn't seen them because she'd been out drinking and had a hangover?

A half-hour after the start of shift, the welfare supervisor Mrs Sparrow came into the pressing hut.

'If I could have your attention please?' she said, and the

girls stopped what they were doing. Lily thought it must be something about the explosion.

'Our new overlooker will be starting today. I'm going over to Goosetown now to collect her. I shall be back shortly. Please try to make a good impression. I know some of you fell short of the standards expected at Greygoose at the weekend.' She looked particularly at Lily, who blushed and looked at her hands, avoiding Nellie's laughing eyes. 'But I am sure you will all be on best behaviour from now on.'

Lily frowned. It was like she was talking to a room of schoolchildren. The woman left and the girls looked at each other, apprehension on all of their faces. Half an hour later and Mrs Sparrow came back in. Lily was just swinging out the cordite press and couldn't take her eyes off it to look but she went cold when she heard a familiar voice call out to her.

'Pavitt?'

Lily looked up and froze: Lady Charlotte Harrington was standing next to Mrs Sparrow, dressed in a shin-length fur coat.

'Pavitt? What in heaven's name are you doing up there?' said Lady Charlotte.

Lily momentarily lost the ability to speak. She looked at Nellie, who was staring at her.

'Oh, of course!' said Mrs Sparrow. 'Yes, of course, how silly of me not to think. Lily here worked at St Clere's Hall, didn't she?'

'Yes, but I didn't know her name was Lily,' laughed Lady Charlotte. 'We all called her Pavitt, except for Mama, who insisted on calling all of the housemaids Jane.'

Jessie, Mabel, Nellie and Marge all looked at Lily in silent support. She was rooted to the spot. Miss Harknett was on pins, waiting to be introduced to the titled lady.

'This is Miss Harknett, the charge hand in this room,' said Mrs Sparrow. 'She will assist you in training the workers, and she will also report to you any irregularities in working hours, uniforms, safe working, attendance and so on.'

'Hello,' said Lady Charlotte. Miss Harknett took her proffered hand and instead of shaking it made a little curtsey and then stood back, looking as though she was in the presence of the divine.

'Lady Charlotte is overlooker for range thirty-eight – she will supervise the workers in all three pressing rooms here and the drying room next door. We are very privileged indeed to have her here.'

With that, Mrs Sparrow started to clap her hands and smiled at the other women, encouraging them to follow suit. The girls clapped and looked at each other in dismay.

'Thank you, it is really rather wonderful to be here,' said Lady Charlotte, accepting the applause. 'Now if you'll excuse me, Mrs Sparrow is going to find me a uniform to put on, which is all very exciting indeed. Oh, and Pavitt?' Lily still couldn't speak. 'Would you be a dear and help me unpack my things in the morning? I'm so terribly inept when it comes to the domestic. I'm in hut one in the colony.'

Lily looked at the wall, acutely embarrassed. Lady Charlotte didn't wait for an answer but left with Mrs Sparrow and Lily could hear her being introduced in the next pressing room. Miss Harknett turned to them with a look of rapture.

'Goodness, what a treat!' she said. 'Now back to work, everyone, we don't want to fall behind.'

Lily knew the others wanted to say something to her, but she avoided their gazes and starting refilling the press cylinder with cordite dough. She wanted to cry. Lady Charlotte being there was going to spoil everything.

When break time came around, the girls rushed ahead to the mess hut to avoid having to walk with Miss Harknett. Nellie linked arms with Lily and pulled her along.

'Bloody cheek,' said Nellie. 'What's she doing here? What does she know about cordite?'

'About as much as I knew when I started, I suppose,' said Lily sullenly.

'She can at least call you Lily,' said Jessie. 'Fancy calling you that and asking you to unpack for her.'

Marge squeezed Lily's arm in silence; she understood better than the others how Lily felt, having come from service herself. The others probably hadn't even met an upper-class lady like Charlotte before, except for those who helped in the YWCA hut. They only had their own notions about such things, but they couldn't know what it was really like to work for a titled family.

'I don't want to do her unpacking,' confessed Lily. 'But what'll happen if I say no? I'll just have to do it.'

'Don't worry, Lil, I've got a few tricks up my sleeve to teach her a thing or two about how we do things,' Nellie said with a wink.

'It's just the way things are,' said Mabel. 'The likes of her are bound to be able to tell the likes of us what to do.'

'Why, though?' said Nellie. 'Because she's had an education and her family's got money, she can patronise us and boss us around?'

'Yes,' said Mabel, laughing. 'Don't act so surprised; you know how things are, Nellie. And the company knows she won't want her job when the war ends, so they'll have less trouble getting the men their jobs back.'

Nellie pouted and tore at her currant bun with her teeth. Miss Harknett sat down with them in the mess hut.

'What's the rush? You're keen to get back to see if Lady Charlotte is there, are you? Aren't we lucky to get her? Wait till I tell Mother, she'll be thrilled.'

The girls ignored her and drank their tea.

'I bet we'll get some attention from the press, now,' gushed Miss Harknett. 'Imagine, a real titled lady working here, and not just in the canteen, but in the factory itself. It's just wonderful, isn't it? I shall have to buy a new hat in case there are photographs.'

Back in the pressing hut, Lady Charlotte appeared in her Greygoose uniform. Hers was khaki with a green trim instead of red, to distinguish her rank. Lily was surprised to see her wearing the tunic and trousers. She even had the cap on.

'Isn't this splendid? I feel like a real munitionette now,' she said. 'This is what I wanted, for us all to be in it together, no matter what our backgrounds. Joined together in the spirit of patriotism, helping our boys stop the war.' She beamed around at the women. Miss Harknett nodded with enthusiasm and Mabel mustered a smile but the others didn't mask their indignation. 'We even have the same colour hair. Astonishing,' she said, pushing her auburn hair into the side of her cap.

'Ours goes orange from the cordite,' said Nellie. 'But you'll not be touching that, I suppose?'

Lady Charlotte turned in surprise at Nellie's tone – she was treading a fine line speaking to a woman of Charlotte's standing in that way.

'Goodness me, is that so? It's terribly hot in here, isn't it?'

'I'm afraid it is, Lady Charlotte,' said Miss Harknett. 'We must cover the windows with the blackouts.'

'And the fumes . . . golly, I can hardly breathe. How do you manage for twelve hours?'

'We don't,' said Nellie. 'At least a couple of us are carried out of here unconscious every night to lie down outside till we feel better and then we come back in and start working again.'

'My goodness,' said Charlotte, frowning. 'Well, I look forward to learning all about cordite now I'm here.'

Mr Nash came rushing into their room looking flustered. 'Air raid. Everyone out,' he said, and hurried through into the drying room.

'Oh, I say,' said Lady Charlotte. 'Oh, I say. Right, yes, right, let's turn off the machinery and leave the building. Miss Harknett, I leave you responsible for checking the machinery is turned off in this room.' With that, Lady Charlotte rushed into the next room.

Lily's stomach turned over with fear. 'There weren't any searchlights when we went on break, were there?' she called to the others as she switched off the cordite press. 'I thought there was something odd.' Everyone around there knew that no searchlights between nine and ten o'clock meant an impending air raid.

Miss Harknett checked both presses and hurried the girls to the hut's exit where they tore off their rubber overshoes and dipped out of the blackout curtain into the cold darkness.

Lady Charlotte was there giving instructions in a loud, authoritative voice.

'Away from the danger area, head for the safe area and shelter under the buildings there.'

'Come on,' said Miss Harknett to the girls, 'get a move on.' They all headed quickly along the tramway, across the road to the safe area and on to the tramway again to get to the administration building. Lily turned to see Nellie, Mabel and Jessie running off down the road towards the factory gates and she wondered where on earth they were going.

Lily and Marge were told to head to the safe buildings. All of the huts there were raised up on brick stilts.

'Get in there,' said Miss Harknett, waving them all into the small spaces between the stilts. 'Marge and Lily, get down there immediately.'

Lily and Marge crawled under the hut. The ground was a muddy bog covered in nettles and Lily couldn't stand up straight but bent over slightly at the waist. She tried to squat down, holding on to the brick support but pulled her hand away when she touched a large slug there. Miss Harknett came in after them and Lily heard Lady Charlotte's voice, clear and strong.

'Under the hut, everyone.' And then the lady herself crouched down and crawled in with them. It was dark and damp in there. Lily felt something move across her foot and in the dim light made out several rats running around them. Lady Charlotte must have seen them at the same time because she started to scream.

'Pardon me, Lady Charlotte, but please do try to be quiet,' said Miss Harknett. 'They are just rats.'

Lady Charlotte clapped her hands over her mouth, her eyes as wide as saucers, and kicked out at the rats with her boots like some sort of frantic Irish dancer. Lily took her chances and ducked out from the hole and ran after Nellie and the others down the road and out through the factory gates. She saw them ahead of her, running across the marshes, and tore after them, looking up at the sky for Zeppelins. The girls appeared to be heading for a haystack. Lily sped up and sprinted across, glad of her football training, and slammed into the side of the haystack next to Jessie.

'What are you lot up to?' she panted.

Nellie laughed, out of breath. 'It's nicer out here than in that hole with the rats and Miss Harknett, isn't it?'

'Isn't it dangerous out here, though?'

'Listen, if that factory goes up we'll all be gonners,' said Mabel. 'I'll take my chances out here, thanks.'

They fell silent, each trying to get their breath back, look-ing up at the sky for signs of the air raid. Searchlights from the Greygoose blockhouses and from the Thames Haven port and the forts by the river were all scanning the sky.

'It'll be ten minutes yet,' said Mabel. 'The wardens at Shoebury send a telegraph message when they see a Zeppelin.'

Lily breathed out and watched the light show in the sky. Munitions factories were obvious targets for the enemy. They could be bombed at any moment.

'I suppose this is as good a time as any to tell you I'm get-ting married,' said Mabel.

'What?' said Nellie.

'Married?' said Jessie. 'Who on earth to?'

'My brother-in-law,' said Mabel. 'I think it's for the best.'

'What do you mean, Mabel?' said Lily.

'I have to think about my kids, Lil,' she said. 'When the war's over and the men come back, I might not have this job any more, and since my John went down with that torpedo, if I don't get work, we could end up in Orsett workhouse.'

'Where is he, your brother-in-law?' said Jessie.

'In France. He's on leave next month, we're gonna get married then. You can all come if you like?'

'That'll be nice,' they all chimed.

'I might get married in my uniform,' said Mabel.

'Ooh yes, I like that idea,' said Nellie. 'Shall we all come in our uniforms?'

They agreed they would. They were proud of being munitionettes. Lily wanted to show off her uniform as much as the others did but felt sorry for Mabel having to marry her brother-in-law out of necessity rather than anything else. She'd get separation allowance, which was more than her widow's pension. She was just trying to make sure her and her children's future was safe.

'Has he got a name, then?' said Nellie.

'George,' said Mabel.

'At least you won't have to change your surname,' said Lily.

Jessie suddenly gasped and batted Lily on the arm to look. The searchlights had picked out an enormous German airship in the sky above the Thames, following the river to London. The stutter of anti-aircraft fire from the Greygoose blockhouses and the forts followed and the girls watched as the Zeppelin swerved to get out of the rays.

'Come on, lads, get it!' shouted Mabel.

There was more gunfire and then the searchlights lost the

airship and the girls peered intently at the sky, wondering where it had gone. A few minutes later they heard gunfire further up the river.

'It's getting closer to London,' said Nellie.

Lily's body tensed, the Zeppelin could drop bombs at any time; it was waiting until it got to London to do the maximum amount of damage. There were people sleeping in their beds. It was too awful.

'I hate those bastards,' said Nellie.

'Should we wait till we know which way they head back?' said Lily.

'Yes,' said Mabel. 'There's always the chance they'll dump any leftover bombs on the way back home. Sometimes they head back over Norfolk way, though.'

'We'd best sit here for a bit to see,' said Jessie.

They sat there in the darkness. Lily fidgeted to get comfortable on the prickly hay.

'You know,' said Mabel, 'back in the day, there were marsh people living out here. The men used to go inland to the hills to find their wives and bring them back here but they would turn sickly and yellow from the stinking fogs and die of the ague. So the men would go back inland to find another young wife and bring her here until she died of the ague too. Some of them would get through twenty-five wives.'

Nellie cackled. 'I reckon we'd be taken for marsh people, we all look sickly and yellow, don't we?'

'Ha ha, I reckon little Marge is one of them,' said Jessie. 'Where is Marge?'

'Down the hole with Miss Harknett and Lady Charlotte,' said Lily.

190

'Oh, poor love,' said Mabel, chuckling.

Lily wondered what Charlotte must have thought about sheltering from Zeppelins in a muddy, rat-infested hole. It was a far cry from St Clere's Hall. She remembered the conversation she had overheard, when Charlotte said she wanted to do war work in France. If she had gone against her parents' wishes to come to Greygoose, she'd be feeling nervous. Lily shook the thought away and stiffened when the sound of a bomb falling reached them. They were all nervous, and Lady Charlotte asking for help to unpack had been shameful. Lily refused to feel sorry for her. In the distance they could hear more gunfire. Soon they saw the Zeppelin heading back but this time going north. It went over Stanford-le-Hope and none of them could breathe. They watched it head off until the searchlights could no longer reach it. They strained to hear the sound of more bombs being dropped but all was quiet.

12

4 April 1916

Dearest Lil,

What a turn-up, having Lady Charlotte at your factory.
Just try and get on with it, love, it'll turn out for the best.
Mum wrote and said they are all right after the Faversham
to-do. Terrible business. I don't wonder that you should get a
different job, love. There's a nice bunch of lads here and we
are all looking forward to getting on the front line ha ha.
    Your loving Sid

Sid's letter arrived the day after the Zeppelin raid and Lily's
heart charged with rage when she read it. Ada hadn't both-
ered replying to her letter asking if the boys were all right
after the Faversham explosion, but Ada had got her sister to
write to Sid about it. Lily knew Sid wouldn't want her working at Greygoose once he'd heard about Faversham, but she
couldn't give it up now, it meant too much to her.

    She'd been wondering whether to ignore Lady Charlotte's
request to help her unpack. With gritted teeth she thought
she'd better do it, and so she walked down to hut one before

the night shift started. When she knocked at the door, it was answered by a girl in a maid's uniform.

'I'm here to see Lady Charlotte Harrington,' said Lily, feeling on ceremony.

'If you'll wait in the sitting room, please, I'll announce you,' said the maid.

Lily was startled to see the inside of the hut, which on the outside looked identical to the others. On the inside, however, it looked more like something from St Clere's Hall. There was a sitting room with wood-panelled walls, electric lights hanging down and painted pictures in gilt frames on the walls. There were two big fireplaces, one on each side of the room, and plenty of comfortable settees and armchairs in clusters around the fires. Fresh flowers arranged in vases had been placed on the tables. Lily was astonished.

'Ah, Pavitt!' said Lady Charlotte, coming into the room.

Lily's back was up straight away. 'Can you call me Lily here, please, Lady Charlotte?'

'Oh, yes, of course, Lily, I'm awfully sorry, old habits and all that. I know we're starting our shift soon but if you wouldn't mind helping . . . ' she said, leading the way. 'Lady Blythe has her maid, who has been splendid helping around the place, but I daren't take advantage.'

Lily didn't answer. Lady Charlotte was oblivious to the fact that she was taking advantage of *her* and Lily certainly didn't want to give her the idea that she was happy to be doing maid's work here.

They went through a door into Lady Charlotte's room, which again, would have looked quite at place in St Clere's. There was fancy wallpaper, rugs, a large bed, wooden furniture. Lady Charlotte's suitcases were open on the floor, clothes spilling out of them. Lily looked at the mess and her guts churned. Why couldn't she just put it all away herself? Why was it so hard for her to do, had she even tried?

'What do you need help with, Lady Charlotte?' Lily thought she would encourage her to do something herself.

'Oh, all of it, Pav— Lily. I don't know where it all goes,' she said, sitting down at her dressing table and taking off her earrings.

'Well, which ones?'

Lady Charlotte frowned and turned around. She stood up and pointed. 'There, all the clothes.'

'Well, you can hang up the dresses in the wardrobe. And you can put your underclothes in the chest of drawers.'

'Oh, Lily, be a dear, would you? Isn't it a pain that we have to remove all jewellery and pins before going to work? I might just stop wearing jewellery altogether,' she said, looking at her reflection and taking out her hairpins.

Lily tutted quietly to herself and got on with putting the clothes away.

'And isn't it wonderful that women are getting a real chance to show what they are capable of, doing men's work in the factory? I think it's just marvellous,' Lady Charlotte went on, winding her hair into a loose plait on her shoulder.

There was a knock at the door and the maid popped her head in. 'There's a visitor for you, milady, a Lord Nevill?'

'What?' said Lady Charlotte, jumping up from her chair. 'What in heaven's name?'

Lord Nevill had been to St Clere's several times when Lily had been there. He was one of Lady Charlotte's suitors.

Lily wished she wasn't there and hurried to put away the clothes. Charlotte looked at the floor and frowned while she recovered her composure.

'Show him to the sitting room and then bring him in here in ten minutes, would you? Lily's here so it's perfectly proper. I just don't want to have to talk to him if any of the other ladies are there.'

'Oh, what does he want?' muttered Lady Charlotte, powdering her nose in the mirror and smoothing down her hair.

Ten minutes later the maid knocked again and showed in Lord Nevill. Lily always thought he looked quite nice. He seemed more relaxed than some of the other suitors who called on Lady Charlotte, and he had a nice floppy fringe.

'Charlotte,' he said, coming forward. She took his hands and kissed his cheek.

'Hello, James. What on earth are you doing here?'

'Are you ill? Going to bed?' he asked, indicating Charlotte's hair.

'What? No, we can't wear hairpins to work and I start my shift soon, so I can't talk long.'

'Oh, you brought your maid with you,' he said, looking at Lily.

'No, but it's the funniest thing, Lily here left St Clere's to work at Greygoose and we've ended up in the same part of the works. She's very kindly helping me to unpack.'

'Oh, I see,' said James. 'Now, Charlotte, I'm terribly worried about you. You know I have something to do with the Uplees factory that blew the other day. I'm frantic with grief for all the men who lost their lives, and when I heard that you were here, I had to rush over immediately.'

'How did you know I was here?' said Charlotte.

'What? Oh, everyone knows you are here. Lord Harrington's daughter doesn't just go missing, you know, however hard you tried to make it appear so.'

'I did not. I am my own person; I simply didn't tell them what I was going to do in case they stopped me.'

'Well, I hope you have proved your point and will come back with me, I'll take you home.'

'James, for heaven's sake, I know Mother has put you up to this. Do you really think this will endear me to you in the slightest bit?'

Just at that moment there was a huge bang, like an explosion, and they all jumped and stood stock still.

'What was that?' said Lily.

'Oh no, is it us this time?' said Charlotte.

'I'll go and find out,' said James. 'Stay right here.'

With that, he rushed away. Charlotte sat down on her bed and looked at Lily.

'What could it be? An accidental explosion? A bomb? It's frightfully scary here, isn't it?'

Lily nodded and played anxiously with the beaded dress she was holding, squeezing the beads hard between her finger and thumb. 'I'm going to go and find out,' she said eventually.

'Yes, so am I,' said Charlotte with determination. 'What are we doing sitting here like damsels in distress?'

They got up to go but James knocked and came back in. 'It's all right,' he said. 'They are just blowing up the waste water pond.'

Lily didn't know what he meant.

'What?' said Charlotte, equally mystified.

'It's the by-product from the nitro-glycerine manufacturing process,' explained James. 'They channel the waste water into a pond and then blow it up with a stick of dynamite every now and then.'

'Oh, thank heaven for that,' said Charlotte. And Lily breathed a sigh of relief too. She looked up at the clock on the wall.

'Milady, we should be going now.'

'Oh, yes, good, well, James, it's time for our shift so I must bid you goodbye. Please do not worry about me,' she said, kissing his cheek.

'I beg you, Charlotte, please just leave this business. I tell you, if you had seen the devastation at Uplees. One hundred and eight men perished, some of them atomised by the blast with no remains for the relatives to bury. One of the ambulance men went home and hanged himself, he was so traumatised by it all.'

Charlotte and Lily listened to his chilling report. His words were deathly. But still, Lily knew she would go back to work. And Charlotte made it clear that she would too.

'I'm sorry, James, I really am. Now we *must* go.'

Lily was dismayed to find herself getting the train to the factory with Lady Charlotte, who wore her enormous fur coat and attracted the attention of all the workers. The women police constables on the factory gates waved her through with smiles and hellos and Lily scuttled away to the change room while Charlotte chatted with one of them.

'I wonder how milady is doing,' said Nellie at work.

'I helped her unpack just now,' said Lily.

'Did you, Lil? You didn't have to do that,' said Jessie.

197

'Why wouldn't she want to help her?' said Miss Harknett. 'We are extraordinarily lucky to have Lady Charlotte here.'

'Have you seen the inside of hut one?' said Lily, and the others shook their heads. 'It's like St Clere's Hall – really grand, with a sitting room and everything.'

'Ooh, I'd love to see it; lucky you,' said Miss Harknett.

'It doesn't surprise me that she'd have better than us,' said Nellie. 'Do the society ladies from the canteen stay there too?'

'Yes, I think so,' said Lily. 'One of them has brought her maid with her.'

Jessie made eyes at Lily, who turned to see Mrs Sparrow and Lady Charlotte come into the pressing room.

'Girls, if we could have your attention for a moment,' said Mrs Sparrow. 'Mrs Hodges, the factory inspector, will be making an inspection of the factory this evening. When she comes, if you would please continue with your work, and express due gratitude for the opportunity to do such valuable war work for a very generous wage,' the welfare supervisor paused for a moment to let her words register, 'that would be splendid.'

'What's all that about?' said Lily when the women had left the room.

'Just as Mrs Sparrow said,' said Miss Harknett. 'We shall continue with our work and if we are questioned we are to express our gratitude.'

'In other words, they don't want us complaining about anything,' said Nellie.

'She's lovely, Mrs Hodges,' said Jessie. 'You can tell her anything, she's on our side.'

'Our side?' said Miss Harknett indignantly. 'Whatever can you mean by that?'

'I mean, if we ever say anything about the factory we get told off for it, but with Mrs Hodges she wants to know if anything's wrong, that's her job,' said Jessie.

'Well, if I hear anything said against the factory or Mrs Sparrow I shall report you at once,' said Miss Harknett.

'Oh, keep your cap on,' said Nellie. 'Mrs Hodges works for the Ministry of Munitions not Greygoose. We're allowed to tell her if we're unhappy about anything.'

Lily could tell from Nellie's face that she wouldn't necessarily go against Mrs Sparrow and say anything.

About an hour into the shift, Mrs Sparrow brought Mrs Hodges round. The welfare supervisor kept a close eye on proceedings as Mrs Hodges walked around the room talking to the girls.

'It's awfully stuffy in here, isn't it? Do you find it difficult to get through the shift? Do you ever faint?' Mrs Hodges asked Lily, and Lily saw Mrs Sparrow boring holes into her with her glare.

'No, missis,' said Lily. 'It's hot but it's all right. I'm glad of the job.'

'Yes, dear, I know you are glad of your job,' said Mrs Hodges, touching Lily's arm. 'And I know you are paid well and are honoured to help our boys end the war, but is there anything you would like to see improved here in the conditions or hours?'

'No, missis, thank you,' said Lily.

And every other girl there said the same thing, Nellie included. It was clear to Lily why they said it. Yes, the place was too hot and they fainted on night shift and were carried outside to lie on the ground to recover; yes they were turning yellow from the poisonous chemicals and their hands were covered in hives and they were terrified about being blown up or bombed by Zeppelins. But, the job gave them freedom. Lily had never worked in a place where she felt important, where she had a bit of money in her pocket to spend on herself, where she had good friends and could even play football. She wouldn't say anything against that.

When Mrs Hodges left, the girls carried on with their work. Lady Charlotte came in and Lily thought she looked uncomfortable about something, agitated.

'How is everything in here, Miss Harknett?' she asked.

'Very well, thank you, Lady Charlotte,' she replied, almost dipping into a curtsey.

'Well, the inspection seemed to go well. Mrs Sparrow was pleased, which means the manager will be pleased. So that is all very well.' It was as if she wanted to say more on the subject but stopped herself. 'There is something I need to tell you all. We are going to be offering paid overtime for the next three months. There is going to be a big push soon in France and we need production to be increased to cope with it. This is all highly confidential and not to be repeated outside of these walls.'

'Is there a choice?' said Nellie.

'What's that, Nellie?'

'Do we have to do the overtime?'

'Well, the company would rather you do it, Nellie,' said Charlotte.

'So how come you waited till Mrs Hodges had gone before you told us? Or is that a silly question?'

'Nellie!' said Miss Harknett.

Alfie ambled in from the pressing hut next door. 'Oh, sorry, milady,' he said when he saw Charlotte there. 'I just wanted a quick word with the girls, but it's about something after work.'

'It's all right, Alfie, if it's quick,' said Charlotte.

'Girls,' Alfie said, and clapped his hands together as though he had something good to say. 'I've set up a first game between shift teams A and B.' The girls stopped what they were doing and cried out with glee. 'Settle down,' Alfie said, grinning. 'It'll be on Sunday the thirtieth of this month, so we've got three and a bit weeks to get ready for it.'

'We won't let you down, Alfie,' said Lily, smiling, her stomach turning over at the thought of playing an actual game for the first time.

'I know you won't, Lil,' he said. He'd never shortened her name before and she found herself glowing with pleasure and looked down to avoid his eye. It was what Sid called her.

'We could make it a charity match,' said Jessie. 'Charge for tickets and give the money to the army hospital. I bet they'd love a gramophone or something like that to cheer the lads up.'

'What's all this?' said Charlotte.

'We've set up a women's football team,' said Alfie, 'and they're doing pretty well, I can tell you.'

Charlotte's eyes lit up. 'Is that so? How splendid. I have heard about women's football teams in other parts of the country and I think it's super.'

The room fell silent.

'I was rather a demon at hockey at school,' she contin- ued, 'and, as you know, they refer to hockey as "rugby with sticks".' She looked around at them all expectantly and Lily's heart sank. Did Lady Charlotte mean to join the team?

'We've got our team, thanks, milady,' said Lily.

'Yes, Lily, but you'll need a reserve team, won't you?'

Charlotte looked around at the rest of the gang. Nellie, Jessie and Mabel were all concentrating intently on their work.

'Alfie?' said Charlotte. 'You'll need a reserve team, won't you?'

'I expect so, milady,' said Alfie, looking at the others uncertainly.

'That settles it, then. I'm very excited to join you. When's your next practice?'

No one answered at first. 'At three o'clock tomorrow, milady,' said Mabel eventually. 'On the marshes by the factory gates.'

'Splendid,' said Charlotte. 'What'll I wear?'

'We wear shorts, milady,' said Mabel.

'Well, I shall have to send out for some. Thank you, Mabel.'

Charlotte left the room, beaming, and Alfie followed her. Lily looked at Nellie and her own feelings were reflected back at her. It was bad luck, it really was. Lady Charlotte was spoiling everything.

'I thought she was gonna tell you to go out and get her shorts,' said Nellie.

'Me too,' said Jessie. 'I don't want her practising with us. She's not one of us.'

No, she's not one of us, thought Lily. She felt a roll of anger simmering inside her, bubbling like a stew in a pot. For the first time in her life, she was enjoying herself, away from a life of servitude, away from the grind of poverty at home and Ada's punishing regime of guilt and housework. Lady Charlotte was going to trample on her happiness, when the lady already had everything, all the privileges of wealth and education and connections. It wasn't fair. And Charlotte thought she'd be good at football because she'd played hockey at school. Well, Lily hadn't told the others but she had often had a kick around with Sid and the boys in the tenement yard of a Sunday and that's why Alfie had said she was a natural. The stew bubbled a little faster in the pot when she thought about being on the pitch with Charlotte. It would be a level playing field in more ways than one – rules of the game and the game only. None of the other rules of life that normally applied to her would come into it.

At the end of night shift the girls made their weary way to the canteen for some dinner, even though it was six thirty in the morning. It was crowded and jolly as usual, despite the hour. Lily sat down with the girls from her pressing room and they broke the news about Lady Charlotte to the rest of the football team.

'Oh, you're joking,' said Eliza. 'Fancy her wanting to do it. Couldn't you put her off?'

'No, we tried,' said Lily. They all looked over to Charlotte who was taking a seat with the other overlookers at a special table that had a tablecloth and nicer settings. One of the society ladies rushed over to take her order. The women who sat at that table didn't go up to the serving hatch, they were waited on.

Nellie scooped some of her mashed potato on to her spoon and catapulted it through the air towards Charlotte. It landed on the back of her neck and she jumped and put her hand there, feeling it squashed into her hair.

'Who did that?' she shrieked. The canteen fell silent. 'Who did it? I demand to know.'

Nellie looked as innocent as the rest of the women there. And when no one was forthcoming, Charlotte sat back down. 'This is outrageous,' Lily heard her say, as one of the women handed her a cotton napkin to wipe the mash off with.

Jessie nudged Nellie and giggled and the noise of chatter started up again in the room. Lily smiled and a look of understanding passed between her and Nellie.

After a decent sleep and breakfast, Lily made her way to the marshes for football practice. The women were standing around Alfie, chattering excitedly.

'The chap who looks after the Grays pitch is ex-army – he was happy to do us a favour,' said Alfie.

There was a properly marked-out pitch on the marshes. 'Oh, it's lovely, Alfie,' said Lily and he grinned.

'Now we've got no excuse not to train properly,' he said. 'We even cleared the bramble bushes off it,' he laughed.

'The farmer didn't mind?' said Mabel.

'No, he said he's doing a bit for the war by keeping us happy,' said Alfie. 'Says we're doing a grand job.'

'Ah, here you are,' said Charlotte, coming along wearing shorts and socks and proper football boots. 'Look at me! Isn't this hilarious?' She did a twirl for them and her face fell slightly when no one said anything.

'Right, let's get on with it. Run around the pitch three times to warm up,' said Alfie, and off the girls went. Nellie and Lily ran behind Charlotte, with Nellie mimicking how she ran with her back as stiff as a rod and her knees high. Nellie scooped up a glob of mud and lobbed it at Charlotte's back. Charlotte swung around but Lily and Nellie raced ahead and overtook her. Charlotte didn't say anything but sped up herself and overtook them. By the time they reached the end of three laps they were all sprinting to the finish and collapsed in a heap, gasping for breath.

'Well, I'm glad to see you're keen,' said Alfie. 'Get in two rows now, we're going to practise tackling.' He lined them up in two rows facing each other. Lily started off tackling Mabel and took the ball off her easily enough, having learned from Sid when he taught it to the boys. 'Good, Lily,' called Alfie. 'Everyone, watch how Lily does it, she's got the knack. Lady Charlotte, you try to take it off her.' Charlotte came forward and ran at Lily but Lily was too quick and went around her, leaving Charlotte slipping in the mud. Before Alfie could call out for them to swap partners, Charlotte ran to Lily and tried to take the ball, but Lily pushed her away and ran away with it. Charlotte went after her and tripped her up, Lily sprawled in the mud. 'That's a foul, Lady Charlotte,' called out Alfie, but Lily didn't care if it was a foul. She went for Charlotte, got an arm around her neck and clawed the ball away with her foot, the two women grappling with each other until they both fell in the mud. The other women were cheering them on but Alfie intervened and broke them up.

They came apart and stood up, Alfie standing between them. 'All right, girls; it's football not rugby.' Lily and Charlotte looked at each other, fierce and panting.

'That's enough of this Lady Charlotte business. Out here, it's just Charlotte,' said the lady, glaring.

Nellie and Mabel were smiling and nodding at Lily; they thoroughly approved of her rough tackle and seemed to have reached an unspoken agreement. From then on, they targeted Charlotte until they were all covered in mud. Alfie called time and they left the pitch to go back to the hut for a bath. Lily was exhilarated. It felt marvellous tackling Charlotte, she couldn't wait for the next practice.

At work, Charlotte didn't mention her treatment on the football field, but she certainly changed her attitude towards the girls: she spoke to them with authority and was no longer familiar. She showed no signs of giving up on football practice, either. Not when she found slugs in her overshoes, or when there were nettles on the toilet seat, not even when Jessie sprayed her with the hose and said it was an accident. She came to the next practice and the next. She even asked Mrs Sparrow for a budget to buy kit, and Mrs Sparrow agreed. They all had new football boots and khaki jerseys and half a dozen new balls.

Lily never said a word to the other girls about their silent campaign to put Charlotte off. But when Charlotte came to them asking about their production levels, the girls would start a rousing chorus of 'It's a Long Way to Tipperary'. When Charlotte had instructions to convey from Mrs Sparrow, the girls would sing 'Keep the Home Fires Burning'. Lily wasn't an unkind person but she had plenty of bad treatment in reserve for Charlotte and meted it out without remorse. At work, Charlotte had authority over her. Just as every other person in charge at the factory was deemed better than the likes of her, and so in a better position to take control. But on the football field, Charlotte was no longer Lily's boss.

With the in-fighting came a higher level of play, the competition spurred them on and they became quite good on the field. They practised hard and Lily felt herself growing more skilled. Off the field they made every effort to make Charlotte's life difficult. They complained to her about the fumes, and about the rashes on their skin. They complained about the state of the lavatory and their sore gums and how they weren't allowed to change the press cylinders or adjust the machine settings themselves. They moaned about the extra hours they had to do and when Mr Nash complained about the girls working too fast, Charlotte turned on him and told him off. They moulded a piece of cordite into the shape of a man's privates and left it on the bench for her to find. Mabel and Nellie told hair-raising stories about their experiences with men to embarrass her. They broke into her locker and hid her clothes. They called her milady in sarcastic tones and they didn't tell her when football practice was. But she found out and kept coming back.

By the time the end of April came around, and the day of the match between A-shift and B-shift, the tension between Charlotte and the others crackled. It was a Sunday afternoon and the girls met in the canteen for lunch before the game.

'I feel sick with nerves,' said Lily, playing with her food.

'You don't look much better, Marge,' said Mabel. Marge looked up at her, her usual nervous laugh missing, her pleasant nature dampened.

'It's my dad,' she said. 'We haven't heard from him. He's been taken by the Turks in the Siege of Kut.'

'Oh, Marge,' said Lily, putting her hand over her friend's.

When they walked over to the marshes it looked like most of the factory were out to watch. Tickets had been sold and money was collected for the army hospital in Orsett. Alfie had prepared the girls as best he could and he looked nervous for them. 'Just do your best, girls,' he said. 'And watch out for Jane and Petra on their defence.'

'Who's that?' said Mabel. Lily turned to see three men setting up their cameras on tripods at the side of the pitch.

'It's the press,' said Alfie. 'They got wind that Charlotte is here and they couldn't miss the opportunity to see her running around in shorts with the rest of you.'

'But she's not even on the team,' said Nellie. 'She's the reserve.'

'Mrs Sparrow said she's to play,' said Alfie, shrugging. 'She said Marge is to sit out.'

'What? That's not fair,' said Lily.

'It's all right,' said Marge. 'I don't feel like it anyway.'

When they jogged out on to the pitch the crowd cheered, and there were some jeers at the sight of the women's knees, and calls of *I can see your knickers,* which made Lily feel exposed and ridiculous. Fancy having to play in front of all these people. She was already nervous and cross that Marge had lost her chance of playing – but the young girl was too nice to say anything about it.

'Lady Charlotte!' called the press photographers, and waved her over for a shot. The others looked on as Charlotte posed and was then questioned by a reporter with a notebook. Even when Alfie blew the whistle, she took her time coming into position.

The girls gave it their all; they made some good passes, despite Jane and Petra from the B-shift team taking the ball off them at every opportunity. Mabel saved two goals, and Lily tried to shoot but couldn't get it past Petra. B-team looked just as nervous as A-team did but it was a friendly enough atmosphere, being a charity match. It all felt like a dream to Lily.

After half-time, Alfie blew the whistle for the game to recommence but Charlotte answered the call for more photos before running on to the pitch. A group of well-dressed girls in fur coats and make-up cheered from the sideline for Charlotte, and Lily exchanged glances of frustration with Nellie. It was like a one-woman show and the game was being affected. B-shift had scored two goals and A-shift had only got one past.

The photographers called Charlotte over and she went back to pose for them, with one foot on the ball. Lily looked at Nellie and shook her head with rage. She ran over to Charlotte and kicked the ball from under her foot. Charlotte stumbled and fell on to one knee. Lily ran with the ball towards the goal, shot and scored. The crowd cheered her and she jogged to the other girls to celebrate.

The whistle blew and Lily made another run, calling to Jessie to pass the ball to her. Jessie made a good pass but before Lily could get her foot on it, Charlotte was there and took it, dribbled around Petra and scored a goal herself. The crowd cheered louder, the photographers called, and Lily wanted to punch Charlotte in the face.

The game finished with the score 3–2 to A-team and the girls patted each other on the back.

'Lady Charlotte, Lady Charlotte,' the photographers called, and she went to them without a look back at her team.

'Bloody well done, girls,' said Alfie, beaming.

'Thanks, Alfie, it was your training that did it,' said Mabel, panting.

'Oh, I feel so sick,' said Jessie, clutching her stomach. She ran to one side and threw up.

'You all right?' said Nellie. 'What is it?'

'Nothing. It's all right,' said Jessie.

'Best get her back for a rest,' said Alfie, 'she doesn't look too clever.'

With a final wave at the crowd, they left to help Jessie back to the colony, each one of them high from their win. Jessie kept a brave face but when they got her into her bed she started to cry. 'Please stop being so nice to me,' she said. 'You're just making me cry.'

'What is it, Jessie?' said Lily, kneeling down by her bed.

'I can't tell you, can I? You'll all think me a terrible girl.'

The jubilation of the football match evaporated in a second as the women welded together around their friend.

'Is it something to do with that sweetheart of yours?' said Mabel, with a knowing look.

Jessie gave a wretched nod. 'Yes, I think so. Mrs Sparrow will sack me, won't she?'

Lily understood what Mabel meant, and her heart went out to the girl. 'Why don't you ask her for help, Jessie?' she said. 'Can't she move you to the safe area for now? You can't stay in cordite like this.'

'She doesn't let you move once you're in a job,' said Mabel.

'You'll have to marry him, Jessie,' said Nellie. 'He can't leave you alone in this state. Then you'll get separation allowance.'

'He won't,' sobbed Jessie. 'And I can't leave work yet, I need the money, and if I leave she won't give me a leaving certificate so I'll not get anything else. I'm stuck in cordite so God knows what'll happen. I've heard of women having yellow babies.'

Lily put her arm around the girl and they comforted her as best they could until she fell asleep.

'It's not right,' said Lily, as they left the hut.

'She'll end up in the workhouse if her family kick her out,' said Nellie. 'Or worse.'

'What could be worse than the workhouse?' said Lily.

But Nellie didn't answer.

13

Mabel had an impromptu May wedding when her brother-in-law George came home on leave. The members of the football team were all invited to the small ceremony at St Mary the Virgin church in Corringham. Mabel had cackled at the irony of it. They all wore their munitions uniforms, even Mabel. And with George in his army khaki, they made a patriotic-looking couple. Mabel's six children were there, too. As Lily watched the couple exchange their vows, she wondered how they would both feel when the war was over. Mabel had explained that she was marrying George to secure her future, and Lily could only guess that George was marrying Mabel at least partly out of a sense of family duty. He would go back to France once they were married and if he came home safely, which wasn't at all a certainty, they would settle down as a married couple when they hardly knew each other. Lily couldn't imagine being married to a stranger.

It was a Sunday and Lily hadn't been able to visit the boys in Kent – they were doing overtime on Sunday mornings now and what with the wedding and the reception, she'd have to wait until the following weekend to see them. From the church they all made their way on the light railway across the marshes to the village hall in Goosetown. The YWCA volunteers had kindly laid on a wedding spread and the girls had lugged the gramophone over from the rec hut. By half past five the party was in full swing and the punch bowl had been refilled several times. The girls not in uniform were done up in their best crêpe de Chine beaded dresses, trimmed hats and silk stockings.

'Fancy a dance, Lil?'

Alfie was there, looking smart in his best suit, and when he asked Lily to dance, the glow of the punch made her say yes.

'Go on, then.'

He took her hand and they moved around the dance floor, Lily aware of his discomfort.

'It doesn't hurt too much to dance?' she said

He laughed. 'Well, I can shift those cylinders at work, can't I? I can do a bit of a waltz. In any case, I wouldn't miss the opportunity to have a dance with you, now, would I?'

Lily smiled. 'What happened? Can I ask?'

He didn't have a chance to answer. Time seemed to hover about them as a terrible pulsing force shook the ground beneath their feet and the needle skidded off the gramophone. In the same second, Lily recoiled as the windows of the hall blew inwards with an almighty smash and shards of glass flew towards the wedding guests. One caught Lily in the side of the face and she was knocked sideways with the shock of it. People screamed and clutched their faces and heads; Mabel and George grabbed for the children. Lily turned around in a daze, seeing blood and expressions of horror, the deafening boom of an explosion crashing in her ears. She dropped to the ground and covered her head, Alfie did the same next to her, putting one arm over her. Another explosion cracked and blew and the building shook. Lily crawled towards the door and realised she was actually crawling over the door, which had been blown off its hinges. She got out of the hall and stood up, her ears ringing, her face wet with blood. An immense spiral of cloud was rising from the factory works.

'Oh no,' she sobbed, 'oh no.' She stood in shock and then started to run towards the factory on wobbly legs, not thinking of anything else, just how fast she could run across the marshes to get there. She sensed others running with her, arms and legs pumping in the periphery of her view. She reached the factory gates and was greeted with a scene of horror. Workers – men, women, teenage boys and girls – running and screaming, some standing still in a daze. Women police constables, bewildered and shaken themselves, were helping the walking wounded. She went deeper into the works, towards the smoke, and the further she went, so the damage to the buildings got worse and worse. The smoke and fire were coming from the danger area. The roof of one of the guncotton huts had blown right off, the wooden walls blown out and Lily could barely see the brick foundation supports. The acrid smell of brick dust and burnt nitro-glycerine was choking her. The Greygoose soldiers were there, getting people away from the wreckage. There were people on the ground not moving. A woman staggered from the scene, her clothes blown off, her face black and burnt, her hair gone. Lily ran to her, took her by the arm. The woman's charred skin came off on Lily's hand and she pulled it away with horror. The woman fell to the ground. '*Help*,' Lily screamed, '*help!*'

A man ran towards them. 'Help me get her up,' he said. Lily lifted the woman's ankles and felt the skin shift beneath her hands. The man picked her up under the arms and they staggered with their appalling load towards the waiting Greygoose motorised ambulance. They got the woman inside and looked for the driver, who was nowhere to be seen. 'Can you drive?' the man asked Lily. She shook her head, panicked.

'I can.' Lily turned to see Lady Charlotte. 'Get in the back with her,' said Charlotte, and Lily climbed in with the woman and sat next to her. She had passed out and Lily didn't know if she was alive. Charlotte got into the driver's seat and started the engine and they headed off slowly, out through the factory gates and on to Goosetown. They arrived at the little Goosetown hospital and carried the woman in. All was a state of emergency.

'We've only room for one more,' said the nurse. 'The others will need to go to Orsett.'

Charlotte and Lily drove back to the factory.

'Good God, this is horrific,' said Charlotte, but Lily was too shocked even to answer her. They got back to the scene of the explosion. By then the ambulance driver had carried another woman on a stretcher to the road and was waiting there.

'Get this one in and take her to Orsett,' he said. 'There's a lorry I can drive.' They got the woman in and started off for Orsett. On the road they passed other vehicles heading for the factory to help, people's cars and carts, two funeral hearses and a military ambulance. Lily sat with the woman, terrified to look at her. Her whole body was naked and charred, her eyes and hair had gone – her whimpers were the only evidence that she was still alive.

'Hold on,' said Lily. 'We're getting you to hospital. Just hold on.' Lily put out her hand to reassure the woman and realised she was shaking violently. She didn't know whether to touch the woman's hand in case the skin came away, so she gripped her own fingers in her lap to try to stop the tremors. They reached Orsett Hospital and when the staff opened the back of the van, Lily told them the woman was dead.

The hospital staff carried her out and told them to go back for the other wounded. Lily sat in the front with Charlotte. 'She stopped breathing,' she said. 'I couldn't do anything, she just went.'

Charlotte reached across and held Lily's hand. 'We did our best,' she said quietly, and Lily saw that tears were streaming down Charlotte's cheeks but she kept on driving.

They went back for more. They made the journey another seven times. One of the men they took had had his leg torn off and Lily held a towel against the bleeding and tried to calm the man's screams with some brandy she found in the ambulance. Finally, they stopped and waited for people with minor injuries to be treated onsite and a man put some petrol into the ambulance. Heads were bandaged, arms were put in slings. They put them into the back of the ambulance four at a time while Lily rode at the front with Charlotte.

It was late, midnight. The fire had been put out and the dead had been carried away. 'Go home,' a man said. 'You've done enough, go and get some rest.'

Lily took Charlotte's arm and they walked across the marsh to the colony. They didn't speak. When they reached hut one, they embraced and Lily's resolve cracked. She broke down and sobbed and she went back to hut ten and crawled into bed. She lay staring at the ceiling all night. Every time she tried to sleep, she saw the woman with no eyes who had just slipped away.

In the morning Lily got out of bed when she heard the sound of others stirring. She felt sick with fatigue and shock. She poured some water into the bowl at the wash stand and held a flannel to her face. She winced and remembered how she had been hit by a shard of glass in the village hall when the windows blew out. Inspecting it in her tiny looking glass, she saw that one side of her face was caked with dried blood. She soaked it away with the flannel.

Her uniform was in a heap on the floor. She took it to the matron, Mrs Pratt.

'I'm sorry, I'm afraid it's stained,' she said, holding it up. The tunic and trousers were streaked with soot and blood.

'My dear,' said Mrs Pratt in a soft voice, 'let me take that for you. May I bring you a cup of tea?'

Lily looked in surprise at Mrs Pratt. Her unusual kindness was enough to make fresh tears fall down Lily's cheeks. 'No, it's all right, thank you. I'll go to the hut for breakfast.' Lily wanted to be around other people, she wanted to sit at the canteen table and pour a cup of tea from one of the brown teapots. She needed to feel as though the world hadn't ended.

In the canteen, everyone there looked the same as her. Silent, strained and slumped. Haunted by what they had seen. With shaking hands, Lily poured herself a cup of tea and she buttered some bread. One of the girls started to sing 'In the Shade of the Old Apple Tree' in the sweetest voice and the girls looked up at each other and joined in the song, with croaky, sobbing voices that became stronger and more resolute with each line. Lily sang too, for the people who had died yesterday. They had died with their hearts full of pride and she owed it to them to go and find a fresh uniform and get over to the factory to lend a hand.

Seeing the devastation in daylight was like walking through a nightmare. Windows had shattered, doors blown off, the perimeter fence was down, part of the administration hut had fallen in. It wasn't the guncotton hut that had blown, they discovered, but one of the nitro-glycerine huts. But no one knew how it had happened. The hut itself was a flattened tangle of burnt metal and wood, the walls of the huts adjacent to it had fallen inwards, despite being two hundred yards away. Thank goodness for that distance and for the earth mounds around the hut, which must have absorbed some of the force.

Lily suddenly remembered Mabel's wedding reception and wanted to find her friend to see if she was all right. What a thing to happen on your wedding day. She'd go over to Mabel's house in Goosetown later. Men and women were helping sort through the debris. Police constables and soldiers were giving orders and supervising the carnage.

'What can I do?' Lily asked one of the copperettes.

'Can you help with sorting out some of the wreckage?' she said, waving Lily over to the edge of the destroyed hut. Rolling up her sleeves, she joined the others, pulling out the charred debris and throwing it into the waiting carts. The pieces of wood and metal were still warm. Lily wondered whether the girl they had transported was still warm or if she'd be cold by now. Lily saw Lady Charlotte there, her sleeves rolled up too, and went over to work next to her.

'Hello,' she said.

'Hello,' said Charlotte, stopping to greet Lily. 'It's a terrible mess, isn't it?'

'How many dead, do you know?'

'They think fifteen. Plus about forty injured. Because it happened at a quarter to six, there were just those working overtime in the hut itself, and the other workers were making their way through the gates. If it had happened even fifteen minutes later it would have been a lot worse.'

The ones working overtime had died. It was a terrible injustice.

'We did well last night, Lady Charlotte,' Lily said, feeling a new kinship with her.

'Yes, we did. Please, I've decided, no more Lady. It's just Charlotte from now on.'

'All right,' said Lily. It was so strange working side by side with Charlotte. Lily felt she should say something about St Clere's Hall but her life there had been so different and she didn't want Charlotte thinking of her in that way, on her hands and knees cleaning up the Harrington family's mess.

They worked until five o'clock, when, with so many people there helping, the site had been mostly cleared and work had started on a new nitro-glycerine hut. They were told to go for dinner and have a proper rest and that the night shift would start the following evening. Charlotte and Lily walked to the YWCA canteen and sat together at one of the wooden tables without a tablecloth. Gradually, the rest of the football team joined them.

'Blimey, Lil, is your face all right?' said Jessie.

They exchanged stories of how they had helped after the explosion. There wasn't a one without a story to tell.

Mabel and the children were all right. Mabel was taking the day off today and would be back at work tomorrow. No one expressed a desire to leave the factory, to seek work elsewhere. They were intent on doing their duty, and even more so now that people's lives had been sacrificed for the cause.

'Well, they don't need us at the factory any more today. What say we have a kick-around?' said Charlotte. 'It'll do us good to take our minds off things for a minute. And, I've decided, it's no more Lady Charlotte, it'll just be Charlotte from now on.'

'All right then, Charlotte,' said Jessie, with a glance at Nellie who made no comment.

They changed into their kits and met on the pitch. The West Kent guards called over to them as they fixed the perimeter fence and watched the girls train.

'You girls all right?' said Alfie, running across to them.

'They don't need us in the factory any more today so we're having a kick-around to let off a bit of steam,' said Jessie.

'Good thinking, I reckon,' said Alfie, checking to see that they were all there and not hurt. 'Terrible business. Lil, is your face all right?'

Lily nodded.

'Look, it seems a bit off to say it now,' said Alfie uncertainly, 'but if you want something else to take your mind off it, there was something I was going to tell you at the wedding. I've fixed up a charity league game with the Tunnel Cement works, for July. I reckon you're up to it after seeing you play the other day.'

'Alfie, we think a couple of the girls on the B-team worked

in the nitro-glycerine hut. We don't know if they're all right,' said Jessie.

'What?' said Lily. 'Who?' she felt herself reeling.

'Didn't you know?' said Nellie. 'Jane and Petra worked in that hut. We just don't know if they were doing overtime yesterday.'

'But I carried two of those girls,' said Lily. 'I couldn't even recognise them, their hair had burned off, and one of them who died in the ambulance next to me, her eyes had burned out. It might've been Jane or Petra . . . oh my God.' Lily covered her mouth with her hands.

'Oh, God. I'll try to find out,' Alfie said, jogging away.

Lily didn't have it in her to play football any more that day.

'Come on,' said Nellie, 'let's go and get some bottles of stout; I think we need it.' She beckoned the team to come. 'You coming, Charlotte?' she said.

'Yes, if you'll have me,' said Charlotte, tagging along. They went to the village shop and bought two bottles of stout each.

'Where shall we go? To my hut?' said Nellie. 'It'll be a squeeze in my room.'

'Will your sitting room be available?' said Charlotte.

'We don't get a sitting room, milady,' said Nellie in a sarcastic tone.

'Ah, I see. Well then, come to my hut, if you like,' offered Charlotte. The others looked at her doubtfully. 'There's a sitting room with plenty of room, the others won't mind.'

Inside Charlotte's hut, the girls oohed and aahed at the luxury of it.

'Why don't *we* get this, then?' said Nellie sourly.

'All right, Nell, it's not her fault, is it?' said Jessie, sitting down on a leather sofa.

'Oh,' said the maid, coming in. She hesitated when she saw the workers there. 'Would you like some tea, milady?'

'Oh, no thank you, just some glasses for everyone, please.'

The maid bobbed her head but didn't look too pleased about having to bring anything for the factory girls.

The girls sat self-consciously on the edges of their seats, but when the drinks were poured, the conversation started to flow and they leaned back a little.

'Alfie won't know where to find us,' said Eliza, scratching her scarved head. 'He's gone off to find out about the girls.'

'Everyone's in a state; he'll understand,' said Lily. She finished off her glass of stout and poured another. Its effects were already helping her relax.

'I am just dumbfounded that this happened,' said Charlotte. 'I think the safety precautions here leave a lot to be desired. A lot.'

'Yeah, well, they don't care about the workers; they care about production, they make no bones about that,' said Nellie.

'I just can't stop thinking about it,' continued Charlotte. 'How much danger we are in. Some of it unnecessarily. I know the management are overworked, but still . . .'

'It's like being on the front line,' said Jessie.

'Yes, indeed,' said Charlotte. 'You know,' she went on with an embarrassed smile, 'I'm afraid I ran away to work in munitions.'

'What?' said Nellie, sitting up.

'Yes, I wanted to go to France to help my friend in a military hospital in Le Touquet but my mother wouldn't allow it.'

Lily remembered overhearing the argument Charlotte had had with Lady Harrington when she was dusting the library.

'So I just packed my things and came here. Not the most rebellious move, considering I am only a few miles from my family home. But I'm sure my parents are furious. And, since this came out, even more so,' she said, smiling and reaching for a newspaper on the table. She opened the paper to the right page and passed it to Lily. It was the local coverage of the football match. There was a large photograph of Charlotte with her foot on the ball, the moment before Lily had kicked it away from her. The caption read: *Lady Charlotte roughing it with the factory workers and doing her bit for the war,* as if the rest of them didn't matter.

'So you're just here to annoy your father?' said Nellie, taking the paper. Her face clouded over when she read the piece.

'Not exactly,' said Charlotte defensively. 'My mother said France is too dangerous for women. I wanted to prove a point by working here. I want to do my part in the war, just like you.'

'Just like me, eh?' said Nellie, with a strange smile. 'I doubt that.'

'I think this is an important time for women,' said Charlotte. 'The war has given us a chance to show what we're made of. I have to admit, even despite the explosion, that this war has given me a new lease of life, I don't know about any of you?'

'That's an insult to the people who died yesterday,' said Nellie.

'Is it?' said Charlotte. 'I don't think so.'

Lily thought she knew what Charlotte meant, but she didn't want to say in front of Nellie.

'Last year I marched for women's right to serve,' said Charlotte. 'Why shouldn't women be able to do their bit to defend the country?'

'You sound like a suffragette,' said Jessie, taking a gulp of her stout.

'What of it?' said Charlotte. 'I believe in suffrage, don't you? Emmeline Pankhurst has done so much for the cause.'

The room went quiet. Charlotte drained her glass. 'I don't know why people are so apprehensive about suffrage. We'd have a fairer and more civilised world if women had the vote.'

'The vote wouldn't make any difference to my life,' said Nellie.

'My Sid can't vote either,' ventured Lily. 'It's not just a woman's thing; it's about the classes too.'

'Yes, that's true, but as things stand, women can't vote at all. You know, I think you are all astonishingly brave. The work you do, your sunny attitudes. You really all are an inspiration to me.'

Lily didn't know what to say, and neither did the others because everyone stayed quiet.

'Well, cheers to that,' said Lily finally, and raised her glass. 'And here's to all the poor souls who lost their lives yesterday.'

Everyone raised their glass to that.

'I will say something. With my position at the factory, I'm privy to certain information that I am uncomfortable with. Certain information to do with wages and safety,' said Charlotte.

'Like what?' asked Jessie.

'Well, I think we should ask Mrs Hodges the factory inspector to visit again; there were certain things that Mrs Sparrow said I shouldn't mention. They change working practices so they don't have to pay women what they are due. They are so worried about upsetting the men's unions, but frankly, when women are doing the same jobs for half the wage men are on, it takes the biscuit to put them in unnecessary danger.'

Nellie frowned. 'You don't think you'll change anything, do you?'

'I don't know,' said Charlotte. 'I think there might be an opportunity here. As I said, I just can't stop thinking about it. But now's not the time, we're all exhausted.'

'Yes, I need my bed,' said Eliza, getting up to leave.

Lily trudged back to hut ten too and lay down on her bed.

'Post for you, Lily,' said Mrs Pratt, pulling the curtain aside and putting a letter on the end of the bed.

It was Sid's handwriting. Lily held the envelope to her face. His hand had touched the paper. She would have loved to see him now.

12 May 1916

Dearest Lil,

I'm sorry, love, they've sent us to France. I didn't get a chance to see you before we left. They promised us leave to say goodbye and I was going to surprise you but then there's this big push planned and they need men desperately so here I am. I'm with Dad, he's written to tell Mum. So now I'm Tommy Atkins and not Sid Pavitt any more, ha ha. Fully trained and off to the Western Front. I've even got my

Trench Orders handbook. I hope you can get down to see the boys soon, love. Give them my best, won't you? Tell them their dad's going to fight in the war. I'm joining the 10th Battalion, Essex Regiment, you can send letters there.

Your loving husband, Sid

It was the last straw. Lily slapped the letter down on the bed. It was too much to take in. Her Sid had gone to France and she hadn't even been able to see him off. Her nerves were strung tight. She should have felt more upset about Sid going but she didn't. Not when it was like she was on the bloody Western Front right here in Tilbury. She was in danger, she was part of an army of women in munitions work, directly supplying the forces, she had bombs dropped around her, explosions and devastation, she felt like she was part of the front line.

She went across to peep around Eliza's curtain. 'You got any brandy?' she asked. Eliza nodded her head and reached into her drawer for some. 'Sid's been drafted – he's in France and I didn't see him before he went.'

'Oh, Lil, what a bloody awful day.'

She gave Lily the bottle. It was what she needed. To numb her thoughts and get some desperately needed sleep.

14

Dearest Lily,

Just writing your name gives me a boost. You should see the mud here, there's no getting away from it. We get animal visitors in our uniforms and in the trenches, so we never get lonely. It's either hellish fearful or hellish dull but we're not allowed to rest and there's always talk of the big push. I think of you a lot. I hope you are safe at work and the boys are well with Mum. I've got a cigarette card with a picture of a munitions girl on it, saying what splendid work all you girls are doing. Here's a field poppy that I pressed for you. It's the only thing that grows here. They are the hearts of men.

Write to me soon, love,

Your loving husband, Sid

Lily sat on the train back to Corringham from Kent. She'd seen the boys for the second time since the Faversham explosion. The first time, she had asked Ada why she hadn't let her know they were all right. Ada had simply replied that there was no need, they weren't close enough to the factory to worry, that the teacups had rattled and the loose kitchen window had fallen out and nothing else. Lily wondered how the woman let it lie on her conscience. She must know she was being vindictive. The satisfaction of it must outweigh all else.

Twelve women and four men died in the nitro-glycerine explosion at Greygoose. Two of them had been found thrown into a ditch a hundred yards away. One of them had no remains at all. The funeral took place the Sunday after it happened. Lily and the other workers from the factory wore their uniforms and walked behind the hearses, which were draped with union flags and pulled by horses in regalia. The dead were buried in one long grave. Seeing the coffins lined up like that was horrifying. Both Jane and Petra from the B-shift football team had perished. Lily would never know if it was them she had carried – but she hoped it was. The thought that she had spoken words of comfort to them was important to her.

They looked for word of it in the papers but all they found was a very short piece entitled *Explosion at War Factory*, reporting that the casualties were not numerous, sixteen killed and forty-five injured. There were no details and no names or tributes. There could be no risk to public morale or workers' spirits. Even the company hadn't acknowledged the explosion or offered any reassurance to the workers. Apart from the new collection of injuries on view in the YWCA canteen, it was as if the explosion hadn't happened at all.

Of course, the girls went back to work as soon as they could. Eliza's words when she had first started rang in Lily's ears – *We just get on with things here.* The boys overseas still needed the ammunition, and they now included Sid and Gerald. Lily was even more intent on working hard in the factory.

Everyone was staggered to read that Kitchener had died. The boat he was on was blown up by a German mine. It struck a new reality into the workers' hearts. If the Hun could kill the mighty Kitchener, they could certainly kill their own boys. Lily wondered how Sid and Gerald had taken the news. They had been in France three weeks and Sid's letters had become less frequent. His tone had changed from cheery to sometimes brooding, and certainly not as jolly as it had been. He wasn't allowed to say anything about the fighting and she could only wonder exactly where he was and what he was doing. She often thought about whether he'd had to kill a German yet, and how much he would hate it.

Relations in the cordite shed had improved since the explosion. Charlotte wasn't such a foreign creature any longer, although Nellie and Jessie were still wary of her. Lily found herself comfortable in Charlotte's presence, and intrigued by her. She wondered what it must feel like to be educated and to have time for political things like women's suffrage. Charlotte had said no more about it since the day after the explosion when they'd all gone to her sitting room to drink their stout.

The B-shift team had decided not to carry on playing football. Losing Jane and Petra had been too much of a blow for them. The A-shift team had considered doing the same but in the end thought that they would continue, that they needed it too much for themselves. And so, for them, football practice continued with zeal and they trained hard, knowing that they would be up against the Tunnel Cement team in July.

When Lily got back to hut ten, there was a note from Charlotte asking her to go to hut one. Lily was tired and wanted to rest but felt a slip of excitement that she'd been invited. She was flattered to think that a titled lady like Charlotte had taken a liking to her. She washed her face and walked down to hut one. The maid let her into the sitting room where she found Charlotte on a sofa with papers sprawled all around her.

'Hello,' she said, distracted. 'Thank you for coming, do take a seat.'

'What's all this then?' said Lily.

'This is what I wanted to see you about,' said Charlotte, sitting up and taking out a cigarette. It was very daring for someone like her to smoke and Lily felt that she'd been let in on a secret. Charlotte offered the pack but Lily shook her head.

'I've been thinking a lot about the explosion and about conditions in the factory in general,' said Charlotte. 'You know, when I first started here, Mrs Sparrow seemed to be very pleased about it, and was, to my shame, rather fawning. She said she needed my help to keep the workers in order, and to make sure that the women kept in line with what the men's unions had dictated.'

'What do you mean, like not letting us set the machines?'

'Yes, exactly. To all intents and purposes, the women in the cordite shed do the same work as the men, with the exception of setting the machines. Now, I've been doing a little research and this is what I have discovered.' She gave Lily an apprehensive look. 'Last year the men's unions made a deal with the government that women would be forced out of their jobs at the end of the war. They don't want women doing the skilled jobs of the men and they don't want women paid the same as men. Putting two and two together, the management here at Greygoose is appeasing the unions by keeping on enough men to be able to break down the jobs into component parts so as not to pay women equal pay for equal work.'

'Yes, but the wages I get here are much higher than in service. I'm happy with the money. It does bother me that we're not allowed to touch the machines, though.'

'Well, the one goes hand in hand with the other,' said Charlotte.

'There's nothing we could do about it, though.'

'Isn't there?' Charlotte took a drag of her cigarette and put it out in the ashtray. 'It's not just the wages that I've been thinking about. You know, there are Factory Acts to protect workers but it seems that the Home Office has been waiving these Acts during the war in order to keep up with demand. As such, the long hours we do and the poor conditions are allowed. The factories, especially the private ones like Greygoose, get away with practically anything as long as they keep up production. Some of us are doing eighty-hour weeks with the pressure of overtime and suffering terrible accidents and illness to boot.'

What Charlotte was saying made sense but she seemed to be suggesting that it could change. To Lily this was a strange idea. Surely you just took your chances and got on with it and if you didn't like it someone else would have your job. And wasn't it unpatriotic to complain at all when there were men being slaughtered in the trenches? Lily felt uncomfortable. But she didn't want to say so – she was enjoying being in Charlotte's confidence.

'I'll ring for tea,' said Charlotte, picking up a little brass bell. When the maid brought the tea and Charlotte poured a cup and gave it to Lily, Lily tried not to smile too much. She wondered what Sid would say if he could see her now, being served tea by a lady in a posh sitting room.

'I know it seems inappropriate to complain,' said Charlotte, guessing Lily's thoughts. 'But this war, like nothing before it, is changing people's attitudes to women. Isn't it our duty to take advantage of this and do our little bit for the cause?'

Lily stared at Charlotte, not knowing what to say. 'But the suffragettes ... the flappers ... people don't take to them, Charlotte.'

'This is different,' said Charlotte, as though she had already considered that. 'This is the same cause by different means. This is all women doing their bit for the war, showing patriotism and bravery. There are women receiving medals for bravery shown in munitions accidents.'

'And it's not as if you get much choice when Mrs Sparrow threatens you with not getting a leaving certificate,' said Lily.

'Yes exactly, it's almost as if we are forced to do the work without complaint else leave without another job to go to. It's akin to men being shot on the front line for cowardice.'

Lily didn't think it was quite as bad as that, but the leaving certificate business did bother her, it was something Mrs Sparrow seemed to hold over them.

'And the hours – I've seen women fall asleep in the canteen rather than eat their meals,' said Lily.

'Yes, with this big push on now, it's all hands on deck to supply the front line, with no thought of how it's affecting the workforce. You know, I've read that some workers in other factories are pushing for three lots of eight-hour shifts instead of two lots of twelve hours. And it's been debated in the House of Commons but nothing has changed.'

Lily was impressed with Charlotte's knowledge and the way she talked about things. She felt herself getting caught up in it all.

'And women don't just have to do their jobs, they've got children to care for and older parents to look after and pay for, and all the housework to do as well,' said Lily. 'No wonder they're tired. I mean, look at poor Mabel.'

'I knew you were the right person to confide in, Lily,' said Charlotte with a smile, and Lily felt herself swell with pleasure. 'Look, I've had an idea. It's direct action and I want to know if you're on board.'

Lily's swell of pleasure dipped into a twist of fear.

'I've drawn up a list of demands and I want to send them to the factory inspector, Mrs Hodges. I think she should be our first port of call.'

'What?' said Lily, going cold despite the heat of the room.

'A list of demands – things we want to see changed,' said Charlotte. 'The things we've just been speaking of.'

'Demands? But I'll get the sack. I can't make trouble, I need this job.'

'I understand that, Lily, and I can assure you, you will not lose your job. I will present the demands and say that I have the support of the other workers, without naming names.'

'Oh, right,' said Lily, looking down at her hands in her lap, at her wedding ring wound with string. She inspected her fingernails, yellow from the cordite, and the livid rash on her hands and wrists. The thought that she would have any say about anything almost made her laugh. Women like her weren't listened to, they were just expected to get on with things and be grateful. 'What's the list?' she asked.

Charlotte pulled a piece of paper off the table and read it aloud. 'Reduce shifts to eight hours; have equal pay for equal work; improve safety and health with daily milk for workers to ward off septic teeth, seats while working where possible, a regular health inspection, gloves, masks and improved ventilation.'

'Blimey,' said Lily, 'that's a lot.'

'I know,' said Charlotte, frowning. 'Too much?'

'I don't know. Ladies like you are used to people listening to you ...'

'That's why I think this will work,' said Charlotte, with a grin. 'They wouldn't dare sack *me* and I am in a position to give you and the other girls a voice.'

15

25 June 1916

My dear Lil,

    Thank you for the football, it's given me and the lads a real boost. And your joke about the girls' football team, that was even better, we do laugh about it I can tell you. The thought of you girls tripping over your skirts after the ball. I sometimes have to stop and remind myself that you're still there, that I'm not in hell. Sorry, love, please write soon.

    Your loving Sid

'Hadn't you better call yourselves something?' said Alfie, in the Bull Inn. They should have been on night shift but there had been a fire in the cordite mixing hut and the factory had been closed temporarily. The football team had decided to take the opportunity to go for a practice. It was nearly the end of June and there was only a week before the big match with Tunnel Cement. Those from the cordite shed had gone on to the village for a drink.

'How about the Greygoose Angels?' said Marge, and everyone looked surprised that she'd spoken out first.

'Yes, I like that,' said Jessie. 'The Greygoose Angels.'

'I don't know,' said Nellie. 'I don't know if the company would allow it, we're supposed to be off the map, aren't we? What about The Tilbury Angels?'

'Angels sounds childish,' said Charlotte grumpily and Nellie raised her eyebrows at her.

'Sid sent me a dried field poppy from France,' said Lily. 'He said they are the only thing that grows over there. He said they are the hearts of men.'

'Our uniforms are trimmed with red,' said Mabel. The pain of the loss of her first husband flickered across her face. 'We could get red football shirts.'

'The Tilbury Poppies,' said Lily.

'Yes,' they chimed. 'The Tilbury Poppies.'

'What's wrong with milady?' said Nellie, looking at Charlotte.

'Don't call me that, Nellie,' she replied. 'I am just feeling a little exasperated about something.'

'Why don't you tell them, Charlotte?' said Lily. Charlotte had shown her the letter from Mrs Hodges, who had taken nearly a month to respond to their list of demands.

'Very well,' said Charlotte. 'You may remember after the explosion when we were talking in hut one's sitting room? Not you, Alfie, you weren't there. We were talking about the unhealthy and unsafe conditions in the factory and also how women are not given equal pay for equal work.' Alfie sniffed and put down his pint glass. 'Well,' Charlotte went on, 'I compiled a list of things that I thought should be changed in the factory, and I showed them to Lily and then I sent them to Mrs Hodges.'

'What sort of things?' said Nellie.

'Having masks and gloves and somewhere to sit down at work, things like that,' said Lily, not sure how the others would react.

'And equal pay for equal work, and shift hours reduced to eight hours, oh, and for workers to be provided with milk every day to help ward off septic teeth.'

No one spoke and Lily took a sip of her drink, and another.

'And what did she say to that, then?' said Mabel eventually.

'She has agreed to the milk and the masks and has ignored everything else,' said Charlotte. 'It's so frustrating. Mrs Hodges should be our ally but clearly she is weak and beholden to the Ministry of Munitions.'

'Can I ask you a question, Charlotte?' said Nellie. 'Why are you roughing it with the likes of us? Your kind don't do this work. We *have* to work, we haven't got a choice.'

'Don't you trust me, Nellie?'

'Well, it's just that we get it from all sides, don't we?' said Nellie, returning Charlotte's glare. 'At work it's Mrs Sparrow threatening us with the sack without a leaving certificate; at the colony it's the matron telling us off for being noisy; when we're out and about, it's the copperettes spying on us, taking us home if we're a bit drunk or swearing or, heaven forbid, having a cuddle with a boy. They are all a better class like you, controlling the likes of us. But at the end of the day, we are risking our lives doing a dangerous job – probably the most dangerous war job, after the Tommies on the front line – and now you're telling us you're on our side?'

'She is, Nellie,' said Lily. 'Give her a chance, will you?'

'Yes, I can see that now, Nellie,' said Charlotte. 'However, ultimately, all of these processes are put in place by men, don't forget. Men in government at the Ministry of Munitions.'

'Men like your dad?' said Nellie.

Charlotte stiffened. 'My father is not in Government. But, yes, men like him make the rules and have the power to stop progress for women.'

Nellie nodded, as though satisfied by what she'd heard. Charlotte had a point to prove to her father, and Nellie must have thought it would work to the factory girls' advantage in some way. The mention of Lord Harrington, though, made Lily clutch up with anxiety. And it deepened her desire to see something done that he wouldn't approve of.

'Don't mind me, will you?' grumbled Alfie.

The women looked to Charlotte and waited for her to deal with Alfie's discontent.

'Alfie, may I ask you something?' said Charlotte.

'Depends what it is,' he said, sitting up.

'Would you say that the girls here do good work at the factory?'

'Course they do.'

'Are you surprised by that?'

He shuffled uncomfortably in his chair. 'Look, when we first started getting all the girls in the factory I wasn't happy about it. None of us were. Yes, they work hard and I see that, but we're worried about our jobs, aren't we? You can't blame us for that.'

'Yes, but were you surprised by how hard the women work and what they are capable of?'

'Yes, very surprised.'

The women exchanged glances and smiles.

'Don't you think they should be able to do their jobs fully, to become skilled workers and be paid appropriately?'

'Now, Lady Charlotte, you're asking me something there, aren't you? It's not a straightforward thing. The unions tell us what to do so we can protect our jobs. But you ask me if they should or if they could do the skilled work? I say yes to both.'

'Oh, Alfie, you little blinder,' said Jessie, slapping him on the back until his face cracked into a grin.

'And the equal pay?' said Charlotte.

'Now that's something else, Lady Charlotte,' he said, rubbing his neck and squirming in his seat. 'You mean for the war or after the war?'

Charlotte hesitated. 'Let's say, for the duration of the war, they would be trained as skilled workers and be paid the same as their male counterparts.'

Everyone stared at Alfie, waiting to hear what he would say.

'I say, it wouldn't happen in a hundred years.'

The women groaned theatrically. Lily could see they hadn't expected him to say yes. But, it was good to hear him say they were capable of doing the skilled work and that they should be trained properly.

'Don't get me wrong,' he said. 'When they tell me not to let you girls touch the machine settings, I don't agree with it, but I have to go along with it or the other lads would see me off.'

'And it's not just that. Mr Nash tampers with the machines to make it look like we can't do the work.' Everyone looked at Mabel. Lily remembered her hinting at it the day she started in the cordite press. It kept going wrong when Mr Nash said he'd fixed it.

'Alfie?' said Lily. His face reddened and he took a lug from his cigarette, looking away.

'What?' he said crossly. 'Do you think I have any say in what Mr Nash does?'

'So it's true?' said Charlotte. 'He deliberately sabotages the girls' work?'

Alfie shrugged, not committing himself. 'I don't do it,' he said.

'I didn't mean to say you did it too, Alfie,' said Mabel. 'But Mr Nash has got it in for us.'

'Well, I just told you how some of the men feel about the girls in the sheds. But not me, not any more.'

Lily gave Alfie an encouraging smile. It was important to hear things like this; it was good of him to confide in them.

'We set the machines ourselves before, though, didn't we, Alfie?' said Mabel. 'That time you came and checked it and it was all right?'

'Yep and I told you off for it, didn't I?'

'What would you think if I told you we've been doing it ourselves every now and again since then?' said Mabel with a cheeky grin.

He smiled and shook his head. 'It doesn't surprise me any more.'

'Is this true, Mabel?' said Charlotte.

'True enough; ask the others.'

Charlotte looked at the others nodding their heads. 'Well,' she said, with a big breath in, 'it looks as though we have a case on our hands.'

'A case?' said Marge shyly.

'Yes, a case to put to Mrs Sparrow. You have shown you

are doing the skilled work of a press hand and you should be paid accordingly. Plus, I would like to see our other needs met that Mrs Hodges has deemed unimportant.'

'You want to go up against Mrs Sparrow?' snorted Jessie. 'I wish you the best of luck.'

'No, Jessie,' said Charlotte. 'I would like all of us to put our case to Mrs Sparrow, not just me.'

'But having you speak with us would make sure we are heard,' said Nellie, nodding, almost to herself.

'Exactly,' said Charlotte seriously.

'Well, bloody Norah, I reckon we should do it,' said Nellie, sitting up and banging the table with her hand.

Lily smiled uncertainly. With Nellie and Charlotte joining forces, anything could happen. But hadn't Charlotte said she would present the demands without naming the workers behind them?

'Right, well, ladies, I wish you the best of luck, but you know I can't be in this with you, don't you?'

'Yes, dear Alfie, thank you for confiding in us,' said Charlotte. 'It means an awful lot.'

Alfie touched his cap and left. The women watched him go.

'It is truly shocking that Mr Nash is sabotaging your work,' said Charlotte.

'You wouldn't be able to prove it, though,' said Lily.

'Probably not. And we have enough to go on now,' said Charlotte.

'I need to tell you ladies something,' said Nellie. She looked down at her lap and frowned. 'And when I do, I don't know if you'll still want to know me, but it looks like it's the time to be honest with each other.'

'What is it, Nellie?' said Lily, touching her friend's hand, wondering what on earth could be the matter. Nellie frowned and drew her hand away.

'It's about what I was before I came here,' she said to her lap. 'I told you I was a flower girl in London, remember?' She looked up to see the girls nodding. 'Well, that's a lie. I wasn't a flower girl. I got into trouble when I was younger, I didn't have a family to speak of and I had to fend for myself the only way I knew how.' She started to cry. Lily looked at Charlotte, who had gone pale. No one spoke and Nellie pushed back her chair to leave. Lily was shocked. The thought that Nellie had been a prostitute repelled her, but the fact that she'd been driven to do it because she'd had no other option overshadowed everything else. Lily knew what it felt like to have no choices in life. She gripped Nellie's arm.

'It's all right, Nellie, you did what you had to. I'm not gonna sit here and tell you you're bad.'

'Nor me,' said Mabel. 'You're a dear friend to me and I don't care about your past.'

'Me neither,' said Marge meekly. 'I think you're wonderful, Nellie.'

'Same goes for me,' said Jessie. 'You hold your head up, Miss Nellie.'

Nellie looked at them through her tears with disbelief. Lily wished Charlotte would say something.

'I got on the training for this job in London,' Nellie went on. 'It took six weeks and didn't pay enough to live on, but I did it and when I came for the job, Mrs Sparrow couldn't deny me it because I'd trained. But she knows what I was and she holds it over me, threatens to tell people what I am, threatens to get rid of me if I make any trouble or corrupt any of you girls.'

'What in damnation!' It was Charlotte. She stood up in a fury and spat the words, banging her arms against her sides. 'Blast that woman, how dare she?'

Nellie looked up at her in complete surprise, her face breaking into a smile, which turned into a laugh. Lily and the others joined her, laughing at the sight of Charlotte in a rage. The lady's wrath melted and she sat back down. 'Don't let Miss Harknett find out about this, she'll have kittens,' she said, chuckling.

'How about we put maternity needs on that list of yours?' It was Jessie, suddenly serious. 'Seeing as we're all being honest.'

'Yes, I think that's a super idea,' said Mabel.

'What's this?' said Charlotte. No one had told her about Jessie's condition.

'I've got myself in a bit of trouble, too,' said Jessie, with a weak smile.

'Oh. I see,' said Charlotte, visibly shocked and looking at Jessie's stomach, which she was covering with her arms. 'And have you told Mrs Sparrow?'

'God, no. She'd have me out. But I can't stop earning yet, I need the money.'

'And what changes would help you at work, particularly?' said Charlotte.

'I don't know. Maybe being able to change jobs so I'm not breathing in fumes in the danger area. And a nursery in Goosetown would mean I could still work when the baby comes.'

Charlotte looked excited. 'Yes, these are exactly the things we need to ask for. Why should women have to make do any more?'

'Do you really think they'll agree to it, Charlotte?' said Jessie in wonder.

'I don't know, but I believe we should present our list of demands to Mrs Sparrow and if she refuses, we shall seek the support of a women's work union and go to tribunal.'

'Blimey,' said Nellie, sitting back and running her hands over her head. 'You don't do things by halves, do you?'

'She won't let you join a union,' said Mabel. 'A girl in guncotton joined one and she got the sack.'

'But surely that's not allowed?' said Charlotte.

'Mrs Sparrow has her own rules,' said Mabel. 'She doesn't care what's allowed and she knows the women here need their jobs.'

'Look, let's just see what she says first,' said Nellie. 'She might be all right about it.'

'Here's to that,' said Lily, raising her glass and clinking it against the others'. The booze had gone to her head, but the sentiment around the table felt very real to her. These women were strong and her friends and she wanted to be involved in this. The idea that Sid wouldn't approve or that it was wrong to complain during the war or that she was getting in above her head, she shoved to the back of her mind.

It was eight o'clock and the bell rang time. 'I won't get used to these war hours,' said Nellie. She seemed more relaxed, and not just because of the drink.

As they left the pub, they saw a young woman being for-cibly escorted away by a copperette. It was a good example of what they'd been talking about and it resonated strongly for Lily; she had a new perception of the way women like her were treated. They just wanted to be allowed to get on with their jobs and have a bit of fun but they were disciplined like children because of their class.

They talked about their list of demands as they walked to the edge of Corringham village, and headed off over the marshes towards Goosetown, not wanting to wait for the light railway.

'Let's add a girls' club to the list, where we get to say how it's run,' said Jessie. 'I'm fed up with those moralising YWCA women who don't let us do what we want.'

'Yes, good idea, and can we put down that the training for this job should be properly paid so we can all afford to do it? That would open up this work to people like me who want to make a new start,' said Nellie.

'Yes, a super idea,' said Charlotte. 'Although you know why the training isn't paid well? It's because they would rather have women who won't need the job at the end of the war.'

A deep and distant rumble of artillery fire came to them in the quiet night. They all paused for a moment. It was the third night they had heard it. Jessie's sweetheart had told her it was a five-day bombardment in the Somme area of France, in preparation for the big push that everyone in munitions had heard about over the past few months. It was the reason they had all been doing overtime. The explosions they heard were very likely blasts of cordite that had passed through their own hands.

'Kill the Hun,' said Mabel, to no one in particular.

'Oh, Sid,' whispered Lily. 'Please God, keep him safe.'

*

The next morning they would ordinarily have been sleeping off the night shift but as they had an unexpected day off, those who had been in the pub made the bold decision to go to see Mrs Sparrow with their list. Charlotte led the way, with Lily, Mabel, Nellie, Jessie and a reluctant and frightened Marge tagging along behind.

'Shouldn't we have asked to see her first?' said Lily, feeling nervous.

'Strictly, yes, but I thought we'd use the element of surprise,' said Charlotte.

They threaded their way through the factory works and into the administration building in the safe area. Charlotte looked back at the others and then knocked at the door.

Mrs Sparrow opened it, a shadow of shock passing across her face momentarily before she quickly gathered her wits. 'Lady Charlotte?'

'Good Morning, Mrs Sparrow. I am sorry to come unannounced but could we possibly come in to have a word about something important?'

'All of you?' she asked, looking past Charlotte to see who was there.

'Yes, if that would be all right?' Charlotte kept her tone professional and clipped and Lily wanted to cower behind her.

'Very well, come in,' said Mrs Sparrow, waving them in with a look of impatience. The six women crowded into the office. Charlotte declined the offer of a chair and stood next to Lily with the others. 'What is this all about?'

'Mrs Sparrow, we are very worried about our safety and health here at the factory. There are a lot of accidents and injuries, never mind the recent explosion. There have been numerous accidental explosions around the country, and I imagine a lot more that haven't been reported in the press. Add to that the ever-present danger of Zeppelin raids.' She paused to take a breath. 'We wish to give you a list of ways in which our lives as valued workers would improve immeasurably.'

Charlotte's voice trembled slightly but she kept her nerve. Lily put her hand discreetly on Charlotte's back to encourage her.

'A list?' A wry smile formed on Mrs Sparrow's lips. She looked down at her hands clasped on her desk and thought for a moment. 'And may I see this list?'

'Yes, here it is,' said Charlotte, passing it to her.

'Thank you,' she said. The women looked on as she scanned the document, her eyebrows rising ever higher as she read. 'I see,' she said, setting it down on the desk. She gave a little cough behind her fist and gathered her thoughts.

'As you know, I am your welfare supervisor. You have come to the right person with your concerns. However, I feel at this important time of war, your demands are rather too, shall we say, insignificant in the face of what must be our most important priority – to maximise production for our boys on the front line. Now, I am sure you understand that I am very busy . . . ' She stood up to show them the door. Lily and Marge shuffled to leave but the other women didn't move.

'Excuse me, Mrs Sparrow, I am not entirely sure you understand the importance of this list. If you would be so kind as to consider each point carefully and address it?' said Charlotte, a hint of anger in her tone.

The welfare supervisor gave a sigh of impatience and an

insincere smile. 'Of course, Lady Charlotte,' she said, sitting back down. 'Now then, *full training in current job and equal pay for equal work,*' she read. 'I don't know where to start with this one,' she laughed. 'For one thing, do you mean to put our men here at the factory out of work? They are here because they have been injured in the course of duty or they cannot enlist for some reason. Do you mean them to be unemployed and unable to feed their families?'

'Of course not, what a ridiculous suggestion,' said Charlotte, causing Mrs Sparrow to look up at her sharply. 'We only mean that the jobs some of the women are doing are partially trained jobs, as a means of not paying them the equal pay of men doing the same work. Why not train them fully and pay them what they deserve? Surely it is their right as a worker?'

'Do you mean to say we are flouting the Factory Acts and Ministry of Munitions regulations here at Greygoose, Lady Charlotte? That would be a serious accusation indeed.'

'Yes, Mrs Sparrow, that is exactly what I mean to say, for it is the truth.'

Mrs Sparrow broke the stare between the two women by looking back down at the list. '*Better provision for maternity problems.* Now, I must say I find this point very intriguing. Is there a maternity problem amongst you that I should know about?' She looked around at them all. Something on Jessie's face must have betrayed her because the supervisor's gaze lingered upon her, and travelled downwards to her stomach.

'Not necessarily, Mrs Sparrow,' said Charlotte. 'But we do feel that if a woman should find herself with child, she should be able to transfer to the safe area to protect her health and that of her unborn baby. Also, we feel that some provision for infant care in Goosetown would be an admirable example to set to other munitions factories.' Charlotte looked at Lily, who nodded her agreement but was unable to speak for fear of being cut down by the welfare supervisor.

'Oh, do you? Do you indeed?' Mrs Sparrow seemed to suppress a yawn and looked down at the list again. '*Better safety inspections of the factory.* Really, girls, do you not think that the manager has safety considerations as a priority here? This is really too much. Please, I must be getting on. Please, if you will ...'

When Charlotte turned around, her face was a picture of stony indignation. She allowed herself and the others to be ushered out of the office and she led them out of the administration building and through the factory gates without saying a word. She didn't stop to check the train times at the little station but proceeded to march across the marshes towards Goosetown.

'Mrs Sparrow does not have our best interests at heart,' she said angrily. 'She's more of a management spy than a welfare supervisor. She wants high productivity above all else, including our safety and our right to a fair wage. We don't need to join a union to go on strike,' she went on as she marched. 'There was a non-unionised strike by women in a Leeds factory. Mrs Sparrow will soon understand the importance of these issues when production is halted. I don't mean to affect supply of ammunition to the front line. It won't be for long, I can assure you. They will soon sit up and listen to us. The men go out on strike when they want to, why shouldn't we? And if that doesn't work we shall join a union secretly. Mary

Macarthur champions women workers – she's the secretary of the National Federation of Women Workers. I'll be shop steward, if no one else wants to,' she added. 'We'll go to tribunal if necessary.'

Lily and the others trotted along after her. Lily was angry too. She believed that the things they were asking for had validity and deserved proper attention and Mrs Sparrow had practically ridiculed them. They hadn't even had the chance to mention the other two demands that weren't on the list: the training pay and the girls' club. The welfare supervisor had dismissed them out of hand, she had belittled them. With Charlotte marching ahead like a general of war, Lily felt empowered. She'd been belittled all her life. She didn't know if halting production was the right thing to do given the situation in France, it most likely wasn't, but as Charlotte said, it wouldn't be for long, and it would make them all sit up and listen. She looked across at Mabel and Nellie, at Jessie and Marge, and the four friends nodded back at her; they were all thinking the same thing.

16

30 June 1916

My Dearest Lil,

    Our Battalion has moved up the lines. We're going into the firing line tonight, ready for whatever is coming very soon — I can't tell you, you know that, don't you? Dad is champing at the bit. We've seen what the Hun are doing and he wants his moment to teach them a lesson, God bless him. I shall need my rum ration, I tell you that. Dearest Lil, I love you. Pray for us and I know we'll make it through and be back to see you and Mum and the boys in no time. Thank you for the cake, it went down well with the lads. We ate it quick before the rats got it. If the rats were German they'd have got us by now — lucky for us they are French. You weren't joking about the football? Well, I'll be blowed. Keep up the good work, love, and keep your chin up.

    Your Sid x

'I wish the pub was open,' said Lily. She and Charlotte had come off shift at six o'clock on a bright and blue Sunday morning. As they waited for the train to take them to

Goosetown, Lily's thoughts were too strong to be drowned in the crowd of workers around her.

'Are you all right?' said Charlotte.

'I got a letter from my Sid yesterday. He said it's the big push in France soon and he'll be in it. Everyone's saying it started yesterday and I haven't heard anything yet. I wouldn't mind a drink before bed.'

'I have some wine in my room,' said Charlotte, leaning in to whisper in Lily's ear. If the police patrols had heard her they might have told Mrs Sparrow.

'Yeah, go on then,' said Lily with a grateful smile.

In her lavish room, Charlotte opened the wine and poured some for Lily.

'It's the football match today. That should take your mind off other things for a moment.'

'Yes, I should think so,' said Lily, taking the glass. 'Funny that you're serving me, isn't it?'

Charlotte paused as she poured a glass for herself. 'Yes, I suppose it is, rather.' She smiled.

Lily took two long gulps. 'Do you remember me coming into your room to make your fire? Or were you always asleep?'

'You were very quiet – most of the time I was asleep, I think.' She blushed. 'I'm sorry I mentioned to Mother that you had dropped the dustpan; I didn't mean for her to say anything to Mrs Coker, I had just made a passing comment.'

'Well, pour me another and I'll forgive you,' said Lily, feeling deliciously tipsy already.

'You know something?' said Charlotte. 'I am really very glad we met on a more equal footing.'

'Me too,' said Lily. 'Cheers to that.' They clinked glasses. 'Maybe we should be blood sisters.'

'What on earth do you mean?'

Lily laughed. 'As kids, we'd prick our fingers with a pin and put them together so our blood mixed. Then we'd say we were blood sisters with someone not in our family. It's like a special bond.'

'Oh my goodness. I'm not sure I like the sound of that very much. But, there is something I've been thinking about doing. Maybe we could do it together, as a blood sister alternative?'

'What is it?'

Charlotte paused for a moment, as though unsure whether to say it. 'I want to cut my hair.'

'What, short?'

Charlotte nodded. 'Yes, I've seen some girls doing it. No one at this factory has, but some girls in London.'

'Oh blimey, Charlotte. What would my Sid say if he saw me with short hair?'

'He might like it,' laughed Charlotte, tipsy too. 'But, after all, it is *your* hair, not his.'

Lily wondered how she would look with short hair. She'd always had long hair pinned up, just like everyone else.

'Unless you're not up to it, it's quite all right,' said Charlotte slyly, with a wicked grin.

'It might be nice not to bother with pinning it up all the time, and it'd be easier for work where we're not allowed pins anyway ...'

'That's the spirit. What do you say?' Charlotte got up to rummage in her dressing-table drawer. She took out a pair of ornate silver nail scissors and held them up.

'Now?' said Lily, blanching.

Charlotte shrugged. 'I'm game if you are?'

'All right, then,' said Lily, with a giggle. 'You do mine first, then I'll know how to do yours.'

Lily sat on the dressing table stool with Charlotte standing behind her. Charlotte pulled out the long metal pins from Lily's bun, letting her orange-tinged hair fall down her back.

'Right, here goes,' said Charlotte nervously. Lily heard the snip as a piece of her hair was sliced off. Charlotte held it up for her to see. They both shrieked and laughed and Charlotte carried on. 'The scissors are tiny, it might take a while,' she said. She cut round from the bottom of one ear to the bottom of the other, Lily watching all the while in the looking glass. She saw herself transform from housemaid to modern girl, her past life dropping to the floor strand by strand. When Charlotte had finished they both fell silent as Lily touched her hair, smoothed it from the top and felt it end abruptly at the nape of her neck.

'God, Charlotte, what do I look like?'

'I like it,' said Charlotte. 'I can't wait for you to do mine.'

'It feels so light,' said Lily, standing up and taking the scissors. Charlotte sat down and Lily took a breath. 'One minute,' she said, reaching for her glass of wine and taking a gulp.

'That does not inspire confidence, Lily,' said Charlotte, laughing and reaching for her own glass.

Lily started cutting Charlotte's auburn hair, nervously at first and then with courage. It gave her a strange sense of power to cut Charlotte's hair and there was also the sense that they were going forward to new frontiers together.

All women had long hair, except for the few Charlotte had seen in London, and a picture of a woman ambulance driver in France that Lily had seen in the paper. Women never cut their hair, unless they'd been really ill. It was the men who had their hair trimmed. Lily and Charlotte would look like the men. And that gave her a strange sense of power too.

When Lily finished cutting, Charlotte stared at herself in the mirror.

'Yes, I like it,' she said. 'I'm glad.' She turned to face Lily and the two of them laughed at their conspiracy. 'It's called a "bob", you know, this style.'

'I know a bloke called Bob,' laughed Lily. She held up her glass. 'Blood sisters,' she said.

'Blood sisters,' said Charlotte.

They finished the bottle of wine. Lily hadn't ever drunk as much. Her speech was slurred and she couldn't stop touching her hair and looking at herself in Charlotte's mirror.

'That bloody Mrs Sparrow,' said Charlotte. 'I've a good mind to write to the Ministry of Munitions about her.'

'Let's break into her office and look for evidence,' said Lily, with a drunken cackle.

'What evidence?'

'I don't know, we might find something in there that she hides from the workers. Some reasons about why we're not paid fairly, or something.'

'Shall we?' said Charlotte, leaning forward towards Lily, her eyes sparkling with mischief.

'Come on.' Lily laughed and stood up to get her coat on, but one of the sleeves was inside out and she turned round and round on the spot trying to get her arm in, like a dog chasing its tail. She settled on having just the one arm in, and followed Charlotte out through the door.

'How will we get past the guards on the gate?' she whispered as they made their way through Goosetown and across the marshes in the bright sunshine towards the factory works.

'I'll have a word with the police constable on duty,' said Charlotte. 'They all know me now. I'll simply say I left something important in my locker in the change room.'

'All right,' nodded Lily, tripping over some ivy.

When they reached the gate, Charlotte turned to Lily. 'Let me do the talking,' she said. She saw Lily's sleeve and turned it out for her, the two of them in a fit of whispered giggles trying to get Lily's arm into her coat.

'Good morning. Lady Charlotte, is it?' said one of the women constables, stepping forward. 'Goodness gracious, have you cut your hair?' she said, staring.

'Yes, it's the new bob hairstyle, have you not seen it in London?'

'No, I don't believe I have,' said the constable, her face a picture of confusion. 'And how may we help you?'

'I seem to have forgotten something from my locker, if we may pop in to get it?'

'Yes, yes of course,' said the constable, giving Lily an equally strange look as she waved them through.'

The two of them walked as carefully down the road as they could, neither of them speaking, until they got to the change room and bundled inside, letting out muted screeches of laughter.

'Right, quieten down,' said Charlotte. 'Let's creep over to the administration building. There'll be no one there now on a Sunday.'

They crept across the road, hunched over and trying desperately to stifle their giggles, reached the administration block and pushed open the door. They found Mrs Sparrow's office, all in darkness, and closed the door behind them.

'We're in,' gasped Lily.

'Let's be quick,' said Charlotte, going to rifle through the papers on Mrs Sparrow's desk. 'You look in there,' she told Lily, pointing at a filing cabinet.

Lily pulled open a drawer and squinted to see inside. There was so much paper. She pulled something out and peered at it. There were lots of numbers and money signs and she couldn't make out what it was, so put it back. The next paper also had money signs and numbers but Lily made out that it was a list of workers' wages.

'Look,' she hissed, and handed it to Charlotte.

'Eureka,' said Charlotte. 'It's a list of wages. Look, look at what the men are earning – nearly twice as much as the women. That's no surprise, I suppose, but let's see, what's Alfie's surname?'

Lily concentrated hard, trying to remember. 'Dunn. Alfie Dunn.'

'Right,' said Charlotte, scanning the pages with her finger. 'Alfred Dunn, here we are, he's earning four pounds, six shillings a week and you are earning how much?'

'Two pounds, two shillings, plus overtime,' said Lily.

'Yes, this is what we need. Can you find a piece of paper so we can write some of these down?'

They set to copying down some of the figures and then carefully replaced the papers in the cabinet.

'I don't know what Mr Nash has got to be so miserable about, the money he's on,' said Lily, and pulled out a document about accidental explosions in British factories. 'I knew it,' said Charlotte, reading over her shoulder. 'There have been dozens of unrecorded explosions and deaths, just look at those figures. Can you write some of them down too? Do we have time?'

Charlotte picked up a book from Mrs Sparrow's desk. 'Look at this: The Welfare Supervisor's Handbook,' she read from the front. 'This is most interesting,' she said, flicking through the pages.

'Come on, I think we should go now,' said Lily, her heart racing at the thought that they might be discovered at any moment.

'Yes, just a moment. Her remit is widespread, there are sections on wages, strikes, leisure, machinery, morality, health . . . Oh my goodness, look at this: "If a girl is pale and withdrawn, she may be suffering from the habit of masturbation. The advisable treatment for the affliction is a series of cold baths, a reduction of meat in the diet, a forbiddance of tea and coffee, plenty of exercise out of doors." Good grief.'

'Come on, let's go,' said Lily.

Charlotte replaced the handbook and they both snuck away, via the change room so as to be seen coming out of it if challenged, and back through the factory gates, saying goodbye to the constables there.

They trudged back across the marshes to Goosetown. Lily suddenly felt exhausted from the excitement and the wine and sobered by the office break-in. She desperately wanted to be in bed. It was already half past eight and they would have to leave for the football match at three.

'What was that about, suffering from what did it say?'

'Masturbation?' said Charlotte, looking embarrassed.

'What is it?'

'It is something the suffragettes talk about. It's about women's sexuality, about pleasuring oneself.'

'Oh,' said Lily, not knowing what to say.

'The puritanical view is that it is something sinful to be punished. The suffragettes believe that this is another way that women are oppressed, that women should not be made to feel ashamed of their bodies.'

'Oh,' said Lily again. 'But it's good that we saw the wages, isn't it?' she went on, keen to change the subject.

'Oh, yes, it is rather. It gives us more ammunition to form a protest. In fact, I am going to write to Mary Macarthur's union about our case, what do you think?'

A deep boom rumbled over the marshes towards them from France. Lily's mind turned to Sid and her stomach sickened at the thought of him there on the front line. She closed her eyes and prayed for him.

'Lily?'

'Yes, I think you should, you should write to the union.'

Lily woke with a sore head and a dry mouth and wished she didn't have to play football today. She was glad she'd written to the boys to tell them she wouldn't be coming to visit – she'd rather face football than Ada with a head like hers. She'd seen the boys last week and although it was lovely, she had come away with a sense of detachment. So much had happened since she'd started working at Greygoose that she felt like a different person. But of course she had smiled and cuddled the boys and gave them presents as though nothing had changed. In a flash she remembered earlier that morning and put her hand up to feel her short hair, wondering what everyone would say about it, imagining Ada's horror the next time she went to visit.

Had she and Charlotte really got drunk and broken into Mrs Sparrow's office? She groaned. It was lucky they hadn't been caught. She closed her eyes and said a prayer for Sid, willing him to be safe. Perhaps she would get a letter from him today to let her know he was all right. She wasn't sure if they were allowed to write letters from the firing line, though.

In the canteen she swallowed a cup of tea as though it was good medicine and poured herself another. She watched as a post woman came into the canteen, spoke to one of the YWCA ladies who nodded and took something from her. The lady stared down at a telegram in her hand and walked slowly back over to the serving hatch. Silence fell as teacups were put down and everyone in the hut watched her.

'Elizabeth,' said the woman, calling a friend to her side, who put an arm around her shoulders while she opened the letter. As she read the words, she uttered no sound but her knees buckled, her friend trying to stop her from falling. Several of the workers rushed over to help, getting the lady to a chair. Lily tried to move but couldn't. She watched the scene play out with a terrible shroud of panic over her. The women took the lady out of the canteen hut and away somewhere, perhaps to hut one to lie down. Lily left her breakfast, peeled herself off her chair and wandered in a daze back to her room to get changed into her kit.

At half past two, the team, wearing their new red jerseys, piled into the back of a hired open-top charabanc with Alfie and were driven to the Tunnel Cement football ground in West Thurrock, followed by a line of supporters in various types of vehicle ranging from horse-drawn bus to motor car. The Tilbury Poppies were in a gay mood, excited and nervous about their first league game, which was also their first away game.

'I can't believe you've done that,' said Jessie, staring at Lily and Charlotte's short hair. 'You look so different, it's strange.'

'I might do it too,' said Nellie, grinning. 'I'd like to look like a modern girl.'

'Nellie, you *are* a modern girl,' said Charlotte, laughing. 'A football-playing munitionette wearing shorts.'

When they got to the ground, they saw the laid-out pitch with two stands full of people. Another layer of fear settled upon Lily's already nervous state for Sid.

'Right,' said Alfie. 'This is our first proper game; let's just stay in it without getting too carried away with nerves. Remember to defend our goal and if you get any chances, take them, but keep it on an even keel and you'll do all right.'

They ran on to the pitch and got into position. Lily and Charlotte were up front and planned to try to pass and shoot together. The Tunnel Cement girls wore white jerseys and grey shorts. They looked like a friendly bunch and Lily suddenly caught sight of her old friend Mary, the housemaid who had left St Clere's to go and do war work. She waved to catch her attention and Mary ran over.

'Lily? Is it really you?'

'Yes,' said Lily, grabbing Mary's arm. 'I'm overjoyed to see you.'

'So you left St Clere's?' said Mary, with a look of expectation.

'Yes, I did. For the same reasons you left, Mary.'

Mary squeezed Lily's arm. 'Poor dear. You're working in munitions now?'

The referee blew a whistle to signal they would soon start and Mary smiled at Lily and ran back to her team calling out, 'Good luck.'

Play started cautiously, with Tunnel Cement passing at the back. Eliza from the Poppies took it away and got it over to Marge, who made a short pass to Lily. Lily ran forward but had it taken by Tunnel Cement. Charlotte seemed impatient and made a run towards the goal, shot and scored. The Greygoose workers cheered from the sideline and Lily ran over to her friend.

'Jolly good show, old thing,' she said, making fun.

Play became faster and Tunnel Cement picked up the pace, shooting towards the Poppies' goal but Mabel saved it and kicked it out. The crowd was lively and loud. Nellie streaked down the field and passed to Lily, who took a shot. It bounced off the bar and rolled over the line and Lily's heart leapt with joy. She wanted to jump up and down on the spot, but settled for a dignified trot over to Marge, who patted her on the shoulder. At half-time, Alfie was jubilant. 'Keep this up, girls. You're doing a fine job, a very fine job. Jessie, your defence is super, keep it up.'

Jessie beamed and drank her cup of water. Lily wondered

how Jessie was doing it, she was four months' pregnant and no one would have guessed – she must have been trussed up tightly into her corset. When the whistle blew they ran back on. Lily felt exhilarated; all she could think about was where the ball was. Tunnel Cement came back with gusto and scored, the home crowd cheering wildly. The Poppies managed to keep them off until the end and they had it, a two–one victory. They patted the Tunnel Cement ladies on the back and ran over to Alfie, who had taken off his hat and thrown it into the air.

'Topping!' cried Charlotte, out of breath, her face red with exertion. 'Simply topping!'

They clambered back into the charabanc and sang their way home to Goosetown, asking to be let off in Corringham for a celebratory drink at the Bull Inn. Nellie pointed out a table of old men who were nodding over at them with looks of disapproval.

'They can't work out if you two are women or men,' laughed Nellie at Lily and Charlotte's short hair. She was merry with drink by then and stood up to perform 'Knees Up Mother Brown', kicking up her bare knees in her football shorts, which caused the men at the table to open their eyes widely. The other girls joined her, even Charlotte, all singing and kicking up their bare knees.

Alfie sat at the table and laughed. 'Come on, you don't wanna be kicked out of here, do you?' he said.

Worn out, they made their way back to Goosetown on the Corringham Light Railway.

'I could sleep for a week,' said Lily dreamily, leaning into Charlotte's shoulder as the carriage rocked them across the marshes.

They said goodbye to Charlotte, who went into hut one – Lily, Marge and Eliza trudging onward to hut ten. Mrs Pratt the matron was waiting for them by the door. Her eyes scanned the girls and fell on Lily's face. In a split second, Lily looked from Mrs Pratt's face to Mrs Pratt's hand. In it she held a telegram and the warmth seemed to drain from Lily's body all at once. She let out a tiny sob as Mrs Pratt handed it to her.

```
Deeply regret to inform you your
father-in-law G. M. Pavitt Pvt 2537
has been killed on active service
deeply regret to inform you your
husband S. J. Pavitt Pvt 2538 injured
in service gunshot wound left
shoulder letter follows shortly
```

'Oh dear God ... Gerald ... oh God he's alive ... Sid's alive,' sobbed Lily and the women crowded around her, murmuring unheard words.

17

2 July 1916

Dear Mrs Pavitt,

I am writing to you about your husband Private Sidney Pavitt. I am a nurse here in the hospital in France and your husband is unable to write. I am very sorry to say that your husband was shot in the left shoulder in the course of duty on the first of July in the Somme region of France. His injury appears to be clean and should heal well, however he is incapacitated and will be sent home to England to recover. I must report that your husband is rather shell-shocked. I understand you have been informed of your very unfortunate loss of your father-in-law, Private Gerald Pavitt. Mr Pavitt, senior, died bravely on the front line serving his King and country. I will try to let you know of any further particulars as they arise.

Yours faithfully
Nurse Streatfield

The day following the telegram, Charlotte granted Lily leave of absence to travel to Nettlestead to see Ada. She went with a heaviness that was hard to bear. Poor Gerald, shot down by the Hun.

Ada's sister Dolly opened the door. She stepped forward to embrace Lily, and showed her inside.

'She won't come down,' she said. 'She won't eat or get out of bed.'

The boys came to Lily, looking in her bag for treats. She hadn't brought anything and they complained. 'Do they know?' she said.

'Yes, of course.'

'Come here, boys,' said Lily, holding out her arms. They came to her, sensing the sadness of the occasion. 'What do you know about Granddad?'

'He got killed by the Hun and he's in heaven,' said Robert.

'Yes, that's right. Your granddad died a brave soldier fighting for us, for his King and his country. We are all very, very proud of him.'

Little Joe put a hand on Lily's knee and looked up at her.

'I'm going up to see Nanny now. You stay here with Auntie Dolly.'

Lily trod the steps of the stairs slowly, hoping not to wake Ada if she was sleeping, hoping she wouldn't have to see the dreadful pain on the woman's face. When she opened the bedroom door, Ada lay flat on the bed with the blanket drawn up to her chin despite the warm weather. Her open eyes swivelled to see Lily come in.

'My dear Ada,' said Lily, rushing to the bedside. 'I'm so awfully sorry. Poor, poor Gerald.' She took Ada's hand but Ada drew it away from her.

'I suppose you're satisfied now?'

Lily started back. 'Ada?'

'He's dead. You'll be satisfied now.' And she turned over in the bed to face away from Lily.

Lily stood pinned to the spot. Ada may as well have pushed a knife through her heart to say such a thing. But what could Lily say? She couldn't comfort her like this.

'I'll come back in a few days, Ada,' she said, her voice trembling. When there was no answer, she left the room and went back downstairs.

'I'll make us something to eat,' said Lily, needing to do something practical. She had bought some bread and cheese on the way and set to work getting out some plates. 'How are you coping with the boys, Dolly, with Ada laid up?' She asked the question with hesitation. Despite the desperate grief in the house, the terrible tragedy falling over them like a thick suffocating blanket, she almost couldn't bear to hear the answer. It might mean her leaving Greygoose.

'I like their company,' said Dolly. 'They are good boys.'

Lily gave her a small smile and said nothing more. She would leave it at that. If Dolly needed her to take the boys, she would say so. Lily cut the bread, the sharp serrated steel cutting through the soft crumb like a bullet slices through a shoulder, like an artillery shell slashes through a breathing body. She gripped the handle to steady herself, waiting for the question.

'Have you heard from Sid?' said Dolly.

The mention of his name made Lily tremble. He was alive, she was lucky. She wasn't lying in bed unable to eat like Ada, although she easily could have been. He was safe, she would see him again. Ada wouldn't even be sent Gerald's body to bury.

'No, but a nurse sent me a letter saying he's in hospital in France. He's been shot in the shoulder but it should heal well. He'll be sent home to get better. We'll be able to see him.'

'There, there,' said Dolly coming to put her arm around Lily's shoulders. 'We all thank God for sparing Sid. He'll see you and his boys before long.'

Lily gave her a grateful nod and wiped her nose on the back of her hand. She put the plates on the table and they sat down to a pensive meal.

On the train back to Goosetown, Lily wondered whether she should have stayed in Nettlestead for the time being to look after the boys while Ada was in mourning. She felt she should have made it her responsibility to do so but something had stopped her suggesting it to Dolly. It was reckless of her but she needed to go back to work. She didn't want to be in Nettlestead with the boys. The realisation made her go cold and she wondered what kind of mother it made her. But Dolly would have asked her to stay if she was needed. The thought of being around Ada for any length of time was awful. The depth of the woman's grief scared Lily – she didn't have the strength to be around it. If Sid had died, the thought of being in that state frightened her. She wanted to go back to where she felt she was a part of something else.

The matron of hut ten passed Lily a note when she returned home.

Mrs S has threatened to sack Nellie. We strike tomorrow. Come to hut one. C x

Lily sat heavily on her bed. So they were going out on strike. Well, so be it. They wouldn't let Mrs Sparrow fire Nellie. They had the power to do something about it. The insignificance of it all compared to what had happened to Gerald made it easier to accept, less fearful than going on strike might normally have been. She walked down to hut one and found Charlotte in her room with Nellie, Jessie, Marge and Mabel.

'How are you?' said Charlotte, standing up to greet her. 'Have you heard anything more?'

'I've been down to see Ada and the boys. Ada's in a terrible state. I got a letter from a nurse looking after Sid in France. He'll be coming home to get better. He'll be all right.'

'Oh, thank goodness,' said Charlotte, and the others echoed the sentiment. 'Do you feel like doing this? It's just that Mrs Sparrow has been particularly unpleasant to Nellie today.'

'She said she's got the power to sack me for immoral behaviour, that she's been wanting to get me out since I started, and now with the demands we made, she's got good reason. Plus she said all these things about the women police reporting to her that I've been out drinking and behaving immorally, like she's been gathering evidence since we went to see her with our list.'

'Well, we'd better do something about it then,' said Lily, buoyed up by being involved in something other than worrying about Sid and the boys. 'After all, if it weren't for me and Charlotte talking about demands she wouldn't have said anything, so it's up to us to help.'

'It's up to all of us,' said Jessie. 'When do we ever get to have our say about anything? The old bat deserves being stood up to.'

'We thought it had better be just us for now,' said Mabel. 'Just our pressing room. We don't want to involve any other workers yet, in case they lose their jobs over it.'

Mabel looked determined but worried. What if they did all lose their jobs over it? Lily thought it was worth the risk. She'd never been able to stick up for herself before.

'Marge? What about you?' Lily asked Marge, who as usual sat on the fringes quietly.

The young girl nodded. 'Yes, I'll do it but I'll not tell Mother. She wouldn't allow it.'

'Splendid,' said Charlotte. Lily looked at her new friend. She was resplendent in this role, as though she'd been born for it. But Charlotte could never understand what this meant to the rest of them.

'If you'll pardon my rudeness, Lily, I think I know what you're thinking,' said Charlotte. 'You're thinking I don't understand what this means to all of you. Am I right?'

Lily gave an embarrassed nod.

'You're right, how could I fully understand what this means to you all? It's bound to mean something different to me, but we're united in our desire for change and I think that will carry us through.'

Lily nodded and smiled. She hoped that was enough to keep them all out of too much trouble. After all, Charlotte had a safety net that the rest of them didn't have.

The following morning, Lily woke up as usual and went for breakfast in the YWCA hut. Her stomach was full of nerves. They had agreed to meet outside the factory gates. When everyone was there, they walked down the road together, past the change hut without getting changed and on to the cordite sheds. Once outside their shed, they stood together and waited. They were all anxious. Poor Marge looked like she wanted to run away.

Miss Harknett came along in her uniform and stopped short when she saw them all there. 'What on earth is happening?' she said. 'Has there been an accident?'

'No, Miss Harknett. We are out on strike,' said Charlotte.

Miss Harknett's face was a picture of confusion. 'Pardon me? Lady Charlotte, I thought you said a strike?'

'That's right, Miss Harknett. Now perhaps you might like to go along and fetch Mrs Sparrow.'

'Oh my word,' she said, blanching white with shock. 'Oh my word.' She hurried away towards the safe area, looking back to check that her eyes hadn't deceived her.

'Right, girls, we shall stick to our guns,' said Charlotte, standing tall.

Lily took a deep breath for courage and stood up straight. She felt as though they were awaiting an ambush and when she saw Miss Harknett returning with a furious-looking Mrs Sparrow, skirts flapping with the speed of her approach, she almost wished she had a real gun with which to defend herself.

Mrs Sparrow stopped before them, a glaze of anger overlaying her usual sardonic expression. 'Now then, what in the wide world do we have here?' she asked, keeping her voice at a normal volume.

Charlotte took one step forward. 'Mrs Sparrow, we are out on strike, in protest at our demands for safety, health and fair pay not being met.' And she took one step back again.

Mrs Sparrow eyed Charlotte and stepped towards her. 'Is

that so, Lady Charlotte? And, may I ask, have you expressed these demands in the order you find personally important? Safety, health and fair pay in that order?'

Charlotte shifted uncomfortably. 'In no particular order, Mrs Sparrow. All of our demands are of equal importance.'

'I see,' said Mrs Sparrow, with a small smile. 'Most interesting. And may I ask, Lady Charlotte, if you were ever involved with the suffragettes and their vulgar movement?'

'What if I were, Mrs Sparrow? It is of no consequence here, except that we are empowered by the knowledge that women can stand up and speak for themselves.'

'Indeed? And who exactly do you mean by *we*? You surely don't think the workers here believe you are on their side?' She gave a cruel smile and looked at the other girls. Lily felt sick.

'We are all in it together, Mrs Sparrow,' said Nellie, speaking up.

Mrs Sparrow directed her attention to Nellie, walking to stand before her. 'Is that right, Nellie? You know I'm very surprised to see you here.' She gave a little laugh. 'I thought you liked working at Greygoose. I mean to say, it is rather a step up for you, dear, is it not?'

'You know it is, Mrs Sparrow, and so do all my friends here.'

'Oh, your friends? It surprises me that they would want to associate with the likes of you, Nellie, when they know where you have been.'

'That's enough of that.' Lily was startled to hear herself speak up in Nellie's defence.

'So, the housemaid is out on strike with her former employer, is she?' Mrs Sparrow stepped over to Lily. 'I suppose all of this makes you feel important, does it? Do you think about emptying the morning slops from Lady Charlotte's chamber pot and consider gleefully how lucky you are now to be shoulder to shoulder with her?'

Lily didn't answer but ground her teeth, loathing this woman who was trying to shame her.

'And with your poor husband lying injured in a hospital in France? What would he think about all of this, I wonder? Would he turn to his fellow comrades in arms and say how proud he is of his wife demanding more money when our boys are being slaughtered in their thousands on the front line?

'And Mabel Jiggens here too?' she said, turning away from Lily. 'My, my, what a morning this is. I do wonder why you would wish to jeopardise your livelihood when you have so many mouths to feed, and living in a house in Goosetown too. Where would you live, my dear, if you lost your job here?'

'You can't threaten us like this, Mrs Sparrow. I must say, your scare tactics are astonishingly unprofessional,' said Charlotte.

Mrs Sparrow wasn't put off. She shrugged and smiled and moved on to speak to Jessie. 'I am still wondering, Jessie Baker, why you are all so keen on reforming maternity rights here. Do I need to speak to a certain West Kent fusilier?'

Jessie avoided the welfare supervisor's gaze and looked fixedly at the ground.

'Miss Harknett,' said Mrs Sparrow, 'be a dear and fetch the police patrols from the factory gates, would you? Please tell them we have some agitators who need dispersing.'

Miss Harknett paled and rushed away towards the gates. Mrs Sparrow paced slowly along the line of women, looking into their eyes.

'Mrs Sparrow, we have the evidence we need concerning the pay level for women doing the work of men, amongst other things. And we mean to see our demands met,' said Charlotte, who seemed to Lily a little less forthright than she had been the night before.

Mrs Sparrow ignored her and stepped towards Marge, who was quivering with fright next to Lily on the end of the line. The woman stood in front of the girl, who couldn't raise her eyes to meet those of Mrs Sparrow. 'And Marge Cuthbert. I am especially disappointed in you. What would your poor mother think of all of this?' Marge started to whimper and cry. Mrs Sparrow gave a big sigh of disappointment.

'Mrs Sparrow, I must insist that you stop bullying these workers, it is really quite unacceptable,' said Charlotte. 'I shall write to the Ministry of Munitions to report your unseemly behaviour.'

Mrs Sparrow turned away from them, not deigning to grace Charlotte with her gaze. The welfare supervisor watched, as they all did, the women police patrols approaching down the road towards them.

'Lady Charlotte, if you think I will not write to your father to express my deepest regret in your being employed here, you are mistaken.'

'How dare you threaten me so?' spluttered Charlotte angrily. 'As though I am a child to be disciplined.'

'Constables, if you would please disperse this unpleasantness. The workers may either go and get changed and report

for work immediately or see me in my office for their papers.'
With that, Mrs Sparrow turned and walked away.

Lily looked at Charlotte and the others for a sign as to
what to do.

'It's all right, girls, I know exactly what to do,' said
Charlotte. 'We have rights as employees and she will not get
rid of us so easily. We shall go and change into our uniforms
and get to work and we shall continue our protest by other
means once we have regrouped. Stand down, constables, we
mean to comply peacefully,' she said to the police constables,
who seemed relieved not to have to forcibly escort a titled
lady off the premises.

18

14 July 1916

Dear Mrs Pavitt,

I write to advise you of your husband Private Sidney Pavitt's progress. He is currently resting in a hospital in Le Touquet, France, and I expect he will be in England in around ten days. His shoulder wound will heal given proper rest. He is writing letters but refuses to have them posted and his state of mind has been affected by nervous shock. Do not expect him to be fully restored when you see him but thank God that he is alive and that you will see him soon. He has served his King and country well and had tried to protect his father, who alas lost his life, as you know.

Cheer up
Yours faithfully
John Frennant, 2Lt Essex

On the horse bus Lily couldn't stop looking at her hands. She laughed at herself trying to rub away the yellow discolouration. She knew it wouldn't come off, but what would Sid say? She wanted to look nice for him, even nicer than he might remember her looking. She had worn her munitions uniform and of course her hair was cropped, but she thought he might see something different in her eyes, a new self-assurance that would make him sit up and cock his head to one side like he did, and then he'd frown a bit and then he'd smile.

A telegram had come from the War Office saying Sid was in England and had been sent to Orsett military hospital. It was a stroke of luck that he'd been placed so close to home. Just a train to Grays then a bus to Orsett. Lily was on pins at the thought of seeing him. She couldn't wait to tell him properly about everything that had happened since they'd last seen each other. Her new job and her new wages, of course, but moving into the colony and how dangerous the job was, and the Zeppelin raids, not to mention the excitement of the strike. She wouldn't say it all at once, it would be too much for him to take in; he'd be so worried about her, he wouldn't understand at first that working in munitions was one of the best things to happen to her.

Lucky for him that his injury wasn't too bad. She kept thinking about what would happen once he was out of hospital. If he'd need to rest somewhere, or if he'd be sent back out to France. She felt guilty at the thought that she might have to leave the colony to look after him and wondered whether he'd be better off staying with Ada and the boys. She shook her head. Getting him better was the first thing.

The bus stopped in Orsett village. Lily asked the way and followed the directions until she came to the outskirts of the village, passed some fields where she saw an old farmer and a young woman haymaking under the July skies that threatened more rain. In long skirts and with her sleeves rolled up to her elbows, the girl bent to slash the grass with a scythe. The man moved slowly in obvious discomfort, stooping to make one slash for every four of hers. Lily carried on down a dirt lane to a collection of buildings with a large chimney in the centre that made up Orsett workhouse. It made her flinch. As a child, it had been her mother's constant threat if Lily didn't work hard. A section of the workhouse infirmary had been converted into a military hospital for wounded soldiers. She thought about making a joke with Sid about ending up there after all.

She was shown from the main entrance to the hospital wing. Stopping at the door, she looked down at her new shoes and took a deep breath, pulled her tunic straight and pushed open the door with her chin held high. It was a large ward with union flags draped on the walls and iron bedsteads lined along each side and also a line of beds back-to-back down the middle of the room. There were perhaps forty beds in all, each with a grey blanket with a red cross on a white square sewn on to it. Nurses in light blue uniforms and crisp white aprons and caps moved about the room. The men lay in their beds, some with bandaged heads or limbs, some with bandages across their eyes. No one approached her so she started to walk down the room looking earnestly for Sid, turning away quickly from each man that wasn't him. It didn't feel decent to stare at a strange man in his bed, and although she was morbidly interested to see their injuries, she didn't want to embarrass anyone.

'Pardon me,' she said to a passing nurse. 'Could you tell me where my husband Sidney Pavitt is?'

She could hear a strange sound and realised it was the

soft whimper of a man crying. She looked away from the dear thing – how awful for him. The nurse directed her to a bed and she saw with horror that the sobbing man was her husband. She rushed to his bedside, aware of the onlookers. Sid's left arm was strapped in a sling and the corners of his mouth seemed to have dropped unnaturally. She took his other hand, which was stiff and swollen. He cried openly, as if he was crying instead of looking or instead of smiling, like it was the natural way of things. He didn't meet her eye, instead his gaze seemed fixed on something far away and she looked behind her to see what it was but realised his stare was blank and unfocused as though the very life had been pulled out of him.

'What is it, Sid? What's happened?'

He made no answer but loosened his hand from hers and put it to her face and wiped his fingers across as though he was a blind man making sure it was her. She gave an awkward smile and glanced at the man in the next bed, who was staring at his newspaper with glazed eyes.

'What is it, dear? What on earth's the matter?'

Sid's sobs calmed. He wiped his nose on his cuff and took on a sudden look of urgency. His fingers reached for the button on the collar of her tunic. He fiddled with it until it came undone. She pulled back, embarrassed, and reached to do it back up again but Sid frowned and pushed her hand away, pulling at her tunic. A nurse appeared, dragging a screen on wheels and pulled it around one side of the bed. She leaned down to Lily and said quietly into her ear, 'Try to discourage him, dear.' And then another nurse brought a second screen and pulled it round until Lily and Sid were hidden from view. Sid didn't seem to notice and was pushing the bed sheet back from his lap.

'Can't you wait till we get home, Sid?' said Lily in a whisper, knowing the screen only blocked the view and not the sound. He made no reply and pulled her roughly by the arm, grimacing at the pain of his injury. Lily started to cry. 'Please, my dear, don't do this. Please.' She pushed down on his good arm with both of her hands and held it there. He frowned, seemed confused, and then he settled again into his former passive state. Lily suddenly retched at an awful stench. He had soiled himself. She pushed through the screens and called a nurse.

'I'm sorry, he needs . . . he has . . . soiled the bed.'

'Oh, it's quite all right,' said the nurse in a well-spoken voice. 'We'll get you cleaned up in no time, won't we, Sidney?' The nurse winked at Lily and went off for some cleaning things and sheets. 'Doctor wants a word,' she said when she returned, and gestured to a man speaking to another nurse who wore a grey dress with a scarlet cape and a large white cap. Lily walked down the ward, shaken by the sight of Sid in such a state. Nothing could have prepared her for it.

'Mrs Pavitt?' said the man. 'Dr Palmer.' He shook her hand. 'And this is Sister Edwards.' He walked them to the foot of the room and spoke in a low voice. 'I'm awfully sorry we didn't greet you before you saw your husband. I'm sure it must have been a shock for you.'

Lily nodded and bit her lips together, not trusting herself to speak without crying. Dr Palmer looked at some notes on a clipboard. 'Your husband has been with us just two days. His shoulder injury is healing well but it will require further rest before he is assessed for service. As you can see, he is also shell-shocked. This condition is something that is not fully understood but has been seen with some regularity in this war. We do not yet know if he is a permanent ineffective and will be invalided out or if he will recover his faculties sufficiently well. Shell shock is thought to be a sign of emotional weakness, a lack of moral fibre, if you will, and the best advice is to speak to him as you normally would . . . to show sympathy . . . but your husband must be persuaded to face his nervous shock in a manly way to preserve his reputation as a soldier and so on . . . '

Lily stared at the doctor, hearing his words but not fully understanding. He seemed to be saying that Sid had suffered a kind of nervous breakdown because he was weak-minded. It didn't make any sense. Her Sid was strong; he was as strong as a horse.

'Symptoms vary between cases. Your husband has anxiety, he is generally mute, but will have sudden bouts of anger and then quieten down again. He has uncontrollable diarrhoea. He more than likely has headaches and hypersensitivity to noise, perhaps tinnitus, perhaps dizziness. And he has the typical thousand-yard stare where he seems to have an unfocused gaze. I advise coming often to see him, but do speak to him normally, as I said, and hopefully that will bring him round. Now, if you will excuse me . . . '

'Yes, Doctor; thank you, Doctor, thank you, Sister.' Lily managed to express her gratitude and was left by herself. She wanted to run out of the door, to give herself time to take it all in, but she was there and the men were looking at her, as if they needed her to be strong for them all, to carry on just as they had to do. She walked slowly back to Sid's bed. The nurse was tying the dirty sheets into a bundle.

'All done.' She smiled and left them alone within the screens. Lily perched on the edge of the bed.

'Hello, my dear,' she said, swallowing hard. 'It's your Lil come to see you.'

She waited for a flicker of recognition but he just stared ahead with those awful haunted eyes. She wondered what he had seen to put him in such a state and whether he'd ever tell her about it.

'I couldn't wait to see you,' she said, making up her mind to chat to him normally as the doctor had advised and wishing the tears would stop running down her cheeks. 'It's a bit of luck you being in Orsett, isn't it? I thought it was funny how you ended up in Orsett workhouse after all.' The joke fell dead in the air and she wished she hadn't said it. 'It was a joke; this hospital is in part of the workhouse, they've taken it over for the war, that's all,' she said, not wanting to add to his worries. She wanted to say how sorry she was about Gerald but she thought it best not to talk about anything upsetting.

'The boys are well,' she said. 'They are so proud of their dad. I wonder when they'll be able to see you. That's a good reason to hurry up and get better, isn't it?' She cast around for something to say, trying to keep her nerve. 'What do you think about my uniform then? And my hair? I'm a proper munitions girl. And you know what? We beat Tunnel Cement in a football match – I scored a goal. But it's dangerous at the factory, and they don't do what they could to keep us safe. And they don't pay us fairly either. Guess what? Me and Lady Charlotte are friends now, can you credit it?'

She chewed the inside of her cheek and looked at Sid. He had closed his eyes and she couldn't tell if he was asleep.

'I'll leave you to rest, Sid dear.' She kissed him on the cheek and left, keeping her eyes fixed to the floor and gritting her teeth until she got outside in the lane where she started to run. She ran until her lungs gave out and she stopped and sat on the grass verge with her face in her hands and she cried for Sid. Her poor, gentle, strong Sid, who had been left behind in France, and this ghost of a man who was now her husband.

19

On a muggy August evening, Lily made her way to the cordite shed for work. As she stepped through to put on her rubber overshoes, Mr Nash hurried over to her.

'You're to report to Mrs Sparrow in her office,' he said, curt and grumpy.

'What's wrong with you?' Lily was surprised to hear herself say it in such a tone but the man had been objectionable ever since she'd started. 'Apart from not wanting women in the factory, I mean.' She gave him a sarcastic smile and he started back.

'I know what you're up to,' he said. 'You and those others causing trouble here. It's bad enough you're taking our jobs, but you want our wages too? It's disgusting.'

'Well, at least you've had the knackers to say it out loud,' she said and took off the rubber shoes and went out to the administration block in the safe area. It was over a month since they had attempted to strike and they had all kept their heads down. Lily had been preoccupied with Sid anyway.

She knocked on Mrs Sparrow's door and wished Charlotte

was there with her. She didn't know if she was equipped to defend herself.

'Good morning, Lily,' said Mrs Sparrow, the ghost of a smile on her lips. 'Please take a seat.'

Surprised, Lily sat down and mumbled a good morning.

'How is your husband faring?' asked Mrs Sparrow pleasantly.

'Not too well,' said Lily. She'd been back to see Sid twice more since that first shocking time and he'd been in the same state. 'But he'll pull through,' she added, not wanting to give Mrs Sparrow any ammunition against her.

'Now then, Lily, you must know that it is within the remit of my job to keep production going with the workers' welfare in mind. As part of that remit, it is my responsibility to smooth out any troubles that may occur and avoid any unpleasantness that may take the form of protest or strike action.'

Lily stared at her and nodded.

'I understand your concerns about the working conditions and pay here at the factory but there is only so much I can do. My hands are tied to a great extent by management, by Government demand, and so on. However, I am willing to offer you an olive branch in the form of a promotion if you agree to desist from any further agitation.'

'Oh?' Perhaps Mrs Sparrow thought they had been regrouping and causing unrest in the factory since the last time she had spoken to them. She was clearly trying to make sure her factory was free of disrupting influences.

'I will see you are promoted to charge hand in one of the workshops in the safe area of the factory. It will mean a higher wage for you and you will no longer need to worry about working in unhealthy conditions.'

Lily looked at the woman. What she was offering was tempting – more money and a safer job. It was what they'd been asking for in the strike.

'No thank you, Mrs Sparrow,' she said. And the conviction with which she said it was like she had been reborn. Her chest swelled with strength and her eyes stayed steadily on Mrs Sparrow's.

'You are sorely mistaken to refuse this chance,' said Mrs Sparrow, her thin veil of cordiality fading. 'What on earth do you think you will achieve by going against me?'

'Not against you, Mrs Sparrow, against unfairness for workers.'

'So be it. You will report to the nitro-glycerine hut in the danger area where you now work. And you are on very thin ice. If there is any more trouble from you, you will be out on your ear. Good day.'

Lily didn't deign to answer her. How dare she think Lily would take a bribe and leave her friends to their fate? She had heard about the nitro-glycerine hut, it was where they mixed the acids. She'd seen the acid burn scars on some of the workers in the canteen. That vile woman was trying to get rid of her by making her want to leave of her own accord. She had been split from her friends in the cordite shed. Well, she would show her. She'd just bloody well get on with it.

She found the nitro-glycerine hut in the danger area. The inside of the hut was lined with concrete walls and floor. Cement partition walls separated large round vats standing about three feet high. The women there wore long white overalls and black rubber boots.

'I'm to report here,' she told one of the women who was hosing the floor with water. The woman called the foreman over.

'Lily Pavitt, is it?' he said. She nodded. 'I've heard about you. I won't have any trouble in here. Come with me and I'll get your uniform.'

When she was kitted out, a woman called Penny showed her how to stir the vats with an ivory stick. The particles of acid in the air landed on her face like tiny lit matches, burning her skin. She winced and rubbed at her cheeks but every time she stirred, she'd jump at the tiny dots of pain.

'I'd say you get used to it but you don't really,' said Penny, stirring the vat next to her. 'We have to change our overalls once a month because of all the acid burn holes on them.'

'It's horrible,' said Lily. 'I can't stand it.' Her overall already had some tiny brown specks on it. She wanted to rub her eyes but daren't touch them with her hands.

'It rots your hankies and gets in your throat,' Penny went on matter-of-factly.

'Haven't you asked for masks and gloves?' said Lily.

'Oh, yes, I've heard about you. Aren't you the troublemaker from cordite?'

'Yes, didn't you go on strike or something?' said another woman, Freda.

'Only to ask for better working conditions and fair pay,' said Lily.

'Fair pay? Don't you think you get paid enough? Greedy cow,' said Freda.

'Equal pay for equal work. Why should men earn double the pay of women when they're doing the same job?'

'Who do you think you are, asking for more money when there's a war on? It's disgusting, I can hardly believe my ears,' said Freda, looking around at the other women for their agreement. She put her hose down and marched towards Lily, her face angry and menacing. 'My husband is missing in the Somme, and you're here going on strike?' She poked Lily in the shoulder.

'Get off me,' said Lily, poking her back. 'If you weren't such a fool, you'd realise that what we're asking for will benefit you in a fair way, but you're too stupid to see past your own nose.'

'You little . . . ' Freda pulled back her arm and slapped Lily's face. Lily was so shocked she stood there with bulging eyes.

'Go on, Freda, get her,' someone shouted. But before Freda came at her again, Lily slapped her back and then they were pushing and pulling each other's overalls to try to get the better of each other. Freda yanked Lily's cap off and pulled at her hair, making Lily screech with pain, and Lily kicked at Freda's shin, making the woman go down on the wet floor. Lily jumped on top of her and held her down until the foreman stepped in and separated them.

'In trouble already, is it?' he said, pulling Lily up by her arm.

A boy suddenly appeared at the door of the shed and shouted, 'Air raid.'

Lily shook herself free of the foreman's grip and ran out of the door. She didn't stop to see where the girls from nitroglycerine sheltered but made for the factory gates and out to the haystack hoping to see some of her friends.

She was the first one there. There was no sign of the raid in the sky yet and the realisation of what had just happened hit her as though Freda had slapped her face again. She thought she might cry but didn't. Instead, she curled her lip and wanted to jump back in the fight again. The stupid woman. Couldn't she see that what Lily and the others were doing was right, that they were risking their jobs to make things better for everyone? Even despite the war, they were all in danger here at Greygoose; why should their lives be endangered more than necessary? And Charlotte was right about the pay. It did seem inappropriate but it was worth fighting for.

Jessie and Mabel came running across the marshes and flopped down by the haystack next to Lily.

'Lil, you're here, where have you been?' said Jessie, out of breath. Before Lily could answer, Charlotte came too.

'Oh, there you are,' she said. 'What is it? You looked wretched.'

'I don't know where to start,' said Lily. 'Mrs Sparrow called me to her office to try to bribe me with a promotion if I stopped with the protest.'

'No, that old bag,' said Mabel. 'Did you take it?' she added.

'Course I didn't. Then when I said no, she said she's putting me in the nitro-glycerine hut from now on and if I make any trouble I'm out.'

'Oh, that vile woman,' said Charlotte. 'She's splitting us up.'

'And then the girls in nitro-glycerine started calling me a troublemaker and I got into a fight with one of them. And then it was the air raid,' she said, taking a breath.

'You got into a fight?' said Charlotte, shocked.

'Did you win?' said Jessie, laughing.

'Where's Nellie and Marge?' said Lily with a grin at Jessie.

'Haven't you heard?' said Charlotte. 'They've sacked Nellie, she's gone.'

'They've sacked Nellie?' said Lily, feeling sick.

'Yes, Mrs Sparrow said she has proved herself undesirable for work here and she sacked her.'

'So she won't get a leaving certificate then?'

'Worse than that,' said Mabel. 'She's going to prison.'

'What?'

'It's all rather delicate, I'm afraid,' said Charlotte. 'Poor Nellie was given the choice of prison or work in munitions when she was found guilty of prostitution in London. It was the courts who sent her on the munitions training course and that meant Mrs Sparrow couldn't refuse her the work, on the condition that she didn't find herself wanting.'

'Oh dear God, poor Nellie,' said Lily. 'So, she was the bravest of all of us, protesting when she knew she could end up in prison.'

'Yes,' said Charlotte.

'It just makes me more determined to see it through,' said Jessie.

'Me too,' said Lily.

'Where's Marge, then? What's Mrs Sparrow done to her?' said Mabel.

'Don't know,' said Jessie. 'I haven't seen her in cordite.'

'How are you getting on?' said Lily, nodding at Jessie's growing belly.

'I'm managing with a corset at the moment,' she said. 'But I won't be able to hide it from work much longer,' she added.

'Your Edward deserves to know, Jessie. He might do the honourable thing,' said Charlotte.

Jessie shrugged and looked away, which made Lily wonder whether she had told him but hadn't got the response she'd wanted.

'Oh, some good news,' said Charlotte. 'The union wrote back to me. They will fully support us and have arranged a tribunal. The date is set for the eighteenth of November.'

'Oh well done, Charlotte, that is good news,' said Lily.

They sat there by the haystack watching the searchlights play across the sky until the siren sounded for the all-clear. Lily went back to the nitro-glycerine hut, steeling herself for more trouble. She took up her ivory stick and began to stir the acid, scrunching up her face to lessen the surface of skin available to the burning particles in the air.

Penny came over to her and Lily braced herself.

'Don't worry about Freda, she has a crack at everyone who starts in here,' she said.

'Oh, how nice,' said Lily.

'Look, I'm interested in what you were saying about masks and gloves. We should have them in here; it's terrible, it really is. We don't mind doing our bit for the war – of course we're proud to do it – but they could do more for us than they do here at Greygoose.'

'I know,' said Lily. 'It's the same in the cordite shed. We pass out from the fumes in there, and look how I've turned yellow. There must be a way of making it better.'

'Well, look, I'll talk to some of the girls. I think you're all right.'

Lily smiled and carried on with her work, wondering how she could make a makeshift mask for now until they could add it to the list of demands.

Around four hours into the shift, the door opened and Marge came in wearing the white overalls and rubber boots.

'Marge!' said Lily, going over to her. 'Has she put you in here too? I'm glad we're together.'

'Yes,' said Marge meekly. 'I'm in here too.'

'You all right? You look like your dog died.'

'No,' said Marge in the quietest voice. 'I'm all right.'

20

Two weeks later, a letter arrived for Lily telling her that Sid had been moved to the auxiliary military hospital at St Clere's Hall. She didn't much like the thought of going back to the Hall but was glad that Sid had made enough of an improvement to be discharged. She was on nights that week and able to visit Sid during the day. He was much closer now, just a half-hour away. She took the Corringham Light Railway and then walked the short distance to Stanford-le-Hope. Approaching the Hall, she couldn't muster the courage to go in through the front door and took the servants' entrance instead. Inside, she passed two maids she didn't know, saw Mr Tween the cook, who glanced up from his mixing bowl with indifference, and then ran into Mrs Coker on the stairs.

'Pavitt? What on earth are you doing here?' said the house-keeper, looking Lily up and down, taking in her new hair and clothes and smart boots.

'Hello, Mrs Coker. My husband is a patient here; I've come to see him.'

'Well, use the front door from now on; you are no longer

a member of staff.' The woman continued her descent down the stairs without a word of sympathy or well wishes.

At the top of the stairs, Lily pushed through the green baize door into the vast hallway. She found the hospital set up in the library. There must have been twenty beds in there. It was unrecognisable. Hospital kit and apparatus everywhere, a man with one leg on crutches being helped to his bed, nurses tending patients at their bedside, a man with his eyes bandaged dictating a letter. One of the nurses saw Lily and came over to her. With a start, Lily realised it was Lady Harriet, Charlotte's sister.

'Hello, Lady Harriet,' she said, stopping herself from curtseying.

Harriet frowned for a second and then smiled with recognition. 'Ah, Mrs Pavitt, we've been expecting you. It must be strange for you coming back here. I'm terribly sorry that your husband was hurt in France. Has he spoken much to you?'

Lily shook her head, taken aback at Lady Harriet's friendly manner. 'No, nothing really. I've seen him three times at the other hospital but he was just staring like a dead man.'

'Yes, all the men who come here are shocked by the horrors they have seen, some more so than others. They primarily want to sleep and we let them do that. Mr Pavitt has been discharged from the district war hospital at the workhouse infirmary but he continues to need care and rest. His shoulder wound will heal – he's lucky it's a clean wound – we've had so many amputees here. He has responded a little more since he came here but he needs bringing out of himself. The VAD nurses here like myself make talking and listening a priority, we try to entertain and amuse the men and help them forget.

If they want to talk about the war we listen but we wouldn't expect them to express their feelings. It is best not to dwell. If you wish I can bring the Super over to talk to you, but I'm sure she will say the same thing.'

'It's all right; I'd like to see him now.'

Lady Harriet nodded and led her over to Sid, but Lily faltered when she saw Lady Harrington come into the room. She wore the bright scarlet dress of the VAD Commandant and the attitude of someone who had taken charge. Lily didn't want to speak to her; she remembered how dreadfully she had been treated as a housemaid there. If Lord Harrington came in too, she'd make a run for it. At the sight of her mother, Lady Harriet paused and guided Lily over to one side.

'I do apologise. I do hope you don't mind my asking . . . have you seen my sister at the munitions factory at all?'

Lily didn't know how much Charlotte would want her to say. 'Yes, milady, I have seen her there.'

Lady Harriet nodded solemnly. 'We do miss her. I'm sorry to involve you in this, but you know us all. Perhaps if there is an opportunity, would you give her my best regards and say it should be awfully nice to see her?'

'Yes, I will try, milady,' said Lily.

Harriet gave her a grateful smile and led her over to Sid, who was sitting up in his bed wearing his hospital blues. He did look a little less rigid and strange than the last time she had seen him. Lily sat down on a chair by the bed.

'Hello, love, how are you today, then?'

Sid turned his head towards her and let his eyes settle on her for a moment before looking away again. It was more than he had done before and Lily's heart leapt a little. She took his hand in hers and spoke to him again, as she had done before, not minding if he didn't talk back.

'Well, they've moved me into the nitro-glycerine shed at work. It's where the acids get mixed up for the cordite. Terrible in there it is; all the little bits of acid in the air land on your skin like hot sparks. I told the other girls we should ask for masks and gloves and one of them said I was being unpatriotic but some of them are all for it and they are going to join the protest. Oh, I didn't tell you about that, did I? Well, you know Lady Charlotte? Well, her and me put a list of demands to the welfare supervisor Mrs Sparrow – you know, the old bag – and then we went on strike. Yes, on strike. I know what you think, that it's not right because of the war, but it is right, Sid. We are working in really awful conditions and it's dangerous and we don't get paid the same as the men doing the same work.'

She paused to take a breath and Sid turned towards her. He was frowning as though he didn't understand something. Lily rubbed his hand and took a cigarette from a pack on the bedside table, lit it up for him and put it to his lips. His face trembled as he took a drag and blew out the smoke and Lily was as pleased as punch that he had let her help him. But all of a sudden he started to cry. His shoulders shook gently and tears rolled down his face.

'Oh, my dear,' said Lily, putting the cigarette down and wrapping her arms around him. 'Oh, my love.' She pulled him towards her and he responded by putting his arms around her too. She clutched him tight and let him cry and she felt his emptiness, his terrible loss of self. Everything had been stripped away from him in France, his very heart and soul had been ripped from him.

'I'm sorry,' he said, pulling away and sniffing to stop his tears. It was the first thing he had said since coming home.

'Sid, love, it's all right, don't say sorry. I'm here for you, I'm just glad you came home. We'll be all right, love, you'll see.'

He gave her the smallest, weakest of smiles and she knew that he was coming back to her.

Back at Goosetown, Lily changed for Saturday football practice. Mrs Sparrow had forbidden any further matches but she couldn't stop them from training. Lily jogged over to the pitch on the marshes to greet the others already there. It didn't feel the same without Nellie, but they still wanted to carry on training, especially since Lily and Marge had been separated from the others at work.

'Where's Marge?' said Lily.

'Don't know,' said Jessie. 'I hardly ever see her these days; she's never in the canteen when I'm there.'

'Charlotte, could I have a word?' said Lily, taking her friend to one side. 'My Sid is at the hospital at St Clere's now.' She let it register before continuing. 'I saw Lady Harriet there, she's a nurse.'

'Yes, I know,' said Charlotte. 'What did she say?'

'She knows you're here. She asked me to tell you they are missing you and it'd be nice to see you.'

'Did she?' Charlotte seemed surprised. 'I'm not sure Mama would have echoed that sentiment. Did you see her?'

'Only at a distance.'

'Well, that's lucky for you,' said Charlotte, running off to kick the ball.

Lily looked across the marsh to see Marge walking

towards them in her football kit with her head down. 'All right, Marge?' she called. Marge gave her a weak smile and nodded. She looked terrible, tired with dark circles under her eyes. She jogged away for the ball before Lily could question her further.

'What's wrong with Marge?' said Charlotte. 'She looks frightful.'

'I dunno but I can't help but wonder if Mrs Sparrow has been pecking at her.'

'Marge.' Charlotte called the girl over to them.

'Yes?' she said, looking younger than her years and truly miserable.

'We are worried about you. What is it, what's wrong?' said Charlotte.

Marge looked anxious at their question. 'Nothing,' she said. 'It's nothing. I'm just tired.'

'Has Mrs Sparrow been on at you about the strike?' said Lily suspiciously.

'What makes you say that?' The girl looked terrified.

'She has, hasn't she? What's she said?' said Lily, taking Marge's arm. 'Tell me, don't be frightened of her; I won't let her bully you.'

Marge broke down into tears. 'It's awful. She's put me on a special diet with no meat and no tea or coffee. And she makes me take cold baths every day.'

'Why? What for?' said Lily.

Marge shrugged. 'Just to make me better. I can't say,' she said. 'I've got to go, I'm tired.'

Lily and Charlotte watched helplessly as the girl trudged back over the marshes towards the colony.

'What's that all about?' said Lily.

'I really cannot think. But the poor girl looks frightful,' said Charlotte. 'She's dreadfully thin and looks like she hasn't slept in a week.'

'Cold baths and no meat?' said Lily, frowning. 'I'll bet that bitch Sparrow is punishing her for being in the strike.'

'Oh, Jessie!' Bonny cried out. Lily turned to see Jessie holding on to Bonny, her face screwed up with pain. Her football shorts were low under her growing belly but Lily saw the red of blood seeping down the insides of her knees. Lily rushed towards her, looked down at her friend's legs, and put her hand on her stomach.

'Can you walk?' she said. Jessie grimaced and nodded. They walked her slowly back to Goosetown and to the little hospital there. Other workers stopped to gawp as they went by.

'It's not a bloody circus,' said Mabel, warning them off.

In the hospital, the nurses took Jessie inside, telling the girls to wait. It seemed like an age and when five o'clock came round they took it in turns to rush to the canteen for some dinner. At quarter to six they told the nurses they had to go to work and they all hurried off to the factory to get changed for night shift, hating to leave Jessie there on her own.

Lily watched the clock and when six on Sunday morning came round, she ran to the hospital as soon as she was changed.

When she got there, the nurses said Jessie was sleeping but they let Lily sit by her bedside. She had lost the baby. Lily couldn't help but think it was for the best. Jessie wasn't married and her Edward had showed no signs of doing the honourable thing. She held Jessie's hand and the girl stirred and opened her eyes. When she saw Lily, her face convulsed into tears. 'It's gone,' she whispered.

'I know, my dear,' said Lily, gripping her hand.

'They said it was poisoned.'

'What?'

'The cordite. The baby was poisoned from me working in the cordite shed. They said it was yellow, like us, and it couldn't have survived. Oh, Lily . . . '

Lily found herself crying too. She tried to imagine how she would have felt if she'd lost a baby at six months. Carrying it in your belly, feeling it move around and kick. Getting those maternal feelings for it. 'Oh, Jessie, I'm so sorry,' she said. 'I'm just glad you're all right. I've been so worried about you.'

'I'm not all right, though, am I?' she said, wiping her tears away bitterly. 'If I could have asked Mrs Sparrow to let me move out of the cordite shed this might not have happened. I didn't tell anyone but I was falling in love with my baby.'

'Yes,' said Lily, understanding. 'Yes, I know.'

'It was a girl,' said Jessie, sobbing again. 'Why did they tell me that, Lil? Why did they have to tell me?'

21

'It's showing!'

Charlotte sat down next to Lily in the YWCA with her dinner on her tray.

'What's showing, Marge's petticoat?' laughed Mabel. But Marge looked down at her plate and pushed her food around with her fork, not seeing the funny side.

'The Battle of the Somme picture. I can't believe it's taken until September to put it on at the Grays Empire. I haven't had a chance to get up to London to see it, what with these wretched shifts. Who would like to come?'

'What, tonight?' said Jessie. 'It's Saturday night, I'm going to the dance with Edward.'

'Jessie, have you said anything to him about what happened?' said Mabel.

'Course I haven't. What would be the point of that?' she said crossly. Jessie didn't like talking about her miscarriage. She was trying to carry on as though nothing had happened. But it had changed her. Lily would catch her staring into space, or not concentrating on what she was doing at work. She was absent-minded; she'd drop things or not hear what was said to her.

'So? Mabel? The cinema?' said Charlotte.

'Sorry, love, I've got to get back to the kids, haven't I? Lily and Marge will go with you.' Marge shook her head and the others exchanged worried glances. 'Go on, love, it'll do you good to have a night out.' Marge put down her cutlery and walked away from the table, leaving them all staring after her.

'Well, it's just you and me, then, Lily,' said Charlotte.

'Yes, all right, I'll go,' said Lily. 'Sid was in the Somme, I'd like to see it.'

'It's actual footage of the men on the front line,' said Charlotte. 'It should be a real insight. Knock at hut one when you're changed and come in for a drink before we go.'

In Charlotte's room they got carried away talking and drinking and after two large glasses of wine each, they left hut one very merrily and made their way on the train to Grays.

'I've never been to the cinema,' confessed Charlotte.

'Never been to the pictures?' said Lily. 'Why not?' She laughed, finding it the funniest thing.

'Well, you know, we'd always go to the theatre and so on . . .'

'Oh, I see, too good for the pictures, were you?' Lily teased her friend. 'Well, get ready to come out scratching.'

'What on earth do you mean?'

'You'll see. Come on.'

They went into the Empire Cinema in the High Street. Charlotte insisted on the front row of the circle and fidgeted in her seat, looking at the upholstery for foreign bodies. Lily was drunk and couldn't stop laughing at her. They watched the copperettes patrolling the aisles, rooting out couples cuddling in the darkness. The title card and music came up on the screen, and Lily settled in her seat. The first shot showed the preparatory action from the last five days of June before the battle began and Lily sat up, suddenly realising what was on the screen before her. This was where Sid had been. How strange to see it with her own eyes now; maybe she would even see Sid on the film.

'That's all the artillery fire we heard, remember?' whispered Lily, her heart racing.

They had heard the sound of the field guns across the channel. The film showed a field and rise beyond, with smoke and horses and men getting carts of ammunition ready to move up the lines, just as Sid had written about in his letter. Lily looked for him, scanning the men's faces. An inter-title card read that a general was addressing the Lancashire Fusiliers and Royal Fusiliers and her heart sank that it wasn't the Essex Regiment on the screen. But she could imagine Sid lining up there with the others in his steel hat, listening to his orders, and it made her shiver. There was a vicar giving a service to the Manchester regiment outside on the mud the night before the attack.

'They didn't know what was coming,' whispered Charlotte. 'I heard that the bombardment didn't work, that's why so many men died on the first day of battle.'

An officer with a pet fox on a lead. Then, Lily's heart leapt, an inter-title describing the munitions dumps along the front with supplies of shells thanks to the British munitions workers. Several people in the audience sent up a cheer and Lily and Charlotte beamed at each other in the darkness. Men in uniform pulled back the tarpaulins to show the camera vast piles of boxes of shells. Then a shot of eighteen-pounder shells pounding the German trenches in the five days before the attack. Lily thought of the cordite in those shells and was proud to have been a part of making them. On screen, men were throwing off the empty cartridges into a huge pile. Had Sid been doing that job? She looked desperately at the men in the film for her Sid. They looked happy enough, maybe they enjoyed being filmed.

Next, swathes and swathes of men moving up on the evening before the attack. Lily could have cried to see them marching cheerfully along the track carrying their kit and rifles, smoking and smiling shyly at the camera as they passed, some waving their steel helmets. She could picture Sid there with Gerald. And now Gerald was gone. A lot of the boys in the picture would be dead now. Lily imagined a mother or wife watching her son or husband marching past, little knowing that he would be dead the next day. The London Scottish, East Yorkshires, the Hampshires, the Buffs, Bedfords, Suffolks, the Royal Welsh Fusiliers, all marching to the front line to defend King and country.

The field guns in action, firing at the enemy trenches. The cloud plumes in the distance. The plum-pudding shells fired from trench mortars. The monstrous mechanics of war. Men having a meal in camp the evening before the battle began, standing in a huddle waiting for steaming food to be ladled into mess tins on the muddy ground. Lily searched their faces, looking for Sid and Gerald. The men wore sheepskins over their khaki and sat on the ground around a small fire to eat their meal.

Twelve-inch Howitzers firing enormous high-explosive shells. The Royal Warwickshires on their way to the front line, smiling at the camera. So many men doing their duty, their families at home. The Worcesters fixing wire-cutters to their rifles for getting through the German barbed wire. More men, thousands of them, marching forward. Horses lying in the grass, dead from exhaustion after hauling the guns.

The morning of the attack. Lily stared hard at the screen. They knew now that nineteen thousand men died on the first day of the battle, Gerald among them. Barbed wire and sand bags and great clouds of earth from artillery fire. The Lancashires fixing bayonets in a communication trench, waiting to go to the firing line. The inter-titles going by too quickly to read properly.

'The trenches are terrible, aren't they?' whispered Charlotte.

Seven-feet-deep gouges in the mud, men running through in single file carrying boxes of ammunition on their shoulders. The Lancashire Fusiliers in a sunken road in no man's land soon to be under heavy machine-gun fire. Lily and Charlotte looked at each other with dread. The men here weren't as jolly as those further back. Some of them stared sombrely into the camera. There was fear in the eyes of these brave souls and it was as if they were asking why they were being filmed in these dreadful moments, perhaps the last moments of their lives.

'I can't imagine,' whispered Lily.

'Me neither,' said Charlotte.

The signal for attack. The inter-title card read that along the whole sixteen-mile front, the troops went over the top towards the enemy lines under heavy fire. One man fell back shot, the rest clambered over barbed wire into the smoke of gunfire.

'That looked staged,' said Charlotte.

Lily agreed that the scene hadn't looked realistic. The man who had fallen back looked at the camera before laying his head on the ground. But then there were scenes of the battlefield, smoke pluming from the enemy lines in the distance, and British Tommies racing across no man's land. A man rescued and the card telling the audience that he died within thirty minutes of being brought back to the British trenches, carried along on a soldier's back. Lily's stomach twisted with nerves. The conditions the men were fighting in. The mud and the kit they had to carry and being under threat of fire all the time. The film showed the wounded being carried down the trench on stretchers. British and German wounded. Men sagging and bloody. The walking wounded with bandaged heads and arms, limping and aided. A battalion returning with prisoners from a successful attack, the Germans injured and haunted, helped along by the Tommies. A group of them standing still for a moment for the camera, our boys and the enemy sharing a joke. All just young men together.

The Royal Field Artillery moving forward where dead men from the Gordons and the Devons lay on the ground. Lily shook her head at Charlotte, put her hand over her mouth and wept. Dead men on the ground, with men marching past and horses pulling wagons of artillery to cause more death. Someone's husband, someone's son. More casualties, on stretchers and walking, Germans and British. Men dirty and dazed and staring. Tommies offering the German prisoners water, a cigarette.

The trenches and dugouts, men living like rabbits in a warren. Shell holes in the mud on no man's land filled with

German bodies. Dead bodies in the trenches. A dog lying dead with his dead officer. The bodies indistinguishable from the mud, the two combined, one sinking into the other. A soldier sitting slumped forward as if napping, but dead. Our boys lined up on the ground while their comrades dug their graves. The landscape broken and scarred, littered with wire and shell cases and forty-foot mine holes. Charred tree stumps and the grass long lost in the oozing mud. The village of Mametz a crumbled ruin. The post arrived on the front line. Lily laughed through her tears. Good old post office; the boys got their letters and their cake and tins of bully beef from their loved ones at home. What relief it must have brought them.

Essex Regiment having a wash in a stream. The whole picture house roared and Lily sat up in her seat, straining to see Sid. The men were crowded on the riverbank, all look-ing at the camera and laughing. Lily was desperate to see Sid there, she could tell him about it. They could go and watch it together. Not Gerald, Gerald wouldn't be there, this was after the battle on the first day, it may even have been after Sid had gone. She sat back in her seat. Yes, Sid would have been in the clearing station or the base hospital by then. He was injured on the first day of battle. Charlotte reached over and squeezed Lily's hand.

'Lovely to see the Essex Regiment,' Charlotte whispered and Lily nodded.

The film ended and Lily applauded with everyone else. She felt as though she had been there in France herself, she was exhausted from the emotion of watching it.

'My goodness, what an insight,' said Charlotte, clearly affected by what she had seen.

'My poor Sid, being in that. All of those poor boys. They are so brave, smiling at the camera like that,' said Lily as they walked to Grays station.

'And to think it is still going on and they have hardly advanced at all,' said Charlotte, scratching her hand.

'How many more dead will there be?' said Lily.

She scratched her neck and dug Charlotte with her elbow, still merry from the wine. 'Scratching, are you?'

'Good heavens, how disgusting,' said Charlotte, wrinkling her nose.

'Quite something to see all the shells in a pile, with our cordite in them,' said Charlotte when they were on the train. 'There was not a single woman in the whole picture but I feel we were there in spirit.'

'And lovely that the filmmaker thanked the munitions workers.'

'It does make one reflect, though, does it not?' They got off at Stanford-le-Hope and walked down the road to the Corringham Light Railway station.

'About all the killing you mean, don't you?'

'Whether it's right and whether what we do is right.'

'I know. But if we didn't do it, the Germans would get us, wouldn't they? Oh, there's no train, we'll have to walk across the marshes in the dark to Goosetown.'

They set off across the dark marshland, through long grass, the ground boggy from the recent rain. It must have been between nine and ten o'clock because the searchlights were doing their usual sweep of the sky. It was a clear night, which meant the Zeppelins would stay away because there was no cloud cover to hide in.

Charlotte gave a big sigh. 'The futility of war. It does make one wonder whether Emmeline Pankhurst is right. I was a militant suffragette before the war, you know. Oh yes, I even threw a stone through a shop window on Oxford Street.'

'I really wish I could have seen my Sid on that film, I could have told him about it,' mused Lily, not in the mood to talk about suffrage.

'Now, Sylvia Pankhurst is an interesting character,' said Charlotte, following her own train of thought. 'She opposes the war and is very interested in conditions for women munitions workers.' She looked at Lily for her agreement. 'I suppose she recognises this war as an opportunity to progress women's rights even though she is a pacifist. Do you know,' she said, stopping still, 'I do believe I may change my allegiance to Sylvia Pankhurst.' She continued walking. 'Her mother has no interest in working women's rights.'

'I don't know if we should be striking. Seeing those men out there . . . '

'But then there's Mary Macarthur,' said Charlotte, disregarding Lily's comment. 'She is a feminist activist committed to working women's issues. It's her union that is going to help us with the tribunal. And don't forget all the women dying from TNT poisoning in munitions factories.'

'It's the workers who need a voice, not just women,' said Lily, her own thoughts on the subject becoming clearer. 'I might tell Sid about it, see what he thinks.'

'I believe we are doing the right thing, Lily,' Charlotte said defensively. 'Yes, it is very difficult in the face of the men's struggles. But this is an unprecedented time for women and we must take it with both hands. We can help the men by making munitions while also fighting the women's war for better conditions and fairer pay.' Lily didn't answer, there was no talking to Charlotte when she started one of her rants. 'You know, the women bus and tube staff went on strike because they weren't given the bonus the men were given. And they got it.'

'My shoes are getting ruined in this mud.'

'Don't worry, ask the hall boy to clean them for you,' said Charlotte, cracking into laughter.

'Oh yes, I bet you wish you could,' said Lily, laughing too.

'It is a beautiful night. You know, that film is most likely from the propaganda bureau; but then we're not to expect anything else, I suppose.'

'Talk in English,' said Lily, nudging her friend with her elbow.

Charlotte looked at her in surprise. 'I only mean to say, from what my brother Bertie tells me in his letters, the film isn't a true representation of the real war. It didn't show any of the real fighting or slaughter, really primarily movement of troops and the enemy dead and taken prisoner. Those German prisoners being put on the train for England.'

'It still looked really awful, though, Charlotte.'

'Indeed, and the way our boys shared a cigarette with the prisoners. It really showed that they are just sons and sweethearts too. You know, I spent quite a bit of time in Germany when I was younger.'

'But what about the tens of thousands of our boys who have perished? Maybe they show that to make sure the Germans treat our prisoners well.'

'Yes, they are all young men, just young men.' Charlotte

hiccupped and covered her mouth. 'There won't be any men left. No husbands left for our women.'

'What about your Lord Nevill, then?'

Charlotte waved the comment away. 'He treats me like a child. He's a good match and that's all. Did you read about the commander of the Zeppelin that was brought down over north Essex?' Lily shook her head. 'He tried to rouse the nearby residents before setting fire to the Zeppelin, to give them a chance to get away safely.'

'Wasn't it lovely to see the Essex boys there having a wash,' said Lily. 'I was looking for Sid but then I remembered he was injured on the first day of battle.'

'And I heard that when the Germans torpedo our merchant ships, the crew are given time to lower their lifeboats first. What was that?' said Charlotte, stopping dead and staring ahead at a dark mound of bushes.

'What?'

'I thought I saw something move by those bushes.'

'Probably just a bullock.'

'Or Gunther Plüschow . . . ?'

'Who?'

'Didn't you hear about the German prisoner of war who escaped from a camp at Donnington Hall and made his way back to Germany?'

'Not sure,' said Lily, screwing up her face and trying to think. 'It might be one of Mabel's marsh men ghosts looking for a new bride.'

Charlotte laughed. 'Yes, that's it. It's a marsh man ghost.'

'You'll make a good marsh man's wife,' giggled Lily.

'Where is God in all of this?' said Charlotte, still ranting.

'How can he allow this war to happen? The death and mutilation – it's against morality.'

'How much of that wine did you have?' said Lily.

Charlotte laughed and took a hip flask out of her bag, took a swig and offered it to Lily, who put it to her lips and spluttered when she found it was whiskey.

'There it is again – something rustled over there, something big,' said Lily.

They crept forward dramatically in the dark towards the sound, scaring themselves and giggling.

'Not many people know that there's a German prisoner of war camp a few miles from here at Horndon House Farm,' said Charlotte.

'Stop it, you're scaring me.'

'My father told me about it. It holds around forty men.'

'Oh, I saw some of them going to the post office on the morning I went to the labour exchange about this job.'

'There you are, then. There might be one of them hiding behind that bush.'

'Oh stop it; let's scare the bullock away so we can get on.'

There was another movement from behind the bushes and the girls jumped. 'Let's run towards it to scare it away,' said Charlotte, looking at Lily until she gave a nervous nod. 'One, two, three, go!'

They ran towards the bush, shouting and clapping their hands. To their great surprise not a bullock, but a man ran from the bush and tore away across the marshes. Lily stopped dead and let him go but, to her horror, Charlotte ran after him. 'Yoo-hoo,' she shouted, drunk and silly, 'you've nothing to fear from us,' and away she ran on her football-trained legs.

'Stop,' shouted Lily, chasing after her friend. 'Charlotte, come back.'

The man ran towards the river and in the darkness he seemed to disappear near a disused blockhouse. Charlotte slowed to wait for Lily to catch up.

'What the bloody hell are you doing?' said Lily, doubling over to catch her breath.

'What'll we do?' said Charlotte. 'Approach him?'

'No,' said Lily. 'What if he's a German?'

'Well, he's not going to hurt us; he must be scared and hungry. I'll bet he was picking blackberries to eat.'

Lily thought about the men in the film, the captured Germans taken prisoner and brought to England on a train. Perhaps he was one of them and just wanted to get home to his family.

'Let's just see if he's all right,' said Charlotte, walking slowly towards the blockhouse, a small square wooden structure. Lily followed her, not wanting to be left alone on the dark marsh.

'Hello?' Charlotte called. 'We shan't hurt you. Are you injured?'

'Hello,' said a man's voice. And he came out from the blockhouse wearing a field-grey German uniform and black boots, his hands held up in front of him.

22

Despite the wine she'd had earlier, Lily didn't think she'd ever been so scared in her life. She, Charlotte and the man stood looking at each other in silence until Charlotte took the initiative and spoke.

'Lady Charlotte Harrington, it's a pleasure to meet you,' she said and Lily wondered if she had gone quite mad. What was she doing telling this man her name? Charlotte held out her hand to him.

'Corporal Viktor Kirschbaum,' said the man in a German accent. He stepped out of the shadows and tentatively took Charlotte's hand. Lily stood by, ready to kick him if he tried anything, but he shook Charlotte's hand gently and stepped back with a small bow. From what Lily could see in the dark, he was a handsome man, with hooded eyes and a generous mouth. He seemed to want to smile but was holding back to judge the situation.

'Cherry tree,' said Charlotte, smiling.

'What are you doing?' hissed Lily.

'You speak German?' said Corporal Kirschbaum.

'A little. I have spent time in Germany. I once went to a party at King Ludwig's castle.'

'Ah, in Bavaria. Our mad King Ludwig.' The man finally let himself smile and he seemed relieved to do so. Lily wished Charlotte wasn't being so familiar with him.

'Are you injured?' said Charlotte, and Lily realised that he was holding his left arm against his body.

'I fell, in one of the holes here,' he said, finding the right words. Lily was surprised at how well he spoke English.

'May I see?' said Charlotte, stepping towards him and shrugging off Lily's grip on her arm. 'Where does it hurt?'

'My shoulder, it is . . . it is out of the . . . '

'Out of its socket? It's dislocated?'

'*Ja*, yes.'

'*Charlotte*,' Lily hissed, but her friend held up her hands and the man nodded in agreement. She felt his shoulder through his uniform. 'I have never done this before but I have seen it done, when I did a first aid course. I can try . . . ?'

The soldier gave a nervous smile and held up his forefinger to ask her to wait while he stepped to one side to grip on to the side of the blockhouse. He nodded and set his face. Charlotte put her hands on his shoulder, felt around a bit, held up his arm and with one sickening push, shoved it back into its socket. The man bent over and let out a growl of agony.

'*Vielen dank*, thank you,' he said, standing up and rubbing his arm. 'Thank you.'

'It worked?' said Charlotte, beaming. 'I rather thought it wouldn't.' She looked at Lily, who glared at her.

'Do you mind my asking . . . ?' said Charlotte. 'What . . . I mean to say, where . . . ?'

'I escaped.' He said it matter-of-factly. 'From the camp at Horndon House Farm. I am trying to get home to Germany. I heard of Gunther Plüschow ...'

'Oh yes, the prisoner who made his way back to Germany from here. Lily, I was just telling you about him.' Charlotte opened her eyes wide at Lily, she wanted her to talk to the man but Lily stayed back.

'Are you hungry?' said Charlotte.

'Yes,' he said apologetically.

'We can bring you some food,' said Charlotte. 'But you must stay hidden. You must be freezing out here.' It was cool for mid September and the wind on the marshes made it more so. 'Do you know where you are? There is a—'

Lily lunged forward and grabbed Charlotte by the arm to stop her talking. Charlotte was going to tell him about the factory. 'Yes, stay hidden,' said Charlotte, stopping in her tracks, 'and we shall bring you some food tomorrow.'

'Thank you, *danke schön*.'

'Here,' said Charlotte, taking out her cigarettes and matches and the hip flask from her bag and handing them to him.

'Come on,' said Lily, pulling at Charlotte's arm. Charlotte smiled at the soldier and came away, the two women heading back over the marshes towards Goosetown.

'We have to help him escape,' said Charlotte.

'Have you lost your senses?' said Lily angrily. 'We'll get put into prison. Why are you helping him? He might have been the one who killed my father-in-law.'

'Lily, after watching that film, I really feel it would be the best thing to do. Look at where we are, right on the river. If we give him some food, we can help him get down to

316

one of the wharves and out to a boat – that's what Gunther Plüschow did – he rowed out to a boat at Tilbury Docks and got to Holland. There's the Greygoose wharf on Hole Haven creek, but that would be heavily guarded. There's the Thames Haven petroleum wharf there on the river. What about that?'

'I don't want anything to do with this, Charlotte, and I think you'll wake up tomorrow and feel the same way.'

Lily was so tired from the wine and the film that finding the German felt almost like a dream. She was angry with Charlotte and she just wanted to sleep. Tomorrow was Sunday. She knew that Charlotte would wake up and know that what had happened tonight was desperately dangerous.

Upon waking the next morning, Lily's stomach convulsed with fear and her eyes shot open. Her first thought was what would Sid say and that she would have to tell him about it. They would all be arrested, the police would find out. The German was a spy, trying to get into the factory. Charlotte had given him a box of matches. He'd blow them all up.

She hurried to get dressed and went to knock at Charlotte's hut. The maid told her that Lady Charlotte was taking breakfast in the YWCA hut. Lily ran over there.

'Ah, here she is,' said Charlotte, who was standing by the serving hatch talking to one of the volunteer ladies. 'Yes, we'll go to the marshes, find a nice spot by the river,' she continued and the woman nodded and handed Charlotte a basket.

'What are you doing?' said Lily, by now rigid with fear and following Charlotte outside.

'I simply told them that we are going for an autumn picnic and could they pack up some food for us,' said Charlotte in a low voice. 'They think I am quite mad to go picnicking in this weather but I told them we need to get fresh air after being in the factory. Quite the stroke of genius, I thought.'

Lily stared at her friend. 'It's for him, isn't it?'

'Yes, of course it is. What on earth is the matter?'

'What on earth is the matter? Are you a lunatic? We have to report this to the police straight away,' said Lily, beside herself.

'Walk with me,' said Charlotte in a stern voice, her face suddenly hard.

Lily went with her, out of Goosetown and on to the marshes where they wouldn't be overheard.

Charlotte put the basket of food down and stood to face Lily. 'If you report him to the police he'll be shot.'

'Well, tell him to go back to the camp, then. We'll be in a lot of trouble when people find out about this. We'll lose our jobs, we'll go to prison.'

'Look, what if this was Sid trying to escape from Germany?' Charlotte snapped. 'You'd want someone to help him, wouldn't you?' She looked at Lily's wretched face. 'Calm down,' she said, trying to do the same herself. 'I know this is a shock. It is for me too, but let's go and give him this food and then we'll see.'

Lily was out of her depth. She nodded and went with Charlotte, scared out of her wits. They made their way south to the river and walked along it, checking that they weren't being followed. Lily hoped they were sufficiently far from the blockhouses on the factory perimeter not to be seen. They approached the disused blockhouse cautiously and when they were near, the man stepped out from inside, careful to stay on the riverside out of view from the marsh.

'Good morning,' he said. He looked frightful, tired and dirty, dark circles under his eyes. Charlotte handed him the basket and he sat on the ground to open it, found some sandwiches and tore at them with his teeth. 'Thank you,' he said around the food.

Once he had eaten and drunk the water in the stoppered bottle, he leaned back against the wall of the blockhouse and took out one of Charlotte's cigarettes to smoke. Lily gave Charlotte a hard glare, urging her to talk to him about going back to the camp.

'Corporal Kirschbaum,' she said.

'Viktor, please.'

'Viktor. May we ask, what do you plan to do now?'

'I want to get home to Germany. I watch for a boat on the river.'

Charlotte glanced at Lily. 'I know you heard about Gunther Plüschow's successful journey home, but don't you think it is safer to go back to the camp and wait for the end of the war?'

'I cannot. At the camp it is . . . the men have . . .' He tapped his temple. 'It is bad in the head. They do not let me work because I am corporal. I know not how long I am there. I want to get home to my family—' His voice broke and he recovered his composure.

Lily's heart sank. Charlotte was right: what if Sid had been captured in Germany and wanted to get home? But what if Sid found out about them helping this chap?

'But every police patrol and army guard will be looking for you. If they catch you . . .' she said.

'Yes,' he said, knowing what would happen.

'In the papers they say Germans like stabbing babies

319

with bayonets,' continued Lily. 'If anyone finds you they'll report you.'

'That is not true,' he said. 'We do not stab babies. It is propaganda.'

'Our men have died, have been killed …' she went on, thinking of Gerald and what Sid and Ada would say if they could see her now, what Mabel would say about the Germans killing her husband.

'Yes,' he said, his expression sad and serious. 'It is war. I despise it.'

Lily looked at Charlotte in exasperation. 'They'll have us for spies,' she said.

Charlotte bit her fingernail.

'I am not a spy,' said Viktor, and they both looked at him. 'But I know they will say it if they catch me.'

Lily needed to get back to see Sid, so she and Charlotte walked back to Goosetown together. She had written to the boys to tell them that she would try to get to see them soon, that she hoped they would be able to see their father, too, before too long. She knew she shouldn't say anything to Sid about the German prisoner, not while he was trying to get better.

At St Clere's Hall, Lily found Sid sitting up on his bed. He saw her come in and followed her progress towards him. She could tell straight away that he had improved. He wasn't staring into the distance any more.

'How are you feeling today, love?' she asked him.

He struggled to give her a smile and put out his hand for her to hold. 'A bit better, Lil,' he said quietly. 'The shoulder's still giving me gyp, though.'

The matron came over when she saw Lily there. 'He's looking much brighter, isn't he, Mrs Pavitt?' she said in a businesslike fashion. 'Your shoulder is doing very well indeed, Mr Pavitt. I shouldn't wonder you'll be out of here soon.'

Sid's face fell. 'It's still giving me gyp, Nurse.'

'You might not be sent back out to France, Mr Pavitt, and these beds are needed. Injured men are coming home in droves.'

Sid looked at his lap and Lily squeezed his hand. He seemed terrified at the prospect of being sent back to the front line and Lily could see that he wasn't up to it, but she'd read in the papers that they were desperate for men, that men considered essential for war work at home were being reassessed to be freed up to go and fight.

The matron went off to attend to somebody else. 'It's all right, love, I think you'll be here a while yet.'

'How are the boys?' he said and Lily was delighted that he'd asked after them.

'To tell you the truth, I haven't had much of a chance to see them lately. I work twelve-hour shifts and I've been wanting to come here to see you. But whenever I've been down to Nettlestead they've always looked happy. I bet they'd love to see you when you're up to it.'

'Not just now, love,' he said with a weak smile.

'Sid, dear, I've got something I need to tell you,' she said in a low voice so the man in the next bed didn't hear. 'Something's happened and I'm stuck in it.' She hadn't meant to talk about it but he seemed a bit better and she was desperate to get his advice about what to do for the best. 'Me and Charlotte found this man on the marshes. He's a German. He escaped from the prisoner camp in Horndon and he wants to get back home to his family. We've given him some food, he was starving . . . '

She watched Sid's face eagerly. He frowned, taking it all in. 'What?' he said. 'A German prisoner?'

'Yes, and he just wants to get back home. He said it's awful in the camp, he's really homesick. Charlotte wants to help him, but I don't know what to do.'

'You want to help him?'

'Yes, well, Charlotte does, he's homesick. We were thinking what if you were stuck in Germany like that; I'd want someone to help you.'

'He's homesick? He's a damned German. He might have killed my dad. Oh no, oh God, oh God . . . ' Sid leaned back against his pillow and closed his eyes, moaning. Tears squeezed through his eyelids and fell down his face. 'Oh, what have you done? Oh no, no . . . '

A nurse rushed over. 'Whatever is the matter, Mr Pavitt?' she said, looking at Lily in consternation. Lily felt sick, she wanted to take it back, she shouldn't have told him.

'It's all right, Sid, I didn't mean it, I didn't . . . ' She didn't know what to say. The nurse was staring at her; the man in the next bed was looking too. No one else could know about the German. They would all be in a world of trouble.

'I think you should let him rest,' said the nurse, giving Lily a strange look.

'Yes, all right. Could I just . . . could I just say goodbye to him please?' The nurse nodded and went away. 'Sid,' whispered Lily. 'Sid, don't worry, I'll sort it all out, just don't worry about it.' He quietened down, whimpered and let his head fall to the side and seemed to be falling asleep. Lily kissed his cheek and got up to go.

Back at Goosetown, Lily got changed for football practice. She jogged over the marsh towards the pitch where a few of the others were waiting. Feeling jittery and worried since seeing Sid, she thought a run around the field would do her good.

'Where is everyone?' she said. Only Jessie, Mabel, Eliza and Bonny were there.

Jessie shrugged. 'Don't know; it's not as good now that Nellie isn't with us. I suppose people have lost interest.'

'Marge is missing,' said Mabel.

'What?' said Lily, frowning.

'Mrs Sparrow came into the cordite shed looking for her. She said she'd been to Marge's family home to look for her but she wasn't there, and she hasn't slept in her hut for two nights.'

'I know she wasn't there last night; she always goes home when she can on a weekend to help with the children,' said Lily. 'But now you mention it, I don't remember saying goodnight to her the night before that. Where the bloody hell is she, then?'

'Don't know, but I'm worried about her,' said Mabel. 'Mrs Sparrow has got the women police out looking for her.'

A shiver of fear ran through Lily. If they were searching for Marge, they might find the German prisoner.

'I hope she's all right,' said Lily. 'Has something happened?' With a jolt she remembered what Marge had said about Mrs Sparrow. That she wouldn't let her eat meat or tea or coffee and she'd been giving her cold baths. With all the distractions of Sid and the German, Lily hadn't given it much thought but it must have been simmering in the back of her mind because now it came to her clearly. The Welfare Supervisor's Handbook that Charlotte had found in Mrs Sparrow's office that time. A treatment for girls who were doing that thing to themselves. For girls who were shy and pale. They should be made to have cold baths and to take exercise and to not be given meat or tea or coffee. With horror, Lily realised that Mrs Sparrow must have accused Marge of it, and was treating her for it, as a punishment for being in the strike that time.

'Lily, what is it?' asked Bonny. 'You look like you've seen a ghost.'

'Nothing, I've just remembered something I forgot to do.'

Lily rushed away, back to the hut to get changed. She needed to go to Marge's family home, she needed to find her. But first she had to find Charlotte and tell her there was a search for Marge. If the German was found, there would be far worse consequences than Mrs Sparrow could ever dish out.

She got changed in a hurry and ran to knock at hut one. The maid answered and told her that Lady Charlotte had gone out. Lily was beside herself. She'd have to go to tell the German by herself. She tried not to run towards the marshes, to avoid being seen acting suspiciously. Walking calmly until she got down by the river, she then broke into a run. When she approached the disused blockhouse, she slowed down, afraid of being there by herself. The sound of a woman's laughter came from within.

'Hello?' she called out.

'Oh, hello, thank goodness, I wondered who it was.' Charlotte came out, followed by the German.

'What are you doing here?' said Lily.

'I might ask you the same thing,' said Charlotte.

'I went looking for you. Marge has gone missing. I think I know what Mrs Sparrow is doing to her. But the copperettes are out searching for her, so they might come here and find Viktor.' Lily frowned when she saw several new items in the blockhouse: blankets and other food they hadn't brought before.

'Oh dear, oh yes, I see what you mean,' said Charlotte. 'Viktor, you need to find somewhere else to hide. This place is too obvious a hiding place if they look around here for Marge.'

'I need to get on a boat,' he said, looking worried.

'What about heading up river to Tilbury Docks like Gunther Plüschow did?' Charlotte suggested.

'It's heavily guarded at the docks,' said Lily. 'I used to live there. They've got machine guns and anti-aircraft guns, there are troops camped in the barracks in Tilbury fort and Purfleet garrison is just a bit further up the river – you can get arrested just for being seen in Purfleet. There's a pier at Coalhouse fort but it's swarming with soldiers – Eliza lived there but was told to move out.' Lily reconciled herself to helping him with this information because then he'd be gone and out of this mess – she'd rather help him that way than harbour him here.

'Oh dear,' said Charlotte. 'I know what. The factory has two barges, to take the cordite up river to Woolwich. Might there be a better chance of getting on a boat in London?'

'London will be guarded like here,' said Viktor.

'You should stay around here,' said Lily reluctantly. 'I reckon your best bet is to try to stow away on one of the petroleum ships going out of Thames Haven pier. They aren't allowed upriver, only down river.'

'Yes,' said Viktor, looking at her with admiration. 'Thank you. But where shall I wait for the boat?'

'One of the old railway carriages down by Shell Haven creek?' said Lily, looking at Charlotte.

'Yes, then if the police come searching, you'll have a chance to move under cover. Here, there's nowhere to go if they come,' said Charlotte.

'You'll have to wait for darkness, though, won't you?' said Lily.

'Yes, I will wait and watch for police and move when it is dark.'

'It's that way,' said Lily, pointing. 'Good luck,' she said guardedly, relieved beyond words to say goodbye to him.

23

It was an hour before sundown when Lily walked through the factory gates for her night shift. She felt paranoid and ill at ease, not knowing if Viktor had escaped or was still waiting on the marshes for a boat to stow away on. When one of the copperettes tapped her on the shoulder she nearly jumped off the ground.

'Search, please,' said the constable. It was standard practice. Workers were picked out at random when walking through the factory gates and searched for contraband. Lily was led to the little hut by the gates and asked to turn out her bag and pockets. She was terrified they were on to her and she was being watched. The constable looked through her things for cigarettes and matches, searched through Lily's hair for hairpins, checked her shoes for Blakeys and asked her if she was wearing a corset with metal boning. Satisfied, the constable told her to proceed. Lily breathed a sigh of relief and hurried on towards the danger area.

Jessie ran up behind her out of breath. 'They've found a body. A dead body has been found in Shell Haven creek.'

Lily stopped, searched Jessie's face. 'What? Who is it?' she said, her mind immediately jumping to the conclusion that it was Viktor.

'Don't know, they aren't saying yet.'

'Where's Charlotte?' Jessie shrugged and hurried on to the cordite shed. Lily went after her, got to the cordite range and saw Alfie there.

'Hello, what brings you here?' he said. 'And why weren't you at football practice? Lost interest, have you?' he went on, his eyes twinkling.

'Sorry, Alfie, I've just been busy, what with Sid in hospital and not being able to see the boys much and everything.'

He smiled and seemed to want to say more but held back.

'Have you seen Charlotte?' she asked, looking around the pressing hut.

'Through there.' He pointed to the next room.

'Have you heard?' said Lily, pulling Charlotte to one side of the room.

'Yes, I'm terrified it's Viktor,' whispered Charlotte.

'I know. It's too awful. I wonder what happened, if he was caught or hurt himself trying to escape or something.'

Charlotte pressed the back of her hand against her mouth. 'Do you really think it's him?' she said.

'Don't know. Come and tell me if you find anything out. I've got to get to work.'

Lily made her way over to the nitro-glycerine shed and pulled on her rubber boots. The women there were all right with her now but the work was awful. Lily had lots of pin-prick burns on her face and hands and a constant sore throat. She had learned to work with her eyes squinted after a particle of acid had gone into one eye and she'd had a blind spot in her vision ever since.

Marge wasn't at work and Lily remembered she had meant to go and see the girl's mum to find out what was wrong with her. She had no doubt that Marge had hidden from Mrs Sparrow when the welfare supervisor had gone to check up on her at home. Poor Marge. Lily's guess that Mrs Sparrow had accused her of masturbation fitted with how awful the girl had looked recently. Lily needed to ask her about it; if she was right she had a good mind to go and confront Mrs Sparrow. How dare she bully them like this just because they had made a stand about the conditions at work?

It must have been around ten o'clock when the foreman came rushing in to tell them all there was an air raid warning. The girls knew the drill. They got out of the shed quickly and over the road to shelter beneath the huts in the safe area. As she usually did, Lily ran down the road, out of the factory gates and over to the haystack. She was used to the threat of Zeppelins by now, accustomed to seeing these strange and enormous things in the sky. Sometimes she saw them, often she didn't. Bombing raids were always in the paper the next day and the grisly body count was mounting.

The cordite girls, Jessie, Charlotte and Mabel, came jogging over to the haystack. Lily was desperate to ask Charlotte if she'd heard anything about Viktor, but didn't dare mention it in front of the others.

'I wish Nellie was here,' said Jessie.

'I know, I miss her too,' said Lily. 'I wish we could find out which prison she's in so we can visit her, or write to her at least.'

'We should start a campaign to have her released,' said Charlotte. 'She should never have been fired in the first place.'

'Can we mention it at the tribunal?' said Lily.

'Yes, I should think so.' Charlotte looked at Lily, and the two women exchanged a private thought about Viktor. The tribunal hadn't been at the forefront of their minds since they had found him.

'Oh God, here it comes,' said Mabel. The sound of anti-aircraft guns reached them and they saw the blue smoke trails of phosphorous bullets in the sky. A huge Zeppelin appeared in the spotlights, going over the Thames. They watched as it moved to swerve the gunfire and Lily's heart clutched tight when it redirected its course and came towards them.

'Oh no,' she whispered. 'It's coming for the factory.'

'It's just swerving out the way of the guns,' said Mabel hopefully.

They all watched, tense with worry, as the six-hundred-foot oblong monster moved slowly towards them, making a deathly humming sound. It was so close that Lily could see the gondolas hanging from its belly and the pilots in uniform.

'It's hit; they've hit it!' shouted Mabel. One of the phosphorous bullets had struck the canopy and set the gas alight inside. It all happened so quickly. The airship burst into flames.

'Run!' shouted Charlotte.

The German soldiers dangled bombs over the side of the gondolas. They were going to do their damnedest to cause some damage before going down. Lily ran and didn't look back until she was at Goosetown. There was a massive explosion and she turned to see a plume of smoke rise above the factory. At the same time the giant Zeppelin was coming down at a sharp angle. It was so very big. Its nose touched the ground at the factory gates, as though it was asking permission to enter, and Lily watched in horror as the rest of it came down in a ball of flame.

She looked at the others, knowing they were all thinking the same thing: was it safe to go back to help?

'Come on,' she said and started to run towards the factory. The whole place was lit up from the Zeppelin fire. It didn't explode but burned away. Already the factory's fire brigade was there with hoses, putting out the fire before it set light to the factory. Lily could see that the bomb had come down in the safe area and she guessed there must be people there desperately putting out that fire too. The police, the army guards, everyone ran towards the Zeppelin.

Four of the Zeppelin pilots had managed to get out of one of the gondolas and were running from the burning wreck with their hands held high. One of them suddenly turned and took out a revolver, brandished it at the armed guards coming for them. Lily and the others ducked for cover.

'Halt, halt.' Another German came running from the direction of the marshes and Lily froze when she saw that it was Viktor, coming towards his countrymen with his hands held up.

'Viktor!' exclaimed Charlotte, and got up to go towards him but Lily gripped her arm to stop her.

'Shut up,' she hissed and Mable and Jessie looked at them and at the scene before them in disbelief.

There was a shot and the man holding the gun went down. The British guards swarmed over them, pinning them all to the floor, Viktor included. Lily and Charlotte watched helplessly as they were manhandled into an army truck and taken away.

'Just keep quiet,' Lily said into her friend's ear. 'Let's go and help.'

Charlotte nodded, following Lily over to the Zeppelin. Guards and foremen and the copperettes shouted instructions to fetch sand and water. The Zeppelin had almost burned out, its metal ribs tangled and smouldering. They managed to get round it and through to the factory, not knowing if the whole place was about to blow. They fetched sand buckets with everyone else and ran for the spiralling smoke coming off the safe area. Within forty minutes it was under control and the danger of the explosives going up had passed. It was a lucky outcome, which so easily could have ended with thousands of deaths.

The workers were told to go back to work. It seemed like a strange thing to do after what had happened. But production was their priority and now they were out of danger they had to carry on. Lily spent her shift scared to death that Viktor would tell on her and Charlotte.

When shift finished in the morning, Lily and the other workers were directed out of the factory by a new route through the perimeter fence. She looked for Charlotte but didn't see her. Everyone crowded to see the dead Zeppelin, its nose crashed to the ground by the factory gates, its girders smoking. They had all seen a similar sight in the papers but how strange to see it there at Greygoose. Lily got back to the colony and fell into bed exhausted. If she'd known she'd be woken up by a West Kent guard come to arrest her, she might have got up and run for the hills instead.

24

'Mrs Lily Pavitt?'

Lily turned over in bed, exhausted from the previous night. She looked at her clock: ten in the morning. Who on earth was waking her up four hours after she'd come off night shift? It was a man's voice, in the girls' hut. She remembered the Zeppelin and Viktor and sat up in bed quickly.

'Mrs Pavitt?'

She pulled back the curtain to her room and saw a West Kent guard standing there awkwardly.

'Would you please get dressed and accompany me to the police station? I will wait for you outside.'

'What's this about?' she said, feeling the warmth drain from her body. The guard didn't wait to explain. So Lily dressed quickly, wondering briefly if she could climb out of a window and run away. Viktor must have told on her. It could be the only reason they wanted to talk to her. She'd be arrested and put in prison. The boys would find out.

The guard nodded when she came out of the hut and she followed him to the little police station in Goosetown. She'd never been in there and looked around with fright, clutching her hands together. They would call her a war criminal. She wished she could talk to Charlotte, ask her what to say.

'Mrs Pavitt, I am Superintendent Haynes. Please sit down.'

The superintendent sat at a desk in a sparse room. He smoothed his neatly trimmed moustache with his fingertips and watched her sit down opposite him. 'I understand you have recently made a new friend? Please tell me about him.' He waited, expectant and stern.

'What do you mean?' she ventured.

'You know what I mean, Mrs Pavitt,' said the superintendent, sighing impatiently. 'You and your fellow worker were seen taking food to him in a basket.'

Lily started to cry. She'd have to tell them the truth. They knew about it already.

'I'm sorry,' she whimpered. 'We ... just gave him a bit of food, that's all. I didn't do anything else. I'm sorry. Please don't put me in prison; I've got two little boys and my husband's in hospital.'

'Calm down, Mrs Pavitt. What you did was wrong. It is an offence against the Realm to aid an escaped prisoner of war. Did you know that?'

Lily shook her head and the superintendent looked with exasperation at his constable standing in the corner.

'He may have passed secret information to his country. He may have signalled somehow to the Zeppelin to bomb this factory.'

Lily's eyes opened wide. She'd been right to be suspicious of Viktor. And Charlotte had been a fool.

334

'Your accomplice is also in trouble, despite her social position. Were you aware that she visited the escaped prisoner twice on her own?'

Lily shook her head. 'How do you know?'

The superintendent sighed again. 'I am not at liberty to reveal my sources. Suffice to say, one of your colleagues had been keeping a patriotic eye on you both.'

Lily wondered who on earth it could have been. Mrs Sparrow?

'What do you know of a certain Marjorie Cuthbert, aged thirteen years?'

'Marge? She's my friend. But she's eighteen, not thirteen. We started working here on the same day. She lives in the same hut as me and works in the same shed.'

'When was the last time you saw her?'

'I don't know,' said Lily, trying to think. 'I've been worried about her, she hasn't been to work. I was meaning to go and see her mother to see what was wrong.'

The superintendent paused, seeming to choose his words carefully. 'Miss Cuthbert's body was found in Shell Haven creek yesterday.'

'Body?' said Lily, feeling as though the floor of the room was tipping at an angle. 'What do you mean, body?'

'Catch her, Constable,' she heard the superintendent say, and everything went dark.

When Lily woke up she was in an unfamiliar little room lying on a narrow bed. There was a chamber pot in the corner. She got to it just in time to be sick. Marge was dead. Young Marge, her body found in Shell Haven creek. Sweet Marge with her nervous laugh. Marge who went home when she could to help her mother. Marge the brave munitionette, the football player, Lily's friend.

Lily sat on the little bed and cried for her. What could have happened? She couldn't imagine her being dead. Lily looked around the room and wondered vaguely where she was, but she almost didn't care. Nothing mattered any more if someone like Marge could be found dead in a creek.

The turn of a key sounded in the door lock. A policewoman came in with a glass of water and handed it to Lily.

'How are you feeling?' she asked.

'I don't know,' said Lily. 'My friend is dead.'

The constable nodded. 'I'm sorry to hear it. She was very young to do such a thing.'

Lily's head jerked. Such a thing? 'What thing?'

The constable shifted as though she had said something she shouldn't. 'Your friend committed suicide. I thought you knew.'

'Committed suicide?' The words were like vile trespassers on Lily's tongue. 'No, she wouldn't. It's a mistake.'

'I'm afraid a letter was found in her room, written in her hand.'

'Oh no, no.' Lily covered her face. She had no proof but she just knew immediately why Marge had done it. Because of Mrs Sparrow and the shame of being accused of something immoral, unspeakable. 'Poor Marge, oh Marge.' Lily felt a hatred within her like she had never felt before. It was burning her insides. A hatred for the despicable woman who had caused Marge's suicide.

Mrs Sparrow.

'You are being kept here for the present time,' said the woman, and she left and locked the door behind her.

She was in prison. Locked in a room. Panic rose up in her. She thought her mind would snap. It was too much. Too much had happened. She couldn't cope with it all. 'Let me out,' she shouted. Then again, louder, 'Let me out.' She had to see Sid. She'd explain what had happened. He would tell her what to do. No one came. She was left there by herself with her terrible thoughts. She curled up on the bed, clutched her knees to her chest, just like little Robert did when he slept. No one could get her like this. She'd just stay here, curled into a ball, and everything bad would just go away.

She didn't know how much time had passed. It had been quiet and felt like night-time. She hadn't slept. She stared at the wall and listened to every sound. The muffled voices, the doors closing. Someone opened her door and she turned to see. It was the woman police constable again. This time she had a tray of food.

'Sit up and eat,' she said matter-of-factly, as though Lily's life wasn't unrecognisable, as though her heart wasn't in shreds, as though she wasn't scared witless.

Lily did as she was told and sat up. 'How long am I being kept here?' she asked.

'I don't know.'

'Can I see my friend Charlotte?'

'Lady Charlotte Harrington?'

'Yes,' said Lily hopefully.

'No. She is being held here, too.'

'Oh.' Lily felt some comfort in that. Charlotte was there, somewhere nearby. It made her feel less alone. She suddenly felt hungry and looked at the tray of food. Mashed potato and some meat. She wondered if Charlotte had been given the same meal or something different, something better. She wondered if Charlotte had a better room than her, she thought she probably did. And she wondered if somehow Charlotte would be able to get herself out of trouble and if she'd help Lily get out of trouble too.

'There is someone here to see you,' said the constable.

'Who?' said Lily.

'A Jessica Baker.'

'Jessie? Oh, please may I see her?'

The special constable nodded and disappeared. She came back with Jessie and stayed in the room while the two friends spoke.

'Thank you for coming,' said Lily, bursting into tears at the sight of a friendly face.

'What's happened, Lil?'

'I don't know; but Marge is dead.'

'I know,' said Jessie, her face twisting with grief. 'Poor, dear Marge.'

'She killed herself,' Lily whispered.

'It's just too awful,' said Jessie. 'Lil, is there anything I can do? Are you all right?'

'Where am I, Jessie?'

'You're in the police station in Goosetown.'

'Oh.' She had felt a million miles away. 'I need to see Sid,' she said. 'Can I see my husband?' she asked the constable.

'You are to remain here presently,' she said.

'Can you go and see him for me?' Lily said it desperately to Jessie. 'Can you tell him I'm in trouble, that it's because of what—' She shook her head. 'No, just tell him I'm sorry I can't see him, I'm busy.' She didn't want to worry him. But she needed to ask him what she should do.

'Course I will, Lil,' said Jessie, putting her hand on Lily's. 'He's at St Clere's, isn't he?'

'Yes, that's it. It's only down the road in Stanford, Jessie. It'd be a big help if you could do it.'

'Course I will. Is there anything else?'

'No, I don't know. Have you seen Charlotte?'

'I'm going in to see her next.'

'Can you tell her . . . ' Lily looked at the constable. 'Can you tell her, I'm all right and I hope she's all right?'

Jessie nodded and said goodbye. The constable left with her and Lily looked at the tray of food. She ate some, feeling better that she'd seen Jessie. She wished she could see Sid.

Jessie must have gone to St Clere's Hall straight away because she was back in what felt like a couple of hours.

'Jessie, you're a good friend to go so quickly,' said Lily, sitting forward to clasp Jessie's hands.

'Lil, love, I'm sorry. He's not there, love. He's gone. He's discharged himself.'

'What? Where's he gone?' Lily burst into tears again. She couldn't take this news. Not on top of everything else. 'Where is he?'

Jessie held Lily's hand. 'They don't know. He just got up and left.'

'Maybe he's better? He's coming to see me?' said Lily, wiping her face with her hand. 'He'll be so cross I'm in here, but it's good that he's better, isn't it?'

'Yes, love,' said Jessie with a strange smile.

A man's voice called down the corridor to the attending

woman constable, who poked her head out of the cell door to see. When she wasn't looking, Jessie quickly took a fold of papers out of her coat pocket and slipped them under the sheet of Lily's bed. 'There are some letters,' whispered Jessie, looking scared. 'Some of Sid's letters. He left them for you.'

Lily shook her head, not understanding. Why would he leave her some letters if he was coming to see her?

25

Dearest Lil,

The bombardment has started. Haig says the wire will be cleared and we'll have a clear run through all the way to Berlin! I want to come home. Dad is ready for it but he's putting on a brave face for me. We're in the support line now and will be going into the firing line tonight. The mud is orange and putrid with shit and rotting corpses. The stink is everywhere. Every man smokes all the time so they can get the stench out of their nose. Please send more tobacco. My skin is crawling with the damned lice. They took our uniforms for washing but it didn't kill the buggers — they lie in wait ready to come back out of the seams as soon as I put it back on. I hate it here.

Your Sid

27 June 1916

Dearest Lil,

It's the third day of the bombardment and the noise is shattering my nerves. I can't sleep. The mud is everywhere.

341

The officer is in a dug-out but we have to sleep on the fire
step in the rain or on the duckboards, and if you fall off them
you sink into the mud. My feet are swollen and sore and
my hands too. The rats here are beyond belief. I thought we
had big uns in the docks but these are like cats – they gorge
themselves on the bodies of the men. I woke up with one
biting my face. I was so cold it must have thought I was dead.

Your Sid

                                                    30 June 1916

Dearest Lily

I don't know if I'll put pencil to paper again. They say
we're going over the top tomorrow. We are all scared stiff
but no one really says it. They threaten us with being shot
for cowards if we don't fight. There are no heroes here.
It's murder. We are being murdered by our own. We are
murdered if we will not murder. God save us.

Your Sid

                                                     1 July 1916

Dearest Lily,

I'm back. I got back. I've never seen the like in all my life.
They told us to go over the top and to keep going. The man
next to me had the top of his head blown off into my face.
The wire hadn't been blasted by our shells, it was so thick it
looked black. We had to keep going, trying to get through,
but couldn't run with all the ammunition we were carrying.
The Boche's machine guns picked us off like a fairground
kiosk. Men would jerk and wheel and look like strange
puppets dancing, caught in the wire with bullets going through

them. Dad isn't back, oh God. I keep walking the trench looking for him. Men are screaming. The stretcher bearers come back laden. I'll keep looking for him. He might be out there somewhere. I have to wait for dark and then I'll go out.

Your Sid

2 July 1916

Oh God, Lily, I found Dad. They got him, Lil. I found him in a shell hole half under water with rats on his chest. Oh God, they were eating him. I can't stop seeing it. It's there all the time. I kicked them off and pulled him out of there. I couldn't see where he'd been shot, he was bleeding everywhere. Lily, I can hardly bear it, he opened his eyes. Dad, I cried, Dad, stay with us, I'm getting you back. I dragged him out of the hole and put him on my back but he let out such a cry of pain I had to put him down again. He looked at me, Lil, with such love and asked me to end it for him. God abandoned us. I had to do it, I had to shoot him. I couldn't let him die like that. I dug a hole for him with my hands. I wouldn't let the rats eat him, Lil. I wouldn't.

Your Sid

17 September 1916

Lil, what have you gone and done? My own wife. How can you take my loyalties and pit them against each other? I can't live with it. God has already put us against the Hun. I'm leaving the hospital and going back out to join my regiment in France. I don't know what to say.

Sid

26

When Lily started reading the letters a coldness spread over her in a second. These were the letters Sid had written in France and not sent. But he wanted her to see them now. He was punishing her. She slapped them down in her lap. Sid had never written anything like that before.

She put her face in her hands and cried. Poor Gerald. Poor, dear Sid. The things he had seen and done. How could he ever be the same again? It was no wonder he couldn't speak to her about it. How could those words ever form on his lips? He was right – where was God in all of this? Having to shoot his dad because the rats were eating him. Lily started to tremble. The trauma of the factory explosion came back to her mind. She had tried so hard to block it out. She saw the girl with no eyes dying in the ambulance. She cried for her. She cried for Sid and for Gerald. This damned bloody war.

He hadn't even mentioned his own injury in the letters. When had he been shot in the shoulder – did it happen when he went out to get Gerald from no man's land? Maybe when he had first gone over the top? Had he dug Gerald's grave with a wounded shoulder? Had he not felt it because of the shock of what he had seen? His state of mind must have been far worse than the state of his shoulder.

Now he was going back out there because of her. Lily moaned and cried, unable to bear this news. Because of what she had done he was going back out to that hell. She wanted to run after him, tell him not to, tell him she'd been stupid. It hit her then. How very stupid she had been. How irresponsible, how foolish. How carried away with her new life and her new friends. She punched her lap, over and over again. She had to hurt herself the way she had hurt Sid. She deserved to see those letters, deserved to be punished by him. What a fool she had been.

She picked up the letters again. Touching the paper, she felt his hand there, wondered at his nervous state as he wrote. She put the letters to her face and kissed them. He wouldn't have been allowed to send those letters from France, they would have been censored. Had he never intended her to see them? Poor darling, had he written those words down to try to get them out of his head? Had he spoken to Lily in that way to comfort himself? He was too kind to let her know the truth. And now, he had been forced to show her them to explain why he'd had to go back to France. What sort of a state was he in now because of her? An even worse one.

Sid, poor gentle Sid. Going back. He'd get killed, or he'd have to kill again. It was against his nature. He'd be shot for a coward if he refused. And all because she had helped a stranger, a German stranger. She had followed Charlotte and got herself into trouble. What had she done?

27

A key sounded in the cell door. It opened and Charlotte walked in. Lily didn't get up from the bed but stayed sitting. She was glad to see Charlotte, but not because she had missed her friend.

'I heard you crying out yesterday but they wouldn't let me see you until now,' said Charlotte. She sat down next to Lily on the bed and held Lily's hand.

'Sid has gone back to France,' said Lily, pulling her hand away.

'What on earth for?' said Charlotte. 'I thought he was still in hospital.'

'He was but when I told him about that German, he couldn't stay here. His loyalties to me and to his country were so torn that he couldn't stay; he had to go back out to France.'

'Oh no,' said Charlotte, covering her mouth and shaking her head. 'Oh, Lily, I'm so sorry.'

'You should be. It's you who got us into this,' said Lily, staring at her.

Charlotte jumped up off the bed. 'Now hold on a minute, we both wanted to help Viktor.'

'Did we?' said Lily. 'On that night, when we were drunk and you were sad about seeing the prisoners in the Somme film, you wanted to help him but I wanted to tell the police and you wouldn't let me.'

'Wouldn't let you? He would have been shot,' said Charlotte, aghast and defensive. 'It is very likely he will meet that fate now, after stepping in to help when the Zeppelin went down.'

'I don't care,' said Lily. 'I care about my husband and whether I'll ever see him again. I care if he is safe or whether he'll die out there. And I care about my boys,' said Lily, letting out a sob, 'and what they'll do without me if I get put in prison for this.'

Charlotte went quiet and sat back down.

'I don't know any more if we should have become friends,' said Lily. 'I've followed you and your whims and look where it's got me. I've been a bloody fool.'

'I don't know about that,' said Charlotte indignantly. 'What whims particularly?'

'All the strike stuff and the German,' said Lily. 'You don't understand what it means for someone like me to do things like that. What it would mean if it went wrong and I lost my job. You've got your position to help you, you've got a safety net. And you might deny it and say you're going against your family, but when push comes to shove I bet they'd get you out of trouble. Who would I have to get me out of trouble? I have to be braver than you; I've got more to lose.'

'What are you saying, Lily? That you don't believe in the things we are protesting against?'

Lily thought for a moment and things became clearer.

There had been an unease at the back of her mind that she hadn't been able to put into words.

'Yes, but not in the same way as you. I can see that now,' she said bitterly. 'You want rights for women. I want rights for workers. I'm a worker first and a woman second. You want rights for women at the expense of workers.' She tried to find the right words; she was explaining it to herself as much as to Charlotte. 'Just like those copperettes, they think they are so modern, the first ever women police, making progress for women. But who do they police?'

Charlotte looked away. She had realised it too.

'They police the working women. They tell them not to swear, not to drink, they tell them not to have a cuddle with a boy in a doorway. The workers work hard for their money. Why shouldn't they have a good time after work and spend their money how they please?'

'And that bloody Mrs Sparrow. She takes the biscuit,' continued Lily. 'She might say she's making progress for women. She's got a high-up position at the factory. But look what she does to the workers. She bullies them and threatens them if they step out of line. She caused Marge's death.'

Lily's blood was boiling. As she thought about it all, she saw it clearly. Women had it bad, yes, they got paid less than men, they'd lose their positions of authority when the war ended, they didn't have the vote. But working women? They had it the worst of the lot.

'The better classes of women are treading all over the working women just to get ahead. And it makes me sick,' she said. 'All these munitions workers, a million of them, they are all from the lower classes like me. It's only a few of

348

the better brought up here and they are our charge hands and overlookers, forewomen. There are a few gentlewomen like yourself, but they are volunteers in the canteen, and you as an overlooker. And the papers love it that you're here, you're celebrated, a titled lady on the factory floor. But what about us? We always had to work before the war, we weren't celebrated, we were treated like slaves by the likes of you and yours. And we're accused of all sorts in this war. The war work pays us too much, we buy ribbons and fripperies, there'll be illegitimate babies and drunk women in the gutter. But the upper class are called modern girls, aren't they?'

Charlotte recoiled from Lily's anger. 'What do you expect me to say, Lily? How could I understand your position when I haven't lived it? My position is no fault of my own, I didn't choose it. I would say I have had immense courage to question the order of things when I am privileged and could simply have a comfortable life without complaining. But no. I recognise the injustice and the chance to grab the opportunities this war has offered us. Look where I am – wearing trousers and working in a munitions factory, playing in a football team and demanding proper pay and conditions for us. Women's rights are vitally important and if the only way to inch forward is for women like me to bemoan the state of things for women like me, then so be it.'

The two women stared at each other. Lily could see her own anger reflected back at her in Charlotte's eyes.

'And to say that we shouldn't have become friends,' continued Charlotte, 'is ludicrous. It's perhaps the best thing to come out of all of this. That we can understand one another, and help one another. As women.'

349

'What about the men?' said Lily. 'Isn't it terrible to be asking for more when they are fighting for us? I've got some of Sid's letters, they are awful, the things he's had to see and do . . .'

'Oh Lily, I'm so sorry for Sid. There is no way of justifying their experience against ours, except to see them separately and unrelated.'

The door opened and a copperette told Charlotte it was time for her to go back to her room. Lily lay down on the bed, her nerves strung tight. She was glad she'd said her piece to Charlotte. Lily wasn't the only one to blame in all of this. She frowned. Perhaps she *was* the one to blame. She didn't have to follow Charlotte's lead; she could have walked away any time. With bitterness Lily realised she had let herself get carried away. Her new job had been such a novelty, so liberating compared to her job in service. She had to admit that leaving the boys with Ada in Nettlestead had been part of that liberation. She'd enjoyed her freedom from the drudgery of family and work. Her new job as a munitionette was hard and dangerous, it could be monotonous, but it was much more than that too. It made her feel important. Needed. And it was exciting meeting all those new girls, playing football, and getting to know Charlotte.

She nodded to herself. Yes, it was exciting. But that was not a reason to get into trouble the way she had, and to upset Sid the way she had. She should have made more of an effort to see the boys; she should have stayed in Nettlestead with them when Gerald died. She hadn't even considered how they would have been shaken up by losing their granddad and seeing Ada in that state. Ada was a mother figure to them,

Lily should have thought more about that. She was in the wrong and she hoped it wasn't too late to put things right.

She woke up, unaware that she had fallen asleep, and wondered what time it was. The door opened and a copperette brought her a tray of breakfast. She must have slept all night. As her jumbled thoughts aligned themselves, she remembered that Sid had gone and she remembered his letters and her talk with Charlotte.

'What's gonna happen to me?' she asked the copperette.

'I don't know,' said the woman. 'The super will speak to you.'

She wondered where Viktor had been taken and whether he had told them about her and Charlotte helping him. An hour later, Charlotte was allowed back in to see her.

'What do you want?' said Lily.

'I want to apologise,' said Charlotte. 'I've been thinking about everything you said yesterday and I want to apologise for not fully understanding the risks you have been taking.'

Lily nodded and moved over so Charlotte could sit on the bed. 'You're right,' said Charlotte. 'I hadn't considered how the lives of working women differed from those of other classes. My view was skewed. This war has given girls like me an unprecedented chance to escape our fates – being married off according to rank and lineage – you can't blame me for grabbing the opportunity to have a different life, an exciting life away from the drawing room. It's not surprising I would be a little carried away by it all. You know,' she said, looking embarrassed, 'it was you who inspired me to do this job.'

'Was it?'

Charlotte nodded. 'I came home late one night to St

351

Clere's and snuck into the kitchen for something to eat. I saw a newspaper there with an advertisement for Greygoose and remembered that Mother had said you had left to work there. I thought the superior vacancy for overlooker was a suitable position for me. I didn't tell the family. I suppose I ran away to Greygoose to teach them a lesson. For not allowing me to go and volunteer in France,' she added. 'When I met with Mrs Sparrow, she was more than happy to take me on, an educated upper-class woman who wouldn't want the job at the end of the war.

'I have to confess to being excited about roughing it on the factory floor,' continued Charlotte, 'with the less-privileged workers, earning my own money. I thought it would be exciting to pull together in doing our bit for the war and to prove what I am capable of. Clearly I was misguided and naive. Why would the workers be happy for a "Lady Bountiful" to waltz in and take charge of them? I can see that now and I feel like a fool.'

'It goes both ways, Charlotte,' said Lily, realising something. 'We judged you the same as you judged us.'

'Yes, I suppose you are right, and it is generous of you to say so.'

'But I've got my husband and children and my livelihood to think about.'

'I know, I understand that now. This war has given me a brief insight. But for you, this is your way of life, having to work and earn enough to live. And I wanted to tell you that I am going to try to sort things out.'

'How?' said Lily suspiciously.

'I'm waiting for a letter to arrive before I can say anything.

But do try not to worry. That damned Mr Nash won't see us off.'

'Mr Nash?'

'Didn't they tell you? Mr Nash is the one who told the police that we'd been helping Viktor. He'd been spying on us, following us.'

Lily frowned. Grumpy Mr Nash who she'd argued with that night in Goosetown, when he said he hated having women in the factory. 'Because he hates having us in the factory? He'd really do something like that?'

'I don't know what his motivation was. A sense of patriotism, perhaps.'

'Bloody hell. You wait till I see him.'

'I think it's probably best to keep quiet about it,' said Charlotte.

Lily ground her teeth. So the miserable bastard had told on them. You couldn't trust anyone.

'I am really very sorry to have dragged you into something and caused you so much upset. It is my fault that Sid has re-enlisted. I knew all along that I had the security of my family, despite our current tensions. I should have been more thoughtful. I am going to do my best to get us out of this.'

Charlotte smiled at Lily and left the room. Lily wondered whether Charlotte would be able to get them out of there. Whatever happened, she felt sure that she no longer had a job at Greygoose. She tried to think about what she would do, where she would work. She wanted to see the boys, put her arms around them and gather them to her. She'd have to tell them that their father was back in France.

28

Lily waited patiently for Charlotte to do what she could. She waited all day and when nothing happened, she fell into a restless sleep and dreamt of rats as big as cats and imagined herself there in the trenches trying to sleep on a muddy fire step. She woke up tired and drained, ate some breakfast and waited.

At mid-morning, the station sergeant came in.

'Mrs Pavitt, you may go,' he said.

'I can just go?' she said, sitting up.

'There will be no charges made against you. You are to remain here as a Greygoose employee.' He looked at a piece of paper in his hand. 'In the cordite shed.' He held the door wide and she went through it and out into the fresh air.

She looked back, wondering whether Charlotte would be released at the same time, but there was no sign of her. She started to walk to her hut in the colony but stopped and returned to the police station.

'Can I see Lady Charlotte, please? Is she still here?'

'No, she has gone.' And that is all they would say. Lily ran to the colony, to Charlotte's hut and knocked at the door.

'She isn't here,' said the maid, and wouldn't tell Lily anything more. Lily ran on to her own hut. The girls were all at work. She'd been in the same clothes for days so she hurried to have a strip wash in her room. Once changed, she ran for the train to Corringham and then trotted along to Stanford-le-Hope to St Clere's Hall, the only place she could think of looking for Charlotte. Making her way to the auxiliary hospital, she just had to check that Sid wasn't still there, that it hadn't all been a terrible mistake.

She went to his bed and saw another man in it.

'Is Sid Pavitt here?' she asked one of the nurses, who frowned and shook her head.

She saw one of the housemaids go by carrying a pile of folded towels, and grabbed her arm.

'Can you tell Lady Charlotte that Lily is here to see her, please?' The unfamiliar housemaid frowned at Lily but then she nodded and disappeared into one of the servants' doors. Lily waited there, nervous that she would be challenged and thrown out but to her great relief, Charlotte appeared and gestured for Lily to follow her through to the drawing room.

'What happened?' said Lily. 'Why did they let us leave?'

Charlotte inspected her hands and when she looked up she was uncharacteristically embarrassed. 'I asked my father to pull some strings.'

'Oh,' said Lily, the mention of Lord Harrington making her stiffen. 'So you're back here with your family? You've left Greygoose?'

'That's right.' Charlotte's face looked strange and Lily realised that she had made a great sacrifice to get Lily out of trouble.

'You took the blame, didn't you?'

'It was the least I could do,' said Charlotte.

'And you left Greygoose and came back here as part of the bargain?'

Charlotte nodded and gave a small smile.

'Thank you,' said Lily, hugging her. 'You're a good friend.'

'I'm glad to hear you say it,' laughed Charlotte. 'I thought I had lost you.'

'No, you'll not get rid of me now,' said Lily. 'And you got me back into the cordite shed, too?'

'Yes, I thought you'd be better off with Jessie and Mabel, and Alfie. I've asked my father . . . ' Charlotte began seriously. 'I've asked him to find out where Sid has gone.'

'Really?'

'Yes, and if he finds anything out, I will tell you immediately.'

'Thank you,' said Lily, clutching Charlotte's hands. 'Thank you.'

Charlotte squeezed Lily's hands and stared into her eyes. 'Lily, I hope you will understand why I am asking you this . . . Please, could I urge you to continue with the protest at the factory?' She faltered, as though afraid of spoiling their trust again, but Lily nodded and thought.

'It would be a pleasure,' she said. 'That damned Mrs Sparrow. Our Marge will not die in vain.' *But I will do it in my own way, not yours*, she thought.

'I think to waste this opportunity would be a terrible shame,' said Charlotte.

'And what will you do now?' said Lily. 'What about Lord Nevill?'

Charlotte shuddered. 'Yes, he has been rather good. He kindly stepped in to help minimise the damage to my reputation. Mother was awfully grateful,' she said, rolling her eyes. 'I don't know what will happen – perhaps I'll give him a chance to impress me.' She smiled.

'Meanwhile, Mother wants me to help in the hospital. So that is what I shall do. Amongst other things,' she said. 'Viktor is being held in prison. He has been charged with spying, which carries a death penalty. I want to help him appeal. I feel responsible for him being caught. Of course, my parents can't know about any of it. And you know, my feminist allegiances are changing in view of my factory experiences. Poor Nellie being sent to prison and poor Marge ... The acute injustice imposed on working women. I'm reading Mary Macarthur and Sylvia Pankhurst now. I'm done with the militants.'

'It's Mary Macarthur's union you've written to, isn't it?' said Lily.

'That's right. I will pass on any letters I receive. You know,' she gave an embarrassed smile, 'when I started working at the factory I was disgusted by the language and behaviour of the working women. Appalled by it. But I see things differently now. How I struggled to live on the meagre factory wage but how much it meant to you all to be earning that amount. Just buying the papers or going to the theatre as often as I might would have been impossible on such an income.'

Lily shook her head. How could two women of the same age in the same country live such different lives? 'And all that stuff in the papers about the munitions girls wasting money on ribbons and new clothes,' she said. 'Why shouldn't we buy the odd fancy when we couldn't have done it before?'

'Exactly right,' said Charlotte. 'Who is anyone to impose notions of taste when taste is an unachievable luxury for many?' She sighed. 'I would never have known any of this if I hadn't had the opportunity to work with you all. The vote has always been my priority, and the right for women to enter the professions. But I can see how that may not benefit working women, not for some time.'

'Will you help me with the protest?' said Lily. 'You've taught me so much, Charlotte. I need to do it my own way, but I still want your help.'

'I'd be delighted,' said Charlotte, beaming.

29

When Lily went back to work in the cordite shed the next day, it felt like coming home. She'd been in the nitro-glycerine shed for six weeks and had the acid burns to show for it. She still couldn't see properly out of one eye. The absence of Nellie and Marge was hard to bear, but to be back with Jessie and Mabel was a comfort. Miss Harknett, however, greeted her with distaste.

'Morning, everyone,' said Lily. 'Where do you want me, Miss Harknett?'

'Oh, Lil, it's lovely to have you back,' said Jessie, coming over to hug her friend.

'We didn't know what was happening,' said Mabel. 'Where's Charlotte?'

'Charlotte's gone to work at the hospital at St Clere's,' said Lily, not wanting to get into everything now.

'On the press, if you wouldn't mind, Lily,' said Miss Harknett with a sour face.

'Yes, Miss Harknett.'

'You'll find we are managing with just the four of us. Mrs

Sparrow will be recruiting a new overlooker and cordite worker in due course.'

To replace our beloved friends, thought Lily.

'And there will be no talk of the recent events while you are at work. It would be highly inappropriate,' said Miss Harknett.

'No recent events, Miss Harknett?' said Mabel with a glint in her eye. 'I had terrible guts in the lav this morning. Shouldn't we talk about that, then?'

Miss Harknett didn't entertain Mabel with a reply and looked like she wished she was somewhere else.

Lily set to work on the press, the strong smell of ether making her lightheaded. She knew they were all putting on a brave face. It was nice being back together but the loss of the others was palpable. At break time they huddled together on the tramway platform with cups of tea in the cold September wind.

'There's been talk of an escaped German prisoner,' said Mabel tentatively.

Lily nodded. 'Yes. But I don't think we should talk about it. Me and Charlotte got ourselves into trouble and Charlotte got us out of it. I'm just glad to be back here; I thought I'd lose my job.'

Mabel and Jessie exchanged glances but neither of them pressed Lily for more information.

'What about the strike,' said Jessie, 'with Charlotte gone?'

Lily was surprised she'd asked about it. She felt Charlotte had put it all on them and they'd be glad not to have to take any of it further.

'I don't know yet,' said Lily. 'I need to think about it.'

'That Mrs Sparrow has got it coming,' said Mabel, looking at Lily meaningfully.

'Yes,' said Lily, and let it be. She wanted to get settled back into work first before thinking about anything like that.

Going back into the shed, Lily saw Mr Nash in the first pressing room. He saw her and turned away abruptly to attend to one of the machines. How he must hate her being there. Was it simply because she was a woman doing men's work in the factory, or was there an added incentive to hate her because she'd been involved in the strike? She resisted the urge to go over to challenge him about it. She could feel the rage boiling in her but she tamed it and told herself she would wait, do it properly when she was ready.

A week passed, then two. Lily went to Nettlestead to visit the boys. She took them presents and sweets. She told Ada nothing of the German prisoner, nothing of Sid re-enlisting. She waited to see whether her mother-in-law mentioned a letter from Sid, but she didn't. Her sister Dolly asked after him and Lily found a way to answer without either lying or revealing the truth.

'His shoulder is almost better, he's bearing up,' she said. 'I'm working long hours and don't see him much.' She couldn't bring herself to tell the boys their dad was back in France and they might never see him again, that she had written dozens of letters to him, sending them to the Essex Regiment and hoping they would reach him, but had heard nothing back. She just put it all off and hoped things would work out for the best.

At work she pulled her weight and did her bit. The long hours were exhausting and it wasn't the same as it had been before when Nellie was there. Alfie tried to get them to start the football up again but it didn't seem right with Marge dead. Lily wanted to talk to the others about the protest but didn't have the energy to give to it. As the weeks went by, so her conviction slipped and her confidence waned. She avoided going to see Charlotte, who she knew would push her into doing something. She wondered whether it was best just to fit in and get on with it; perhaps she had caused enough trouble already.

'I wonder how Marge's mum is doing,' said Mabel at work one day. Lily pretended not to hear and swung round the cordite press so that Mabel had to attend to the cords coming out the other end. Lily hadn't gone to see Mrs Cuthbert when Marge was missing; she hadn't got around to it with everything else going on. And when Marge's body was found, she offered her condolences to Marge's mum at the funeral but didn't have the heart to go and visit their home. She had avoided it but now she thought it was time to go – she didn't want it on her conscience that she hadn't offered her support. After all, it was because she and Charlotte had dragged Marge into the protest that Mrs Sparrow had taken her revenge on the girl. Lily was a conspirator in Marge's death. It was a hard thing to face.

In late October on a week of night shifts, Lily gathered her resolve and asked the matron of hut ten for Marge's address.

'I want to take some flowers,' she said. She looked at the address. Fobbing. She took the Corringham Light Railway and walked north, asking directions along the way. Coming to a little row of run-down cottages on the edge of the village, she knocked at the door. A small boy answered and Lily thought he looked familiar. He let her in and she was shocked by the state of the place. The floor inside was compacted earth. It smelled strongly of damp. The children were barefoot.

Someone coughed in the back room. 'Hello?' said a woman, suspiciously, coming through, dabbing at her mouth with a handkerchief. Her clothes were shabby from wear, her teeth bad. She coughed again. Lily had heard the sound before. A consumption cough. The woman looked exhausted and thin, wasted. There was a hard look about her as though she thought Lily might take something away from her.

'Hello, Mrs Cuthbert? It's Lily. Lily Pavitt. I worked with Marge at Greygoose factory.'

'Oh,' said the woman, shoving a child from a chair and sitting down, the little life left in her seeming to evaporate at the mention of her daughter. Lily held out the flowers she had brought and Mrs Cuthbert took them, looked at them so intently as though expecting to see a better life in there, something new that would make her smile. But she didn't smile. 'Thank you,' she said. 'It's not the same without Marge. She was a dear thing.'

'Yes, a dear friend. I'm so sorry. I'm so, so sorry,' said Lily, wanting to say the words without explanation and feeling her eyes burn with hot tears.

'She was too young. Thirteen years old,' said Mrs Cuthbert, shaking her head. 'I've lost others, but Marge . . . I thought she would—'

'Thirteen?' said Lily, taken aback.

'Yes. She lied about her age so she could work the night shifts and earn more. She was a good girl.'

Lily sat down on the edge of a wooden chair laden with clothes, remembering the superintendent at the police station telling her Marge's age. Lily had assumed he'd got it wrong. 'I didn't know.'

'Just push that off,' said Mrs Cuthbert, indicating the clothes. 'It's laundry I've taken in but I can't manage it today. She loved it there,' said the woman. 'I said to her it's a waste of money living there when she could live here and walk in, but she said she wanted to, that she'd do overtime to make up for it. Said the food was good and plentiful. Used to stuff her pockets with bread to bring back here.'

Another little boy came in and Lily started back. 'Hello,' she said to him. 'I've seen you before—' She stopped herself when she saw the look of shame on Mrs Cuthbert's face. Lily was horrified – the two little boys who begged at the factory gates were Marge's brothers. They had no shoes. They must have walked five miles across the marshes to get there, and five miles back. For a bit of bread and the odd coin. The loss of Marge's wages must have been devastating for Mrs Cuthbert.

It made Lily hate Mrs Sparrow even more for what she had done to the poor girl. Lily wanted to ask Mrs Cuthbert how much she knew about Marge's death but couldn't bear it. Jessie's Edward had told her that Marge had left a note in her room saying she couldn't live with being accused of immoral things. It was proof of Lily's suspicions. Lily couldn't bring herself to ask Mrs Cuthbert if she knew the truth. What good would it do to talk about it?

'How is your husband, Mrs Cuthbert?' Lily remembered Marge being worried about her father fighting in Turkey or somewhere.

The woman looked at her hands, looked over her shoulder as though she wanted to escape from the question. 'He's missing; they don't know,' she said.

'Oh, I'm sorry, I hope . . . I hope you hear something soon,' said Lily, wishing she hadn't said anything. 'If there's anything I can do to help,' she went on, looking around the hovel. 'I could wash the clothes?' she said weakly, not knowing if it was an intrusion to suggest such a thing. Mrs Cuthbert just looked up at her blankly as though she had misheard her. Lily stood up awkwardly, not knowing what else to say. Neither of the women spoke further. Lily smiled and let herself out.

She walked quickly down the road away from the feelings of injustice and pain and helplessness she felt for Mrs Cuthbert. She had to get away from the reminder that people like Mrs Sparrow had so much control over the poorer classes, and how fragile the working-class existence was. Something could happen, a wage could dry up, and there would be no shoes for the children and they would start begging for their bread. What would happen when Mrs Cuthbert died of consumption? The children would go to the workhouse. Mrs Sparrow had used her class to bring devastation on this poor family, to control someone beneath her. Poor Marge, only thirteen years old, working hard to support her mother and now dead from the shame of being accused of something she wasn't guilty of.

Lily walked fast and didn't stop until she came to Corringham station. Breathing hard, she looked across the marshes towards the river, towards the creek where Marge had been found, towards Greygoose factory where Marge had worked so hard. Lily realised that *she herself* wasn't helpless in the face of Mrs Cuthbert's pain and injustice. Lily had an opportunity, a unique chance for someone like her. She could do something about it. She could put things right.

30

'I'm joining a union.'

Jessie and Mabel looked at each other and smiled. They had been waiting for Lily to say something like this.

'Good. We will too, then,' said Mabel. 'We'll need a shop steward. You can do it, Lily.'

Lily smiled at their response. She had been anxious about how they'd react; she needed their support if this was going to happen.

'I'll go and talk to Charlotte about how to do it and I'll write to the union. It'll be Mary Macarthur's one, the National Federation of Women Workers.'

'Good,' said Mabel, putting her hand on Lily's shoulder.

Lily found Charlotte sitting by a soldier's bedside at the auxiliary hospital at St Clere's Hall. Her face lit up when she saw Lily.

'How the devil have you been?' she said. 'I miss you all so much. How are things at the factory?'

'Not bad,' said Lily, following Charlotte into the privacy of the drawing room. 'I'm going to join a union.'

'The NFWW?' said Charlotte and Lily nodded. 'Jolly

good, I was wondering when you were going to do something.'

'What shall I do, write to them? I can offer to be shop steward if they need.'

'Splendid idea, Lily. Yes, wait a tick, I'll get the address.'

'Have you the support of many others?' said Charlotte, coming back and handing Lily a piece of paper.

'Only Mabel and Jessie so far. I need to start talking to people about it.'

'I'd ask people to be discreet. When Mrs Sparrow gets wind of it she'll try her best to squash it as soon as possible.' Lily nodded. 'You know,' Charlotte went on, 'she must still be fuming about my father talking to the factory manager.'

'How do you mean?'

'Well, that's how he managed to secure your job, by speaking to the factory manager, who in turn told Mrs Sparrow. She was undermined. By a man. It's rather ironic.'

'Well, there's no hope that she'll take any of it well.'

'Best of luck. If there's anything I can do to help . . .'

Lily spent the next week talking to women quietly about conditions in the factory, about being undermined by the men's unions not allowing them a skilled wage, about joining a women's union. Jessie and Mabel spoke to the girls too. Some of them recoiled from the idea, not wanting to upset what they believed was a good thing. Some saw the chance to improve the safety in the factory and to be trained fully. Some had been bullied by Mrs Sparrow, had been threatened with the sack without a leaving certificate or with having their separation allowance taken away because they were having too much of a good time. She would accuse them of flaunting their wages with new clothes instead of buying war certificates, of being late when they had a family to look after at home with no help. Some had lost friends in accidents, some had liver disease from the cordite or epilepsy from the ether, some had lost fingers, some had been scalped. Some wanted the chance to stand up and be heard for the first time in their lives.

Lily wrote to the NFWW union and they wrote back with her membership and instructions on recruiting other women and collecting the union dues. It was exciting and illicit and it lit a fire in Lily's belly. The union confirmed the date of the tribunal that Charlotte had arranged – 18 November, only eleven days away. Lily would be the representative of the workers. They advised her to speak to the factory manager and welfare supervisor. It was time to go and see Mrs Sparrow.

Clutching her papers tightly to steady her shaking hand, Lily knocked at Mrs Sparrow's office door.

'Come in.'

When the welfare supervisor saw it was Lily, she put down her pen and leaned back in her chair, surveying her opponent. She waited for Lily to speak first.

'Mrs Sparrow, I have come to tell you that I am going to represent the women workers of Greygoose who are members of the National Federation of Women Workers at a Ministry of Munitions tribunal to . . . ' She faltered. She'd rehearsed it all but the sight of Mrs Sparrow's hard glare put her off. 'To put our case that our demands for improved safety conditions and fair training and equal pay for equal work have not been met.'

Mrs Sparrow maintained her stare but sat forward. She put her elbows on her desk, and rested her mouth against her clasped hands, considering her next move.

'And what does your husband think about all of this, Lily Pavitt?'

Lily took a deep breath. 'No, Mrs Sparrow, I will not be bullied by you. My husband is none of your business. It is time you stand judgement for what you have done.'

The woman laughed out loud. 'And what, particularly, is it that I have done, Lily Pavitt?'

'You were treating Marge for . . . for masturbation, when she was simply shy, pale and overworked.'

Mrs Sparrow couldn't disguise the look of surprise on her face. But she recovered quickly. 'I might ask how you came into possession of such confidential information, but it is of no consequence. I acted in the girl's best interests; I have nothing to be judged for.'

'You are wrong, Mrs Sparrow. Your actions caused that girl's death. Did you know she was only thirteen?'

Again, the woman looked visibly shaken but masked her thoughts quickly. 'And what about the part you played in the girl's situation? It was you who involved her in your so-called strike action. It was then that I diagnosed her condition.'

'She was so ashamed she killed herself and you'll have that on your conscience for ever. If you have one, Mrs Sparrow. A conscience.'

'Was there anything else, Lily Pavitt?' said the woman, feigning boredom.

Lily smiled. 'You know you've gone too far. Well, it's time the workers had a voice, it's time they spoke out. You judge us for our class, our upbringing, how we spend our money, how we dress and how much we drink when a lot of us have come from a kind of slavery working in service for a pittance. How dare you look down your nose at us? Who are you? Why are you so special? You call yourself a welfare supervisor but you take pleasure in threatening to sack us without a leaving certificate and no livelihood, with taking away our separation allowance, you tell us to spend our hard-earned wages on war certificates. I will tell you who I am,' said Lily, leaning forward over Mrs Sparrow's desk. Her fear had gone, evaporated in the heat of anger. 'I am a worker. I am a mother, a wife, a patriot.' She jabbed the desk top with her finger. 'I am a woman. I am a person.'

She straightened up. Mrs Sparrow's expression of disdain had slipped.

'Don't you see that these women have the chance of a new kind of life?' continued Lily. 'Why can't they have ambition? They are good, capable workers. If they all went back to their past jobs, who would make the munitions? Look at what these women are doing for our country, risking their lives in these dangerous conditions. Doesn't it stir a pride in your chest?'

'As a woman of a better class,' said Mrs Sparrow defensively, 'it is my duty to impose social and moral order on those unable to do so for themselves. You'd all be running around drunk in the streets wearing gaudy clothes and going with men if women like me didn't extend an arm of educated guidance. You have no notion of how best to use your increased autonomy. I and the women police service are here to help the women workers from going astray.'

Lily ignored the woman's nonsense. She wouldn't allow it

to shake her new-found sense that her existence had meaning, as a worker and as a woman. She had learned how to use her new freedoms in the right way to have proper control over her own life, she was more confident in herself and that was worth gold.

'Lady Charlotte may be gone but I am taking up our campaign. I am going to speak at that tribunal and you may or may not support us. Whatever you wish. Just don't get in my way, Mrs Sparrow. And don't judge your own career to be more important than mine or more important than the needs of women like me.'

Lily gave her one last look and turned away, clasping her hands together to stop them shaking. She walked out of the door and didn't look back.

31

'I think I might be sick,' said Lily.

'Come on, buck up, you're here now,' said Charlotte, look-ing just as nervous. They were waiting in the hall of Grays police court for eleven o'clock, the time of their tribunal hearing. 'It's not a police court today, it's a munitions tribu-nal, it's different. You're simply here to state your complaint against your employer.'

'But I can't remember anything. I'll forget what to say.'

'You've written it all down and rehearsed it. We are here for you. I don't know when the union representative will arrive,' she added, checking the hall again for the NFWW rep.

'Workers against Greygoose Munitions?' a court clerk called out and a jolt of fear went through Lily's body. She looked at Charlotte, who gripped her arm and steered her forward. They went through into the court and Lily felt like a little girl. The men sitting at the tables at the front looked official and stern.

'Where the devil is she?' hissed Charlotte. 'We need our union rep up there or they won't hear our case.'

Lily was led to a seat and placed under oath. All the while

she looked at the officials. All men, the one in the middle had fur-trimmed scarlet mayoral robes and a heavy gold chain of office. He was looking at some papers and talking to the man on his right, in a suit. There was another man to his left in a suit, reading some papers.

'Oh my goodness,' Charlotte suddenly whispered into Lily's ear. 'It's only Mary Macarthur herself.'

Lily looked up to see a pretty middle-aged woman walk into the courtroom. She had fair hair piled high beneath a plain, wide-brimmed hat, and wore a long skirt and smart cropped jacket. She turned to Lily and smiled, a glow seeming to radiate from her, and took her place at the table. Charlotte looked overcome. She gripped Lily's shoulder and went to sit down to watch the proceedings.

'Mrs Lily Pavitt, munitions worker at Greygoose Munitions, Corringham,' called out the court clerk.

Lily stood up, worried that her legs would give way. The panel of men and Mary Macarthur waited for her to speak but she couldn't utter a single word. She frowned and swallowed and tried to make a sound but couldn't.

'Please state your case, Mrs Pavitt,' said Mary Macarthur in a quiet Scottish accent.

'Yes, miss,' said Lily, relieved that her voice had returned. She looked down at her notes and started to read. 'I am Lily Pavitt, cordite press hand at Greygoose Munitions factory. Me and my fellow workers want to see improved safety conditions in the factory, we want to be paid a fair wage equal to that earned by men for the same work . . .' She paused as the men on the panel looked at each other with raised eyebrows. 'We need a factory nursery for women with children, we want a fair welfare supervisor, we want our work shifts reduced from twelve to eight hours, we want seats while working where possible, and we want gloves, masks and improved ventilation.'

The room fell silent. 'Oh, the factory inspector Mrs Hodges gave us masks for the cordite shed,' added Lily, 'but we need them for all the areas where we breathe in dangerous gases, and we need gloves for all areas where we have to touch dangerous chemicals and acids.'

'You have consulted the factory inspector on all of these issues?' said the mayor.

'Yes, sir, yes, Mr Mayor, but she only gave us milk to drink to stop septic teeth and as I say, she gave us masks for the cordite sheds. Well, she said we'd get masks but we haven't had them yet and it was a while ago now.'

The mayor held up his hand for her to stop talking while he consulted his panel.

'Would you elaborate on the improved safety conditions you require?'

'Yes, sir. We work with dangerous chemicals and gases. You can see me, look, my skin's turned yellow from the cordite, and they say it gives you heart problems and liver problems and girls in other factories have died from working with TNT and we have to touch the cordite with our bare hands to load up the presses and pull out the cords for drying. And it stinks in the sheds. Lots of workers faint and have to be carried outside to lie down in the fresh air and then they come back in to start working again.' She paused for breath. 'And in the nitro-glycerine sheds we have to stir the acids together and it spits up and makes tiny little burns all over our faces and hands and gets in your eyes and it burns inside your nose and mouth and throat and makes you go half mad.'

The men on the panel became quite animated, talking in quiet voices together, but Mary Macarthur just sat silently in her seat and smiled at Lily and nodded.

'Would you clarify what you mean by needing a fair welfare supervisor?' said the Mayor, consulting his notes. 'I believe your current welfare supervisor is Mrs Sparrow?' Lily nodded. 'She was supposed to be sitting on this panel to represent your employer but she seems not to be here, so we shall have to consider your case without her.'

Lily hadn't realised that Mrs Sparrow was supposed to be there. What did it mean that she wasn't? Was she afraid of being found out about mistreating Marge? Whatever the reason, it would certainly help their case by her not being there. Lily risked a glance back at Charlotte, who gave her a nod of reassurance.

'Mrs Sparrow has treated us unfairly, sir. She threatens to sack us without leaving certificates if we complain about anything or refuse certain work; she bullies us to control us. She mistreated a young worker who then committed suicide because she was so ashamed—'

The Mayor held up his hand.

'This is a grave accusation. What was this mistreatment exactly?'

'Marjorie Cuthbert was a young girl, shy, thin from poverty and pale. She joined us in asking for better conditions and pay and she was punished by ... Mrs Sparrow accused her of an immoral act and treated her for it ... '

'Mrs Pavitt, please state the immoral act.'

Lily looked down and twisted her hands. She couldn't bring herself to say it out loud. Mary Macarthur pushed back her chair and stood up, walked purposefully over to Lily and bent down to her. 'Tell me, my dear, and I will relay it to the Chairman.'

Lily swallowed and whispered it into her ear. Mary Macarthur looked into Lily's face for confirmation and went back to the panel. She stood behind the Mayor and said something quietly into his ear. He jerked back in surprise, disconcerted. He in turn relayed the information to the other officials on the panel.

'This accusation must receive a separate hearing, Mrs Pavitt. And as regards the leaving certificate system, the Munitions of War Act of 1915 empowered the Ministry of Munitions to implement this system.'

'I'm sorry, sir,' said Lily, emboldened enough to interrupt. The Mayor nodded. 'The system is open to abuse of power. It is used to bully workers in an unfair way.'

He held up his hand and nodded as though he had heard this particular complaint many times before. 'And your case regarding equal pay?' He said it as though he was bound to hear her view but didn't really want to.

'We are paid less than men when we can and do do the same work, when as widows we support our families and our aged parents. This work isn't a novelty for us, we do it to survive. We have proof that Greygoose Munitions break down men's skilled jobs into parts so that women cannot claim a skilled wage.'

'What proof?' said one of the officials.

'If I may, sir, could I ask a male worker to come and speak?'

The panel conferred and agreed to call the man forward. Alfie stood up from his seat and walked ahead to be sworn in. He was as pale as his shirt. Poor Alfie, Lily had begged him to come to court to tell them about it.

'Please state your name and occupation,' said the court clerk.

'Alfred Dunn, cordite press hand at Greygoose Munitions.'

'Go on.'

'Yes, milord, well, milord, I'm a press hand and Lily here, and Jessie and Mabel there sitting down, they're all press hands too but Mr Nash the foreman told me not to show them how to set the machines so we don't have to pay them a skilled wage. But, milord, they only went and set the machines themselves anyway when I was busy and they did it all right too.'

'Thank you, Mr Dunn,' said the Mayor, waving him back to his seat.

Lily gave Alfie a grateful look. They had agreed beforehand that he wouldn't mention Mr Nash sabotaging the women's work. They had no proof of it and it might have made them sound churlish and untrustworthy.

'Mrs Pavitt,' said the Mayor, looking at his papers, 'would you please clarify whether yourself and five co-workers staged a strike action at the factory and refused to work on the fifth of July this year?'

'Yes, sir.'

'Taking part in a strike is a Ministry of Munitions offence under the Munitions of War Act 1915 with a maximum fine of fifty pounds. Were you aware of this, Mrs Pavitt?'

'No, sir,' said Lily in a tiny voice, wondering why Charlotte hadn't mentioned that before.

The panel conferred. Mary Macarthur wasn't consulted

and didn't attempt to attract the attention of the men but sat there silently. She gave Lily an almost imperceptible nod. When the men had appeared to have come to a decision, Mary Macarthur spoke out, without consulting them.

'Mrs Pavitt,' she said in a clear voice, 'have you anything further to add to your case?'

Lily looked at her. There was something else that Lily wanted to say, but she wasn't sure if it would sound right, or if it was official enough. She turned to look at Charlotte, who gave her another nod of encouragement.

'Yes, miss, there is.' Lily cleared her throat. 'Is it all right if I bring some of the workers forward? It shouldn't take too long,' she added, seeing the look of impatience on the faces of the officials.

'Yes, Lily, of course,' said Mary Macarthur.

Lily turned around and gestured to a group of workers she had brought with her and were sitting down. 'This is Eliza, she got her hair caught in a drill machine in the cartridge workshop and it ripped part of her scalp off.' Eliza came forward and gave a little curtsey. She pulled off her headscarf and showed the panel her scarred, puckered scalp where the hair no longer grew. She went to stand at Lily's side.

'This is Jessie and Mabel, they've got yellow skin from touching the cordite, and their hair has turned ginger and Mabel's got septic teeth.' Jessie and Mabel took off their hats to show the discolouration of their hair and Mabel gave them a strange smile, pulling her lips away from her teeth to show her gums and her one missing front tooth. 'And Jessie here, she was in the family way.' Jessie blushed red but stood at Lily's side and nodded. 'And she lost her baby and the doctor said it was yellow and couldn't have survived. He said it was because Jessie works with cordite.' Lily gave Jessie a smile of thanks.

'This is Mary, she got her arm caught in the cordite press and had to have her hand amputated.' A girl came forward with one coat sleeve rolled up to show a bandaged stump. It was the girl who'd been in hospital when Lily started at Greygoose, the girl Lily had replaced.

'These ladies are Mrs Tapsell and Mrs Golding. They lost their daughters, Jane and Petra, in the nitro-glycerine explosion in June. Jane was nineteen and Petra was twenty-two years old.' The two women were dressed in mourning clothes. They held on to each other and came forward, their faces wretched with grief.

'This is Mrs Thurgood. Her daughter Emily died in the Zeppelin bombing last month. She was twenty-five and had two young daughters herself.' Mrs Thurgood walked forward grimly, clutching the hands of two small girls who looked pale and frightened.

'This is Ella Packard, she used to work in the cordite shed but the ether gave her epilepsy and now she has fits all the time.' Ella ducked her head and scuttled over to join the rest of the women.

'These are Alice Pearson's parents. Mr and Mrs Pearson lost their daughter in a crane accident in the factory earlier this year.' Lily put her hand on Mrs Pearson's arm as they went by.

'This is Marie Laver. She lost two of her fingers in the black powder mill.' Marie came forward shyly, held up her hand and went to stand with the others. 'And look at me, I'm yellow,' said Lily, 'and I've got tiny burns all over my face and hands and I've always got a sore throat and a cough. A bit of acid got in my eye and now I can't see properly out of it.'

'I think you have made your point, Mrs Pavitt,' said the Mayor. 'Would you please go back to your seats,' he told the other workers.

'Please don't mistake me, sir, milord,' said Lily, afraid she hadn't made her point the way she had wanted to. 'We are all patriots, we love doing our bit to help our boys in the services. We are needed. We want to work but we want to be treated fairly. We do manual labour with dangerous machinery, chemicals and gas, in fear of explosions, accidents, poisoning, Zeppelin raids. When there was an explosion in May, twelve women and four men died. We were there, clearing bodies and wreckage with our bare hands so we could get back to work. We are not so afraid of the danger that we don't want our jobs, our livelihood, but we need our safety to be protected and we deserve to be paid the right wage. We are the girls with yellow skin and acid burns, we are the women's army, willing to do or die.'

Lily sat down. She had nothing left to say, she had no more breath in her body to speak further. She put her head down and wanted to cry. She had done her best. At the sound of low voices and shuffling papers she looked up and watched the panel conferring. Finally, the Mayor spoke.

'Mrs Pavitt, we commend you and your fellow workers for the important war work you do at Greygoose Munitions. These tribunals are for the purpose of complaints lodged by aggrieved workers or employers. You have listed a string of such complaints that fall within the remit of this court and many that do not, within the context of war and the complexities of unionism and national gender pay structures. Productivity must be the first priority of any munitions factory.'

It was Mrs Sparrow's old refrain, productivity must come first. Lily's heart sank.

'However,' continued the Mayor, 'we do wish to grant you permission to demand safety equipment.' A cheer went up from the workers and Lily looked around at them. 'We do condone the working of shorter shifts,' another cheer, 'and in view of the fact that many national munitions factories have subsidised nurseries for workers' children, we do recommend that Greygoose factory does the same. The Ministry of Munitions will pay seventy-five per cent of the cost of the nursery as well as seven pence per child per day or night. Remaining costs will be met partly by the mother and partly by Greygoose factory. Thank you, Mrs Pavitt. Case dismissed.'

The workers clapped and cheered. Lily sat, dazed, not knowing what to think. She looked at Mary Macarthur who beamed at her, got up from her seat at the panel and left the courtroom without a further word to anyone. Charlotte grabbed Lily in a hug. 'Well done, you were marvellous, you were marvellous.'

Charlotte was pleased and people were cheering. Lily hadn't mucked it all up. The workers crowded round, congratulating her and themselves. She beamed at them, hardly able to process what had happened. They hadn't got everything they wanted, but they had asked for it and that meant the world.

32

Lily couldn't believe how far she had come. From cleaning out chamber pots at St Clere's Hall to representing the Greygoose workers at a munitions tribunal. It didn't seem real.

Poor Marge would forever be on her conscience. She felt she had made amends in some small way by standing up in court and telling everyone how the young girl had been wronged. But it still didn't take away the fact that Marge had been ashamed to the point that she had taken her own life.

Charlotte had been devastated to learn that Viktor Kirschbaum, the German prisoner, had been accused of spying and shot by firing squad at the Tower of London. Lily tried to comfort her, but she refused to admit how terrible she felt about it. Her appeal to the courts hadn't worked. Lily reminded her about campaigning to have Nellie released from prison, to give her something else to think about, and Charlotte took up the challenge sooner than Lily thought she would. Charlotte also became Marge's mother's patron. Mr Cuthbert had been reported dead. He had been taken prisoner by the Turks and had died of starvation. Charlotte helped the family get on their feet and she started a local widows' fund and paid for the family to see the doctor and bought them new clothes and shoes. She made sure the Cuthberts wouldn't go to the workhouse. If Marge was looking down on them, she wouldn't have to worry.

'My father's just glad I'm under the St Clere's roof and not in trouble,' Charlotte told Lily. 'He is keen to help with the widows' fund and, after all, charity work is what a Lady like me should be doing,' she added drily.

Lily had never told Charlotte what Lord Harrington had done to her behind his bedroom curtain. Perhaps in some way he was making amends and paying his dues for what he'd done to her by assisting Charlotte with the widows' charity and helping get them out of the trouble with Viktor.

Going back to work after the tribunal, Lily was anxious about how she'd be treated. Mrs Sparrow hadn't appeared at the hearing and Lily didn't know if it was because she was worried she'd be in trouble for bullying the workers or because she was showing them her support with her absence. If she'd gone to the tribunal, she would have been expected to contest their demands. But when Lily turned up for work at Greygoose, there was no sign that Mrs Sparrow would make life difficult for her. In fact, the welfare supervisor helped get the plans for the new nursery underway. And she sorted out the new safety measures – the masks and gloves and ventilation – without complaint. She even seemed to go out of her way to do so.

To Mr Nash's consternation, and Jessie and Mabel's delight, Lily was promoted to charge hand in the cordite pressing room. And Miss Harknett was promoted to overlooker, Charlotte's previous position. Lily was beside herself with joy.

It was the ultimate vindication that she'd done the right thing by the workers, that someone like her from such humble beginnings could represent them in a position of authority. She had proved her worth. Poor Alfie was demoted to general labourer in the black powder shed. Mr Nash was furious that he had spoken up for the women at the tribunal. But Alfie didn't seem to mind too much. He started up the football team again and was determined to win the local league. He told Lily he knew what he wanted to do after the war: he was going to be a professional football coach. He'd come full circle since leaving his mining village to be a footballer.

Charlotte had said all along not to expect to keep the munitions jobs when the war was over, that the men would need their jobs back and the women would no longer be needed. Lily couldn't imagine not working at Greygoose now. The thought of going back to domestic service was chilling. Her mind immediately ran to the demands she would make. Respect from the mistress, higher wages, more freedom. How she had changed.

The one dreadful force that pushed down on her shoulders every waking minute was the fact that she hadn't heard from Sid since he went back to France. Lord Harrington's enquiries had amounted to nothing. All he could say was that Sid wasn't with his regiment in the trenches and that he hadn't been reported missing. Lily had to tell Ada that Sid had gone back; she took it badly. It was terrible expecting bad news every time the post woman came to the colony. Lily dreamt of him every night pulling Gerald from that shell hole. Where was her Sid now? She prayed for him to come home safe.

385

33

15 January 1917

Dearest Lily,

    I got your letters, I'm glad you've sorted it all out and it's all right now. I'm in France. They let me stay at the base instead of joining my regiment at the front line, because of my injury. I'm a bit better. I've learned how to drive, I'm a driver now and I'm glad to be of help here. I'm due some leave, they said I can have it soon, so I'll come and see you and the boys, shall I?

    With love from your Sid

Getting the letter from Sid was like being pulled out of the shell hole that invaded her dreams. Lily sobbed with joy when she read his words. He sounded like his old self again.

She went to see Ada and the boys in Nettlestead to give them the news. Ada still blamed her for Gerald's death, even though Lily had had no control over Sid being shown the white feather that time. The woman was bitter with grief but when Lily showed her Sid's letter, she couldn't conceal her relief. They were united in their desperate joy that Sid was alive.

386

'I might take the boys back when the factory nursery's finished,' Lily told Ada and her sister Dolly.

A flicker of sadness passed across Ada's face, but she turned away and said nothing.

'Oh, what a shame; we like having them here,' said Dolly, pulling Robert towards her. 'They're good at taking our minds off things.'

'I'm going to try and get a house, so the boys can be with me. And for when Sid comes home. And I'll still be able to work if there's a nursery at Goosetown.'

Dolly smiled and nodded, patted Lily's arm. None of them knew whether Sid would really come home. The casualties in France were staggering and nothing was guaranteed.

In the garden, Lily helped Dolly hang out the washing on the line. She sat on a bench in the late January sunshine and watched it flap in the wind – it looked like the ghosts of people, living lost lives.

It was impossible to know how much longer the war would go on. The battle of the Somme was over at last. It had ended the day of the tribunal. General Haig had declared it a success but his many dissenters called him a butcher. The numbers spoke for themselves. More than nineteen thousand British Tommies died on the first day of the battle, the day that Gerald had died and Sid had been shot. They said there weren't enough explosives in the shells to reach into the deep German trenches during the five-day bombardment and that's why the first day of battle was such a disaster. Lily wondered whose fault it was that the British didn't know how deep the German trenches were and whose fault it was that not enough cordite was put into the shells. The battle lasted for one hundred and forty-one dreadful days with the British army advancing only seven miles and sustaining over four hundred thousand dead and wounded. The Germans were sending aeroplanes to drop bombs on Britain now. Lily was glad to be doing her bit to try to stop the enemy.

Although Charlotte held with her justification for the protest at work, it still didn't sit well with Lily when she knew how many men had been slaughtered in France and elsewhere. The working women of Greygoose had gained a foothold of control over their existence but at whose expense, the men on the battlefields? Lily wondered why it took a war to make a difference to women's lives. It cheapened the progress somehow, made it a guilty endeavour.

She'd been given the chance to change and grow; she was one of the Tilbury Poppies. But what about the men who'd never be brought back home, the men who could only make the field poppies grow? Would she give up the achievement if she could bring back the lives of the boys on the front line, of the girls who had died in the munitions factories around the country? Of course she would.

Indoors, Ada cried out. Lily jumped up from the garden bench. She must have banged her knee on the table or seen a rat. Ada never was very good with rats. Her mother-in-law cried out again and Lily sped up to get there. She ran into the kitchen but Ada wasn't there. She ran into the hallway and she stopped dead when she saw the silhouette of a man in uniform at the front door. Her blood ran cold. Ada was slumped against the wall with her hands over her mouth. The man took off his army cap and he smiled. His face was pulled and gaunt but there was an old familiarity about that smile, like a ghost of times past. It reminded Lily of a time when there was no talk of war, just talk of work at the docks, and the 'old bag' at St Clere's Hall. It reminded her of something that was missing. That pushing force on her shoulders lifted away. It was her Sid. He was home.

A Letter from Sue

Dear Reader,

I hope you have enjoyed reading *The Tilbury Poppies*.

When I was growing up in Thurrock I had no idea there used to be a munitions factory down the road during the Great War. This is what I love as a writer, doing research and learning about our recent history, especially the social history of women. I find myself delving obsessively for facts and getting frustrated if I can't find out what I need. But this time I figured: if the Imperial War Museum, Thurrock Museum and Devil's Porridge Museum don't know how a WW1 cordite press was operated then I think I'm safe to make an uneducated guess!

Of course I also use a healthy dose of artistic licence to create story and character. I'd love to hear what you think of Lily and Charlotte's stories. If you have a minute, please leave a review online – even a one-word review can really help a new book on its way.

My next novel will also be set during the Great War, in 1918, a fascinating year when (some) women got the vote, the war came to an end and the munitions girls lost their jobs. Perhaps one of those munitions girls took a leap of faith into a new career where she wasn't entirely welcome . . .

Many thanks again,
Sue x

https://www.facebook.com/SueWilsherWriter/

Acknowledgements

Thank you to: my editor Maddie West and the wonderful team at Sphere, my agent Laura Longrigg at MBA, beta readers Louise Ryder and Shapla Hodges, my writing group Allie Burns and Tanya Gupta, friends and family for supporting my writing efforts, especially Mia and Molly, and Kevin for his great feedback.

Invaluable research resources included exhibitions, archives and a guided walk of the Corringham Light Railway by the Thurrock Museum volunteers and staff, memories of local Thurrock people, the Devil's Porridge Museum, the Essex Regiment Museum, a guided walk of Stanford-le-Hope by the Tilbury Riverside project, Thurrock Libraries' Gazette archives and Thurrock Historical Society Journal Panorama archives, maps and local history books and the many brilliant books about life on the British home front and the Western Front during the Great War. A note on the title: my publisher and I loved it so much but it did mean I had to squish Thurrock's geography somewhat to make it work.

Finally, a grateful acknowledgement to the courageous women munitions workers, who played a vitally important part, alongside the suffrage movement, in paving the way for women's emancipation.